Two Masks
A Lawton Close Mystery

It's only rock and roll but I like it

Joseph F. Hanna

iUniverse, Inc.
New York Bloomington

Two Masks

It's only rock and roll, but I like it

Copyright © 2008 by Joseph F. Hanna

All rights reserved. No part of this book may be used or reproduced by any means, graphic, electronic, or mechanical, including photocopying, recording, taping or by any information storage retrieval system without the written permission of the publisher except in the case of brief quotations embodied in critical articles and reviews.

This is a work of fiction. All of the characters, names, incidents, organizations, and dialogue in this novel are either the products of the author's imagination or are used fictitiously.

iUniverse books may be ordered through booksellers or by contacting:

iUniverse
1663 Liberty Drive
Bloomington, IN 47403
www.iuniverse.com
1-800-Authors (1-800-288-4677)

Because of the dynamic nature of the Internet, any Web addresses or links contained in this book may have changed since publication and may no longer be valid. The views expressed in this work are solely those of the author and do not necessarily reflect the views of the publisher, and the publisher hereby disclaims any responsibility for them.

ISBN: 978-1-4401-0675-0 (pbk)
ISBN: 978-1-4401-0676-7 (ebk)

Printed in the United States of America

iUniverse rev. date: 11/04/2008

1

A GREAT SIGH WENT UP from behind the bamboo desk. It was a sigh that cried out for acknowledgement. Since the perpetrator of the sigh signs my paychecks (such as they are) every two weeks, it fell to me (ever mindful of my professional responsibilities) to enquire as to the cause.

"What's the matter?" I said, not looking up from my laptop (it's wireless). I was hoping he would answer "Oh, nothing."

But of course he didn't. Instead, he said, "The governor has a tart."

"A what?" I said.

"C'est le scandale du jour!" he said loudly, waving the front page of the paper at me. "Haven't you read the headlines? A great firestorm is gathering flames unto itself, tongues of flames. The talking heads and writing hands are aglow with the flickering of scandal! The governor has a tart!"

"On the Internet, it's all Delicia Fatale going back into rehab," I said. "Her new video is entitled Point Spread. It features the new quarterback for the Giants, and the tight end."

"That's perverse," he said.

"I haven't seen it. She is only wearing a football jersey. The number on the front is double zero..."

"Stop! You are making me imagine something I don't wish to see. That woman child should have been sent to a home and straightened out, not photographed to within an inch of her ..." he stopped and cleared his throat.

"Yes? Her what?"

"The subject is closed. I just don't understand the appeal. She is a troubled child. Her behavior is irresponsible."

"She's a celebrity," I said.

"The subject is closed," he said, returning his eyes to the governor's tart.

"The rules apply differently to celebrities," I said.

He sighed. There was a pause, and then he said "And, alas, to government officials."

"Oh!" I said. Google had produced for me an image of the governor's tart. "Here it says she wants to make a video."

"Who?"

"The governor's tart. She's tough looking."

"The governor apparently has …" there was a long pause, "issues." He hissed the word and drew it out. "There must be some real news," he said, turning pages and scanning the contents anxiously.

We had only moved out to LT's summer house-and-office in the Hamptons 76 ½ hours before. I was online for the sports scores. The Yankee season was young and they already were showing weakness on the pitching staff. I usually don't pay much attention to celebrities, but you have to sort of elbow them aside to get to the news of interest. They are everywhere, like street beggars in some dark, exotic city. I didn't realize I was about to become involved in the celebrity murder investigation and media event of the new century.

The phone had been dead-quiet for hours. That was unusual. People were probably still calling the office on Madison Avenue that LT calls 'the shop'. That's where we spend our time from September to May during the heating season. LT calls heating an interior space "hydrocarbon profligacy" and this is usually followed by "Who spun the thermostat all the way up to 70?" This is always followed by Teddy saying, "I was chilled." Teddy is his love interest. Her fingerprints are all over the thermostat, and just about everything else.

It was just a little tootle from a two-line office phone, and yet …

I came to think of it as a classic example of what some call the Butterfly Effect. A gaudy little piece of eye-candy flaps her wings on one side of the world, air begins to move in a new way and patterns are disturbed. Three weeks later, in an unbroken chain of events, a tornado descends from the heavens, swirls off a nice little town in Oklahoma, and no one's life will ever be the same. From tiny little disturbances, dangerous forces can be released and people can get killed, smashed beyond recognition with only an article of clothing left to identify what had once been a human being. Kidnapping; murder; deceit; and earthly remains dumped in the woods like an empty

Happy Meal box with just the stains left to show where a Happy Meal had once been, all come into the world because a woman changes her mind.

I was bored that day. We did not have a project and I was getting anxious, as I always do when boredom is in the vicinity. I needed to do something. When I have time to think, the mental trouble starts. I much prefer the physical trouble that starts when I have to act.

I picked up the tootling phone.

"Lawton Close and Associates, good morning, How may I help you?" I said as cheerily as I could fake.

"Max, it's Carrie."

So much for cheery.

"For real? My Carrie? The always professional, personal assistant of Rodd Rock, world famous rocker, and former member of the Lobes?"

"I don't have time for it today. Is Lawton in?"

"You are speaking with Max Kelly. I am Mr. Close's personal assistant and general man-of-action. How may I help you this morning? Need any hearts broken? Oh no! You are more the hands-on type. You like to do that yourself."

"Can we try to keep this professional?"

"I'm sorry," I said. "I am forgetting myself. I have been drinking to forget. Your name again, please?"

"Max. It was never going to work out between us. You know that. You knew it the night you left me in the Catskills. I really need to speak with Lawton. I am scared. Rodd is acting crazy. He and his wife are fighting all the time, twenty million dollars are missing from the accounts, and there is a dangerous stalker loose in the area. Are you going to give me a hard time?"

I looked at LT. He had raised his head in curiosity until he heard me say "Carrie," then he went back to reading about the governor's tart. He was no longer present in the present. He was wallowing in weeks-old gubernatorial carnality.

"Rodd Rock," I said to LT.

He looked up and shook his head.

"Mr. Close is in a meeting with the governor's mistress. May I take a message?" I said into the phone.

"I am not," said Mr. Close with a tone of mild indignation.

"Excuse me, one second," I said into the phone to stop Carrie from continuing with her message. I couldn't hear what she was saying because my boss was speaking to me. I turned to him.

"Why didn't you let Dickie pick up in the kitchen?" he said..

"I was expecting a call."

"On line one? You know that line one is for business."

"Carrie?" I said into the phone. "Could you hold, please? I'm having two conversations at once here." I punched hold.

"I thought it was Rodd Rock. Is that his personal assistant? " said LT. He knew who she was. It was his way of beginning a cross examination.

"Remember, she lived here briefly? You know, Carrie with my old car. You got her the job as Rodd Rock's personal assistant. She is about to give me a message for you because you are in a meeting."

"Am I?" he said. He raised one eyebrow.

"I was about to take a message," I said. "You shook off the call. You seemed engrossed in the Governor's sex life."

"Grossed is an apt term. The man is either a fool or a cretin. What is the nature of the message?" said LT. His brain was so packed out with intelligence there was no room left over for patience. "Is it from Mr. Rock? Hasn't he retired yet? Is it about the problem with his management and the missing twenty million dollars? Didn't he just get married?"

"I don't know, do I? I haven't taken the message yet," I said to him. I hit line one. "Carrie?" I spoke into the phone, "Mr. Close has just broken free for a moment. I'm going to put him on." I could hear her other line ringing when I finger-jabbed the hold button again.

"I'm busy," he said. He looked at his folded newspaper, his comfort zone, dry news on crisp paper. The actual bodies involved, with their various odors, moistures and unhappy endings, were sanitized by abstraction. He looked at his newspaper longingly.

"No, you're not. It is for you, line one," I said. I nodded toward the blinking light on the phone console.

"Take a message," he said, picking up the paper, beating it once with the back of his hand to take the kinks out and raising it to the level of his half-frame reading glasses.

"It's for you," I said, shaking the receiver at him.

"Why are you always so difficult?" he said, as he brought the paper down low enough so that he could peer over it without exposing his well-bred nose.

"Boredom makes me crazy. I do crazy things like answering line one when Dickie is in the kitchen. Pick up the phone or I might do something really startling."

"Like what?" he said.

"I haven't thought about it yet," I said.

Line one stopped blinking.

"Now look, she's hung up," I said. "Maybe it was a case?"

"You mean a project. I don't take cases," he said. With the phone line now dark and the discussion rendered moot, he started to pull on the right-side desk drawer that sticks. Inside it were a couple of cigars and various lighters along with desk-drawer debris: old pennies; a letter from his ex; a five-dollar bill; twelve ballpoint pens (some with the names of local businesses - three are dried out); a map of the London subway system; two unsent sympathy cards now ruined by cigar ash powder.

"Uh huh," I said. If he was going to set off one of his stogies, I was not going to hang around. Nobody smokes them anymore. LT doesn't care what others do. He never did. "Maybe Rodd wants you to have his management people knee-capped," I continued, "or torn limb from limb in the court of public opinion."

"Maybe you should get the number and call her back," he said. He took one of the pens out, tried a squiggle on his desk blotter, found that the pen was dried out and *put it back in the drawer!*

"Why don't you?" I said.

"I'm in a meeting."

"Oh, yeah? Whom with?"

"An employee who is about to be in serious trouble."

I dialed 411.

"No! That costs money," said LT. Did I mention that he is cheap? "Look it up in the database! You used to call over there all the time."

"That's the old number in the database," I said to him over the handset. "They changed it because they were getting weird calls from some pervert." He grunted and sat back heavily on his Louis-the-someteenth chair. He started arranging the catalogs, previously opened mail and his magnifying glass on his desktop. This was in preparation for the re-opening of the newspaper. His curiosity had gone limp. Once his blue, blue eyes were stuck again in the still tacky details of wanton flagrancy, nothing short of murder, maybe even his own, could pry them out. I had to act quickly.

"In East Hampton, for Rodd Rock," I said into the phone. Then I waited for it while LT frowned at all the money I was frittering away by using directory assistance. "It's unlisted."

"I can't believe you thought it might not be," he said. "He's the biggest celebrity in the Hamptons. You *are* slipping."

"I thought ..."

The phone rang. I was not going to touch it. It was line one. It was business.

It rang some more. I was looking at the blinking LED. LT was looking at me and he was frowning. It rang four complete times and then stopped, but the line one light stayed lit. Dickie had picked up in the kitchen. Then I heard him shuffling in the hall that leads from the kitchen to the study. We call it the summer office when there is business to do. It was just the study that day. It was about to become the summer office.

"Mr. Close?" said Dickie. He was breathless, but it could not have been from exertion. He was scuffing his feet he as if he had not lifted them more than a millimeter above the almost hundred-year-old parquet flooring as he snailed his way to the office doorway. I looked to see if he left a silvery trail.

"Yes, Dickie?" said LT.

"It's Carrie, Max's old girlfriend, on line one and she would like …"

"We went out!" I said. "I am not sure she rose to the level of girlfriend. Now she's Rodd Rock's very personal assistant."

"I would love to meet him," said Dickie, with a small flare of excitement. "Do you think you could ask her if I could meet him?"

"What does she want?" from LT.

"I don't know. She asked if you were still in the meeting. Is there someone here?" said Dickie.

"No."

"Because if there is going to be anyone else for lunch I have to go to the store …"

Line one was blinking. It was almost hypnotic.

"That was one of Max's little fibs," said LT.

"Are you going to pick up?" I said.

"Thank you, Dickie. I'll take it in here," said LT. He moved the blinking phone closer for an easy snatch. Then he prepared his mind for work. He posted an anemic professional smile on his baby face. He ran his fingers through his dark auburn hair that he keeps combed straight back (looking like he had stepped out of a novel from the Great Depression). He inclined himself forward on his chair so that he balanced on the edge. He can be surprisingly graceful. He and Teddy, his girl friend, like ballroom dancing, if that tells you anything.

He was ready. He lifted the handset.

"Carrie, this is Lawton. How have you been?" He waited and then said, "Good. Things are working out with your job?" He listened for a beat and then said, "I am sorry to hear that. I always get nothing but compliments about your abilities and your demeanor. What can I do for you?"

They were off. I looked over for some sign from LT that I should stay in the room. He ignored me. I did not even get a raised eyebrow. After a minute or two of listening to one side, and not the informative side, of the phone conversation, I got bored again. I needed to move.

I left the summer office and went into the kitchen to see if Dickie had eaten all the rice pudding. There was a little bit left. Dickie was watching the food channel on his little portable TV.

"Who is that? She looks familiar," I said.

"Ina Garten. She lives in East Hampton," he said. He was too enthusiastic for my mood.

"You know LT hates it when you watch TV in the kitchen," I said.

"This is different. I get recipes."

"Have you ever met Ina Garten?" I asked him

"She was here for dinner last August. Where were you?"

"That was her?" I said.

I took my bowl of what was left of the rice pudding to the little breakfast nook. I hate that word, but that is what they call it. Dickie had the paper all messed up. I started sorting through the litter for the sports pages. The scores you can get online, but the in-depth is still better in the paper. In the car I listen to WFAN.

"Hey! I'm doing the puzzle," he said. I do not use the word "petulantly," but if I did, I would use it here to describe Dickie's plaintive cry. I don't use the word plaintive either.

"No, you're not. You are watching TV," I countered.

"I'm not done with the puzzle," he whined.

"Well, I'm not done with the sports…oh crap…" I said.

"What! What's the matter?"

"I got some rice pudding on the paper…"

"What do you mean? Not on the puzzle?"

"What's a four-letter word for there's rice pudding on the puzzle that starts with S and has a T at the end and H-I in the middle?"

He actually came over to see how bad it was. He looked down. There was nothing to see. He grimaced and then he turned his back on me. He padded back to the granite-covered island he calls home. Dickie is not much of a challenge.

A shadow appeared in the doorway to the hall. LT glided into the room. I looked up. Dickie switched off the TV and hustled it out of sight into the cabinet below the island where he keeps his food processor.

"What did Carrie want?" I said.

"Hmm," said LT, frowning. "There's trouble in paradise. Dickie?"

"Yes, Mr. Close?"

"You will have to go to the store."

"What am I getting?"

"I'm not sure. There will be seven for dinner. Rodd Rock, his new wife Arlene, Carrie, Teddy, myself, and Max."

"Rodd Rock? Here? Tonight?"

"Yes, Dickie. I hope you will control yourself and not do anything … ah … to embarrass the firm. We are always professional, are we not?"

"I try to be, Mr. Close, but the Lobes! They changed music for all time."

"What year did the Lobes break up? I think it was the year I got married...," said LT.

"Oh!" I said. "She called again. I forgot to tell you."

"She is not supposed to call. Only her lawyer is supposed to call. She knows that. Why did you take the call? We have discussed this."

"Because you cancelled caller ID during the last episode of grim austerity."

"But Dickie answers the phone," he reminded me. Dickie nodded his agreement. What was I thinking? I must have been crazy to answer the phone. Maybe I was having some kind of bi-polar ADD Obsessive Compulsive episode triggered by acute boredom.

"Dickie was at Pilates class in Sag Harbor. He's studying to be a pill-lah-tay when he grows up," I said. "Can we get caller ID back, please? I thought we were off austerity."

"We may be soon. I will think about it. Mr. Rock wants to talk to me about a small project on his behalf. In fact, I have accepted. He is coming here tonight to drop off a retainer and to ... discuss ... things."

"Rodd Rock? Here? This is going to be ah...*mazing*," said Dickie, with the saddest little, happy-puppy smile on his little face. "I can't wait to meet him. I'll have to make something special, something fantastic."

"Dickie, I didn't know you still followed the music scene," said LT. "I never hear you practicing on your guitar anymore."

Dickie has a room over the garage that LT and Teddy call the carriage house. He takes down a ratty old Fender Stratocaster from the wall where he has taped up promotional posters from when he used to hire bands for a music bar he owned in Florida. The posters are creased and faded, the guitar would look better faded. The guitar is a kind of eye-hurting turquoise blue with two long cigarette burns near the pickups. Dickie has a board full of weird pedals that he stomps on when he is playing. They make him sound like...I don't know what. He wears his headphones and prances around like ... I don't know what. It's like watching an old Sex Pistols video with the sound off.

"I got headphones so I wouldn't disturb anyone," said Dickie. "Rodd Rock is a ... he's a legend. He's awesome." Dickie stressed the first syllable of awesome, sounding like a cross between a cartoon character and a ten-year-old.

"I thought he had three good tunes," said LT. He was making his discerning face where he tilts his head to one side, his eyes look up and he compresses his lips. "Cranberry Moon was a classic. They still play it. What has it been? Thirty years? Good Lord, I was in Miss Meggers School the first time I heard Cranberry Moon. Teddy used to sing that song. Max, would you call Teddy at her office and tell her to be here by six thirty? I may need her sense of ... whatever it is she does."

"She's your girl friend. Shouldn't you call her?" I said.

"Would you mind? I have ... things ... to do."

"What if she says no?" I asked. When Teddy digs in her hooves, that is it. It is over.

"Tell her Rodd Rock will be here. That should be sufficient. Now, Dickie!"

"Yes, Mr. Close?" Dickie had tried to pad quietly out of the kitchen. I can't imagine where he was going to go in the middle of a conversation with his boss. Maybe he needed to light up a joss stick and put some paisley fabric over the little window in his room to make it dark and weird enough so he could sit cross legged in the middle of his littered room and pick out some of the notes to Cranberry Moon, while he tried to remember scenes of his drugged out, blissed-to-hell, early Dickiehood.

"There is a difficulty," said LT. "Mr. Rock and Arlene are ... ah ... they don't eat meat."

"That's cool," said Dickie, with a shrug. He is celibate and he practices some oriental martial arts scam. Vegetarianism is right up his cul-de-sac. "Do they eat lobster?"

"I don't know. Rodd was part of that *Save the Whales* concert series, so maybe we had better not chance it. Do you know any good tofu recipes?"

"There aren't any." Dickie's mood collapsed suddenly. He was dead in the water.

"Well. Be creative. Think about what you can make that will be nice. Maybe some of your Mexican specialties?"

"Indian would be better. I can do a nice curry. I'll see what I can come up with, Mr. Close."

"Just make sure you tell me before you go shopping. Bring me your proposal, and I'll check it over before you go."

"Yes, Mr. Close."

Dickie had gone from Christmas Eve excitement and sugar plum dreams to thoughtful. LT wasn't about to let Dickie have his head when the guest was to be one of the most famous rock stars in history. Dickie came from a wealthy, and, I guess, important family in West Palm. He practices humility and celibacy and does something weird with crystals, but he can't quite get rid of the last stubborn stains of a privileged childhood. He has what Teddy calls the inalienable dignities of entitlement. Dickie is a pain in the ass.

Dickie's path to enlightenment was been strewn with tripping stones. According to the little he has leaked out on odd nights, when he was in one of his rare nostalgia moods (usually brought on by some oldie on the local oldie station) he was thrown out of some of the best schools in the country. All he cared about was a garage band he started, and scoring various substances to abuse. I have heard cassette tapes of the band. They played with tremendous energy unfortunately. They were of the slash and crash school of rock with a lead singer that sounded, as if he was possessed by an unclean spirit named Gogg who was still smarting over an exorcism that went horribly wrong. Now, of course, Dickie was done with all that. He was celibate, he had his martial arts and his humility and all the rest of his tricks that make my skin crawl. He is so damned earnest.

I was not sure if I was excited or not about having Rodd Rock and LT in the same room. LT was at one end of some weird spectrum and Rodd Rock was at the far, far other end. I doubted you could see from one end to the other. The horizon gets in the way. I also wasn't sure what I would feel seeing Carrie again. She traveled a lot with Rodd in circles that I can't even imagine, from London, where he has an apartment, to the Virgin Islands, to Los Angeles, where he has a suite in a very expensive hotel that was first famous in the thirties. LT is afraid to fly, although he will if he has to get somewhere to golf. I hadn't been out of the tri-state area in years. Rodd Rock was here, there and everywhere. He took Carrie with him.

"Look, LT…" I said.

"Max?"

"You're not going to call Rodd Rock Mr. Rock, are you?"

"I shouldn't?"

"I don't think so. That's not his real name, you know."

"It isn't?"

"He was born Sidney Porkhouse."

"And your point …?"

"I don't know. I just don't think you should call him Mr. Rock. It grates. I don't know why. Just call him Rodd."

"I don't know the man that well."

"You do whatever you want," I said, "but I'm telling you, the whole Rodd Rock thing is … you know … stage thing. He plays a character. It's shtick. I mean, what kind of a drug and sex overlord doesn't eat meat? You know?"

2

"Is that thing going to go off?" said LT. He was frowning at a small silver device next to the half-empty plate in front of Rodd Rock. You've seen Rodd Rock's rugged, but handsome face on a thousand pages and flickering screens. He still had his glorious mop of hair, though it had thinned some. It stuck up in front, as if a silent and imperceptible wind had it by the roots. The roots, even in candlelight, were grayer than the tips and that can only mean one thing. The only real change, other than the slight sagging under the eyes and the lazy lids, was how the tendons in the neck stood out like ropes when he moved his head. Still, if you squinted, it was *the* Rodd Rock. His body seemed youthful. Carrie had mentioned that he has a personal trainer who comes to the mansion three times a week.

"I don't know," said Rodd.

"I don't usually allow mobile phones at my dinner table."

"Yeah, well ..."

"You didn't finish your dinner," said LT, with a sad little point of his index finger at a smeared, but still loaded dish.

"It's good. I had a late snack. Do you have any more of the wheat beer?"

"Dickie!" said LT, in a voice loud enough to carry to the kitchen.

Dickie appeared suddenly and immediately. He had been nearby. Dickie has been known to lurk.

"Another wheat beer for Mr. Rr ... ah ... for Rodd. And?" LT looked over at Arlene and smiled deeply while inclining his head to invite a response.

Arlene smiled and shook her head anxiously. I wanted to put my arm around her. She was young enough to be my daughter. Well, maybe if I started in high school, and I might have except that Louise Czbek told me she was not that kind of girl. She changed her views somewhat after she met Carl. That was the year The Lobes had their comeback tour. Arlene would have been in diapers. Poor Arlene.

I was trying to figure out if Arlene was pretty, or just interesting looking. Her hair was expertly cut. You see that in the Hamptons. People pay a lot for a good haircut and sometimes they get one. You would notice the hair right away. It was reddish brown. I don't know if it was colored or not. I would say that it probably was. If so, it was well done with realistic highlights. It was shaped so that it cupped one side of her face and puffed out on the other side. It looked natural and that said more about the skill of the cutter than anything else.

Her eyes were almost green and wide set. They were expressive, always changing, but private. She only glanced at her target when she began to speak. As soon as the words were coming one after another, she looked away. It was weird. She had nice skin and was well rounded without anything sticking so far out that additional bracing was required. From what I could see, it was all as her creator had made it. She was a pleasure to look at. I would have picked her for a softball team choose-up before I would have offered her a prom corsage.

I think I must have been staring, because Teddy kicked me under the table, not that it hurt. She had taken off her stiletto spikers as she always does at the dinner table and her legs have almost no meat on them. There's not much in the way of inertia to Teddy. It wouldn't take a tornado to blow her to Kansas. All I got was the business end of her big toe. It cracked a little on impact. I turned to her. Her eyes were shining more than they usually shine. She raised two eyebrows at me. She made it a small and private gesture. LT noticed it. Not much gets by LT.

Then I realized that Carrie was staring at me and there was a little frown darkening the windows to her soul. I felt my eyebrows going up a couple of degrees. She did not look away. I did not look away. There was a lot going on at the table that night. Only Rodd Rock seemed to be completely relaxed.

Suddenly there was a small celibate breeze and Dickie was standing next to Rodd with a beer held out, as if it were a bottle of LT's 1961 Chateaux Margaux. Rodd seemed startled by the materialization of Dickie and beer.

"What?" he said as he spun his head to one side. "Oh! Thanks."

"I have all of your tapes," said Dickie. He spoke as if he were three hours into the night of the living dead. It was a dull monotone of celebrity-induced near coma.

Arlene looked frightened. She actually jerked in her seat. I thought it was odd. Maybe it hinted at something. No, it certainly hinted at something.

"Tapes!" said Teddy. "Dickie! Nobody has tapes! What do you do with tapes?"

"Cassettes," said Dickie. "I have a player." I have seen the player. It is a Denon. It is connected to a Kenwood amp and tuner and that is connected to two ratty old KLH speakers with cigarette burns and water marks from sweating glass bottoms all over the veneer.

"Thank you, Dickie," said LT, in a certain voice that I know very well. There was a smile and a threat in his voice. The smile was for the guests. The threat was for Dickie, but Dickie is strangely deaf to threats. Dickie was standing in front of one of the Lobes and probably the most talented one depending on who you pay attention to in the music press. He was beyond most earthly threats.

"I have your solo album," said Dickie. His voice was leaden and monotonic. It was now apparently midnight in the night of the living dead; time to go to work on the graveyard shift.

"I'm sorry to hear it," said Rodd with a big smile. He sat back and spread out his elbows like a street merchant opening for business. "I never cared much for it. The producer and I didn't get along and I rather think you can hear it in the work."

"It sold three million copies," said Dickie.

"Have you put water on for coffee?" said LT.

"None for me, thank you," said Arlene. "Dinner was spiffy!" Her hands came up when she spoke like flushed doves. The word "spiffy" stuck in my ear. I could not remember ever hearing anyone use that word before. Spiffy?

"Dickie, sweetie," said Teddy, "I would adore a double espresso."

Dickie was never one for mere hints. He responds better to blunt instruments. He kept his gaze securely engaged with Rodd. It was now three o'clock in the morning in the night of the living dead. They say the darkest hour is just before dawn. He kept talking. "Blue Roller on your solo album is my favorite. It changed my life. It changed my point of view."

"I liked that song. We did a much punchier version with the rhythm section from Belle Crank. Did you ever listen much to Belle Crank? Too bad about Belle, but my god! She had a voice."

"Dickie?" said LT.

"I thought," said Dickie, ignoring the man who makes out his bi-weekly check, "the version on your solo album was better. Belle was too LA Ronstadt for me, too clean. She once played at a club I had in Florida before she was famous, when she was with the Gneiss Brothers. We hung out. Would you autograph my tape?"

Dickie reached behind his back, I guess to his back pocket. As he reached, I heard a quick intake of breath from Arlene. When I looked at her, I could see she was highly anxious, perhaps even afraid.

"Dickie," said LT.

Dickie had produced a cassette box. He fumbled with it for a moment and then pulled out the label. He put the label down in front of Rodd and then reached in his shirt for a pen.

"Dickie," said LT, "what are you doing?"

"Happy to," said Rodd. He was smiling hugely. "By the way, I'm told that you are responsible for this marvelous curry. You know, I've had curry at the best places in London and this is every bit their equal." He then made a little show and a flourish of putting his name on the label. I noticed how he watched Dickie closely. Dickie watched his hand. No sooner was the signature laid down than Dickie scooped it up, grabbed the pen with his little chicken–claw karate hand, and actually backed out of the dining room muttering "thank you" repeatedly. Rodd had made another conquest. Granted, Dickie isn't much of a challenge, but Rodd was so efficient, I was impressed. For the cost of two yards of shopworn smile, a very small compliment, and a soothing tone of voice, he clapped another soul into his tote bag.

"Oh," said LT. "I have to apologize for Dickie. He has never done anything like that that before. As you may imagine, I have entertained my share of people in the public eye."

"No harm done," said Rodd. His face collapsed. The professional smile was gone. He seemed to age ten years in an instant. "I'm used to it, but Arlene …"

All of us turned to Arlene. She had her head down. "I had no idea," she said.

"No. It's been tough on Arlene," said Rodd. "That's why we rang you up. Arlene doesn't think she can take it anymore, isn't that right, Muffin?"

"The life of a celebrity is not what I thought it would be," said Arlene. "People think they own you."

"I tried to tell her," said Rodd, looking from Teddy to LT, " but what do you say?"

"The lack of privacy?" asked LT.

"Privacy! I don't know what that is anymore," said Arlene. I thought she might actually produce tears,

"You see," said Rodd, while looking intently at LT, "she fell in love with Rodd Rock and ended up with me. Now three years on, she wants out. She wants to cash in her chips, don't you, luvvy?"

"I can't live like this," said Arlene, shaking her head so quickly it resembled a slow shiver. "I am not like this. I studied piano…"

"She plays rather well," said Rodd to LT. Then he swept his face around to take in Teddy and me. Carrie had not said a word. She was holding her fork and looking at her plate, which was clean. She tapped her fork lightly on the plate. I was the only one who noticed.

Rodd sighed and then said, "We had an incident or two with a stalker. It puts you on edge if you are not used to that kind of thing. Poor Arlene has been at her wit's end."

Rodd then turned back to LT and spoke directly to him. "I believe you did some work for Senator Pendings. His daughter is someone I know. We ... ah ... knew each other, a while back. She told me that I ... that we ... needed to consult somebody. You're a consultant, aren't you?"

"Yes," said LT.

"And you come most highly recommended by our own Carrie," said Rodd, with an oddly outsized smile. It was a kind of a Jumbotron smile for the cheap-seats in the bleachers. "You would blush to hear the things she says about you. I know I do. She said you can do anything and you are afraid of no one. Well ... I think we may just need your services."

"What sort of program do you have in mind?" said LT.

"It's complicated. You know I have children by my first wife. Well – she's actually number two. I was married to the silly one for six months when I was twenty, but she has been out of the picture for years, decades actually. My God! So much time! I mean the mother of my children. You see - there's a prenup in force, but she gets a very good slice of the pie each month. Now, the pie isn't what it once was. There is money missing from the accounts. You have probably read about that in the paper recently. I don't know anything about money. Since I was eighteen there has always been enough around so that I never had to worry. But here's the deal. I do not own the rights to my own songs. The entire catalog was sold off to a corporation a couple of years after we broke up the band. The sale generated a quite respectable amount of cash. There was a bit of a contretemps among the band members about the various assets, and the thing about it was, that I used a lot of that cash to buy off the band members, you know, to settle the dust. It seemed like a good deal at the time. There was no way one could have predicted that classic rock is about all anyone plays anymore, or the existence of iTunes or the Internet or any of it.

"When we sold off the catalog, pop tunes had a life of about a year or two years with occasional play thereafter. In those days, it was all about the new thing, the next thing, the new wave. You might get a check from ASCAP for a couple of hundred bucks each quarter for a song that was only played on oldies stations, but was not in rotation in any of the major formats."

"What is ASCAP?" I said.

"The American Society of Composers, Authors and Publishers," said Carrie. "It's an organization that collects royalties for performers and composers." I had heard the name for years, but I never knew what they did.

"That's right," said Rodd. "These days, songs we recorded 40 years ago are getting played daily. I heard "Blanket of Tears" at the chemists the other day while I was waiting for my bloody prescription. It was unsettling. I mean, I'm there waiting in line for Singe to get me my stool softener or whatever the hell, and there I am singing on the Wellmart Drug Superstore sound system about a broken love affair with a Swedish Hooker when I was just a lad! Talk about doing the time warp again. My God!"

He shook his head.

"I don't know what you want me to do," said LT. "Do you want to begin an action to recover the song catalog? It might be possible. I would have to brush up on the intricacies of copyright law. If I remember correctly, there was a change in the law a while back. You can assign rights to an intellectual property, but you can no longer assign authorship. In the old days, you could actually sell off the authorship. That is no longer true."

"That's the thing," said Rodd. "I don't know what we want you to do. It is all such a bloody mess. First, I need to gain control of what assets I have. I need to know what is there. I don't trust my management. It's run by Mel Viktor. Do you know Mel?"

"I know of him," said LT. He made an involuntary face. He is usually in better control of his features.

"Exactly," said Rodd. "If Muffin, Arlene, wants out, I would like to see that she is comfortable. But I don't want this to turn into a, you know, how Entertainment Wrap Up will want to shine the big light. This just in! Rodd Rock and his much younger wife have filed for separation! Tape at eleven. Poor Arlene has had about enough. You should have listened to me, Muffin. I tried to tell you …"

"What do you want, Arlene?" said LT. He pitched his voice low and calm.

"I don't know … I just … want … to … I just want my life back. I want to be able to sleep at night and go to the store without worrying about… everything. I want to be able to open my big fat mouth and say something and not have people call me up about it because they read it somewhere and they are either hurt or angry or they are disappointed or they thought I should say it another way. I want to be able to walk into a get-together without a lot of people, strangers with cameras, yelling at me like they know me … like I owe them something. Hey Arlene! Look over here! Hey Arlene! What did you think about the picture of your husband and that singer or that actress or that model or … I don't know how other people deal with this stuff."

"Most people in the public eye," said LT, looking up into the middle of the air, "have their time, a year or two at most, and then they fade back into the crowd. And yet in every generation there are a rare few who, for reasons that are at least partly a mystery, become so identified with a people and a time and a cultural climate that they are set apart. I rarely refer to an individual as a star, the term has been squeezed of most of its meaning, but that is what these individuals become. They become stars. They rise above the rest of us and remain distant bright lights that we can only wish upon. I wish I may. I wish I might ... and you made that wish."

"I didn't make any wish. I met Rodd in the South of France when I was on vacation with two friends from work. We just happened to be walking past his trailer or bus or whatever and ..."

"Yes," said Rodd, smiling suddenly. "I saw them there. I thought I'd say hello. I had my eyes on the tall dark one, what was her name?"

"Marcie."

"That's right. Marcie. She knew how to display what she had on offer ..."

"It was a hot night," said Arlene.

"Oh, it was all of that," said Rodd. He looked at each of us for a moment to make sure he had our attention. He was an old-fashioned storyteller. He obviously enjoyed it. "I didn't even notice old Muffers at first."

"No. And I thought you were a stuck-up, self-satisfied ... and you were married then!" said old Muffers.

"Well ... in name. She had already moved in with Dennis." Rodd made a terrible face when he said the name of his ex-wife's next husband. It was the kind of a face you make when you realize the half-and-half you put in your coffee has lumps. "I was away a lot, on tour. That was when I was touring with Oakie. That was a good tour. The frogs couldn't get enough of us ..."

"Please don't use that term," said Arlene. She sounded weary, as if this was an old issue.

"Sorry. Muffin thinks I'm racist, don't you? I don't know, maybe I've seen too much. Maybe that's what it is. I like the frogs. I like the food. I like the wine, the women ... don't care much for the song. Have you ever heard of a performer named Johnny Hallyday?"

"Yes," said Teddy. "I have a number of his albums. He has a new one out ..."

"Well, that's it then," said Rodd.

"He's no Rodd Rock," said Teddy. She waved at something in the air in front of her face.

"That he is not. Maybe that's why we were such a big deal in Cannes and Nice and all the rest."

"It was always my impression," said LT, with his head tilted up and his eyes focused on something in the air about five hundred feet out and above, as if he could see through walls, "that you could have any woman or nearly any woman in the world. I have seen you photographed with movie actresses, singers, models, and daughters of the wealthy. What made you propose to Arlene?" Arlene first turned to LT as he was speaking and then she turned an intense look on Rodd for his response.

"There's a funny answer to that, actually. Have you spent much time with performers?" said Rodd.

"A dalliance, when I was younger and she was a bit older than I," said LT.

I looked back at LT. He would not look at me. This was new information. It was something else I would have to lean on Dickie to find out more about.

"Someone we all might recognize?" said Rodd.

"In her day, she was quite well known," admitted LT.

"Why didn't you … ah … pursue the relationship?" said Teddy

"Well … it was … crazy," said LT. He was feeling around for words, in the dark.

"The frantic, almost maniacal coupling?" said Rodd. This caused both Arlene and Teddy to look at him. Carrie looked at me. I do not know why.

"One doesn't say," said LT.

"And right afterwards," Rodd continued, "the sullenness? The picked fight? Fights that are carefully engineered, like little clockwork mechanisms with jeweled movement. Then the compulsive purchases? Then the other compulsions including the sugary vodka drinks. Then the scene in the restaurant when the desired table is occupied? And then the vendetta against the restaurant owner and the bad-mouthing of rivals and ultimately the betrayal with one of your own rivals or someone so unsuitable that it becomes a kind of punishment for all concerned …"

"Is it possible we have been with the same woman?" said LT. "Did she speak of me?"

"No. It could be any number of them. One must not generalize, I suppose, but there are patterns and one would be a fool not to see them. I am a performer. I understand that I am acting out a role that is not actually me. There was a time, however, when I tried to live the role. I thought it was expected, that I had to be real, genuine, live on the edge, that sort of thing. One day I woke up in hospital with no concept, no memory, and no way even to imagine how I got there. Ever happened to you?"

"No," said LT, with an auctioneer's finality when all the bidding is done. He likes to drink and he doesn't like to talk about it.

"Well ... at a time like that, you have a choice, don't you? You can either jump from the out-of-control train or ride it down into the big smash-up. I was a jumper, but you know? The riders ... they think that they are going to survive the smash-up, that maybe it won't be so bad. It is though. Ronnie Urskine dead at 27. Belle Crank found in her hotel room, she was not yet thirty. We all know the litany."

Rodd fell silent for a moment. I looked at Carrie. She had turned her eyes down. She was looking at her empty plate. Then she reached for her water glass without raising her eyes. She **was** hiding.

"You haven't answered the question," said LT.

"About why I proposed to Arlene?"

"Yes."

"I thought I had. Here's the deal. There is a lot of control in what we do for a living, performers. We are master manipulators actually. Our job is to create an emotional moment for a group of strangers, but not a static moment, no. We have to give the moment some shape, some narrative, some tension and then, if we are any good, we have to release that tension. I think of poor James Brown who acted out the hideous power. He would sing until he had slumped to his knees. His handlers would approach him with the mantle. They approached warily and slowly because it's the power and the power can turn on you. And then, they would drape the mantle over his shoulders and they would pat his back because he was been spending himself wrestling with the power. And they would lift him up so tenderly and they would lead him just out of the spotlight, away from the glare, into the safety of the shadows. The mantle is at once his protection and his warmth and also the outward sign of his priesthood. And there in the shadows, his back would stiffen. The power, power was upon him once again! He would fling off the mantle, cry out and stride to the microphone and he would sing once more from deep in his flayed vocal chords. It was enough to give you the chills. It was bloody marvelous!

"It is very intimate actually. You act this out for the watchers. You are a symbol and in some odd way, a sacrifice. You give them their own heart's desire, and then they give back the one thing you, we all, want over anything else ..."

"Yes?" said LT.

"Approval."

"I can see that," said LT.

"But it isn't real approval, it's just applause. Still, you get hooked on the stuff. You have to have it.

"And then I met Arlene. I found myself talking to Muffin here. And she seemed so damned normal. And I realized that was the thing I never had, not from the time I was a little child. Arlene was to be my guide for a return to the world of steaming pots on the stove and a quiet chair by the fire. I thought it might be time for Mr. Porkhouse to hang Mr. Rock in the closet, and bar the door against all the pirates and dragon masters. Trouble is, they all think they own you. You, I mean me and Muffin, us, we belong to the fans and the news cycle and they want what they want. They want their Rodd Rock, sword raised and glinting in the setting sun! He stands against the Pirates and dragons and investment bankers, which are nothing but pirates in pinstripes … I'm afraid that dear Muffin has taken fright at the pirates and dragons. It all makes her so anxious. She's not equipped."

"Are you anxious, Arlene?" said LT

"I hate it," she said, "all of it. It is not what I expected. It is hard work. You have to think about everything, all the time. Everything counts. Everyone is watching."

"Tell them about the stalker," said Carrie. LT and I both jerked our faces in her direction. There was a dead silence for three beats.

"What a load of tripe," said Rodd. "It comes with the territory."

There was a genuine look of alarm on Arlene's face. Her lips were parted, as if a word had slipped silently out. Her face was thrust forward. She was looking at Rodd. She was looking intently at him. LT caught it. He spoke to Arlene.

"Arlene. Are you anxious about a stalker?"

"Yes. I'm scared sometimes," she said, quietly.

"Is there one, more than one, or one that stands out?" said LT.

"There are a few people who act as if they have a relationship with Rodd. They send letters and they stand for hours near the house and the apartment. It is one of the reasons we have the security system, but there is one, who I believe is crazy. We found him in the house one night. Rodd had to hire a bodyguard to live in, and we have had to get a court order of protection."

"So you know his name then?" said LT.

"Yes," she said.

"What is his name?" asked LT. He sounded fatherly.

"Thomas Valderben," said Carrie. Arlene nodded.

"What do you know about him?" said LT to Arlene.

"He's already been arrested," she said. She seemed very close to tears. She was knotting and unknotting her napkin. It looked as if she might actually poke her thumb right through it. "He broke into Rodd's apartment once when we weren't there. He took some things, nothing important. He used to appear in the neighborhood and run up to us on the street and…"

"Oh, Arlene, he's a fan! He gets a little carried away, but … really," said Rodd.

"Then he showed up in our bedroom," said Arlene turning suddenly to LT. "He had a *knife!*"

"It was a pocket knife," said Rodd. "Mind you, it was larger than what you or I might carry, but still…"

"For what was he arrested?" said LT, paying no attention to Rodd and keeping his eyes on Arlene.

"Assault or something; something nasty," said Arlene. "I don't know. He's a complete creep."

"He's a harmless obsessive, that's all," said Rodd broadly and somewhat grandly. "He wouldn't hurt a fly."

"He would tear the wings off one at a time, *slowly!*" said Arlene turning to Rodd. She said it with anger that seemed to be left over from a previous discussion.

"You see?" said Rodd, looking at LT and turning up his palms.

"Hmmm," said LT. "There is no point in attempting to reconcile the irreconcilable. You were right to have come to me. I think we should start by developing some preliminary concepts that may become the basis for any future settlement. I will need to know more about your individual expectations and in some detail. If you could give me an hour or so tonight I would like to begin immediately.

"Max? I would like to see Rodd and Arlene in the office for a bit. Could you please drive Carrie back to her room at Rodd's house?"

"I should be taking notes," I said.

"No. This is exploratory. I don't think we will require notes."

"Can I take the Caddy?" I asked him.

"I'd rather you didn't."

3

"I THOUGHT HE WAS GOING to get rid of this old car." said Carrie.

I was on the third try with the ignition key. A fog had rolled in. As I twisted the key for the fourth time and played toesie with the accelerator, I looked at the house. Everyone had moved into the summer office. The room has been soundproofed. You would never know just by looking at it. When the door is closed and latched, you could scream your head off in there and no one would ever hear you.

The car finally started with a grunt and a pop.

"This is a Peugeot 505," I said. "It's LT's idea of a German car."

"Isn't Peugeot French?" she said.

"Yes. Very."

"How old is it?"

"A little older than you," I said.

We began to roll out of the pea stone driveway. It makes a nice sound. I turned on the wipers, but they just smeared the fog drops. The windshield looked like a screen dissolve in a bad movie from the sixties about psychedelic drugs.

"Can you see?" she asked.

"Sort of. So, what's it like working for Rodd Rock?"

"It's been two years. Can you believe it? This may be my last year. He doesn't leave me much time for myself," she said. She was looking out the window. She didn't look at me.

"Is he demanding?" I asked.

She didn't answer. I looked over. She was biting her lip. She saw me looking and turned her face to me. There were things she wanted to say.

"You can talk to me. This isn't Page Six. I am a card carrying professional assistant to a famous lawyer consultant who wouldn't get any work at all if his help blabbed about what they saw and heard. In this business, in the Hamptons … I think we've seen it all and heard more. Is Rodd Rock tough to work for?"

"Not as bad as Mr. Taylor. Do you know anything about the music business?"

"Not much," I said and shrugged.

"Have you ever worked for a show-business type? Somebody really well known?"

"We've had famous clients. Last year we worked with a Hollywood money guy. He was … colorful. He had a personal assistant. He liked to call her up in the middle of the night and ask for things that were right in front of him."

"So you know a little about what it's like," she said.

"Is it that bad with Rodd Rock? He was always known as the nice one in the Lobes. I thought he was clean as well, I mean in real life. I've heard he plays golf. Hard to picture the sex and drugs overlord swinging a nine iron for a little chip shot to the green. Does he really play golf?"

"He's a member of that new club, the one that was started by people that were not allowed into Maidstone. He plays, but not very often. He says it is strictly for professional reasons. You have to play to get along with certain people in the business. The truth is I think he secretly likes it. When his father died two years ago, Rodd flew everyone over to England. I had to make the arrangements on short notice. He wanted multiple planes in case one went down. The money he spends… Rodd's father had once worked as a greens keeper. Did you know that?"

"No," I said. I knew nothing of Rodd Rock's past.

I turned my head to her. She was looking straight ahead through the smeary glass at passing lights and the shadows of restless trees. She had recently had her hair done, maybe that afternoon. In the mountains, her hair had been long and straight. Now it was short and ball shaped. It emphasized her round face. In profile, her nose was slightly too prominent. It resembled the bow of an overturned sailboat, a racing boat. The nose created a small tension that was resolved with a tingle when she turned full face and smiled. The smile was so rewarding, I used to find myself thinking up ways to make it appear. Then she went to work for Rodd at the mansion. Our schedules didn't match up well and she traveled a lot.

She was well tanned and her body was tight, as if she had been working out. She had a silver and turquoise bracelet that looked old and no other jewelry except for two small silver earrings. She wore almost no makeup. Her lips could have used a little color. Her legs looked a little too thin, unhappy thin. They were nicely formed legs that I hated to see touching the old French seat covers. She had a whole new thing going since she left the Catskills. It was hard to imagine her there now. She had made the change to life in the Hamptons. Hiking shoes had been tossed aside for elegant little toe gloves. When costing out woman's foot leather, I have often found that less is more, a lot more. In the millionaire's playground, she fit right in.

"Rodd and his father didn't get along," she said, still looking straight ahead.

"Oh. What about his wife? I mean the one with the kids," I said.

"She's OK. You know she is married to that architect. They have achieved a kind of smug contentment. I hate his design sense, but he is great looking and he does not lack for clients. I see her every now and then if there is something involving the kids. Only one is still in school. The others are out on their own. Mark, the oldest, has a restaurant in the city. Ever tried it?"

"No. Is it good?" I asked.

"It's like Bobby Flay without the subtleties."

"What's it called?"

"Table Rock," she said.

"I get it. So. What's going to happen with Arlene?"

"I don't know. It has been tough. She is a nice enough person, but she got in way over her head. Rodd's clean now, but it's a dirty business. Some of the people in his world are ... trouble. You can't get away from it, I guess. There's a lot of money and a lot of ego, and anesthesia seems to be a way of life."

"Drugs?" I said.

"Everything. Whatever. Someday I'd love to tell you all about it."

"Since we seem to be getting involved in all of this, could you sketch out some of the characters, especially anyone that we shouldn't rile? You know how LT likes to wade right in and start splashing around before separating the crocs from the mud puppies."

"Well, I have to be very careful about anything I say. Did you know he made me sign a non-disclosure agreement?" she said.

"No, but it makes sense. He has an image to protect. Hey! Is it too late to get you to sign one for me?"

"Way too late. That horse cleared the stable door going about sixty. No sense closing that door now. Let the stall air out. I wouldn't go back to the Catskills if I were you. Your name is ... well ... if you were really nice and gave a lot to charity? Up there? You could get it back to just Mud."

"Uh huh. Now what about Rodd?" I said. I did not necessarily want to get into the whole Catskill thing.

"I will say that you should be very careful of the money people behind the label. The label people are OK for the most part, but some of the investors are a little edgy."

"You mean talk loud edgy or dangerous?" I said.

"Both. There's a lot of money at stake and a lot of other things that go on behind the scenes. Watch out for Mel Viktor. The talk is that he looks like a mud puppy, but he snaps like a croc. He manages Rodd's appearances and most of the money. He is one of the people involved with the song catalog. I have heard that he is connected to drug money people, so if Mr. Close wants to start stirring things up with Mel, he should be careful. Have you ever heard of a man named Carlito Penumbra?"

"Oh, yes. I've been to his house in Greenwich." I said.

"He sounds scary."

"He is. You meet people like that in the big leagues."

"Meeting all the people that were just names in the newspaper before has been exciting," she said, "but I don't like where things seem to be going. Mel Viktor has business dealings with Carlito Penumbra. I have read that Carlito Penumbra is being investigated for connections with FARC and Latin American drug money. I'm worried, but I don't know exactly why."

We arrived before a couple of stone pillars with fancy iron grillwork above. The iron gates were wide open. On one gate was a large frowning mask in gold. On the opposite gate was a large smiley mask, also in gold. I had seen them in theaters representing tragedy and comedy. Parked across the street and up about two hundred feet was a light blue Saturn. They don't come in that color, which is why I noticed it. I remember thinking, why would anyone choose that color blue? I could understand taking the car off the lot, because no one wanted it and the sales manager was willing to knock an additional five percent off the already low-low price for ugly *and* throw in a zero percent five year financing, so they could move the eyesore out of inventory, but to go to a paint store and look through hundreds of paint samples and pick that color blue? Rodd Rock's mansion was in one of the most expensive neighborhoods in the world. A Saturn was out of place in the surroundings. The color blue would be out of place in any surroundings. Still, it was just a car on a street, or so I thought. Carrie didn't see the car. For some reason, she was staring at my face. I don't know why. She's seen it before.

"This is it, isn't it?" I said as I turned the Peugeot into the driveway and stopped in front of the open gates. A small sign on one of the pillars read, "Rock Pile," I had been to the gates before to pick her up for one of our evenings of excited promise, expensive food and long silences on the way back to the mansion. That was nearly three years in the past. I was never allowed behind the gates.

"Rock Pile?" I asked.

"Yep. It's a play on his name and a tip of the cap to Nick Lowe. You can drop me here if you want," she said, "just like old times."

"No. I'll take you in, but why are the gates open?"

"I don't know. They shouldn't be."

"What's the deal with the masks on the gates?" I said.

"Rodd said they came from some music hall that was being demolished in London. He rescued them and then sent them out to be gold leafed."

I pulled in and onto the driveway. It began with a skirt of Belgian blocks and then became white pea gravel, just like LT's. It was long and curving. The house was revealed slowly in little teasing glimpses as we drove around some large trees. When at last the thing was fully visible I think I sucked in a breath involuntarily. The sex and drugs overlord lived in something that would have been perfectly suitable dropped down in nineteenth century Newport. The center stood slightly forward from two wings, which spread to each side before turning and coming forward to enclose a kind of courtyard, Attached to one of the wings was a glass structure. I could see that some very large specimen plants, and what appeared to be full-sized trees were growing up to the glass from the inside. I counted seven chimneys. The roofing looked like thatch, but I could see that it was composed of cedar shingles. They had been laid on heavy and apparently bent down at the eaves to resemble thatch.

"Wow! That's some statement. Is the whole thing stone?"

"A lot of it is just faced with a thin marble veneer. It was inspired by a house in England by Edwin Lutyens. Have you heard of him?"

"Me? No."

"Rodd's father had once worked for the groundskeeper at the house. Rodd drove me past it one day when we had to pick up some furniture in Hampshire. It overlooks the River Test. Rodd had been to the property in his childhood. He said that it meant a lot to him. Whethers and Banyon were the architects for the re-creation. You want to see it?" she said. The house did not have the same effect on her, she was used to it.

"You know… I was going to say no, because of what happened the last time you asked me to see where you lived, but I don't like the fact that the gate was open and that's a big house, so I might just make sure you get in OK."

"There's always someone around," she said. "One of the reasons I want to look for another situation is because Rodd wants everyone to live with him."

"Some control issues there?"

"You didn't hear it from me, but … duh."

I pulled the acid green French car alongside a Black Viper. Its top was down and it was getting moist. The ocean was only a block and a half away, generating an evening mist that was falling invisibly. No one seemed to care if the car interior was damp. Why should I?

"Who owns the Viper?" I said.

"I've never seen it before. Maybe it's one of Paul's guys. He's the head of the security service we use. I haven't met him, but I speak with him on the phone."

"That's a fairly extreme ride for a guy that works for a guy. Could it be a friend of Rodd's?"

"I don't know. Whoever drives that thing knows the gate code."

"Do any security people live in?" I asked.

"No. Well, there is Marcus. He's the bodyguard. He works directly for Rodd. His room is on the second floor at the back of the house so he can get to the master bedroom if he's needed."

"What does Marcus drive?" I asked her.

"He likes cars. Rodd bought him a Porsche Boxter after a … after he did something for Rodd that was a big help. He was hired right after they found the stalker in the bedroom."

"What? Here?"

"Last summer. Arlene was a little crazy afterwards. Rodd took everyone to England until it was time to move back into the city."

"What did the stalker do?" I asked. "Did he say anything? Was he threatening in any way? How did he get past the security system?"

"Nobody knows. That's what was so scary. He had to go right past my room and I never heard a thing. What if he had come into my room? They found he had a knife in his pocket."

"You can't have people walking around the house at night with a knife. Was he arrested?"

"No. Rodd told him to leave. He and two of his friends, who were staying here at the time, walked the intruder to the gates. When Rodd came back in the house, he told me to call the airlines. We left the next morning. He had someone come and spend the night on the driveway."

"Did the stalker say anything?" I asked.

"He was just standing there in the dark in the middle of the room. It was crazy."

She opened her door and turned to put her feet on the driveway. She hesitated for a moment, as if she was going to say something, but then she moved without another word.

As we walked toward the house, I looked over at the Viper and the lime green Peugeot parked next to it. There are those that believe you are what you drive and there are those that want others to believe it. I don't know what LT is thinking. The two cars together looked like a New Yorker cartoon where you think there might be a joke, but you are not sure. Then we were at a little flagstone terrace.

"Come this way," she said as she turned toward a row of lighted windows with a small covered entrance beyond. "We use the service entrance."

I wasn't going to get the full effect of walking through the big front door and into the big front hall, but even the service entrance was impressive. We came in through a kind of hall of pantries to a large kitchen in which the lights were on, but set to moody. The pantries were like little walk-in closets. One had two refrigerators and some shelving. One had a chest freezer and some more shelving. One had two professional dishwashers and even more shelving. One just had shelving and cabinets.

"This is set up like a catering hall," I said. I was impressed and I have gotten pretty used to big and over-done architecture.

"Rodd likes to entertain," she said. "There is a lockable door to the kitchen; I guess for security. The delivery people can unload whatever, and not have direct access to the house. There are security cameras in each room and in the hall."

"I saw them," I said. The camera housings looked like little black blisters in the ceiling. It was the same kind of system they use in casinos. The system isn't cheap. You can remotely move the cameras and zoom in on anything that looks interesting.

"They were put in to stop pilferage. Things had a way of disappearing," she said and then she shook her head.

"That would explain the little plastic "Surveillance by Camera" signs."

"It works pretty good. One time Rodd was caught on video eating donuts that the cook had just made. He claimed he had no memory of it. His trainer made him do an extra twenty minutes on the treadmill."

"The stalker hasn't been caught on camera?"

"Not since the system was installed in late April."

"Big Brother is definitely watching," I said. "Who has that duty, by the way, and where is the monitoring system?"

"It's in the basement in the audio equipment room. No one is ever in the monitoring room unless there's a party."

"So the cameras are just for show?"

"No. Everything is stored on the servers. If there is trouble, you just have to play back the video, but it's a pain. It stores up to two weeks before it starts to record over what's there."

"Technology," I said.

I shouldn't have done it, I suppose. It was just curiosity. I have a little LED flashlight on my keychain. It isn't very big, but throws a surprising amount of light. I wanted to see what kind of camera they were using. If you hold a light at just the right angle, you can see through the black blister, enough to make out the shape of the camera or lens.

"What are you doing?"

"I just want to ..." I didn't say anymore because the camera was moving. It turned to face me and I could see the focusing mechanism working. They don't do that by themselves. "Somebody is in the monitoring station right now and they are watching us. They just got a big close up of my face."

"Nobody is supposed to be in there, now," said Carrie.

"How do I get down there?" I said.

"The door there, across from the window on the other side of the kitchen, but I don't think ..."

I saw it. I went to it and pulled it open. The light was on in the basement. The stairs went straight down. The stairway was nothing but blank white sheetrock. The door to the kitchen was self-closing and it clicked behind me as I started down the stairs.

From below, I heard a door slam and then the lights in the basement went off. I was reaching in my pocket for the LED light when someone started up the stairs, coming right at me, and moving fast. Instinctively I moved closer to the wall. It was a wide staircase but it was a tight squeeze when he went by me and I was knocked back into a sitting position. I reached out for a piece of him and got a handful of some pant leg. It was nice material, maybe silk. The grab slowed him down enough that he started to lose balance. I could feel him catch himself with his hands. Then he started kicking. He got in a couple of quick jabs to my shoulder and neck. In the darkness, the impact of his leather shoe was a shock. I let go and tried to back down and away from his kicks. I was also aware, the way you are when things are in slow motion, of the smell of a certain aftershave fragrance. It stirred a memory, but there was no time for memories or even thoughts. I pushed myself away from the wall and tried to grab his kicking leg from a new angle. It was gone. Then there was a quick flash of light as the door above me opened and slammed closed. He was in the kitchen. I heard a crash and a scream. I used my hands and feet to scramble up the remaining stairs to the little strip of light beneath the door. I ran my hand up the door until I felt the doorknob, and I gave it a turn and shoved the door out of my way.

Carrie was sitting in the floor in the middle of the kitchen with her legs splayed. She was just pushing herself up to a sitting position. Her face was twisted up in a question. She didn't say anything, but her face yelled out, "What the hell?"

I heard the Viper start up. You can't miss the sound of a V 10.

"Are you all right?" I said to her, reaching out to pull her up.

"He scared the crap out of me!" she said. "I've never seen him before! What was he doing in the basement?"

"Are you OK?" I asked again.

"I think so," she said. There were no bones sticking out or blood gushing. She felt around the back of her shorts. She looked OK to me. I started for the door. The Viper was leaving in a big hurry. It wasn't being quiet about it at all.

By the time I reached the Peugeot, his brake lights lit up and he was at the gate. By the time the Peugeot decided to run, he was gone. He had turned right, toward the Montauk Highway. By the time I urged the Peugeot to the gate and turned right myself, he was as gone as gone could be. He did leave some nice new rubber stains on the old highway. The Peugeot cannot do that. I know, because I tried.

I pulled over and brought out the cell phone.

Dickie answered.

"It's me. Where is he?"

"He's still in the summer office with Rodd and Arlene."

"Tell him to pick up."

"He said he did not want to be disturbed."

"Yeah, well ... tell him to pick up." I said.

"Hold on."

I had a moment alone to think. I didn't use it. I didn't know what I might want to think about. That's the trouble with a man-of-action.

"Yes," said his voice in my ear.

"I thought you and Rodd might want to know that we surprised an intruder in the house when I dropped Carrie at the door."

"What?"

"I'll let it sink in," I said.

"The stalker?" he asked.

"I don't know. He was driving a Viper. I didn't get the plates because I thought the car belonged to ..."

He was gone. He had put his hand over the mouthpiece of the hand set and he was talking to Rodd. I keep telling him to just press the hold button, but he uses the hand. I could hear every word he said and half of what Rodd said..

"It's Max. There was an intruder in the house. I don't know what, if anything, was taken. Do you know anyone who drives a car called a ... what was the car, Max?"

"Viper," I said.

"Wiper?"

"Like the snake," I said.

The hand went back over the mouthpiece. "Max said it's a Viper, like the snake." Then the hand came away from the mouthpiece. "What color?"

"You mean he knows more than one person that has a Viper? Of course he does! It was black or maybe dark blue."

The hand was back. LT's voice was slightly muffled when he spoke to Rodd, "Max said it was a dark color." The hand was removed. The voice said clearly, "Hard top or convertible?"

"Convertible." I was going to say more but I would have been talking to the hand.

"Was anything taken?" said LT.

"How the hell would I know?" I said.

"Were things in disarray?"

"Disarray? The silverware drawers weren't turned over empty on the kitchen floor if that's what you mean, but it was odd because ..." I was talking to the hand. Then he was back.

"What were you doing in the house?"

"Me? I was dropping Carrie off. When we got there, the gate was open ..."

There was a muffled pause.

"Max," he said.

"Yes."

"Mr. Rock tells me you should not concern yourself with this matter."

"What? The guy knocked Carrie down, scared her half to death and he was inside the room where all the video surveillance equipment is installed. He was watching us on the system when we came in!"

There was another muffled pause.

"Max. This is none of our business. It is an internal matter."

"Something stinks here, LT," I said.

"I want you to come straight home. Also we have had a message from Mr. Bells. I want you to replay it when you get in."

That was LT being cute. Joody Bells, not his real name, is a mob guy who has been missing for three years and presumed dead. We used to have some dealings with him at the time Packy Merino was shot. If we got a message from Joody ... let's just say LT was showing me a yellow card and saying that I had to play ball his way or I would get the red card and be ejected from the game. He was also letting me know that some of the fans on the sideline were armed and also connected.

"OK. I'll be right home. Tell Dickie to leave his ouiga board out so I can get my message from Joody."

"Just come straight home," he said.

The connection went dead. I put my hand on the gear selector to put it back into Drive. Then I looked around to make sure the road was clear before leaving the shoulder. It wasn't. An old Saturn with baby blue paint that had never been waxed and was starting to oxidize, drove past and slowed a bit. The driver looked over at me. This was the car I had seen parked on the street outside of Rodd's mansion. It wasn't the neighborhood for a Saturn, even a new one with all the accessories. This car was the bottom of the line. So why is Mr. Saturn giving me the eye? And where did he come from? There were no other cars on that street at that time. It was so early in the season, most of the big homes were not yet occupied. It was a such strange moment that I thought of following the Saturn just out of curiosity. I wish I had, but I also thought of Carrie,

I turned the car around and went back to see how she was doing. When I got to the burly gates, they were closed. I called her on the cell phone.

She didn't answer. I left a voice message for her to call me as soon as she got my message. I was halfway home when my phone rang. It was Carrie.

"Where were you?" I asked her.

"In the monitor room. That's where the recording computer is."

"What did you see on the video?" I asked.

"Nothing. The removable hard drive is gone."

"I called it in. Rodd seems to know who it was and I think he may know why he was there. He told me through LT that it was none of our business."

"Max, I have a terrible feeling something awful is going to happen."

"So do I. Why don't you quit and get the hell out of there?"

"I'd like to. I should … but I can't," she said.

"Sure you can. Just quit. You don't have any kids or responsibilities. You don't even own your own place. You have no expenses. Just quit."

"You don't know. It's complicated. I can't right now," she said.

"I'd get out of there," I said. "Hey. Do you know anyone that drives a light blue Saturn?"

"What? Where was it?" Her voice was urgent. She knew something about a light Blue Saturn.

"I was pulled over to talk on the phone and some guy drove by slowly and looked me over in a way that seemed oddly aggressive. Do you know who it might be?"

"No!"

"Are you sure?"
"I *said* no!"
"OK, but …"
"Max," she said in a new tone of voice.
"Yeah?"
"Thanks for being here," she said.
"Sure."
"And…"
"Yeah?"
"Oh …"
"What?"
"Just … thanks."
"Carrie?"
"What?"
"Are you OK?"
"I don't know. I'll call you. Goodnight."
And that was that.

4

LT, RODD AND ARLENE WERE still in conference when I got home. I knocked on the door to the office to tell him I was back. I thought he might invite me in, but he said he would see me in the morning. I went to my room.

The next morning I was up first, even before Dickie. I got to play with a pristine newspaper. It was nice. There was also a short postcard from Lyon Biltmore. She had been thinking about me. I had been thinking about her, too. I have been bothered lately by a question that is inspired by her. I find myself wondering if her tragedy came out of her personality or if her personality, formed by a loveless, vanity-filled life and a weird kind of desperate greed for attention, made tragedy of one kind or another inevitable.

Dickie had laid out the card from her for all to see. There would be comments. The fact that I saw the card at breakfast meant that Dickie had taken it to his room for an afternoon and evening. Mail comes around one o'clock in the country. Dickie is a star hound. He loves reading about vanity, emotional greed, the failure of good looks, and human frailty in all its wide assortment. Dickie is weird. I might have to have the card dusted for lip prints! Eugh!

Dickie came down about 7:30 and Teddy appeared 15 minutes later. LT didn't show until nearly 10:00.

"Good morning, Max," he said. "Sleep OK?"

"I guess I did."

"You have a slight bruise," said LT. He was peering at my neck. Then he reached out and pulled my collar to one side so he could see the rest of the discoloration toward my shoulder.

"Yeah. He caught me with his shoe on the stairs, real leather," I said. Then I pulled the collar out of his hand. I hate it when someone grabs at you like that.

"How did things go with Rodd?" I asked him.

"Interesting," he said. That is his version of saying "no comment."

"There's something weird going on over there at his big house on the pond," I said. I was hoping my comment might dislodge something from the boss. Some little crumb from the night before.

"Yes. There are many compartments in Mr. Rock's life. Some are better left unopened. He certainly did not want to talk about the incident. What do you make of it?" LT asked me.

"Me? I don't know. It doesn't make sense. Why have a security system if someone can break in and use it to surveill the people who live in the house? That's really weird."

"I believe, from things that were said last night," LT continued, "that the person you encountered was the gentleman ultimately responsible for the security of the premises. His name is Paul Williams. He runs the Paul Williams agency in East Hampton."

"A security guy? That makes even less sense. Why run out of there? Why would he knock Carrie down? Why didn't she recognize him?"

"I gather she has never met him. He rarely comes to the house. He functions as a kind of contractor. He has a staff of bonded personnel. I don't know why he bolted. That is certainly suggestive. It did not seem to surprise Mr. Rock. It upset him. That was visible, but it did not surprise him. That is also suggestive. I would like you to meet Paul Williams. I would like your assessment of his character."

"What am I meeting him about? Do I have a story?" I asked.

"Tell him that I am taking a hand in security matters. Tell him there was an intruder at the house that was neither prevented by, nor recorded by, any of his expensive security gear. He probably believes we are unaware that he was the intruder. Question the value of his services. Put him on the defensive. See how he handles himself. I don't know. Stimulate!"

"I get it."

"In the meantime," he continued, "I have to look into what has been happening with the missing money. Rodd's financial situation is a complete jumble. Rodd Rock is typical of many artists for whom the subject of money is considered to be either boring or unseemly. Such individuals are prone to the thoughtless corruption of others when those others find that they can misappropriate money with no apparent consequences. Rodd has been foolish in his abundance. He suffers from the tragic though sentimental notion that if others steal from him that which he does not miss, no evil exists. And yet it does. The thief is corrupted, his greed is inflamed. He begins to imagine that what he has stolen is his by rights. When suddenly cut off from what he now regards as his entitlement, the corrupted personality is capable of …"

"Yes?" I said.

"You know," he said.

"Packy Merino," I said. "bleeding to death on a sidewalk in Queens."

"Something like that. I wish you would stop bringing his name into our conversations, may he rest in peace. I feel badly about how that turned out and I would prefer not to be reminded of those unfortunate and now distant events."

"Sorry."

"Rodd Rock has been irresponsible with his financial arrangements. Unfortunately, he has granted Mel Viktor fiduciary powers over certain monetary arrangements and instruments. I am going to have to begin to pick away at a cat's ball of entwined relationships. It appears to be a daunting task. Mr. Viktor likes complexity. There are dozens of entities involved. He uses ink much like a squid. I am about to sever one or two of Mel Viktor's tentacles. I doubt he will like it We must be prepared for a counterattack when he realizes what is happening."

"Be careful. Carrie told me that he has business dealings with Carlito Penumbra."

"That is not happy news, but I might have suspected as much."

"I didn't realize the music business is so dirty," I said.

"Any time large amounts of cash are pooled together, one may expect predators to gather. Money smells like blood in the water. Unfortunately, this task will involve many hours of reviewing financial records."

"You hate accountancy," I said.

"I do," he said sadly.

"You are going to be in a bad mood for the duration," I said.

"I am," he said with a grim nod.

"Great."

"In time, I may ask you to pay a visit to Mr. Viktor. Discretion will be key at this stage."

"You don't want me to stimulate him?" I asked.

"No. And I don't want him to know we exist until I have had a chance to feel about in the dark for an opening with some purchase."

"So, we are back in the shark tank with our bucket of dead fish," I said. "Just like old times," I said. "Like this was a real project."

"Yes," he said thoughtfully.

We had had a long run of dull projects. Filing the results was about the most exciting part of what I had been doing since the winter holidays.

"When you had your…ah…breakdown and…" he began.

"*Breakdown?*" If I had been drinking something. I would have sprayed him with a fine mist from the violent explosion of air from my lungs.

"When you took your hiatus," he said more soothingly.

"I was driven to my hiatus by a scheming, spluttering, rage-aholic, who…"

"Enough. That is a subject neither of us wishes to re-visit at the present. I've missed the excitement you bring to our little explorations. Bobby Dunton is not satisfactory in the role of a stimulator. He seems to be incapable of the implied threat. People don't take him seriously. He is too obviously anxious for approval."

"Dunton? Threat? You would get more results with Dickie."

"No. You have a true talent. Your demeanor makes certain personalities uneasy. I've tried to analyze it and so has Teddy, but we can not articulate whatever it is you project. You have a grating kind of self-assurance, a hyper awareness and a certain physicality…no…these are just words. It cannot be described. If it could be described, it could be taught and it cannot be taught. It is something with which one is infused at birth or else will never possess."

"Stop, I'm blushing," I said.

"Don't use sarcasm. You know what I think about sarcasm," he said. He has told me countless times that sarcasm is a child's toy.

"It's the weak person's wit," I said. "OK. I have to go see Paul Williams. Does he have an office? Can I take the Caddy? The Peugeot had trouble starting last night. I did not mention it before because it always does and is not what you would call noteworthy. I did note, however, that the intruder was halfway to the gate in his 500 horsepower Viper and I could not get a read on his plates because the 35 horsepower Peugeot failed to start in what you would call a timely manner. What if that had been a real intruder? What if we had come in on a crime, bodies laid out on the floor and the perp rushes past us and is going to make a clean getaway because the company car won't start?"

"We have had this discussion and it always ends badly. Take the Peugeot."

"Why can't we get a real car?"

"We have two real cars. They are both luxury automobiles."

"When? Maybe in the previous century!"

"I am a lawyer, not a Stock Car Racer. I use my wits. Any situation that has to be brought under control by dangerous driving is already hopeless."

"I just wish you could experience the world the way I do."

"You are a man-of-action. If I had your considerable physical capabilities, I wouldn't need to employ your services and I very much doubt I could pay for them."

"Why is it that every time you give me a kind of a compliment, I end up feeling dissed?"

"That is not a word," he said. He's a lawyer. He likes misdirection, to deflect thought from a weakness in the case he is presenting.

"People use it," I said. I am not a lawyer and am easily misdirected. "That makes it a word."

"Word up."

"Yes?"

"Don't."

There was silence for a moment. He pretended to look at something on his desk. I was thinking of a suitable comeback. Then he seemed to remember something and said, "There is a bright note." He attempted a smile. It almost seemed genuine.

"Yes?" I said.

"We are all going to a Rodd Rock concert at Jones Beach! We will get the full VIP treatment. Rodd has arranged everything. You might be called upon to restrain Dickie when I tell him. We have backstage passes. Teddy is looking forward to it."

"But not you?" I asked. I am not sure how he feels about music. He usually listens to jazz on the college station.

"Not my scene really. I can't remember the last time I went to a rock concert. I think it might have been the Allman Brothers or Lynyrd Skynyrd," said LT. He was looking up and away, as if a picture of the memory was being projected on the far wall.

"I can't imagine you at either," I said. Then a picture came into my brain. I did not invite it. LT was waving a large cigar in time to "Free Bird" while all of those around him held lighters. Now, no one carries lighters anymore, and LT's favorite cigar store in midtown had had to move to the cheaper rent district. It is now just one move away from liquidation.

"It was a woman from South Carolina with whom I was interested … tangled up in … at the time," said LT. His voice sounded strangely (for him) thoughtful.

"That makes more sense," I said. "I guess it didn't work out?"

"It did not, as you say, work out. She became a governor's wife, unhappily for all concerned."

"When is the Rodd Rock concert?" I asked. I wanted to pull him out of his memory before he went under.

"This Friday night. I've invited Tyrell," he said briskly. He was back in his New York Consultant-on-the-job voice. His eyes were focused on the present.

"You think there might be trouble?"

"I don't know what goes on at a rock concert these days," he said.

"Why the muscle?" I asked. I had a sense that he was hiding something from me.

"It's just me being prudent. And I think Tyrell will enjoy the music. He used to play the saxophone."

"How did you find that out?" I asked. I had a new image in my mind, of Tyrell prancing across a stage in gold lame', his cheeks puffed out like the north wind on a pirate's map.

"He played one night for Teddy and me when you were on your hiatus in the Catskills."

"I miss all the fun. Was he good?"

"I haven't a clue," said LT. "I think if Bruce Springsteen was singing along with guitars, drums and bass it would have been delightful. A nine-minute saxophone solo leaves something to be desired. I don't care how many margaritas one has consumed."

One hour or so later, I was creeping around a filled parking lot in East Hampton looking for an open spot. I couldn't see one, but someone had to be leaving soon. There were three of us on the prowl. You look for people carrying bags and walking at an angle through the lot. Then you try to guess which row and column they are heading for, and you have to beat the other two (a land rover and a BMW) to the controlling spot, far enough back so the person can get their car out and yet close enough that the other prowlers can't jump in first.

On that day, I guessed well. The spot was mine.

It took a couple of minutes of walking to find the little office suite with the Alpha Bravo Charlie Security sign in the window. I entered. It was a world of white sheetrock and closed doors. The sheetrock slabs were unbroken by moldings of any kind. The reception area was like being in a magician's blank white box. The trick started when one of the hidden panels opened. There was a young and attractive woman sitting at a white laminate counter held up by more white sheetrock. She gave the illusion that she had been sawed in half. It was the nice looking half and she might have stolen my heart away if she had never spoken. Her up-island accent destroyed the illusion and most of the attraction.

"Can I help youse?" she said. She wasn't chewing gum, but she seemed like she should be. In a movie scene she would have been.

"I'm here to see Paul Williams."

"And you are?"

"I work for Lawton Close who has been contracted by Rodd Rock to look into some security issues. I understand that Paul Williams is currently handling security for Rodd?"

"Oh, yes! Rodd Rock is our biggest client. I'm supposed to act normal when he comes in the office, but…I mean it's Rodd Rock and I'm like it's Rodd Rock! You know? And he goes like hello and I go good morning or whatever and inside I'm like *oh my god. It's Rodd Rock!*"

"I feel the same way. Is Mr. Williams in?"

"I'll have to ask him. I won't be a moment."

She got up and went to door number three. She disappeared behind it. What was behind door number three? The big deal of the day?

While she was gone, I turned around and looked over some photographs on the walls flanking the entry door and display window. When she came out, she had the "oh, I'm so sorry" look on her face. It was not supposed to be my day.

"Mr. Williams was called away," she said as she walked back to her reception counter. "He is not at his desk."

"Is that what he said?"

She looked at me for just a microsecond and had the intelligence to crack a smile. "He's like so busy. He said to tell you that he was out, but I figured you already knew that he was like not really out, but I'm sorry he just can't see you at this time."

"I can come back. You have Rodd's picture on the wall."

"Those are some of our famous clients. Did you know there are a lot of Hollywood people moving onto the area? I'm sure you will recognize some of the faces."

"I do! Who is that with Rodd? I think I know him."

"That's Mr. Williams!" she said. She almost giggled with pleasure.

"Paul Williams?" I asked.

"Of course. They are like so close. It's like they are like split up at birth or something."

"That's Paul Williams?" I asked. I was aware that my head was at a weird angle when I said it.

"That's him. I think they were golfing when that picture was taken."

"And he told you to tell me he was busy?"

"Well, you know, it's like he's in a meeting or he's like away from his desk."

I just stood there for a moment. When she sat down and grabbed her mouse, I moved.

"Hey! He said he can't…see…you…" she called out. She even stood up.

Too late, he was already seeing me.

"Dominic Pancetta!" I said. "When did you get out? And don't even tell me it was for good behavior."

"Jesus! Close the door! Will you?" he said. His hands were pushing in the air. He was ten feet from the door he wanted closed.

"Who did you have to rat out to get an early release?"

"Max! Keep it down, will you?"

"You're not going to shake my hand?"

"Why should I? What are you doing here?"

"I wanted to talk to you about last night."

"Last night?" he asked. It was a stall.

"At Rodd Rock's place? Or was that some other Dominic Pancetta in his Viper. You think I'm stupid?"

"I work for Rodd. I see him all the time."

"You left in kind of a hurry last night," I said.

"Yeah?"

"You weren't very polite. You were kind of rude."

"I get that way," he said. He had his face stuck out at me like a challenge.

"You were unprofessional. If you want to hold on to an office like this, you have to start thinking like a business man and not some twelve-year-old spray can artist."

"Look! Here's how it is. Out here I am what I say I am. Got that? My name is Paul Williams. I have a nice thing going here. When I saw you at the house ... let me put it this way, If you blow this gig for me, I will come down on you like a shit tornado." He was moving closer for emphasis.

"With friends like you who needs enemas?" I said. It just came to me.

He was real close now. "Cute. Keep it up."

He was practically kissing my neck.

"Lilac Vegetal!" I almost shouted.

"What?"

"That's the scent I caught last night when you went by me like a turd twister. Can you still buy that stuff?"

"I got a guy. You want some? I can get you some."

"I haven't smelled Lilac Vegetal since I used to go to Carmine the Clip over on Oriental Avenue in the old neighborhood. He had three chairs, no waiting, and if you wanted to put a little money down on the Super Bowl, that was OK too. Did you ever go to Carmines?"

"I grew up in Bensonhurst." He said, with a frown.

"Yeah. That's right. Remember Ritchie G?

"Are you kidding me? One night he and I boosted six cases of Medaglia D'oro from the storage room of the Three Brothers Market. Remember old man Puglia? I'm still drinking that stuff. Now Ritchie's a lawyer and I'm head of security for some of the big players in the Hamptons."

"Doesn't anyone do a background check anymore?" I asked. It was a rhetorical question.

"Look. You're not paying attention. Here's the way it is. I need this gig. You know what happened to my last big client because you were the one that found the body. Every time you show up, I get hit in my wallet. Look! I don't want anybody messing this up. You got that?"

"I'm not here to bust your bubble. I'm sure that in time you will bust your own bubble. I am here to tell you that Mr. Close and I…you remember Mr. Close?"

"LT! How is LT?"

"He's doing good; real good"

"Is he still with Teddy?"

I could see the look in his eye. You can't. His eyes were bright. His lips were apart. His face was slightly forward, as if he was trying to catch some distant sound or a scent.

"Yes."

"I would like to get her alone for twenty minutes …"

"She's ten years older than you and her boyfriend is a powerful consultant who surrounds himself with hired muscle."

"The age doesn't mean anything. She keeps herself real good. And don't make me laugh about the muscle. You make me laugh. You're a freaking Comedy Central. You know that?"

"But seriously folks, LT has signed on with Rodd Rock to help out with certain … ah … matters. Security is going to be part of it. We are going to want to know who is going and who is coming and who shouldn't be hanging around. Like, the missing hard drive from the security computer. You wouldn't know anything about that, would you?"

"It was broken. That's why I went over there. I wanted to see if it was fixable."

"Is it?" I asked.

"What?"

"Fixable."

"What do I look like, a freaking IT guy? I sent it out."

"So it's not here then. That's not it over there on the desk?" I asked. He looked behind at the desk too quickly. His reaction told me that the disk drive was in the room, somewhere.

"What did I just say?" he said as he satisfied himself that the drive was not in plain sight and turned back to me.

"There would have been a record of you entering the house last night. What is it that you don't want us to see?"

"You got to see an ear doctor. You don't hear anything. It was *bro*-kin. There was nothing to see because it wasn't working. That's why I went over there."

"How did you know it wasn't working?" I asked him.

"Because Rodd, ah ... because somebody told me it was broken. I don't know who it was. What are you here busting my chops about? Leave me out of this, will you? I'm warning you, you and your boss, don't be messing with my job security. I can show you what real muscle looks like. You know what I'm talking about."

"Didn't your probation officer mention to you that you are not supposed to associate with known felons?"

"Associate my ass. One phone call and you and your boss are like ... you know ... M.I.A., you know ... missing in action. Now, you know what I'm talking about."

"Who are you going to call, Dom?"

"Look around you," he said. Then he looked around. I did too.

"What am I seeing?"

"You know what this real estate is worth?"

"Tell me," I said.

"A lot. You think I could put up the money to start a business in the Hamptons?"

"I don't know. There was that big robbery in Newark. They are still looking for those guys."

"I could book you into Caroline's as is. You wouldn't even need to audition. I'm wetting my pants here. Who writes your stuff?"

"What was all that about at Rodd's last night?"

"I remembered I had an appointment to see a guy. I had to leave suddenly. Sorry I couldn't have stayed to listen to your jokes."

"You had to run over Carrie and knock her down?"

"She was in the way," he said. Then he compressed his lips and gave me the face. The face wanted to know what was I going to do about it?

"She's Rodd Rock's personal assistant."

"I'll apologize," he said.

"You'll do better than that. Carrie is a friend of mine. LT got her that job. If you come anywhere near her ... listen ... I don't like to make threats because that's just talk. You don't have to worry about talkers. The guys you have to worry about, you never see coming. Now you know what I'm talking about."

"I didn't know there was a connection," he said. He had put the face away and was now paying attention. What the hell, there might be some new strings to pull.

"There are connections all over the place. This is the Hamptons. You are not in Brooklyn anymore. Let me tell you something. In Brooklyn you listen to the street, you hear the names, and you know the set-up. It's different out here. You got people from all over the world who have money on this horse or that horse and you have to know a guy to get the odds. You know what I'm saying?"

"I'm doing all right," he said, "I got a silent partner. If I told you who it was, you would shit in your pants. Just so you know. So, as long as you or your boss don't do anything to make trouble…"

"My motto is live and let live," I said, "but you got to know this isn't Brooklyn."

"You know what this is out here?" he said, crowding my space, not just a little. He apparently thought he had now taken control of the conversation. "This is Candy Land. These people are living in freaking Candy Land. This whole place is so wide open … these people don't know shit about security. You could walk in here and just scoop the shit up."

"It only looks that way," I said. "This is a whole different way of thinking. You can't slip the local cop a couple of comps to Atlantic City and expect him to watch your back. Your brother-in-law doesn't have any mojo out here. This isn't about a couple of free steaks." We retreated from each other. Things eased up a little.

"I'm doing all right as long as nobody screws it up," he said.

"You certainly have a nice ride," I said.

"The Viper? I'm thinking of trading it in."

"What are you, bored with it?" I asked.

"It's fast as hell, but, I don't know, I like to have a little plush. The traffic out here…freaking unbelievable! If I'm going to have to sit behind some rich bitch in a Land Rover for two hours I might as well be comfortable. You know?"

When I got back to the house, I did not give it to LT word for word. He detests vulgarity. I just gave him the highlights. The highlights were enough to make him frown.

"Dominic went to prison for what?" he said.

"They got him on receiving stolen goods, but it could have been for just about anything. He was a punk."

"I don't like it. I have to talk to Rodd Rock about this. I hate to stir up trouble needlessly. Complications! Just when I thought I had something workable…"

"Something workable? You have something working? Care to let me in on the deal?"

"It's in the schematic design phase. It is nothing I care to discuss at present. It will probably change … no … this will change it. I can't have uncontrolled elements in play."

"You want to give me a hint?"

"Later. Let's take a ride over to Rodd's house. Call him and see if he will be in."

5

We took the Cadillac. I drove. LT sat in the back. I don't know why he does that.

"Why don't you sit up front?" I said to him.

"You know I much prefer the back."

"It makes me feel like a chauffeur. It's creepy."

"I'm sorry, but I prefer the back. I will only sit in the death seat if Teddy is driving."

"Why? I'm a better driver than Teddy," I said.

"You have your own style, and admirable reflexes. However, if I am fated to be crushed in a flaming road accident, it is only fitting that Teddy should be at the wheel."

I shut up. What do you say to that?

When we got to Rodd's the gate was closed. I pushed the speaker button and said, "I'd like a happy meal, two guzzlers, some chicken nuggets and thick shake. I have to spackle a wall. Be sure it's thick."

Carrie's voice through the speaker said, "You want fries with that?"

"Super size me."

"Please proceed to the pick-up window. I'm off duty at three."

LT sighed a large, pointed sigh in the back seat. I ignored it. The gates swung wide. We were in.

Carrie came out to meet us and to tell us where to park.

"Hi, Max. Hello Mr. Close. Could you put it there on the far side of the carriage house next to Arlene?"

"It matters?" I asked.

"The landscape guys are going to be here soon. They have big trucks with trailers and they have to swing them around the circular drive. Rodd is in a nasty mood. Did either of you see Page Six this morning?"

"Someone at Page Six knows about the marital difficulties?" said LT, from the back seat.

"That's bad enough, but there have been some phone calls this morning. It's going to be on Entertainment Wrap Up, tonight."

"There's a leak," said LT.

"Rodd isn't happy. He was just going to call you when Max called me. He's in the studio. He's anxious to talk to you."

We parked the Caddy and followed her back to the house. We used the service entrance. We passed through to the kitchen. It looked smaller in daylight. The refrigerator door was open and someone was bending into it, someone less than half clothed. She straightened up at the sound of our footsteps, and she turned around. It was Arlene.

She had a towel wrapped around her from the bellybutton down and a bikini top above. She was fleshy in a nice sort of way; more comfortably endowed than buff. She had two glass bottles of Iced Tea caught under one arm. She had a jar of something in one hand and a tote bag in the other. The ice tea bottles were starting to sweat. She spoke.

"Carrie?"

"Yes," answered Carrie.

"Did you order the water like I asked?"

"Oh, I'm sorry. There's been so much going on. I can get a couple of cases this afternoon."

"Thank you. I'm walking down to the beach; it's such a spiffy day. Hi, Max! Hi, Lawton!"

"Hello, Arlene," said LT.

"Nice meeting you at dinner," I said.

"You too. I wanted to get a chance to speak more with you. I think we know some people in common from Sheepshead Bay."

"Well, I'll be around," I said.

"Yeah. We'll see you at the concert, right?" she said.

"I'm looking forward to it," I said.

"I haven't told Dickie about the concert yet," said LT. "Keep it to yourself for now. I want to tell him myself, quietly and calmly," said LT.

"Whatever," I waved it off. I had other things on my mind.

Arlene looked down at her tote bag and said to Carrie "Tell Pica I'm taking what's left of the lobster salad and a baguette." She bent down to put the bottles in the tote bag. Two ends of a baguette that had been folded in half stuck out like bunny ears.

"Well!" she said as she stood up, holding the tote bag loosely. "See you guys."

And then she turned and went for the door we had just come in. When the door closed, and I heard her feet on the gravel of the driveway I said to Carrie, "did she say spiffy?"

"Yes. You are not going to get me to say anything about my employer. Arlene is a nice girl. She just …"

I waited. LT waited.

Carrie turned and began walking toward the door to the basement.

"She just what?" said LT.

"Rodd is in the studio. I told him you are here."

We went to the same door to the basement and down the same stairs that I only got halfway down before the lights went out. At the bottom of the stairs we turned right. To the left, there was a large pit filled with reclining chairs behind a little handrail. The lights were out in the pit.

"Does Rodd have the local Lazy Boy concession?" I asked. "Is that a showroom?"

"That's the media room. It's like a home theater. Rodd previews all of his videos there. The studio is just here."

She stopped in front of a plain door. There was a red flashing LED labeled RECORDING next to the door. We waited.

"He's recording," she said.

No one spoke, not even LT. That was weird.

Then the blinking stopped and she opened the door. The first thing I felt was cool air. As the door swung wide, I could see a large control board, racks of equipment and bunches of wires. The lights were dimmed to a kind of eternal twilight. Rodd was sitting behind the control board holding a red electric guitar. He put the guitar down by his side and leaned it against his chair when he saw us, but he didn't get up.

"I was just adding a guitar line to a little thing I'm trying to demo. Come in!" he said.

Carrie stayed by the door. "I'll be upstairs if you need me. I have some calls to make. Rodd? If I can't get you out on the seven o'clock do you want to go out of Newark?"

"No. I won't go out of Newark. They'll have a seat. They always do in first class."

"OK," she said and then she was gone.

"Carrie tells me that she used to know Max when she worked upstate?" said Rodd.

Before I could respond, LT said, "I had asked Max to look into a situation involving some gentlemen from the Middle East. He was working undercover."

That wasn't entirely true. In fact aside from the part about the Middle East, it was a complete fib. You can get the real story in my report entitled *RSVP Deceased*.

Then LT reached into his blazer pocket and pulled out a thick fold of legal papers.

"I need you to sign some papers," said LT. He pressed them down onto the top of the mixing console and tried to smooth them down. The papers wanted to fold back up. Holding them down with his left hand, he pulled from his blazer one of his collection of French fountain pens. He de-capped it with his teeth and handed the pen to Rodd, who looked confused.

"What is all this?" said Rodd.

"You are giving me powers of attorney. We are about to begin to rein in some of Mr. Viktor's excesses."

"I hope you know what you are doing," said Rodd, as he began signing. LT indicated the spots with a silent pointing of his elegant finger. Pages were turned, new spots were pointed out and duly signed. "Mel has a bit of a temper. He's touchy about money."

"Yes," said LT, "but it's your money and I am just trying to plug some leaks."

"Speaking of which!" said Rodd straightening up and handing the pen back, "I was dismayed this morning to see that my marital concerns have made it all the way to Page Six. I thought it was odd since we spoke just the other night and almost no one else in the world has been told about this. Then I got a phone call this morning from a guy I know who said that there would be an item on Entertainment Wrap Up, about me and Arlene!. And then the phone started ringing. Carrie has been besieged by people calling for confirmation of various horror stories about my marriage. Gentlemen! I ask you! What the bloody hell is going on?"

"There is a leak," said LT.

"That's obvious. Tell me something I don't know. Now you told me this wouldn't happen! Why is it happening? I mean, *Page* Six! Entertainment Wrap Up! It really is the lowest of the low. This doesn't come from your office, does it?"

"My entire livelihood is built on discretion," said LT.

Their eyes turned to me. Me?

"Don't look at me. Why would I want to jeopardize my bi-weekly pittance?" I said. The tone was defensive. I couldn't help it.

"This can be bad for me," said Rodd. "I gather that tonight's item on television will focus on the money. You know I have an ex-wife and children and each and every one of them has a team of lawyers … Good lord. It's a disssss…*aster!*"

"I'll put my people on it," said LT.

I looked at him and raised both my eyebrows and I didn't care if the overlord of sex, drugs and rock and roll saw it or not. LT doesn't talk that way. He never puts his people on anything. He brings his resources to projects. Finding a snitch is not a kind of a project that LT takes on.

"I can't overstate the importance of keeping a proper lid on things," said Rodd. "There's more than just money at stake. You must know that show business is mostly about perception. I hired you because you came highly recommended by people whose judgment I believe to be sound. Carrie is one of them. But we have to manage this thing properly. I don't like loose ends. I can't afford loose ends. I don't want this thing getting out of hand. Am I clear?"

"Yes," said LT. "In the interests of full disclosure I would like to mention that Mr. Paul Williams has a bit of history, some of which includes time spent in a penitentiary."

"Yes, yes. I know all about that," said Rodd.

"Then you know what he was charged with?"

"I believe he was caught with things that didn't belong to him."

"Yes, but that was merely the charge of convenience. It was the DA's best evidence. They had a roomful of articles and no need for easily intimidated witnesses. There could have been other charges. Mr. Williams led a very colorful life back in the day. He was then known as Dominic Pancetta. It could well have been two counts of murder. Where you aware of that?"

"I wasn't. Thank you for bringing it to my intention. You must think me mad to have someone like that on the payroll. Perhaps I should tell you something about the music business. Have you heard of Smash City, the recording studio on Ninth Avenue in New York?"

"LT hasn't, but I have," I said. "Dickie talks about it. It's one of the top five studios in the city."

"That's right. I can't tell you how many hits have been recorded there; many. I built that studio. I hired the best audio guy in the country to design the acoustic characteristics of the rooms and to install the equipment. You see that tape deck over there? The big one with three inch tape? That came from Smash City. It's German, the finest in the world. Everything was the best I could get. I had a Neve 64 track console. I had Penny and Giles faders and the mic pre-amp on each channel cost over two hundred dollars.

"Here," he said as he stood and walked three feet to a small built-in cabinet. "Do you know what this is?" He pulled a worn cardboard box out of the cabinet and showed it to us. It had the name *Dirk* written on the top of the box in fading ink from a felt tip marker.

LT and I shrugged.

Rodd removed the cover of the box, as if it were covering the largest ruby ever found. Inside the box was a metal tube with a wire mesh top.

"Take a look," said Rodd. I was looking and so was LT. I didn't know what I was looking at, except that the thing was probably a microphone.

"Does Dirk refer to Dirk Redland of the Lobes?" said LT.

"This is his very own Neumann U-87. This is the vocal mic he used when we recorded *Lolly*. That went triple platinum. He is the only person to have used it. No one else was allowed to touch it."

LT crowded in for a better look. I did as well. *Lolly* was almost an anthem for a certain age group. It was covered by hundreds of people. It was a classic among classics.

"Is this expensive?" said LT. Money is never far from his thinking.

"It would set you back about five grand today. It is German, the finest microphone made. There's a little tube amplifier built into the microphone. Now the thing about a tube amp is that when you overdrive it, when it saturates, it generates even order harmonics. A transistor, on the other hand, when you push it too hard, will generate odd order harmonics and sound very harsh and cutting. That's why studios still use these tube mics today. This one is more than 40 years old."

"So this is special, then." Said LT.

"Dirk Redland's mic with which he recorded Lolly? And all the rest? I think it is. This is a bloody museum piece. It's priceless."

"So much history," said LT, wagging his head from side to side. "Was *Lolly* recorded at Smash City?"

"No! That's the thing. One month before we were to open our doors, some people came in. They were unhappy about our new studio. They tied up my man and they took axes to the equipment and the rooms and the wiring conduits. Do you know what a patch bay is?"

Both of us shook our heads.

"Here's a small one. Every line from every piece of equipment in the building is brought in to this one panel. It allows me complete freedom to run my signals wherever I want. Each jack in this patch bay is hand soldered. Imagine, if you will, what an axe would do to all this spaghetti. Needless to say, we didn't open in a month or even four. Luckily I had the money to see it through, but I got the message.

"You know what the cops told me? They said good luck. They filed a report. To my knowledge, they never questioned a single person. I felt I had to fight fire with fire. There was almost two million dollars of my money in that studio. What was I supposed to do? Walk away from it? I asked around. I met with some people. Money changed hands. I now have a security team. Mr. Williams or whatever his name really is, is the local manager."

"Bit of irony, the name Smash City," said LT.

"Yes. It wasn't lost on me," said Rodd. He then made a grimace, as if the memory was still painful.

"Why break it up?" asked LT.

"How much do you know about the music business?"

"Almost nothing. Teddy sometimes buys Rolling Stone and keeps up with things. I never have time to listen to music. I haven't paid attention in years."

"There's loads of back room deal-making in the music business," said Rodd. "Airplay is everything. Getting a tune on the air can be tricky. You may not realize that most of the independent radio stations have been snatched up by the big boys. Vertical integration they call it. The big boys control the product from input to output. Professional studios charge hundreds of dollars per hour for use of the facilities. Even so, they have to be kept booked to make any money. Usually commercial bookings are during the day. That's when they record the latest jingle for your magic floor sweeper or room deodorizer or what not. The artists, that's the creative work, they usually like to record at night. Say I was a typical band signed by a major label. Now, they will want me to record a CD. The label would buy a block of time for me at a studio for a flat rate.

"The studio likes to look forward in time and see everything blocked out. Now, New York is a big market and there is a lot of business, but less than you might imagine. There were only four big studios when I started construction of Smash City. People looked around and didn't like the idea of dividing the pie up in smaller pieces. Therefore, somebody called in the goons. The whole distribution end of the business is filled with … ah … you know …" He touched his nose and raised his brow, "thugs and such like. There's a lot of cash in the business, especially in the venues. Cash flows back and forth like a river-tide.

"Performers are notoriously naïve about the money side. I thought I knew the ropes after more than twenty years in the business, but … There's my recent contretemps with my management and the famous missing millions.

We talked about it the other night. The truth is, sometimes, the whole thing just makes me sick."

"Is there any possibility that Williams is the leak?" I said. Both men turned to me, as if I had just asked the number to call for 911.

"What are you thinking?" said LT.

"I don't know." I said. "He was in the house. Maybe he was talking to one of the staff?"

"We will have to take a look at every possibility. We should probably begin with the staff. Do you have any recently disgruntled employees?" said LT, turning to Rodd.

"The line forms at the right. People come to me all humble and looking for a job. Then after they are here a couple of months, they start resenting that I have things they don't have and won't have as a gardener or house painter or electrician. I don't make the rules. I pay good money, better than anyone else around and it somehow makes the problem worse, not better. I don't understand it."

"I think I would like to have Max interview the people that you employ. Could that be arranged?"

"Done! I'll tell Carrie."

"All right Max, take me home," said LT. "Rodd, you and I can stay in touch by phone. Max, make your arrangements with Carrie and start as soon as you can; this afternoon if possible."

"To do what?" I said.

"We are looking for a leak," he said.

"What leverage do I have?"

"I don't know. Use your wits," he said. I could have used a little more in the way of guidance.

"You know what my chance of success is?" I asked him.

"No one knows until you try," he said with a shrug. He had already dropped out of the subject. He didn't seemed to care. It was unusual.

"You want the odds?" I asked him.

"This isn't a game of chance. This is a game of skill. I have every confidence in your abilities."

"I don't like it. I need some kind of pry bar, something to work into any cracks that I might find."

"Tell them there was a blackmail attempt. Tell them that someone at Page Six offered to kill the story for a monetary consideration. Tell them the police are going to be involved, maybe the FBI. What the hell, Stimulate!" He was impatient in a way that I had never seen before. He usually covers up his emotions like a cat kicking sand over lumps in the cat box. I sometimes think that LT sees emotions as lumps in his cat box.

"Man, this could get ugly," I said shaking my head.

"Before you go," said Rodd, "do you want to hear some of the new tracks?"

LT looked pained, but he had to say yes. I was interested. I actually wanted to hear what he was recording. Masters of rock and roll rarely make great music when they have all the time and money in the world. I don't know why, but it seems to hold true.

Rodd suddenly looked ten years younger. Enthusiasm is a great antidote for age. He started pushing buttons and playing with sliders and the whole board lit up with dancing lights and there was music.

All I can tell you is that it was very loud. It sounded great as far as I could tell, but I had heard something similar too many times before. There was no singing yet. That would probably come later. LT looked bewildered. Rodd was watching the lights and bobbing his head in time with the beat. I was trying to look like I was enjoying it. I was, on some level. It wasn't bad. I'm sure it will be better with words.

"What do you think?" he said when it ended.

"Very professional," said LT.

"I can't wait to hear the words," I said.

"You think there should be words?" Rodd said. "Oh! Before I forget, see Carrie on your way out for your passes for the show. Do you need a car? We have a couple of limos going from here."

"I'll take my car," said LT.

"Please try to be early. Security is tight as we get closer to show time. I don't want to have to worry about all of you. I will have my own worries. It should be a good show. The sound guys are terrif. There is also going to be a surprise guest. It's supposed to be a surprise, but our management boys have been chewing over the details of this thing for months. It should be fun. You are in for a treat."

6

Dickie was in the kitchen opening oysters. He is proud of his ability to open oysters. I learned years ago that if you are good at something, people will ask you to do it. I am very bad at opening oysters and I work hard to stay that way. LT, Teddy and I were in the summer office. I was going through LT's American Express bill for the month. Teddy was doing something on her laptop that was actually on top of her lap. Her legs are so thin, it appeared that the laptop might slide off. I tried not to look at it. LT was reading something about the Bush presidency that made him grunt from time to time. He was becoming agitated. Finally he threw the book down on his blotter and said, "I wonder if Rodd's ex-wife could be the leak?"

"Mmmmm," came from Teddy. The way she inflected it indicated that she thought LT's question could possibly be answered in the affirmative, but probably not.

"Does she know about the problems with Rodd and Arlene?" I asked.

"She must." asked LT. "Rodd mentioned that her lawyers have been consulted."

"Do you want me to see her?" I asked.

"Not yet," said LT. "Dickie tells me that in the martial arts, when a stronger opponent comes at you, the trick is, rather than trying to block his energy, to go with it and direct it. There's something profound in that. One doesn't waste all one's strength going against a bigger strength, one steers the bigger strength to one's advantage. I can see it."

He picked up his book, frowned at it and set it back down.

"Why do people leak?" he asked the room.

"Revenge," said Teddy, "or a desire to participate in reflected glory, or control."

"I wonder if the stalker knows about the marital difficulties?" asked LT.

"I'm sure he does," said Teddy.

"How would he find out?" asked LT.

"He is concentrating obsessive attention on the object of his mania. Believe me, sweetie, marital difficulties are not that hard to spot." Teddy spoke with an edge to her voice. LT picked up on it.

"We're not married," he said.

"Relationship difficulties then, like the one that seems to be forming right now."

There was an immense billowing, volcanic cloud of silence. It lasted for about forty seconds and then the phone rang. No one moved. It rang again. LT sighed, but no one moved. It stopped ringing. There was the padding of new age slippers on the parquet floor.

"Mr. Close?" said Dickie at the doorway.

"Yes?"

"There is a Mr. Viktor on the phone."

"Yes?"

"He's very angry about something, he called you a …" Dickie stopped when he saw Teddy look up with cheerful expectation.

"Yes, Dickie?" said LT.

"I better not say."

"Thank you, Dickie. I will pick up in here." LT pulled the phone in close and pressed the speaker button. "Yes?" he said. "Can I help you?"

"Close?" said, or rather screamed, Mel Viktor. "I've just come from the bank! They told me that there is a hold on one of the accounts and that the house account now requires three signatures for a withdrawal! What the hell is going on? I've got people I have to pay!"

"That shouldn't present a problem. Please forward all disbursements to my office for the counter signatures and they will go out the same day, overnight if you prefer," said LT, calmly. "I can send a messenger if you can't wait for the mail."

"I don't have time to screw around with this! You're killing me here! What's going on? I've got people crying to be paid and I'm not going to send the damned checks all over the goddamned place to get signatures. What the hell? I called Rodd about this and he told me to talk to you. Let me tell you something. You better get this straightened out and straightened out fast. I can't run a business this way. You don't know the trouble you have caused, but this is serious. Listen to me! This is serious like you don't even know. I can't have this!"

"I am sorry that you have been inconvenienced," said LT, in his most soothing tone. "Rodd has asked me to help him bring order to his financial arrangements and …"

"Rodd doesn't know anything at all about financial arrangements. That's what I do! Let me tell you this, I am very territorial when it come to money. Here's what you do. You call the bank and get those signatures the hell off of that account and remove that hold or by God there will trouble and you won't like it one little bit."

"The bank has closed for the day," said LT, evenly. "I'll take this up with them on Monday."

"Monday! Bullshit. I want this cleared up right now! This minute! Don't give me this Monday shit. I've got people that have to be paid!"

"I'll see what I can do," said LT.

"You better see what you can do," said Viktor. He hadn't calmed down any.

"I'm sure everything can be resolved," said LT.

"It better be. I'm going to be watching," said Viktor. He hung up.

There was another little moment of silence during which LT placed the handset in its cradle, as if it were a sleeping baby he didn't want to wake..

"Snip, snip," said LT. Then he picked up his book.

"Mmmm," said Teddy.

7

When Lawton Close travels with Teddy, Teddy drives. Teddy likes it hard and fast in the passing lane. She likes to talk her way through traffic situations. "Any time, Ms. Bumpersticker, you can move it back to the middle lane." She will blink the headlights when someone dawdles in the fast lane. It's a trick she learned in Germany. It doesn't go over well in New York.

I managed to get a window seat. Dickie got the hump because he's only five foot six. Tyrell had the other window and LT was riding shotgun. On the way through Southampton Teddy kept up a running commentary.

"Nice driving. Love the turn signal. Did you see that?" Driving in the Hamptons on a Friday night in the summer is always an opportunity for social intercourse of one kind or another. "Sweetie," Teddy intoned to LT in her sweetest Hamptons voice as we were passing the Lobster Inn and there was some jockeying for lanes at the start of the Sunrise Highway, "would you kindly flip off the guy in the Beemer for me? He's nice looking, but badly raised. I would do it, but you are closer."

LT looked over at the maddened driver of the silver BMW. The driver looked back. LT prepared his digit just below the glass in preparation for the reveal.

"Are you crazy?" I said loudly from the back seat. "If you flip that guy off wearing that hat, I'm getting out of this car. I'll walk home!"

LT turned his eyes to the road. The Beemer shot forward into a tiny opening in traffic and cut in front of the Caddy. Teddy didn't lift her foot and for a brief moment, I thought there was going to be some NASCAR style bump drafting. Then the Beemer saw a parking space length opening in the right lane and he veered into it, causing brake lights behind him. With trouble now in someone else's lane, LT sat back and closed his eyes.

He likes it when Teddy is at the wheel although that doesn't stop him from pressing his little, tasseled loafer foot on an invisible brake pedal when he thinks she needs to slow down. That particular night, however, he went into some sort of pre-concert meditation state.

Unfortunately, he was wearing the hat. I had been serious when I said I would walk home if he caused a heated exchange while wearing it. It was a raggedy maggoty hipster's hat. I tried to talk him out of it, but he gets stubborn. Teddy found it at the hospital thrift store and they laughed about it for days, but then he actually started wearing it to places, real places where people could see it.

"You don't have a hat face," I said to him as we assembled in the kitchen in our concert wear. "And even if you did, you would still look stupid in a stingy brim con artist's hat."

"I look stupid?" he asked , threat-fully, I thought.

"I overstated. You look … uncomfortable. You are not a hipster hat guy. You are a high powered consultant with a law degree."

"It's a rock concert. And anyway, Teddy loves it."

"I know. It's a gag. I get it. Teddy gets it. I don't know about Dickie. I think he has been looking on eBay for his own hipster hat, but the rest of the world … I don't think they get it."

"I like it," said LT, running his thumb and two fingers around the brim. It was his conversation ender. He liked it; enough said.

"Well, then don't tilt it forward. It just doesn't look right," I said.

"You're supposed to tilt it forward. That's how it's worn," he countered.

"If you have an IQ of 24 and you spend your afternoons running numbers for Mr. Goombah from the back room of a deli … maybe."

"It's fun," he said. He almost pouted, almost.

"OK. I give up. Wear the hat."

"I intend to do so," he said. And that, as they say, was that. The cat was in the hat.

We made quite a car full. Dickie had selected his better silver dragon jacket that has the name from some Dojo across the back in letters you could read from the 32nd floor. He covered his thinning spot with his formal baseball cap that he saves for special occasions. Teddy was styled-out in her sparkle hose and her mini-skirt outfit from the sixties. It was the real deal, some famous designer from that era that you would know if I could remember his name. It didn't mean anything to me but Carrie nearly fell over herself gushing about it. I just wore a polo shirt and nice slacks. Tyrell had on a brown sports jacket over a Hawaiian shirt of muted earth tones .

"Isn't that hot for you?" I said to him.

He unbuttoned and pulled back the jacket to reveal his shoulder holster and the butt end of his nine-millimeter automatic. If he is carrying, it is usually the little revolver.

"What's the deal? What are you expecting?" I asked. My voice was pitched higher than I intended. Sudden anxiety does that. I don't have a poker face, either.

"Mr. Close said to bring it."

"Wait! I should go back for my Colt."

"You don't need your little pop gun," said Tyrell, with his big easy grin. "You just stay close to me."

"What the hell? Why would he ask you to come dressed heavy?"

"He didn't say."

Dickie was unusually quiet during the ride. He was too excited to chatter. He had his iPod buds in his ears the whole way and I think I heard some old Lobes numbers. He must have had it cranked.

I didn't talk much either. I'd like to say I had a lot on my mind, but I couldn't get started piecing it all together so I didn't have anything on my mind, but I felt like I should have.

We were about fifteen minutes from Jones Beach when Tyrell's cell phone went off. He fumbled for it in his jacket pocket, flipped it open, peered at the number and then put it to his ear. "What's up?" he said. Then he listened for about a half a minute. Then he said, "Thanks. I owe you." Then he closed up his phone and put it out of sight.

"Mr. Close," said Tyrell.

"Yes?" said the hipster hat as it rotated to expose LT's face.

"I just got a call from a guy named Lenny."

"Who's that?" said LT.

"Just a guy. He tells me things he hears on the street. We go back a long time."

"What did he tell you?" asked LT.

"The word is that someone hijacked a shipment of cocaine from a couple of amateurs."

"Why is that of interest to me?" asked LT.

"The word is that Mel Viktor was the banker for the operation."

"Mel was buying cocaine?" asked LT.

"It's complicated. Mel had formed a production company to make a movie. The drug deal seems to have been a sideline. Either way he is out the money or the drugs."

"Was it a big shipment?" asked LT.

"Sizable. That's what I was told."

"Tomorrow, I would like you to develop that line of investigation," said LT. "See me in the morning. Tonight, I want to go to a concert."

Teddy made it to Jones Beach in under two hours. It was good driving for a Friday night, though most of the traffic was going the other way, towards the Hamptons. We parked in a special VIP area and fell out of the car.

"Do you know where to go?" said LT, to Teddy."

"Follow me," she said. We followed her up and around to the back stage area. There was a lot going on. The band and the technicians were just finishing sound check.

"I can't hear a bloody thing!" screamed Rodd, while poking a rigid finger at his ear. He was dressed in loose-fitting silk pants and a wild print shirt. It wasn't the usual Rodd Rock costume. He looked more like a guy from a retirement village in Sri Lanka.

"How about now?" said an amplified voice from somewhere.

"I need more bass," said Rodd. He kept jerking his thumb up in the air. "More!"

The bass player was playing a series of notes. The drummer was hammering away on the bass drum with his foot.

Then Rodd started to sing into a microphone. His voice sounded raspy. He stopped singing and pointed to his ear and then jabbed his thumb toward the sky a few times.

"Oh, come *on*!" he said. "How the hell am I supposed to do this if I can't hear myself at all?"

"How about now?" said the amplified voice.

"I've got too much of the keyboard, much too much of the rhythm guitar and I need more of myself and the bloody bass. I think this ear piece is blown out," he said, digging something out of his ear. "Can I get another one?"

Arlene appeared across the back of the stage, and waved and walked over to us. She was wearing jeans that must have been genetically engineered for her body. She was holding a handful of identification cards to put around our necks. LT started to protest, but she said they were important. Dickie never stopped fiddling with his. He still has it. He spent a week's salary to have it framed in a shadow box. Dickie needs help.

Arlene led us back to a little room with some seating. "You can wait here until Rodd is done with sound check," she said. "There's something to drink and the caterers have sent over this fruit and salad platter. Feel free."

I had never seen Arlene so energized. Her eyes were flashing with excitement and something else. It was the same look with everyone I could see. It seemed like the entire crew had pre-show jitters.

There was a commotion at the door of our little waiting room. Somebody was yelling for Arlene. He was a short guy, but round and had a baby face with short dark hair combed straight forward like a Roman Emperor. He stuck his head in, saw her and said loudly, "There you are! I've been looking all over for you. Rodd had me hold some passes for him and I need them back. The box office said you picked them up. You got them?"

"Yes, Mel," said Arlene. Her voice was edgy. She obviously didn't care for Mel. "I have some friends coming later."

"I'm sorry, babe, but I got to have them back . Hi, folks," he said scanning the rest of us quickly. He wasn't looking for a reply and he didn't get any.

"Mel! I asked for those tickets three weeks ago!" said Arlene. Both her hands came up. "What am I going to do with my friends?"

"I need those tickets, babe, got to have them. There's some label people coming and some other very important people."

"Mel, these are close friends. What am I supposed to do with them?"

"Bring them backstage," said Mel with a condescending smile. His tone of voice suited the smile. "They'll get a kick out of meeting everyone."

"No! Not this time. Make some other arrangements. I've promised these people good seats and they …"

"Listen, babe, I got to have those tickets and I don't have much time. You want to hand them over? Or do you want to hand them over?"

"I'm going to tell Rodd about this. He's not going to like it."

"Hey! Babe! Don't screw with the talent. You can tell him any damn thing you want after the show, but if you screw with his head before the show … I'll make you wish you hadn't."

"Hold on!" said LT, getting up out of an old ratty leather couch he had settled into. He advanced.

"Sit down," said Mel to LT.

"I suggest you alter your tone," said LT.

"Who the hell are you?" said Mel, looking intently at his security card. I wish LT had taken off his hipster hat. It's hard to come off as threatening in a thrift store hipster hat. "Oh! You're Lawton Close! We talked on the phone. I'm Mel Viktor. I haven't heard from the bank yet. When am I going to hear from the bank?" Mel moved away from Arlene and began to crowd LT's space.

"Banks can't be hurried. My card," said LT, handing one of his embossed cards to Mel. He took it, looked at one side and then flipped it over, as if there might be more information on the back.

"I've seen you around."

"I've been around. These are my associates," said LT, nodding his head at his crew.

"Uh huh. That's great," Mel leaned to put his mouth next to LT's ear and said quietly, "I want that money, or I promise you won't like what happens next." I heard the words because I leaned in as well. If Mel had put a quick hand to one of his pockets or behind his back he wouldn't like what would happen next either. He saw me lean in and he backed off. Out came his professional smile. "You're new. I should sit down with you and tell you how things work around here. And look, you have to clear up this business about signatures with the bank. I can't have this. You got to fix this thing and fix it fast."

"I am trying to fix a lot of things," said LT.

"I mean now," said Viktor.

"I'm doing what I can," said LT.

"It's not good enough. I'm not kidding. Believe me, I'm not kidding."

They stood there for a moment eyeing each other like a couple of rutting stags. No one noticed that Arlene had slipped out of the room. We noticed when she came back because in front of her was a giant black gentleman with no neck and arms the size of sea lions. His oversized head was mostly covered by a NY Giant's hat with an oversized and flat bill. The hat was cocked at an angle and turned sideways. Below it, more properly aligned with his massive geometry, was a black do rag. He was jangling with neck chains. When he walked, he led with his shoulders. He kept his hands in front of him at all times, palms turned in. He spoke, using a quiet, almost pleading tone, "Mr. Viktor, I'm going to have to ask you to leave the immediate premises."

"Marcus, you are not going to throw me out of my own show, are you? You want me to bring *my* security guys in here?"

"Mr. Viktor, Arlene has asked me to ask you politely to leave this room. I'm asking you."

"All right. I'll tell the label people that Rodd Rock is too big time for them, that he's forgotten how the game is played and that his wife is a … "

"That's enough!" said LT, stepping up to the two men. "You have been asked to leave the room. I suggest you do so at once."

"Or?"

"My associates will help this gentleman physically remove you."

He looked around at the room. He looked at Tyrell, who wasn't smiling. He looked back at Marcus, he looked at me and he finished up with LT. His entire mood changed. "Hey!" he said, "I'll make other arrangements. Enjoy the show, folks." He was smiling broadly. "I have a lot to do. Marcus? We'll talk."

He was gone. Marcus stayed behind.

"Arlene," he said softly, "one of the guys thought he saw the stalker."

"Here?"

"In the parking lot. I'm having someone check on it. Do you want me to call the police?"

"No. I don't know. Maybe. Tell me if they see him in the seats or anywhere near the stage. Does everyone know what he looks like?"

"We showed his picture at the security meeting. He's not hard to spot."

"OK. Keep me informed," said Arlene.

"I better get back out front," said Marcus. The name had been playing in my head and then the association popped. Marcus O'Brien had once played for the Giants.

"Thank you, Marcus," said Arlene. Suddenly she seemed apprehensive.

He turned and left with more grace than I would have expected from a big man.

"Was that Marcus O'Brien?" I said.

"You know him?" said LT to me.

"Yes, that's him," said Arlene.

"He played a couple of seasons with Giants," I said.

"Rodd pays him to live-in as a kind of bodyguard," said Arlene, "since the … incident."

Just then Rodd entered. He was muttering to himself. He was sweating and he looked sick.

"Arlene dear, where the bloody hell are my pain pills?"

"I don't know, Rodd. I thought I put them in the cooler."

"Where is Carrie?" said Rodd. He was so keyed up his entire body was moving, but not in any coordinated way.

"She's out front with the concessions," said Arlene.

"Does she know where my pain pills are? I can't play my bloody guitar. Somebody better find my pain pills. Where is the guitar tech? My Strat has a loose saddle and the B string keeps going out of pitch."

"I don't know where he went, "said Arlene. She sounded annoyed. "Is sound check over? Maybe he went to get something to eat?"

"I can't play tonight. This is a bloody fiasco. Could you send someone out to get some pain pills?"

"I have aspirin in my purse."

"You know what aspirin does to my stomach. I have to have my pain pills. Where the hell is Mel?" said Rodd.

"Mel tried to take back the tickets," said Arlene. "I told him he couldn't have them."

"Look, honey, there's going to be twelve thousand people out there in another hour and I have to find some way to make them happy they spent a hundred dollars a seat to see a elder gentleman with arthritis pretend to make music. Can we put Mel and the tickets aside until later?"

"Fine. Fine! I'll go get your damned pain pills," said Arlene. She was almost yelling. "I hate the pre-show anxiety. I hate the whole thing. I need a breath of fresh air anyway." She stomped her heels on the way out. Rodd followed after he, saying something that sounded like an attempt to appease. His appeasing tone seemed to fall flat.

"Oh, boy!" said Teddy, when they were out of hearing.

Dickie said nothing. He looked, as if he had just seen a puppy run over by a speeding car.

There we were.

"I'm going to have a beer," said Tyrell. "Anybody?"

There were no takers.

We sat fairly quietly for a while. Dickie plugged his ear buds back in and soon his head was bouncing. Teddy went out to find a rest room. LT pulled his hipster hat lower on his forehead and slumped into the ratty leather couch. I just waited.

It was nearly two hours later when the opening act went on. We went out to the edge of the stage to watch. It was a small band, backing up a girl with a guitar. She had a smoky voice and plenty of it and she used it effectively. At one point Teddy leaned into us and shouted "She's good."

LT nodded blankly. He had brought little cotton balls with him and he was trying to shove bits of cotton in his ears below the brim of his hipster hat. It completed the picture in a weird way. It looked like his stuffing was showing.

The warm-up act played for about forty minutes. The audience was enthusiastic, but half missing. When the warm-up group had left the stage and the stage hands were taking their equipment and drums away, the rest of the people who came to see Rodd Rock began to wander slowly down the aisles to their seats. Most of them were carrying items from the concession stand.

We couldn't see Rodd. He was in his own private area getting ready. We couldn't see any of his band members. I could see Marcus talking to someone with a security badge around his neck and then he pointed at us. The man with the badge came over to us from the other side of the stage. "Uh oh," I said to myself, "here it comes."

The man went directly to LT and started talking. LT had to stop him and pull out his ear cotton and then tell him to repeat what he had been saying.

"Thomas Valderben, he's a stalker, has been sighted in the audience. There is a court order of protection against him. He's not supposed to be here. Marcus has asked me to ask you to keep an eye out for him."

"What does he look like?"

"He's about five, five, heavyset, short dark hair. He is wearing red running shoes, tan cotton pants with a stain and a checked shirt. If you see anyone like that, give me or Marcus the sign. I'll be right over there and Marcus will be at the back of the stage. There will be security guys down front."

"OK." Said LT. He looked genuinely worried. I can tell when he's anxious. "Is there a metal detector here?"

"Not tonight. We usually don't set up screening for a Rodd Rock concert, he usually draws an older crowd."

"We'll look for him," said LT. Then he nodded at me and waited for me to nod in return. Then he nodded to Tyrell, who touched his jacket where his automatic was hidden. Then LT turned to nod to Dickie. Dickie's eyes were closed and his head was rocking from side to side. LT started to move toward him, then stopped and just shook his head. We would have to face our dangers without the assistance of the velvet black-belt.

"Thanks. I don't expect any trouble, but this guy is definitely a loose cannon," said Marcus. He turned and skipped back across the stage.

A guitar tech was going down the line of Rodd's seven guitars standing upright at the base of the drum riser. There were another ten or so in a walk-in shipping container back stage. The tech was checking the tuning with an electronic tuner and wiping each one with a cloth. Two guys were setting up a drum kit on the top of the riser, that looked a little like a Mayan pyramid. It was actually a series of steep risers that ran almost to the back of the stage. I could see that the risers were wired for pyrotechnics. A guy in a pony tail was checking wires and connections that led from the fireworks to a bank of switches and a computer backstage. Something slammed into my back.

"What?" I said to Dickie, who had come in close and punched me.

"I just saw Eric the Red!" he said, pointing to the other side of the stage.

"Here?"

"I think he might be going to play tonight, maybe sit in for a few songs," said Dickie.

"That would be cool," I said just for something rock concertish to say. Eric the Red played on the fourth Lobes album, back when they were still pressing vinyl. He was a flamboyant keyboard and guitar player who also wrote a couple of their early hits. His real name, as most of you will know, is Eric Reed. When I looked where Dickie was pointing I saw a tall shadowy figure in a black cape with a hat like LT's only much, much bigger. He resembled a Doctor Seuss character.

"Max, Tyrell, Dickie…" said LT.

We gathered around him.

I want you to go down into the crowd and circulate. If the stalker is here tonight, I don't want him anywhere near the stage. Dickie?"

"Yes, Mr. Close?"

"This is serious business. If you see him, signal me. Stay away from him. All of you. Go now before the place fills up."

"Can't I look for him from the stage?" said Dickie. He was obviously upset that he was about to give up his special place just before the music started.

"Sorry, Dickie, but no. I want all of you to move through the crowd. I want coverage. You understand? I want you to check out the whole audience. Does anyone need to hear the description again?"

Tyrell and I shook our heads.

"What description?" said Dickie.

LT told him about the stalker. Dickie looked thoughtful. Looks can be deceiving.

"How did we get involved in concert security?" said Tyrell.

"Because we are working for Rodd Rock and this is what he needs right now," said LT.

"I'll take the left side," I said. "Dickie can have the middle and Tyrell, why don't you take the right side." He nodded, but Dickie screwed up his forehead and said, "Stage right or audience right?"

"I'll be there," I said pointing. "What do you care? You are in the middle. That's stage middle, not audience middle."

"It is? Oh! Duh." He said. Whoosh! Even sarcasm passes over Dickie leaving him untouched.

"Get going." said LT. Something was bothering him.

It was strange working against the crowd. They were coming to their seats and looking for a good time. I was trying to go the other way and I was looking for a stalker. There was a funny smell in the air. Someone or two was lighting up a bit of devil weed. There was beer; a lot of beer and I saw at least one bottle of Wild Turkey that had slipped out of its brown paper covering.

It was a hot summer night and there were unbounded, lightly covered chesticles on display; big ones, small ones, shapely ones and fallen arches. I didn't have time for any of that, I was looking for red running shoes.

The audience was more than half female and many of them came in groups. They were beyond the first blush of youth; in fact some of them probably couldn't remember back that far. A number of them smelled nice. This wasn't the patchouli oil crowd. This was more like desperate housewives and company.

I was still wandering and looking when the lights came down and there was a commotion on the stage. A local Deejay was being introduced. He was there to bring on the main act. The Deejay had his own local following who yelled their greetings back to the stage. He cracked some lame jokes and nodded to the shouters. He was so loudly amplified I could hardly understand him. I forgot about the stalker for a moment and watched the stage.

The Deejay said some nice things about the charity for sick children that was to receive a portion of the gate. The night was billed as a charity concert. Then there was a little joking around about the Lobes. Then the Deejay raised up his voice and screamed out an intro for Rodd Rock that got the audience cheering and standing. There was a big crashing guitar chord, some drums and Rodd, dressed in white, came skipping across the stage, as if he were twenty-two years old. I had to shake my head and refocus to make sure it was the same person I had seen an hour and a half before complaining about his arthritis.

He grabbed the microphone from the stand and started singing the first line of "Blue Roller". The audience sent up a cheer, as if he had just scored a World Cup goal. By then, the entire audience was on its feet. I couldn't see Dickie, the stage, Tyrell or anyone except an occasional flash of white from the front of the stage. It was hopeless.

There was this funny little moment at the end of the first song. It stuck with me. "Blue Roller" is on three different albums, CDs or whatever. It has a fast dance tempo, but live, the band kicked it up. It was racing right along when they got to the end and they did one of those hold-the-last-note crash tingle finale. Rodd was waving his pick over the strings and the volume of the final chord was crushing. The drummer was hitting everything he had. Rodd looked down at his guitar for a moment, just a short moment, but when he looked up again his eyes were crazed. The power of some demon was upon him. When he looked up, his expression was maniacal. He appeared transfigured. He had gone over some well-guarded border into a dangerous place. When the audience saw the look, they went wild. Their voices rose up like a storm wind. This was what they had come to see. But what was it? I felt my follicles stir.

Then it was over. The overlord of sex and drugs had had his look-in. It only lasted a second or two. The applause and cheering were long and loud. The audience and the performer were hooked up to some giant energy source.

After the applause died a little, Rodd looked back at the drummer, who raised his sticks for a count off. The audience recognized the intro chords to "Belinda" and another cheer went up, even before Rodd started singing. The ballad, as they played it live, had a much longer instrumental intro than the recorded version and people had calmed down a little before Rodd gave them a look over his raised microphone and spoke, "Oh, Belinda…"

A synthesizer took up the tune and repeated it a few times before Rodd began to growl, "The rain was like pain on the Salisbury plain and the moon lost its way in the sky. I saw her first while dying of thirst for a spoonful of potion to buy."

The audience began to sway, still on their feet. I started back to the stage since I couldn't see anything down in the crowd. I had just flashed my badge at two of the temp security guys when Rodd kicked off a bluesy version of "My Connection." The audience responded with whistles and shouts. As I went up the side stairs to the stage, people directly in front of the stage were beginning to surge closer. Now they were moving their fists in time with the music. People were bumping each other in the tangle of bodies below the stage. I could see that the security guys were getting tense.

In the middle of the song, just at the end of the chorus where Rodd screams about the sons of bitches with their addiction to riches, there was a sudden howl of lead guitar and the lights began to strobe and flicker. Then a blue spot light raced around the back of the stage and came to rest on a strange figure in a black cloak with a tall, sky-scraping, furry hipster's hat that made LT's hat look like a beanie. The crowd screamed out approval. Eric the Red was making his well-rehearsed surprise entrance. He began to wander forward on the stage as he slashed at his guitar. He was making little spastic motions with one leg and bending strangely, as if under some unspeakable and invisible weight. He lashed his guitar and smashed it with his pick, making exaggerated moves with a rigid forearm. His elbow went up and down, as if he was jamming it into the windpipe of a mortal enemy. Then he played a succession of notes too fast and too complex to take in. The individual notes cracked together and became a texture of noise. Then Eric held a high note and bent it until it rose up and warbled. Then he shook the guitar, as if to see if there was any more music in it and then he took a stance and leered at the audience. They seemed to surge forward once again as a mass. Eric raised his hand almost like a challenge and he seemed to have to fight his own hand to bring it down onto the strings to set them off again. His hand flashed down out of the lights like an assassin's hand. The guitar screamed again. He spread his legs and shook his head until the giant hat swayed so violently that it seemed as if it must fly off his head or maybe take his head with it. The massive speaker towers trembled with power. The bass notes were fists. The high frequencies tumbled the boundary between sound outside and sound inside the head.

Suddenly Rodd appeared in the intense circle of white light. He had snatched up his red guitar. It flashed and glinted like a blood-mirror. The two men began to slam each other around the stage. Now two guitars were moaning and howling and buzzing and crashing. I'm not sure it was music, but it was exciting. The lights began to strobe, smoke began to emerge from under the stage. Laser beams created strange runes in the air above the heads of the two men. The music grew louder, with a synthesizer riding over the guitars like an air raid warning and the bass guitar thudding like a stick of five-hundred pound bombs.

Suddenly bodies were leaping up on the stage and security men were rushing forward. One of the bodies was wearing red running shoes. I broke into a fast trot toward the pile-up. As I started to move, I saw Dickie jumping up on the stage and then I saw Arlene. Her mouth was open in a scream. Her hands were in front of her face. She turned, it seemed to be in slow motion, and disappeared into a crowd of fans and security people. It was like seeing some sea creature entangled and them consumed by the waving arms of an anemone.

I was now running to where I had last seen red shoes. He had also disappeared into the crush at the back of the stage. When I reached a mass of squirming bodies, I began to shove them out of my way. Some of them shoved back. I was yelling for Dickie, but he never heard me.

Ten or twelve huge security guys began clearing the stage. They were not being gentle. Fans toward the back of the stage began to stampede toward the exits in the back of the stage. I went with them.

The middle of the stage was now clear. The band had never stopped playing, but Rodd and Eric had wisely stepped out of the lights. I saw Rodd's giant bodyguard with his arms out like a gate. Over his head, in the stage-side gloom, I could see a bit of furry hipster hat and the head of a guitar.

The stage was nearly empty when Rodd and Eric stepped back in the lights. A roar went up from the audience. A stage tech ran out from the side and picked up a fallen microphone stand. Rodd strode to the microphone and grabbed it. Eric played another little flourish while nodding to the drummer. He had his back to the audience. The song changed and slowed. I could hear that they had worked the chords around and the tempo to set up Eric's big hit, "Spin Doctor."

Rodd began singing Eric's song. Then Eric joined him at the microphone and they sang together. It was a mid-tempo song and the audience had calmed down enough to listen to the words about how everything they thought they knew was a lie. I never cared for "Spin Doctor," but it has a catchy tune. I sometimes find myself playing the tune in my head.

I was still working my way to the back of the stage.

When I got through the backstage doorway to the outside, I saw Tyrell waving at me and pointing to the VIP parking area.

I looked to where he was pointing and saw some commotion and headlights coming on in the VIP parking area. It didn't look right. I ran over to Tyrell.

"What is going on in the parking area?" I said, pointing to the cars.

"I'm not sure. I think the stalker is trying to get to his car." said Tyrell.

"Did you see him?" I said.

"Yes," said Tyrell, "but people were running from the stage. Mel Viktor disappeared with the gate. I know he has his gun, but he shouldn't be running around with all that money in this mess. Some other people were in a big hurry to beat feet out of here. When the kids rushed the stage, they must have scared some of the VIPs because a number of them ran out of here. I saw at least three security guys after them. With everything going on, I lost track of the stalker and Arlene."

Just then a large black town car slid out onto the entrance to the highway pointed toward the Hamptons and started chirping its tires as the axle bounced from the heavy acceleration. It was too far away to see who was inside. A limo followed it out and also lit up the tires, but going in the opposite direction toward New York. It was followed closely by a black GMC Denali that didn't turn on its headlights. Then I saw a light blue Saturn pass under one of the overhead lights. It was also heading for the highway to the Hamptons. It was the car that had passed me on Rodd Rock's street after the incident with Dom.

"Why are they all leaving?" I asked. I was asking myself, not looking for an answer, but I said it aloud.

"Something is going on," said Tyrell.

"Is the stalker in one of those cars?"

"I think so," said Tyrell. He looked worried.

"What's bothering you?" I asked him.

"I don't know. I got a bad feeling."

"About what?"

"I just don't know."

A security came trotting toward us from the parking lot. He was speaking into his walkie-talkie. We heard him say that the stalker was gone. Tyrell put out his beefy arm and stopped him.

"You say he's gone?" said Tyrell.

"Yeah," said the security guy. His badge told me his name was Peter. He looked at our badges and said, "Who are you guys?"

"We're with Rodd," I said. "You saw the stalker leave?"

"I saw his car leave," said Kenneth.

"Was he driving?" said Tyrell.

"I don't know. It's dark. Someone was driving."

"Was he alone?" said Tyrell.

Why wouldn't he alone? I thought to myself.

"It was dark." said Kenneth.

"So there could have been somebody else in that car," said Tyrell.

"There could have been a party in that car," said Peter. He tried to shove Tyrell to one side. "It was dark. I had the headlights in my eye. It was his car, because we saw him drive in."

"How was he allowed into the VIP parking area?" Tyrell asked.

"Somebody let him in," said Kenneth. "Maybe he had a VIP ticket. I have to report in. Are you going to let me by?"

"Did you recognize any of the other cars that left?" asked Tyrell. Something was certainly bothering him. He was acting like a grand inquisitor.

"One was Mel Viktor's town car. I didn't recognize the other cars."

"Was Mel Viktor alone?" asked Tyrell.

"I didn't pay any attention," said Kenneth. "Mel comes and goes as he pleases."

"He had all the gate receipts. How close was he to the other cars? Could he see into the other cars?" asked Tyrell. I couldn't see what he was getting at.

"I doubt it. His car was off to the side," said Kenneth.

"Could the stalker see the other car?" asked Tyrell.

"You'll have to ask him," said Kenneth. "Now, look, you are going to have to let me by. I have to report in."

Tyrell stepped to one side and Kenneth began to move. He had the walkie-talkie up to his mouth and he was chattering to someone. I looked at Tyrell. "What was all that about?" I asked him.

"LT was worried that the stalker might try something tonight," said Tyrell.

"Like what?" I asked.

"Make trouble of some kind," said Tyrell. "This is Rodd's only public concert for the rest of the year."

"What kind of trouble?" I asked again.

"Trouble," was all Tyrell said. Then he slapped me on the back. "You go tell LT he has gone. I'm going down into the parking lot to make sure he doesn't come back."

"Is that why he wanted you to bring your weapon?" I asked.

"One of the reasons," he said.

"You don't want to go back in and see the rest of the show?" I said.

"I must be getting old or something, but I don't care much for this kind of music," said Tyrell sadly.

"It's not about the music, it's about the show. The music is just the excuse. Most of the audience is older. I think they want to re-enact something, maybe the first time they got, you know, into it. It looks like they came here to drink and act up a little. Everyone was just going through the motions until Eric the Red showed up. He's something."

"He's something all right," said Tyrell. "My ears are still ringing. You scoot back to LT and tell him that Valderben is gone. I'm going to hang out in the lot for a while. I have to catch my breath anyway."

8

"It's the new liturgy," said LT. He had finally removed his silly hat.

Teddy was at the wheel. She had a cigarette hanging out of her mouth. She hardly ever smokes. Dickie kept asking for a hit. I was about to give him one. Teddy had the window cracked.

"They all have their parts to play," said Teddy. "I agree with you. It is like a liturgy. Every concert has the same structure, only the words change. The audience always waves and stands. It's expected. It isn't spontaneous at all."

"No," said LT. "There is nothing spontaneous about it. It reminds me of the people who stand and scream praises at the end of a so-so opera. They want to believe that they have participated in something special. They paid all that money and ... well ... I find it interesting. The concert was very good theater. Rock musicians have become stock figures like something from the commedia dell'arte. They are our masked clowns representing ..."

"Lawton Dear, you are losing your audience."

"They each have the same style. There are slight variations in costume, but it is all the same look. The movements and gestures are completely studied. The scales they play are complex and have a similar structure to an aria. Rock and Roll has entered its baroque phase."

"You are speaking to yourself," said Teddy.

"I enjoyed the staginess. Eric the Red, politics aside, was quite entertaining. I think he has taken movement classes. Everything was so studied. Still, I thought Rodd was terrific, really super."

"Where does all that energy come from?" said Teddy.

"That was nothing," said Dickie. "You should have seen him at Shea Stadium. Why couldn't we go to the party after?"

"Because," said LT, "I have had quite enough rock and roll for one night."

"Did anyone see Arlene?" I said. "I wanted to thank her for the tickets."

"I think she left," said Teddy.

"With who?" I said.

"I don't know," said Teddy. "Rodd always keeps three or four cars available. She rarely goes to the after-parties."

"What did you think, Tyrell?" said LT. "You are being very quiet back there."

"Tyrell is asleep or pretending to be," I answered for him. "I enjoyed the show. At least I know why Rodd is a star. I couldn't believe it was the same guy we saw backstage an hour before the show."

"He works out," said Dickie sullenly.

"I don't care if he runs marathons, he's not a young guy anymore and he was up there acting like he was twenty."

"He's Rodd Rock," said Dickie, as if that was all that needed to be said on the subject.

"He's very exciting to watch," said Teddy, expelling little wisps of smoke.

"I wish you wouldn't smoke in the car," said LT.

"I have the window cracked and the AC blowing," said Teddy.

"Can I have just a hit?" said Dickie. I punched him low by his hip. "Hey!" he squealed.

"You are not bringing that thing back here," I told him. "There's such a thing as second-hand smoke."

"Settle down," said Tyrell. He did not even open an eye or move. His head was resting against the window. "Don't make me come over there."

We rode in silence for a moment or two and then LT turned on the reading light and turned to us in the back seat.

"Hey!" said Teddy. "Turn that light off. I can't see the road."

"In a minute. We have to discuss tomorrow. Max?"

"Yes."

"I want you to continue talking to the staff, first thing in the morning. Well, you can sleep in a little because of the hour, but as soon as you are up and dressed …"

It was nearly noon before I was up and dressed and read and coffeed and rice puddinged. I was alone most of the time in the kitchen. I had called Carrie to set up a couple of interviews and was halfway through the sports pages when Dickie came down. The second batch of coffee was just gurgling to a finish. I think he woke up and smelled it.

"You weren't going to smoke last night, were you?" I said to him.

"I just wanted a hit for old time's sake. I used to go to a lot of concerts. I smoked a pack and a half a day then."

"I'll bet you smoked some of those funny cigarettes, the ones you roll yourself."

"I did," he said. He was peering at Mr. Coffee, as if it might have been someone he once knew too well, but whose name had been forgotten.

"Don't start up with the cigarettes again. They're a gateway drug," I said over the last page of the sports section.

"To what?" said Dickie, as he lifted the carafe and swirled it. Then he smelled the swirl through the spout and frowned and put the carafe back on its little hot plate.

"The next thing you know you are hanging out in front of bars at night with other smokers and then you go back in the bars and you make weird dates with the kind of women who hang out outside of bars to smoke and the next thing you know you wake up in a flat screen TV starter home filled with colored plastic toys, hooked up with a tattooed lady who has a child by a previous marriage and a little Dickie who looks just like you but is an even bigger pain in the ass."

"I've chosen the path of celibacy."

"Watch out for the detours."

"Oh, Mr. Kelly, your cynicism is going to make you very unhappy some day."

"Oh, Mr. Douglas, you already are."

"Where did you find Mr. Coffee?" he said as a comeback. Dickie's comebacks are like a lobbed tennis ball that dribbles over the net and lies there while you are back waiting for the smash.

"In the closet. Why?"

"I thought Teddy threw it out when LT forbid its use."

"I found it in the trash can," I said.

"Did you wash it first?" said Dickie.

"Dickie! You never wash a Mr. Coffee! You destroy the essential oils that coat the sides of the carafe!"

"Really?" he said. He is just too easy.

Then I felt bad. The poor guy was going through something. I clipped him on the shoulder and went to look for the keys to the Caddy.

When I had my back turned, he cleared his voice and said, almost whispering, "Was that Mel Viktor who had the fight with Arlene at the concert?"

"Yes, why?" I asked him as I grabbed a handful of keys on a ring.

"He called this morning for Mr. Close," said Dickie. I turned to face him. He was looking nervous.

"What did he want?" I asked.

"He was hot about something. He was swearing a lot," said Dickie. "Should I wake Mr. Close?"

"I wouldn't. Let Mel Viktor marinate a little, but do tell LT he called."

"Mel Viktor was very angry," said Dickie.

"He gets that way," I said with a shrug.

"I've never heard anyone so angry, not even my father when he was drinking."

"Did he scare you?" I asked him.

"A little," he said.

"Be sure you tell LT as soon as he comes down."

I drove into the village to begin my interviews with the staff of the Rock Pile. The first on my list was Jorge the gardener. Who would know more about the action at the mansion than the gardener? Well, besides the upstairs maid, if such things still exist.

It was his day off, but he agreed to see me. Carrie told me to meet him at a bus stop in Bridgehampton. When I got there, people were waiting for the Jitney and I stood behind them. When the bus arrived and scooped them up, I had the wooden bench to myself. I thought that Jorge would get off the local bus, but he rode up on a bicycle. He saw me and nodded questioningly. I nodded affirmatively. He nodded more and smile broadly.

He parked his bike against a fence and came over to the bench. I was standing by then. He nodded again. I held out my hand.

"Jorge?" I got the H sound of the J OK and the H sound of the G, but I'm not about to start rolling my Rs. There is no way I am going to roll an R. It's a gateway sound. The next thing you know, you go on to the hard stuff like trying to pronounce the difference between por que and porque.

"Yes. You are Max?"

"Yes. Thank you for meeting me. Did you have to come far?"

"No. Two miles only."

"You don't have a car?"

"My brother took the car."

"You and your brother are from Mexico?"

"Yes. No, we are Guatemalan. But everyone thinks Mexico."

"How long have you been here?"

"I come four years. He come two years."

"Does he work?"

"He is a carpenter. He works for a builder. He took the car because I have the day off."

"We should find a place to sit down. You want some coffee?"

"No, thank you."

"We could sit in a booth across the street. Would you like a sandwich? I'm buying."

"Maybe a lemonade," he said.

We walked across the street. Traffic was so slow, it did not actually stop for us when we walked into the crosswalk, it just did not inch forward as impatiently while we were between the bumpers of the cars on the crosswalk. You could not get another car onto the highway unless you started a second layer.

The Candy Kitchen was at capacity as well, but a mother and her two young kids got up from a booth as I was scanning for vacancies and we moved over and hovered while she picked over the table looking for ice-cream-sticky action figures and two rolling crayons. She did not like us hovering, but I did not like the idea of losing her table so I hovered. She sighed when she finally grabbed her purse and two sticky little hands and entered and exited my personal space on her way to the door. Jorge and I sat. We kept our hands off the mess on the table. A waitress called out that she would be with us in a moment as she breezed past on her way to the mysteries behind the counter. I began.

"How long have you been with Rodd Rock?"

"He hired me when I first come."

"How did he hire you? Were you introduced?"

"We used to wait at the train station for work. Mr. Rock sent one of his people to the train station. We work for while and then no work and we wait for work at the train station. Then there was much work and we work every day until the snow comes."

"But at some point he made you the head guy?"

"Yes, he like what I do. He say to me, 'Jorge, you have hands of the earth. You make the earth talk and sing.' I try to do my best for Mr. Rock."

"How many people work for you?"

"Five or six."

"Are they from Mexico?"

"No. Two of us from Guatemala. One is from Dominican Republic. One is from Columbia and the others from Ecuador."

"Is there a lot of work to do for Rodd?"

"Oh yes. We are planting every day. We are cutting the grass. We are trimming the trees and cleaning around the pool. We are fixing the terrace. We are always busy."

"Does Rodd have a big garden?" I asked him.

"It's big. There are three gardens. One in front for the people to see. One in back by the pool and one behind a fence for the house. Every day we cut the flowers for the house; whatever is blooming. Arlene will tell us what to cut and she puts the flowers together and puts them around the house - inside. The garden for this house is planted so that always there is some flowers. There are herbs for the kitchen also. The cook makes us grow some tomatoes and the chili peppers."

"What's in bloom right now?"

"The roses are nice. The annuals are blooming good right now. Lilacs are over, peonies and cat mint are good now and irises.

"Do you know why I wanted to see you today?" I asked.

"No. Carrie say you want to talk to me. It is important to my job, so I come."

"Do you know that the papers are saying that Rodd Rock and his wife are having marriage problems."

He paused a moment before answering. "People talk about it."

"Do you talk about it?"

"I don't talk," he said. I looked for a smile. There wasn't one. He was being serious.

"Have you seen any fighting between Rodd and Arlene?"

"Why you ask me?" he said. Then he rocked his head to one side and waited.

"My boss has been hired by Rodd Rock to help him. People are saying things about Rodd and Arlene. Some of the things are getting into the newspapers. This makes Rodd and Arlene very unhappy. What do you think of Arlene?"

"She's good," he said. He said it simply, with no inflections.

"You like her?" I asked.

He paused again before answering. He seemed to be considering. "She's good," he said again.

"Have you ever seen the two of them fighting?"

"I have seen them angry."

"Fighting angry?" I asked.

"No hitting," he said. "Speak very loud, argument. She cries. He goes away from her."

"Who do you like better?" I tried.

"This, you can not ask me," he said. He was definite about it.

"No. You are right. You like Arlene," I said.

"She's good."

"And you like Rodd Rock?"

"I work for him," he said, evenly.

"Rodd thinks that someone may be trying to cause him trouble. Do you think someone could be trying to cause him trouble? Does Rodd have enemies?" I said.

"I am just the gardener," was his answer. It was a dodge.

"Have you seen Rodd have a fight, or an argument with other people who work for him?"

"Mr. Rock wants everything done very good."

"I'll take that as a yes?" I said.

"Not all people want to do things so good," he said. Then he dropped his head.

"So are there people that work for Rodd Rock that say bad things about him when he cannot hear them?"

"There are always people who say bad about the boss. All my life this is true."

"How many people work for Rodd? Not just gardeners, but everyone."

"Many," he said.

"More than ten?"

"I think so," he said and nodded.

"What do they do?"

"There is cook. There is assistant. There is manager. There is cleaning woman. There is driver…"

He was interrupted by the waitress who began grabbing and dabbing. We waited. As she skim coated the drippings from the previous occupants using a damp cloth, she said to me, "You know what you want? Or do you want to see menus?"

"Two lemonades," I said, "one grilled cheese on whole-wheat with tomato slices and the biggest platter of fries you can put together."

"Nothing else?" she said cheerily.

"Maybe dessert later. You guys make your own ice cream, don't you?" I asked. Up close, she was…she had something. I don't know what it was. Maybe I just like the stink of a deep fryer and a you-can't-phase-me attitude coasting on weird white comfort shoes. Vivid, quick eyes and a standout figure did not hurt.

"That's what the sign says," she answered. I found myself wondering why she did not just say yes or no.

"We'll talk about that later," I said. When our eyes met, I did not have the brainpower or the patience left over to dig any further into the matter of the homemade-ness of the ice cream. What is it about waitresses?

She departed.

"So there is a bodyguard, isn't there?" I said to get Jorge and myself back to something like a professional inquiry into serious matters.

He nodded. He couldn't keep himself from frowning. "Since the man ... a man was in the house."

"The man they call the stalker?" I asked.

"Yes. Senor Stalker. He was in the house at night. It was bad."

"You don't like the bodyguard?" I asked him.

"Mr. O'Brien? We are not friends."

"Why not?"

"When I come first from Guatamala, I stay with my cousin in California. It was a bad neighborhood. You know these gangs? I don't like these gangs. They have guns and they make trouble. My cousin was walking with a friend and some gang people shot him; shot his friend for no reason. The Latinos and the blacks don't get along in the projects; different gangs."

"Is the bodyguard in a gang?" I asked.

"I don't know. He dress like a gang."

"Do you ever talk to him?" I prodded.

"I stay away from him, but he talks against Mr. Rock. I hear these things," he said.

"I'll have to ask him about that," I said.

"Don't say what I have said."

"No. I won't mention you at all. What about the cook? Does he talk bad about Rodd?"

"He is she. She has fight with Mr. Rock about what to cook," he said. He was anxious in some way about the cook. I could not get a sense of why.

"She's a she?" I said.

"Yes. She is from Guatamala. I am from Guatamala. Her brother told me to come here from California. He works for a restaurant. He has been here many years."

"What is the cook's name?"

"Frieda, but everyone calls her Pica; is short for Picante. She likes the chili pepper. Mr. Rock likes the chili pepper; not so much Arlene. Sometimes Pica and Arlene fight about the chili pepper and Pica quit. Then Mr. Rock calls her and tells her to come back. She comes back. Pica has a big temper. She is strong.

"Pica left Guatamala to make a good life for her children. She had a bad husband in Guatamala. He did not work. So Pica took the bus to Mexico. In Mexico a bad man took all her money. She have nothing. She hitchhike, you say this?"

"Yes, hitchhike," I said.

"She gets a ride in a big truck and the truck takes her to North Mexico. When the truck stop, Pica had nothing, so she work in restaurante for many months to save money to go to America. She learns all about cooking for many people. She cooks good. Then she give her money to some men who promise to take her to America, but they do nothing. They keep the money. She go anyway. She go across the border at night with others, but this night, was not a good night. The police catch them all. Pica was questioned by a man in an office. He was very smart man. He asked her if she had children and she answered that she had children, but she use the Guatemala word for children, not the Mexican word. The man say "So! You are Guatamalan! You have to go back to Guatemala. I send you back on a plane to Guatemala!" and Pica yelled at him that she was Mexican. Pica yells good. She has a temper. She is strong. She did not want to start all over again from Guatemala. She want him to send her back to north Mexico so she could try again to cross the border.

"They argue. He knew she was from Guatemala, but Pica win the argument. He sent her back to Mexico. Everybody lies at the border. He knew she would try again. The next time, no one was looking and Pica find my brother in California. He sent her to me because I had room at the house for one more. Ten of us live at the house, but we had a place for one more to help with the rent. Now Pica lives at the big house with Mr. Rock. I laugh how things happen."

"Does Pica talk bad about Rodd?"

"I don't think so. I think she likes Mr. Rock very much. She talks bad about Arlene. I think she is jealous."

A shadow across the paper placemats meant that food had arrived. The plate of fries was the biggest I had ever seen. "Wow!" I said when it was placed in the center of the table.

"You told me you wanted a platter," said the waitress. She was smiling a challenge at me.

"I better call my broker and buy some potato futures because I think you've created a shortage."

"Enjoy," she said, with her palms spread at nature's abundance. She would be fun to have around, but her work at our table was done and she left us.

"Jorge, you are going to have to help me with these. I can't eat all of this myself."

He only hesitated for a moment. Soon he was working the pile with both hands.

"Do you know Paul Williams?" I said after we had eaten in silence for a moment. The fries were good.

"I see him. He has the car, the Viper. I don't talk to him."

"So you wouldn't know if he was saying bad things about Rodd?"

"I think he's a bad man," said Jorge.

"Why do you say that?"

"One of my men was using a trimmer, you know the weed whacker?"

"Yes," I said.

"And Mr. Williams run out from the house and yelled at my man that he is making stones in the driveway hit the car. He say terrible things. My man did not want to go back to work. I think Mr. Williams is violent. I don't like him."

"How about the assistant?" I said. I hoped I sounded bland. I probably didn't.

"Carrie?"

"Does she say bad things about Rodd?"

"All the time," he said.

"She does? I was only asking because I know her. It was sort of a joke."

"No joke. She is not happy. I think she will leave Mr. Rock."

"Is he mean to her?" I asked.

"Not so much. Not angry so much, sometime, but he all the time asks her to do things. In the middle of the night he asks her to do something. If she is at the beach on her time off he calls her to ask for something. It is always something."

"So Carrie talks bad about Rodd?"

"Yes," he said.

"To who?"

"To anyone. To herself. To the gardener. I am the gardener."

"What about the cleaning woman?"

"Maria."

"Does she get along with Rodd Rock?"

"He likes to have everything perfect. His friends don't respect his things. They make a big mess. Maria has to clean up the big mess. Some of Mr. Rock's friends are like animals. They make a mess like animals. Some of Mr. Rock's friends are important people."

"Do the important people make a mess?"

"No! But everything has to be perfect for the important people and the other friends come all the time and make a mess. Sometimes Maria has to bring her baby sister to help. The mess is so big."

"What about the driver?"

"I don't see him. He comes and they get in the car and he goes. I don't know the driver."

"Did you ever meet Rodd's manager?" I asked.

"I don't like the manager. He is not nice."

"So it sounds like almost anybody could be saying bad things about Rodd Rock?"

"It is hard to be Mr. Rock. Everybody wants something. They think he has everything, so why shouldn't they have something? You understand?"

"Yes, I do. What do you want?" I asked him.

"From Mr. Rock?"

"Yes."

"A job," he said.

"Is there anyone else who might want to get even with Mr. Rock?" I asked.

"Senor Stalker!" he said. His eyes were wide.

"Have you seen him?"

"I catch him twice on the grounds, at night," he said. He was looking for a reaction.

"What did you do to him?"

"I showed him my pruning knife and he ran away."

"You were on the grounds at night?" I asked. It was curious.

He blushed. He put his eyes down. He clammed.

"Jorge! What were you doing on the grounds at night?"

"I was … to visit Pica."

"Oh!," I said. "Did anyone speak to the cops about the stalker being on the grounds?"

"No. Mr. Rock said it was nothing, but I don't like the stalker being outside at night. I think he is trouble. He will make trouble. Why is he outside at night?"

"I'll have to ask him," I said. "Do you know where he lives?"

"He live in the city," said Jorge. "Why is he here?"

"I don't know," I said.

When most of the French fries and all of the lemonade were gone, we did decide to try the ice cream. It was pretty good. It tasted homemade. Dickie's is better. Dickie's tastes like the best gelato in the best restaurant in Brooklyn.

LT scowled slightly when I put the receipt in his in-basket. I never worry about a slight scowl. It is no more important than an eye blink when there is dust in the air.

"What's that?" he said, looking at the little piece of paper. I had slipped it in, print-side down..

"I took Jorge the gardener to the Candy Kitchen for a little snack."

"Why?"

"I needed a place to sit him down."

"Why did you expense it?" he said.

"Because I was on duty." He sighed and lowered his eyelids a fraction of an inch.

"What did he say?"

"Everyone hates Rodd Rock. They are all talking to anyone who will listen. You don't have a leak, you have an irrigation system."

"That's hyperbole."

"So?"

"You should know better by now," he said.

"I know. 'Purple prose is like a rose that smells so sweet pretty, but in time like too much wine it leaves you feeling awful.' You are just changing the subject because you don't like what I am saying."

"I don't," he said. Then he tugged at the sticking drawer at his elbow. If he was going to start fiddling with one of his toys, the rituals could go on for tens of minutes. I wanted to get on to the next activity. I hate watching him try to remove tobacco crumbs from his cigar cutter with a used Q-tip, or fill his ancient Zippo lighter with lighter fluid and fidget with the non-working flint wheel *that hasn't worked in more than ten years*, but he loves to fidget with it.

"Well, what do you want me to do next?" I asked.

"Give me a full report. I want to know everything he said with commentary about how he said it. Then you can take the rest of the day off. I have to think about where we go from here."

I reported while he took apart an antique fountain pen to see if the ripped bladder had miraculously healed itself in the last four years. He looks like he is distracted, but he catches every word and inflection. At least I think he does.

9

SOME AFTERNOON OFF. I WAS at K-Mart in the automotive aisle when my cell phone started vibrating in my pants. I took it out. I flipped it open.

"Yeah?"

"Max?" said a voice. I recognized the voice. It belonged to LT.

"Yeah."

"Come home. There's been a development."

"What happened?"

"Arlene is missing," he said.

"What do you mean, missing?"

"I won't discuss it in an open broadcast. Come in. I need you here."

He hung up.

I put the cell phone away, pulled out the keys to the Caddy and started to walk toward the exit. There was nothing I wanted to buy anyway. Out at the back of the crowded lot, heat waves were rippling in the air above the midnight blue car. LT only uses the Caddy in the summer. It stays in a parking garage in the city all winter. I have told him he needs a white car for summer, or silver; something that reflects light, not a midnight blue heat soaker. He huffs and does not answer. He is a midnight blue kind of guy.

Fifteen minutes later, I was toying with an iced tea and LT was frowning. Teddy was out in her boat with Dickie. Tyrell was out in the field somewhere. I was not told why. Little Bobby Dunton was with him. I hadn't seen Tyrell since the ride home from the concert He must have left the house before I got up the next morning..

"So that's it?" I said to break the silence. "She's gone missing. That's it?"

"She left in the middle of the concert. Rodd was on stage and he did not see her go. She did not show up at an after concert party, but that is not unusual since she hates that part of the business and often does not attend. Rodd slept late, into the afternoon I gather, and when he woke up and she was not around, he assumed that she was out, at the beach or shopping. They have been sleeping in separate rooms for the past year. He wasn't concerned until the security people from Jones Beach called to say that the cleanup crew had found a tote bag in the VIP parking area. It contained Arlene's purse, all of her identification, a sweater, her diamond earrings and her three-carat engagement ring. She never came back to the limousine. The driver never saw her."

"And…"

"There's no and. She never showed up," he said. He sounded grim.

"Any blood? Any sign of a struggle? Any witnesses? Any bloody clothing thrown from the window of a speeding Lexus with blacked out windows?"

"No. Nothing more than what I have told you," he said evenly. He was watching me very closely, even for him.

"If she was going to split from Rodd, she wouldn't leave her things. What do you think?" I said.

"I don't know what to think. It certainly looks … I can't think of the proper word."

"You would usually say "suggestive," I suggested.

"All right, that will do for the time being."

"Why would she take off her engagement ring?" I asked.

"Apparently, she stone was so large it was uncomfortable to wear it. Rodd says that she often took it off and put it in her purse."

"And the money and jewelry were still in the purse?"

"Apparently it had nothing to do with robbery," said LT. He was still staring at me. It made me feel odd.

"Robbery hell, the clean-up crew let that one slip past. They probably thought it was zirconium it was so big. I hope no one tells them it was real. It would bother them for years."

"You are too cynical. The tote bag was from Coach and had a little leather flap with a lock. I'm told they find a lot of things in the parking lot after a big concert."

"So who knows about this?" I asked.

"Well, that's the difficult part. Someone in security decided to alert the authorities. Very shortly now, the whole world will know. It may be too early to get on the six o'clock news, but certainly by ten. The leak is no longer our primary concern. This will most likely become a catastrophic flood of unhappy publicity. Tragically, it will come along before the story about marital and money problems has had a chance to recede. You know what's going to happen, don't you?"

"Wow! People are going to think that Rodd ... had a motive."

"Exactly," said LT.

"This is bad!"

"That's right," he said.

"Do you think she might be ... ah ... in trouble? Or worse?"

"I don't know what to think," said LT. "I need some facts to process. Speculating without facts is like trying to fill an inside straight."

"Teddy beat you at cards again?" I asked.

"Yes, but that is not our concern at the present. We are going to have to deal with a lot of possibly unfavorable publicity."

"What is your hunch?" I asked. "Is she in trouble?"

"Let me state something clearly for you. This project is the most media sensitive operation I have ever undertaken. I will not permit speculation of any kind. I have already spoken to Dickie and Teddy about this. Let these remarks be your warning. We work from facts here, not imagination. You must be very guarded at all times. You must not, under any circumstances, speak to anyone in the news or entertainment business or anyone in law enforcement or anyone with official standing of any kind. You have no idea of how damaging an ill considered remark could be. When we have facts we will act in accordance with them and with our interests. In the absence of facts we will keep our mouths shut. Each of us, every one of us. Am I clear?"

"I hear you," I said.

"Good."

"What about the stalker?" I asked.

"Yes," said LT. "There's the stalker. We will have to pay close attention to the stalker."

"There were a number of cars that left the VIP lot at about the same time," I said.

"Yes," said LT. "I have people interviewing the attendants. I want to know anything I can find out about what and who they saw in those cars."

"People? Who?"

"Carol Prankham sent a couple of her freelance operatives." Carol runs the detective agency we use when we need to rent some operatives. She calls it a duty office, but it's still a detective agency.

"Tyrell and Bobby Dunton?" I asked. I get along good with Tyrell.

"I told you, they are otherwise engaged on my behalf," said LT.

"Where is this thing headed?" I asked him. "I am starting to get the tingle. Should I be getting the tingle?"

"It's too early to know anything. I am not prepared to say anything more on the subject until I have a new fact. I certainly will not indulge my anxieties. I suggest that you do not as well, even with Dickie. We have never been involved with a client with such a high media profile. Rodd's career is going to suffer, no matter what happens. If Arlene is not found soon there could be a hearing or perhaps even an arrest. The media will make the most of it for their own purposes. The circumstances may become overwhelming. For once I may be in the deep end without a ladder."

"Twice, counting Packy Merino," I said.

"I wish you wouldn't bring that up."

"Three times if you count Senator Pendings ..."

"I think I would like quiet now. I would like to stay centered. I would like to be alone. Please close the door on your way out."

"We don't really have a project, do we?" I said. I was getting up slowly from my seat.

"What do you mean?"

"If you were hired to sort out the marital split and one of the parties goes missing, what happens to the project?"

"Rodd wants me to stay on. No one knows where this could end up. The project is much bigger now. It may involve a criminal investigation."

"We have to find her," I said as I stopped next to the door.

"It may be difficult. We may not like what we find," he said sadly and then sighed.

"So you think she's ..."

"Shhhh!" He shushed me and put up the finger, the one he uses to end conversations.

"Before I go, and assuming for a moment that she may indeed be ... ah ... no longer with us ... do you think Rodd Rock is capable of murder?"

"Max. You and I have seen a lot together. The one thing I have discovered about human nature in my experience as a consultant, is that most people keep secrets about themselves and most people are capable of more than we might imagine."

"So, you think..."

"That is all I'm prepared to say at the present. This thing could go in a number of directions. I have asked Rodd to come here to discuss some items that Tyrell has turned up. Could you please keep yourself available for a meeting at three-thirty, here in the office?"

"OK."

I closed the door.

I had time to drive into the village and take care of some personal needs. I also had time to drive over to the ocean beach parking lot and call Carrie.

"Hey. How are you?" I said.

"I'm OK. It's crazy about Arlene, isn't it?"

"When did you find out?" I asked her.

"When the driver called to say he found her things. Until then, I figured she was just … looking for another place to be."

"Has it been bad?" I asked.

"Yeah, it has been pretty bad. Rodd was quite drunk when he finally got home early in the morning. I mean the sun was up. Before he went to bed, he had me make him some eggs. Pica had not arrived yet. I can't do this anymore. I'm putting my resume' together. I can't send it out from here because Rodd's people can see everything that goes in or out. You want to meet at Starbuck's at two and I can bring the lap top?"

"I can't. Rodd's coming over to discuss the Arlene thing. Why don't you just quit?"

"And go where? You know what rentals are like during the season."

"Maybe you could stay here, at LT's." I said.

"You'd like that, wouldn't you?"

"I'm just saying…"

The phone call was unsatisfactory. She sounded distant and distracted. I probably did too. The truth was I did not have a good feeling about the immediate future. Unless Arlene turned up with amnesia in some care facility or showed up on Page Six on the arm of some cabana boy in Cabo or sent a note from an undisclosed hideaway saying "don't try to find me." Rodd Rock was in for a rough time. He would be worked over good by the media and probably the legal system as well. Celebrity has two cutting edges. It slices cleanly on the upswing, but the other side is more blunt. It makes a bloody mess on the downswing.

At 3:45, I was freshly showered and re-shaved and sitting in my usual chair in the summer office. Rodd was slumped back in the big wicker chair LT reserves for clients. Rodd had his large feet stretched out in the middle of the room. He was wearing what he calls his trainers. They looked like a normal white sneakers to me. LT was behind his desk taking notes on a legal pad. Rodd had expressed his anxieties for his missing wife and said all the things a guy might say in a situation like that, but I did not get the feeling he meant any of it. It is true they weren't getting along, but she was part of his world and she was missing. I didn't like his attitude. I was starting not to like Rodd Rock.

When we had gone around the room with compliments and thanks for the concert. Rodd kept it going a little longer than I might have, by saying things like, "Do you really think so?" and "It wasn't too much where I was dancing with Eric the Red, was it? Not too over the top?"

"Very exciting to watch," said LT.

It was and it was also way over the top, but it was a rock concert and people pay money to see way-over-the-top. Everything was too much. The sound was too loud, the lights too active and bright, the fireworks too everything and too smoky as well, the laser display was too distracting and the audience too enthusiastic for what was happening on stage. In short, it was a rock concert.

I would always have my memories of Rodd Rock in his white suit, slam dancing with Eric the Red by the shore of the Atlantic Ocean on a night when even the moon was full. I was in that memory for a short refresher and I could have stayed for a moment longer, but LT's voice turned hard and brought me out of it.

"… it is important, crucial, that I am kept aware of anything that could negatively effect the manner in which you are perceived by the public. Max has informed me that many, perhaps most of the gardening staff have no papers. This would not play out well in the public forum. Small-minded individuals with an agenda could use this to make a great deal of mischief for you and, since we are now involved in a contractual relationship, for me and for my entire enterprise. Arlene's disappearance changes everything. This is no longer a postnuptial negotiation. You could be on trial for your life. I am not sure you fully comprehend your vulnerability to the media."

"Sod the lot of them," said Rodd. He did not stir from his slouch.

"While I find myself in agreement with your sentiment, I also find my attention drawn to certain professional considerations. All the signs point to the unhappy possibility that you may soon be undergoing trial by public opinion."

"Well, a guy's innocent until proven guilty in this country, right?"

"In theory. I don't want to bet your life on it. Your biggest problem in the near term may be how the media decides to play this thing. They will seek to establish a narrative. In it, you will either be portrayed as a victim or a predator. They are not given to nuance. Their usual method is to first simplify and then exaggerate. It is now my job to do everything I can to try to influence the narrative for your benefit. We can't make the media go away, so we have to attempt to manage it. It could mean the difference between you spending the rest of your life at home or in a federal institution."

"All right," said Rodd. He seemed bored. "So, do your thing."

"But I can't do my thing if there are trap doors waiting to spring open beneath my feet."

"You know, you could have been a song writer," said Rodd.

"I doubt it. I am trying to make a serious point. Why do you hire illegal immigrants?"

"Well, it's obvious, isn't it? I have work that needs to be done and they are all standing down by the train station waiting for something to do. They have nothing and I'm set up pretty good. How could I not?"

"So your feeling is that you are doing a positive good. You are providing work to individuals who are desperate for employment," said LT.

"Something like that."

"But it is illegal to hire undocumented workers."

"Well, I'm the overlord of sex, drugs and rock and roll. If you read the crap they write about me I have orgies and Druid rituals with virgins and if you play cut five on the Green LP backwards, I am invoking Beelzebub to run for the senate. Why would I care about a law that no one pays any attention to?"

"It's the narrative! Take the same set of facts and spin them. You hire people who do not speak the national language. They are vulnerable in many ways. They are here illegally and subject to blackmail. You pay them off the books, with cash. Those are the facts.

"Now, depending on the motives of the person reporting these facts you are either, on the one hand a great humanitarian who is providing needy people with gainful employment that they cannot find in their place of origin and you are disobeying (ignoring is a better term) what are, in their essence, unjust and exclusionary and perhaps even racist laws, or on the other hand you are a rich exploiter of the downtrodden of the earth, getting even richer on the backs of their toil. You are a cultural imperialist who uses English as just one more tool to take advantage of people who by definition are politically disenfranchised, because they have no vote. Cash payments further disadvantage the workers because they exist outside all government regulations and safeguards. You are not paying into their retirement accounts, providing them with benefits.

"Same facts, but depending on the spin you are either Mother Teresa or a vicious Robber Baron. Since no one but you can know your actual motivations, and there are psychologists who argue that even you are only half-aware of them, those with an interest in a specific outcome and the power to do so will assign your motivations to you. It is all in the narrative. Rodd the pig? Or Rodd the dove of peace? Which way will the wind blow?"

"All right, you've got my attention. What do we do?"

"It is too late to do anything about your hiring policy. We can only hope it does not become an issue in the media. However, I would like to know if you have any other trap doors."

"Like what?"

"Since you are a high-profile performer, a typical narrative line would include an intimate acquaintance."

"You mean, a mistress? A girlfriend?"

"I could. These days we must include all possibilities, boy friend, treasured pet, the little neighbor child down the street."

Rodd did not answer right away, but glared at LT and shook his head. Then he said slowly, "You know … you're really quite nasty."

"I merely observe. Surely you read the papers."

"There was a time in my life … I haven't been a saint."

"By that, I understand you to mean that there have been a significant number of intimate acquaintances?"

"Beyond counting. There was a time in my life when … what the hell, I was young and they were willing. You know what one of the saddest days in your life is?"

"What?"

"The first time you do something despicable and … you get away with it. No parent to throw open the door to your little room and say "What have you done? You should be ashamed!" Then you realize something dreadful, stunning really. It brings you up short. You are alone in the universe. It's just the saddest day."

"Growing up has its downside, I suppose," said LT. His tone told me he was being sarcastic. I do not know what it told Rodd.

"Never cared for it myself," said Rodd.

"So, to get back to the subject, could I say that there are (could it be dozens?) of people who could be discovered, by anyone sufficiently interested, and used for the purpose of creating in the public's mind an unflattering portrait?"

"Hundreds. Maybe thousands. I don't know. Mostly women. The odd dealer. I'm afraid I indulged in the generational passtime. Mind you, I bloody well inhaled."

"What about the present? Are you seeing anyone?"

"In what sense?"

"In the tabloid sense."

"I don't know."

"What do you mean, you don't know?"

"I'm Rodd Rock. If I have a cup of coffee with a female at the Pomme d'Or and someone snaps a picture, the next day it's on the cover of the tabloids as a picture of my latest doxy. It caused no end of trouble when I was entertaining the wife of a prominent person in politics. He was sleeping it off in the cabana and she and I just went out to get some coffee."

"That's not it," said LT. "You know what I mean. You know what I want."

"Look, I have always had and continue to have deep personal relationships with women. If talking heads want to make something of that, they probably will. If I had ever done half the things that have been reported ... well ... there just isn't enough time in the day to get it all done. Now, there could be some nonsense about Carrie."

I sat up a little straighter and looked carefully at our client. He was leaning back with a little smirk on his face.

"I mean she lives at the mansion. I rely on her in ... many ways. We share ... ah ... our inner thoughts. People have seen us together in all sorts of places. She photographs well. If both of us deny it, well, that's to be expected, they'll say."

"Hmm," came from LT.

Then he tuned out for a moment. Rodd looked at me. I shrugged. "He's thinking," I said.

"Oh."

Then LT returned his gaze to Rodd and said, "Violence? Is there any history of violent outbursts of any kind?"

"The old lady, my first wife ... well, my second really. I don't count the first. That was more of an extended date with papers. The mother of my children once called the cops for a domestic."

"Where charges made?"

"No. It wasn't much. She slapped me pretty good and I slapped her back. I talked to the cops. They were awfully good about it, but they did write it up."

"So someone could say there is a history of domestic violence ..."

"Not really. We had our spats. Oil and water really. Actually more like vinegar and water. She was quite bitter back then. She came out of a bad scene, ran away from home when she was sixteen. I met her when she was working in a club in London. Funny thing, we thought we had so much in common ... and we did, I suppose. Don't know what happened."

"But someone could say there was a police report of domestic violence and then produce that report, yes?"

"I suppose. If anything, she was the violent one. Her father was a violent man. He was thrown out of the British army for fighting. Can you imagine it? Here now, this won't do. You are too violent for the army. We are sending you back to civilian life where they tolerate this sort of thing. Makes you laugh sometimes."

"This fellow Viktor, he seems like someone who could be trouble."

"Oh, yeah, he's trouble. You don't want to cross old Vik."

"Have you been associated with him in the past?" asked LT.

"Look, here's the deal. When you are young and someone gives you too much money and people pay too much attention to you … I don't know … it's tough on a lad. It would seem to be the answer to all your hopes and schemes … I mean it's what we all work for isn't it? I guess that's success. But it doesn't feel that way. It feels like … I don't know … there's a lot of anxiety involved and … you start feeling like you are special. I mean everyone is telling you are special. That's their job. So when someone says, here, smoke this, it will take the edge off … well, it does. You wind up giggling in a corner like you were ten again. So you start buying the stuff. And someone has to retail it and that's your buddy, your connection. And he's getting rich, too, because you are giving him a lot of cash. You know there's a kind of expectation that the big star buys goodies for all the hangers-on. They tell you how special you are and then they submit the bill on a nightly basis. A little champers and maybe some caviar, a little weed and maybe some poppers and … well … Laissey le bon temps rouler; let the good times roll.

"Then one day your connection is on the front page of *Billboard* because he has invested in some talent. It's command and control, mate. He already owns them in a spiritual sense, if you believe in a soul. He is turning his cash into a business position. He buys up acts on the way down. They've had their hit and their follow up and now they're just a commodity. So he puts them on the road and he keeps the books and he handles the cash. And he stuffs a good bit into his pockets before the act even knows it exists. After the Lobes broke up, Vik promised me the moon. He's done all right. He's kept me going, got me gigs, produced some music. We had a gold record together. I can't really complain except that there is a small mountain of cash that has never been accounted for. And I might complain more than I do, but he still has friends from the days when he was in the retail business; the wholesalers. And they are a nasty lot. And when Vik needs a favor … ah … well … he can call in the artillery. I am a little concerned about the fact that you have cut him off from control of the cash. He calls me three times a day. He sounds desperate."

"I'm sure he is. He was there at the concert when Arlene disappeared. He left early. That is suggestive," said LT.

Rodd had the oddest reaction. He started to dismiss what LT was saying, even frowned about it, but then, almost as if he suddenly thought of something long forgotten, he sat violently forward.

"Damn! It is suggestive! You're on to something."

"I want Max to meet him. Is that possible?" said LT.

"Certainly. He has an office right on West 57th Street and he has a fake castle on the beach in Westhampton. But you don't want to wind up old Vik, because he can do a lot of damage. Trust me on this."

"Will you set up a meeting for Max?"

"Right now," said Rodd, as he reached in a pocket and came up with a cell phone. He pressed a single button and held the tiny phone to his ear. Then he looked at me and winked and said, "It's your funeral."

10

I WASN'T SURE ABOUT SEEING Mel Viktor. I was not sure about anything, but I did not see the point of meeting with him. Arlene was missing and some were presuming the worst. If Mel had snatched her, he was not going to throw up his hands and confess when I pressed him hard for an alibi. If he had done something to Arlene and I pressed him hard, he might feel the need to take a few decades off my life by bringing it up short on the spot. You never know with people.

"Why am I doing this?" I had said to LT.

"You are fishing."

"For what?"

"For whatever is biting. We don't know yet," he said. He spoke evenly while he tried to stuff some stamps back inside the roll out of which they had spilled.

"What's my bait?" I said.

"You have none." The stamps went in the roll until one bent. LT frowned and ripped off the remainder.

"OK. What's my lure?"

"The eternal lure," he said, "The classic treble hook shiner in murky waters; money."

"Whose money?" I said. LT was trying to smooth the bent stamp. I was beginning to want to take it from him and slap his hand.

"Rodd Rock's, of course. Mel Viktor stands to gain or lose significant money based on how this current situation plays out. He owns, in part or wholly, the entire catalog of Lobes' hits. He is involved with the management side of the business and therefore he is involved in some manner in the missing money that the news commentators have been discussing ad nauseum. You could hint that we know more than we know. Viktor's name has been associated with the wholesale side of the drug business. He has not faced a conviction to date, but one might easily hint at possible revelations to the press of an unsavory nature. Mr. Viktor may be teased with his own past."

"Why is his past an issue now, if it never was before?"

"Because, he is tied to Rodd Rock. Rodd Rock is the big story. It is likely that the reporting frenzy will only increase. Viktor is a colorful and sordid figure, an attention getter in a business that demands constant attention. Put Viktor into the Rodd Rock narrative and you can advance the process of the demonization of Mr. Rock handily. There is a little window here, where Mr. Viktor's past can be played out as big news. You have a number of approaches open to you. Use your initiative. You stimulate and I, as I always do, will observe the response."

"OK, but be sure to tell my next of kin that I went out with my boots on, stimulating to the end."

"You don't own boots," he said. He was done with the stamp. In triumph, he opened his sticking drawer and cast the lonely stamp into the utter darkness within. The stamp was doomed. The cigar ashes, toast point crumbs, used old ink cartridges, and blackened pocket change would soon reduce it to litter.

"No. Maybe I should get some."

Mel Viktor had boots and they were … I cannot think of a splashy enough word. They were made of some reptilian hide and the poor creature must have thought he had been dyed and gone to heaven; pearly gates had nothing on those boots. But I didn't know about the boots when I pulled up in front of the castle.

The houses along Dune Road in Westhampton are a little weird. A few years ago the road was washed out entirely by the ocean after a series of winter storms. For a long time the road was closed. You could drive down to where the road was blocked off and look over at the falling down houses. The waves, at high tide, came right up to them and under them.

The storms were forgotten and new houses built. The new houses were packed next to each other like old suburbs from the turn of the last century. Each house cried out in as loud a voice as architect and builder could summon, using the breath of bank accounts that had inhaled violently during the bull market, "I am beach house, hear me roar in numbers too great to ignore …"

Most of the houses were what Teddy calls Boast Modern. Even I can recognize in-your-face conspicuous consumption when I see it. It isn't subtle.

Still, driving along the bright row peering at house numbers, I had gotten somewhat used to fake columns, glass walls and sweeping rooflines. When Viktor's number came on a pair of stone gates holding up rampant unicorns, I was startled by house beyond. It was out of rhythm and out of character with what I had been seeing. Mel Viktor's summer home was his castle and I mean the real deal, with cone roofed towers and long dark slit windows and weird little details that were supposed to look like carved stone.

Cars driving by in the other lane slowed to rubbernecking speed and no one, not even the drivers, were looking at the road. The Viktor Castle was an eye catcher. I felt a little surge of misplaced pride when I put on the turn signal. Hey! Suckers! I get to go inside the thing!

No one was looking at me or my turn signal. They were looking at what Prince Charming might have built if his father, King Klaw "The Hammer" Charming had made his fortune in the carting business and crooked municipal contracts.

When there was a break in the rubberneckers parade, I flipped the wheel and pressed the midnight blue snout of the Caddy between the iron castle gates. The drive curved up and to the right as it ascended the modest rise of the remaining sand dune. I drove past the entrance and parked with some middling luxury cars that all needed a wash and wax, in a little parking area the size of a Staten Island Ferry. As I walked back to the entrance, I realized the structure was stucco. The stone wasn't real. Probably nothing else was real The slits in the stone walls where you fire arrows and pour boiling oil were, when you got up to them, windows tinted almost black. It made the hulking mass look even more sinister and yet more fake at the same time.

As walked, I could hear the surf. Looking toward the East, I could see a kind of halo around the morning sun made of sea mist formed by the smashing of waves on the beach. Sea mist has a smell. It's a little hard to describe. It smells like life and it smells like death. That's what I smelled when I walked to the entrance of the multi-million dollar "hey-I've- got-an-idea! Let's build a castle!" To Viktor belongs the spoils.

He had good surveillance equipment, the best, and it wasn't obvious. I knocked on the big wooden door, studded and strapped with metal. A voice to my right told me to please use the service entrance. I looked to my right and there was a tiny speaker grill I hadn't noticed.

"Where would that be?" I inquired.

"Go back along the walk until it forks and bear right."

"Thank you."

I walked till I got to a large bayberry bush and then followed a fork in the asphalt path around and down until I came to a little stucco archway. Below it and behind it was a regular double door. A little sign showed me where to press the buzzer. I waited only a second before the door buzzed back at me and I tried the handle and I was in. Three strides brought me to an all-white area that was three stories high. A high ceiling like that is usually called a cathedral ceiling, but this really was a ceiling like they have in a cathedral. At the top of the walls were old (looking) timber beams. Each beam was painted with bright colors that looked like they might have represented family colors – if the family had been many generations in the clown business. There was a lot of yellow and red. At the far wall on a small raised area a suit of armor stared back at me. The suit had a large sword.

"May I help you?"

I looked to my right and there at a small desk with no computer visible, but four commercial phones, was the most beautiful large woman I have ever seen. She was at least two-eighty, but her face was perfectly formed and her hair had been fussed over by someone who knew what he or she was doing.

"Thank you. My name is Max Kelly? I'm here to see Mr. Viktor?"

"Yes, of course. Take those stairs to the next level and someone will announce you."

One of her phones signaled a call and she gave her attention to it. I turned, found the stairs and started up. Above my head was a giant candelabrum, seemingly made of bent iron. The bulbs and holders were shaped like candles. It had gold touches and there were concentric rings pierced with red stones or glass. It suited the space I guess. I would hate to have to replace the bulbs.

On the second level, which was actually the main floor of the structure, there was another little desk (this one had a computer and only two phones), another beautiful large woman and in a little raised niche, another suit of armor.

"Mr. Kelly?" Both of the beautiful fat women had beautiful voices with no trace of any accent. On the phone I might have fallen in love. Out of eye-shot, she was a knockout. Under scrutiny, there was a lot to love. You would have to start at the foothills.

"That's me."

"Could you have a seat, please? Mr. Viktor is on the phone to the coast."

"Do they still say that?" I asked.

"What's that, Mr. Kelly?"

"A guy is on the phone to the coast?"

"How would you say it Mr. Kelly?"

"I don't know. He's got a call from California? Hollywood? Burbank?"

"That's what we call the coast."

She smiled and I think she meant it to look sweet, but I could see that we weren't going to get anywhere.

"Is that security?" I said and tilted my head toward the suit of armor. Every floor seemed to have one.

"Yes, Mr. Kelly."

No sense of humor at all. But then I saw something astounding. The suit of armor sneezed. Then a steel scaled hand reached up and opened the visor and stuck a piece of Kleenex in there and snot was blown. It wasn't just another empty suit. I got the tingle.

A door opened. Another super-sized woman, this time with dark bangs of hair, fabulous cheekbones, well highlighted with make-up, eyes that laughed and a perfect nose emerged onto the little corridor reception area. She smiled my way and then turned her attention to the beautiful woman at the desk. They exchanged file folders. Then the dark-haired one gave me a big smile (I returned it with interest), turned and went back to the door from which she had first emerged. She pulled it toward her, and like a horizontal sunset, she went out of my life. The door closed with no sound.

I sat. The walls were covered with pen drawings, caricatures of famous people. I could recognize about half of them. Some of them have been out of circulation for years. Three or four of them were dead.

A door opened. A guy stuck his head out. It swiveled. It spoke. "Max? Come on in. I only have a second." The head disappeared behind the still-open door.

"You may go in now," said the beautiful receptionist.

"Thanks. That was Mr. Viktor, right?"

"Oh, yes!" She was as cheery as the good witch in the Wizard of Oz. She had almost the same face and hair. She was at least a size twenty.

Mel Viktor was a lot different in his office than he had seemed at Jones Beach. Then he seemed crazed and I could almost say vicious. I was expecting a tough time, but he decided to use charm instead of intimidation, at least in the beginning.

"So, Max! Rodd says you wanted to see me about something?" He lit off a 2000 watt smile. There was nothing Energy Star about it.

"Yes, I ... "

"Hey! What did you think about the show?" he said, coming toward me. "Great, wasn't it?"

"Yes, I..."

The next thing I knew an arm was around my shoulder. I wasn't expecting or prepared for it. He shook me toward him. "Hey!" he said. "What would you like? A little espresso? I got a machine. Some pastries? I get them sent out from a deli in Lawrence. You like rugala? This is the best! I'm telling you. Apricot?"

"No, thanks, I ..."

"Something stronger? A little pick-me-up?" he said, beaming with some weird pleasure. He sniffed twice suggestively and flashed his eyebrows.

"Not for me," I said.

"Max," he said and put on a big fake pout. Then he backed off two feet and shook his head slowly. "You should eat."

"Later," I said. "Who is the guy in the iron suit?"

"Bertram?" he said and then he giggled. The weird part is that I wanted to giggle with him. There was something crazy and attractive about him. It was like we were both ten years old and meeting for the first time in a steel-fenced playground. "I'm doing a favor for an old friend. Bertram didn't have a job and as a joke I told him he would have to wear a suit of armor and he said OK. He was serious! It started out as a gag, but I like it. The magazines love that shit. One thing I know is how to generate publicity. Have you got a girlfriend?" he said. I would love to know how he jumped from one subject to the other. There was obviously a link in his mind, but I couldn't see it.

"Me?" I responded. The question hit me when I was already off balance from his strange manner.

"Hey! I'm having some people over on the weekend, entertainment people," he said and gunned me down with his index finger like he was emptying a clip at me. "You would go over real big with a couple of the girls that like to hang around. Yeah. I can hook you up with ... Roger! How the hell are you?"

It took me only a half a second to realize that he was talking into his ear phone. He nodded at me and smiled to show me that he had just taken a call. He then pointed to his ear. I waited. His ear was glowing with a blue light.

"Suzy was asking about you, big guy," said Mel, his eyes sparkling with what looked like merriment. He waited for a moment and then said, "That's not the way she told the story. You have to lay off the mojitos, big guy. Your jito can't take no mo!" At this Mel laughed heartily. I was just starting to like old Mel, when his smile tightened into a grimace and he said, "Oh, cut the crap, Rog. Turn up the heat and tell them they can talk to me or they can talk to my lawyer. I don't care either way. I want that venue. OK. Call me back." He shifted his gaze back to me and his momentary frown became a brilliant smile once again. He was back.

"Had to take that. So ...?"

"Mr. Close asked me to ..."

"Has he talked to the bank yet?"

"I don't know. That's not why I'm here."

"I should call him. He's got to talk to the bank. I got people that need their money. These are people you don't want to mess with. You really don't."

"I'm sure he's doing everything he can," I said.

"What's with the hat?" said Mel.

"Mr. Close's concert hat?" I said, to buy time. There is no answer to the question, at least not in this universe; in one of the other universes maybe."

"Does he wear that often?"

"Only for rock concerts," I said.

"Does he ever get in fights?" said Mel. The was a small and questioning smile trying to bend his lips.

"All the time. He beat up a guy in Chelsea so bad they had to put him on life support," I said. I was playing it broadly. It was a funny concept.

"Close did?" Viktor said seriously. In his world this sort of thing seemed to happen regularly enough to be a possibility. He had moved over behind his desk and now he sat. His eyes never left my face.

"He's thin, but he is a Jokido master," I said, matching my tone to his concern and then overdoing it a little for comic effect.

"You're kidding!" he said. He pointed a finger at me.

"Jokido is no laughing matter."

We both waited for it. He stared at me and cocked his head to one side a couple of degrees. He was waiting for some indication on my face that I was kidding. I stared right back at him, wondering when the obvious would hit him over the head with a sock full of lead shot. Then he broke out a sly smile and shook his head and said to himself, "Jokido master." Then he changed his face to a look of unsmiling, professional interest and said, "So he asked you to see me? What about?"

I started to tell him when he held up a finger and pushed it at me. Apparently there was another call.

"Cyril! Talk to me! What can I do you out of? Uh huh? I don't think so. I can't do that. I'm barely holding my head above water over here." This caused me to look around. I could see the ocean through the smoky glass window behind me. It looked like it was behaving itself. The view cost more than I will make in my entire life even if I don't have it cut short while stimulating for LT. There were gold and platinum records on the wall. I did not get up to look at who recorded them. There was a suit of armor in the corner, but I could see into the visor and it was empty except for the little video camera in there. Most people would miss it.

"Look, Cyril, you are asking me to dismember myself. You know I would walk through fire for you, but … come on! Come on! OK … I'll talk it over with my guy. Schmeckle deckle. Later, babe."

He flicked his head my way to show that he was back.

"I don't suppose you could turn that thing off for a minute?" I said. It doesn't hurt to ask.

"No," he said, smiling.

"Well, the reason I'm here ..."

A buzzer sounded. He suddenly looked like a lab rat that knows a big shock is coming whenever the buzzer goes off. I sat up a lot straighter just because of the look on his face. I know fear. It wasn't the smell, that came later, it was the involuntary muscle spasms in his cheek and the look in his eye.

We both turned toward the closed door. Something big was coming. It came. The door was pushed aside as if by a tsunami and she imploded into our space. It was another beautiful large woman and this one was pissed about something.

"But ..." was all he got a chance to say. This was her show.

"You little creepy-dog! You told me you were done with that! And now I find out it's been going on for the last two months."

"*What?*" said Viktor, almost yelling to match her tone.

"You and that Charlynne slut, the little piece of tail that caused all the trouble last summer. She's a freaking dancer, for cry-sake! And I had to hear about it from Mary Anne! That's it, buster! You can screw all the tramps you want because I'm moving the hell out and I'm taking Tommy and you can screw yourself for all I care, because I have had just about enough."

While she was yelling, her hands were waving at his face. She was trying to get a slap in, but he was good at ducking and covering. He hadn't gotten out of his chair yet and it had a ludicrously high back, She was having a hell of a time trying to land a flat hand.

He was making little noises that might have become words of self-defense if she had allowed them to develop. All of a sudden he held up the finger to her and pushed it at her. She stopped for a moment. He had a call.

"Eddie!" he said into his headset. "What do you got?"

She watched for a moment longer, but I could tell from the venting gasses she was going to blow.

"I can't do twelve percent," said Mel Viktor. "Tell him to refigure and get back to me. I think I can maybe go ..." He was so intent on his call that he made the mistake of leaning forward. He was exposed.

With that, she swiped him one across the side of the head and the little phone set flew across the room and landed on the floor. It was still glowing with a weird blue inner light. That was it for Viktor. He jumped out of his chair waving his arms. "Hey! Hey! What the hell! This is *business!* You can't come in here like this in the middle of business! What are you thinking?"

"I'm leaving you. I'm through with this," she said.

"OK! I got it. But you can't be messing with a guy's business. Are you nuts?"

"I'm taking you to court," she said. Then she punctuated the threat with a face.

"I've been there before over bigger deals than you," he said right back to her.

"I'm gonna make you do nice for Tommy if I have to hire every lawyer on the East coast," she said.

"Go ahead. Now get the hell out of here. And once you walk out that door, don't even think about trying to get back in because I'm going to tell security that you're a crazy bitch and I'm going to authorize deadly force. I'm going to make out a police report that you are a sick and violent crazy person!"

"You go to the police," she said with a sarcastic laugh. "Go ahead, and when they come to talk to me … Guess what? I will depose your ass so deep in crap, you will end up in a cell and you won't see the light of day till your teeth fall out! You think I don't know what goes on? I know what goes on."

"Get out of here. You make trouble for me or my business and see what happens. If you know what goes on, you think about that before you do anything stupid."

"Everybody told me not to marry you," she said.

"Well, why did you then?" he said.

"You know why."

"Show some respect. I got a guy here," he indicated me with his upturned hand. I had thought he had forgotten I was in the room."

"I'll be at mother's. Don't try to call."

"I won't."

She turned to go. Just before she got to the door, she said in a mumble, "pig."

"Bitch," he answered her. His mumble was a little louder.

She didn't look back. She opened the door, went behind it and she left it open. He followed her to the door at a safe distance and closed it quietly. Then he walked softly back to where the phone had ended up. He picked it up as if it were a baby bird fallen from a high nest. He caressed the earpiece into place and put his head to one side, as if listening. "Eddie?"

I waited. He waited.

"He's gone. He'll call back. Excuse me one moment." Up came the finger. Then he began to diddle with something on his belt. I guessed he was making a call.

"Hello? This is Mel Viktor on Dune Road in Westhampton. I am going to need three temps as soon as you can get them here. They should be presentable, very presentable. Don't send anyone older than forty and they should be skinny...uh huh? That's your problem, figure it out. I don't want to see anyone but thin and presentable. You'll find a way. If you do this for me there will be a nice cash bonus. If the temps work out we can talk about a permanent gig. I'll need them for at least three weeks, but if they work out, we'll talk. Thanks. And you are? OK Cheryl, see what you can round up."

He looked at me and smiled. I had been in his office only a few minutes and I had seen almost every emotion and tone of voice there is.

"I'm sorry about this. You picked a busy day. I have to make one more call." He diddled some more with the thing on his belt. Then he made a face like someone who sees the bus coming and wants to be sure it's the right one. Then he said, "It's me. She just left. She knows about you. Keep your head down. You want to come over for dinner? No. She's gone. Do me a favor, call Minky's Moving and Storage and tell them to have two trucks over here tomorrow morning ... babe, she's gone. I'm telling you. It's over. Yeah. Same here."

Then he turned his face to me and he was smiling professionally.

"So Rodd Rock says you want to talk to me? What about?"

"About the missing money."

The smile vanished. He actually blushed. I hadn't seen a man blush in a long time.

"Oh, fuck-a-rat I need this now! There's no missing money. There never was any missing money. Doesn't Rodd think he has enough, money for god's sake?"

That's when he flashed the boots. I had a little preview of them when he went to close the door and pick up his phone, but most of the time they had been stowed away under his Louis the Sun King of Miami (and Los Angeles – fine furnishings for less) desk. With the subject of money now on the table, as it were, he retracted his feet, brought them up to eye level and then folded them out and dumped them onto the top of the desk. Louis would have been perturbed, but he was in Miami and it was Mel's desk now. If Mel wanted to put his shoes on the desk, he damned well would.

Now that they were fully revealed, I had to stare at the boots. I had never seen anything like them; not that I have spent much time looking at cowboy boots. These would be hard to miss in the dark on a moonless night. He saw my reaction and smiled a little.

"You like 'em?" he said.

"What are they?" I asked.

" Komodo Dragon hide; custom made. I have a guy down in Nashville, Dore West. What's your size?"

"I don't wear boots."

"You should. You have a nice line," he said.

I had to get the conversation back to something like reality, if I could remember a way back there. "So you are not concerned about the missing money?"

"Should I be?" he said, still admiring the boots on his own feet.

"If it's missing."

"What do you know about the entertainment business?" he said, looking up.

"Not much."

"That's right. You don't know shit about what I do or how I do it. If I took the time to explain it to you, which I'm not going to do because I'm a busy man, you wouldn't get it. I'll tell you this. It's expensive to make entertainment. Most projects lose money. Some band has a hit. They tour. Tickets go for forty bucks and up. Right? You think the tour is making big money?

"Sounds like it to me," I said. "That's a lot of cash flow."

"What if I told you that the tour is a loser, and that the management only sends the band out to support product sales and that a lot of those tours are sponsored by big corporations who want the public relations and are willing to put out big bucks to buy the association."

"Sounds crazy," I said.

"It's a crazy business. What if I told you that you have to pay for airplay?"

"That sounds illegal," I said.

"Illegal? I'm glad you brought that up. If I told you about the after-hour, off-the-book expenses ... ah ... I'm not going to do that, but you can use your imagination. Rodd Rock has done all right for himself. He costs a lot to handle. I'm the best in the business, but I have ..." He swiveled his head around the room. Mine swiveled as well just to see what he was looking at. "... expenses."

I shuddered. The last time I heard someone say that was when LT was explaining why I could not have a raise.

"You have receipts?" I asked him.

His jaw dropped down, as if something had snapped in the mechanism. He just stared for a tiny moment, but in that tiny moment, I got the tingle. I felt the menace.

"What are you?" he said, "Internal Revenue?"

"Over the years you have done everything for Rodd Rock, isn't that true?"

"Everything. Everything," he said with a lot of hand motion indicating complicated activity.

"What if he called you up and said he wanted his wife to disappear …" I said.

"Hey! What the hell! I thought you came here as Rodd Rock's guy? What kind of a question is that? You don't know what you're getting into asking a guy something like that. Let me tell you something and you should listen up. I don't know what happened to Rodd's wife. I don't keep track of his personal life, but if I did have something to do with whatever … and you come in here like this asking me about it … what do you think I'm going to do?" The boots went back under the desk and he was leaning toward me with his forearms on the desk, as if he was ready to spring.

"Make a phone call to Dominic Pancetta?" I suggested.

"Hey! I don't like where this is going. I'm a busy guy. I only agreed to see you because …"

Up came the finger. This time he turned his head toward the earpiece and frowned. "Yeah, I'm on," he said. There was a moment while he listened. "When?" he said. The he listened for another second. "I can't talk now. I'll call you. I'll call your land line. Stay there till I call. Don't touch anything. Stay by the phone."

Then he turned to me and said, "Something has come up. I'm going to have to ask you to leave." He stood up. I stood up. "You know what I hope for you?" he said.

"What?" I said.

"I hope your boss or someone teaches you some manners before you have to take remedial lessons. It's a tough world out there. There's a right way and a wrong way to do business. You got a lot to learn. So does your boss. Tell him to talk to the bank. I'm running out of time here. Tell him this for me. If I run out of time, so does he. Tell him. "

He held out his hand. I almost didn't shake it, but I was learning. He gripped my hand a little tighter and looked me in the eye. I looked him in the eye. I do not know what it is I saw there.

11

"So what did you find out at Mel Viktor's?" said LT. He was playing with his mail. "Where's Dickie?"

I was looking at my Palm Pilot where I had made some notes. "Dickie went into town," I answered him. "He is going to the liquor store and the farm stand. Mel Viktor is a character. He wants you to call the bank. He was emphatic about that. In fact I think he threatened your life if you don't. And his marriage broke up while I was sitting in his office. And I might have overstimulated."

"What do you mean?" said LT, putting down an unopened bill. He frowned at it.

"I mean his wife came in the office while I was there, she's a bruiser by the way, and she tried to slap Mel around for adultery. Then she walked out and took the kid. As soon as she cleared the doorway, he called his girlfriend and then ordered up a couple of moving vans."

"While you were sitting there?" said LT. Now he was frowning at me.

"I was invisible. I was a fly on the wall."

"Could it have been staged for your benefit?"

"No," I said.

"You are certain?"

"These people don't really believe that other people are real. They do what they feel and say what they feel whenever they feel like it. I do not know about her, but it makes him dangerous. From what I could see of her, she is dangerous too. No wonder he could get involved with what you would call unsavory types and survive. Life? Death? It's all just a game unless it's his life. He is the kind of a guy who could rationalize anything if it gave him an advantage, and I mean anything. If he wanted you or me messed up, he makes a call and he doesn't break a sweat. I tried out Dominic Pancetta's name and there was a reaction. I could not read it, but there is a connection there. My guess is that they have done business in the past together, maybe the recent past. I may have used too much leverage ..."

"What did you do?"

"I prodded him about the missing money and asked him if he would remove Arlene if Rodd asked him to do it."

"Why would you do such a thing? Mel Viktor hardly needs stimulation at this point, quite the opposite! I didn't send you over there to start a barroom brawl. What were you thinking?"

"I don't know. Arlene is missing and he was in the parking lot when she disappeared. So I asked him about it."

"And his reaction?"

"Stimulated."

"It may get worse," said LT, while fingering an unopened letter.

"Why?"

"I may have inadvertently sent the IRS in his direction."

"Inadvertently?" I asked.

"I was consulting an old acquaintance of mine who works for the IRS. I tried to keep names out of it, but he knows we are involved with Rodd Rock and he connected some dots. I was attempting to find out about the status of Viktor's offshore entities. You would be amazed. There are more than a dozen. Mr. Viktor is in a vise. He doesn't realize it yet, but the jaws are coming together slowly, but inexorably. The lever is in my hand. If his marriage is breaking apart as you say, then Mel Viktor's financial health will be taking a turn for the worst. I suspect there will be a pernicious inflammation."

"Will he know that you are the one applying the pressure?" I asked.

"Only by inference," said LT, slitting open the envelope with a vicious swipe ending in a kind of flourish. He used his jade letter opener, as if he were cleaning a fish. He usually uses his finger to open an envelope. He was in a weird mood. "Mel Viktor has been getting away with murder for years," he said.

"Literally or figuratively?" I asked.

"We will see," said LT.

That is when the doorbell rang.

"I'll get it. Dickie's in town."

They were the two saddest people I have ever seen. There were nice looking and decently dressed; he in lightweight summer gear and she in a breezy kind of skirt and blouse. He had a deep tan. She was more the pink type.

"Is Lawton Close available for a consultation?" the man said.

"He is in the middle of some paper work. I can ask him. Would you care to give me your names?"

"Just tell him that we are the parents of Arlene Bourges."

"Oh. I'm so sorry about the news. Please come in out of the sun. I will go ask him if he could give you a moment. I'm sure I can get him to see you. Could you wait here a moment, please? You can sit if you are more comfortable. I'll be right back." I waved my hand at the loveseat Teddy found at the thrift shop that turned out to be the real deal. She is good that way. His eyes took in the offer and he nodded. His wife's eye stayed on him.

LT had his reading glasses on. He had picked up the bills again. He had his little printing calculator out and he was frowning. He looked up when I entered. Then he pulled his glasses down a half an inch and looked over them.

"What is it?"

"Arlene's parents are here."

"Here?"

"That's right. They want to see you."

"I can't see anybody now. I'm not prepared to see anybody now. Look at this desk."

"I'll clean up the desk. I'll put the bills away. You can slip into the kitchen and have Dickie receive her parents while you freshen up."

For once, even though he is one of the greatest lawyers I know, he didn't argue. He started to argue, but got no further than a tone of voice grafted onto a sigh. No actual word was produced. It was more like an argumentative whimper. Then he stood, twirled as a soldier on parade might do, and then he was gone.

It took me a minute to get the torn envelopes into the waste basket and the bills basket put away in the bottom of the file drawer in the little closet that LT converted to a wall of file cabinets that he can hide just by closing the door. I closed it. Then I got down on my hands and knees and picked up all the paper bits created when LT opens envelopes with his finger. He only uses the jade letter opener on certain mail. I don't try to figure it out. He's eccentric.

I went back through the kitchen to give the all clear. LT had found his seersucker jacket. It was wrinkled, but hell, it was a jacket. He dialed his bow tie into a horizontal alignment, and then nodded to me and brushed past my shoulder on his way back to the office through the back hall. I heard Dickie in the front hall. From the evidence by the sink, it appeared he had taken them some iced tea. I went to the sound of the voices.

They all looked up when I entered the foyer. She was seated. He was standing and they were cradling their iced teas, as if they were buckets of quarters from an Atlantic City slots payout.

"Thank you, Dickie. Mr. Close will see you know. He had to finish speaking with a client on the phone. This way, please."

LT is a master of many things. One of them is how he stage manages the meeting of people. He waited the exact amount of time before rising so that their first impression was of him at his desk. When he rose he showed the physical grace that has made his dancing with Teddy a local legend (ballroom dancing, the real thing). He also arranged his features into a look of deep concern and yet it was inviting at the same time. He spread his hands slightly in welcome and told them to come in and find a seat. I don't know how he does it. You might think it was phony, the face of concern, but I know him and he manages to work up some kind of actual concern.

I put Mr. Bourges in one of the wicker chairs and drew up Teddy's little French chair for his wife. In the city we have a coil built into the big wing back chair to sense metal such as a gun. We don't have that capability in the country. I doubted either of them was armed.

"You've met Max. He tells me that you are Arlene's parents. This is a dreadful time for you. Have you traveled far?"

"Just over from near Boston. We took the Cross Sound Ferry," said the husband.

He seemed to be in his mid-sixties. He was thin, had quite a bit of thick gray hair brushed up in almost a flat top and he was surprisingly well-tanned for so early in the season. Maybe he golfed or fished. He didn't dress like the Hamptons. He seemed more the New England country club type with summer weight sensible slacks and a cloth belt with designs on it. They were probably nautical designs. I didn't stare.

His wife did stare wherever she looked at someone. She looked at her husband when he spoke and she looked at him so hard I thought her eyes were going to telescope in his direction. When LT spoke, she switched her look to him and it was even more intense. Her long summer skirt was bright yellow and her blouse was white. Cut down penny-loafers covered her feet. She weighed a bit more than her husband. Her hair had an unnatural brown tint and was close cut. Her days of fussing with hair were evidently past. You could see the resemblance to her daughter, although her daughter's features were much finer. That must have come from her father.

"We understand you are looking for our daughter," said Mr. Bourges.

"I have been retained by Mr. Rodd Rock ... that is a difficult name under the circumstances ... to provide professional services. I am a consultant in matters of law."

"We have asked around," said the father. "You have a reputation as a man who gets things done. We'd like to hire you to find our daughter."

"Yes ... well ... you see ... as I am already retained by Mr. Rock, it would be difficult to ..."

"Are you talking about a conflict of interest?"

"That's a good part of it," said LT. He was actually squirming.

"There's no conflict of interest. He wants to find her as well, doesn't he? Unless he did something to her, in which case ... would you represent him in court if he were accused of ... some sort of foul play?"

"Probably not. I rarely appear in a courtroom. I don't usually practice as a trial lawyer. I am not comfortable in that role."

"Would you represent a man you knew, or honestly considered, to be guilty of a terrible crime?"

"You raise an interesting question. Certainly a person who is guilty of a terrible crime requires representation and should have it. That is how our system works. But ... no ... I prefer not to act in the role of a defense lawyer. I have, in rare instances, appeared in court as defense counsel, but only as a part of a team and only in a support role."

"Then I don't see the problem. We need some consultation. You are a consultant. You charge a great deal of money and we have prepared a great deal of money to be made available for your professional services. There should be no conflict of interest with Sidney Porkhouse AKA Rodd Rock because, presumably, he wants to find his wife and we want to find our daughter. Think of us as part of the team. We are happy to take a subsidiary role. I brought my check book." He reached into his jacket and drew forth a leather covered checkbook with a little flourish and slapped it down on the desk. "I assumed you would need a hefty retainer."

"Stop! Are you always this ... ah ... direct? What do you do for a living?"

"I am a professional negotiator," said Mr. Bourges.

"Ah. Then it is useless for me to attempt to deflect you from your purpose ."

"Absolutely."

"You would gauge each of my maneuvers and prepare a calibrated response, would you not?" said LT.

"That's what I do."

"Until at last I would find myself ... ah ... with very little room to maneuver."

"That's how it works."

"My position is hopeless."

"Nearly so."

"Max."

"Yes?" I didn't understand what LT was up to. We can't have two clients for the same job.

"Prepare a standard contract for Mr. and Mrs. Bourges."

"What do you mean?" I asked.

"What did I say?" he responded. There was a little bit of "not now" in his tone.

"You said to prepare a standard contract for Mr. and Mrs. Bourges."

"I did. Why are you still sitting there?"

"But …"

"Yes?"

"You want me to use the standard form?"

"That's right. I will make some small changes to the boilerplate by hand and everyone will sign. Please leave the space for retainer blank."

"On my computer?" I asked.

"Yes. The one in your room, or you could use Dickie's in the kitchen. If he's online, ask him to get off. When you have it completed send it to the printer here and I'll take care of everything else."

"Do you want me to do that later? So I can take some notes?"

"No. Please do it now."

I got up. The Bourges nodded to me solemnly. I nodded to them and left the room. I went to the kitchen and saw that Dickie was downloading something for his iPod. He wasn't actually snapping his fingers, but he was bobbing his head and he had his weird white ear buds in. I thought of telling him again about what Peter Townsend said about going deaf, but he looked so pleased with himself and he smiled up at me when I came over to him that I just couldn't.

I went to my room and turned on my lap top on the little desk by the window. It took a while to boot. It gave me a moment alone with my thoughts and my thoughts were darkening. LT had lost control of his greed. It was always there. It is a chronic condition, but he usually keeps it under control with various self-medications. Now, in his weakened state, his defenses had been overwhelmed. There had been a flare up. His fever was high. He was feverish and delusional and … there was going to be trouble.

It took about fifteen minutes to get the agreement in shape and to send it down to the printer in the summer office. I sent three copies. Then I followed the electrons down to the office. When I opened the door I saw LT arranging pages from the first of the copies and Mr. Bourges was saying something that ended with the words, "… and if you could indeed do that … that would be spiffy."

At almost that exact moment there was a pounding on the front door. I heard Dickie pushing back his chair in the kitchen as he stood to go for the door, but the pounder couldn't wait. The door was coming open and the pounder was coming in. I was out of my seat and moving to the office door and then through to the hall. He was already in the house and moving toward me.

"Whoa! Where are you going?" I said to Rodd.

"The cops are at the house and they have taken all the video disks from the security system. Can they do that? I mean they did and they had papers, and they took my lap top and computer. Where's Close? We have to talk."

"He's with some people. You are not going in there, so you might want to slow your adrenal system down."

"I have to see him," he said. He was agitated.

He was still moving. I had to stand in front of him to get his attention. He thought he was still going to move and I had to hold his arm. It was stringy, but there was a lot of muscle for a skinny older guy.

"You are not going to see him now," I said.

"I have to!"

"No, you don't," I said. "You can either go back to your house and wait until LT is free or you can come out the back door with me and wait on the porch."

"What are Arlene's parents doing here?"

"Why do you say that?"

"That's their car outside, the one with the Massachusetts plates. What are they doing here?"

I began steering him to the kitchen. As long as he was talking, the steering was easy. When he stopped talking and could concentrate on resistance, the steering became problematic.

"They are talking to LT," I said.

"What about?"

"About their missing daughter, what do you think?"

"I should be in there!" he said, almost violently.

"I don't think so. If they wanted you in there, they would have invited you in there."

"What are they saying?" he demanded.

"I don't know. I am not in the room."

"You came out of that room!" he said. He was angry and fidgeting. Most of his body parts were in motion.

"Yes. I was only in there for a moment. LT had me making up some paper work for …"

"What kind of paper work?" he demanded.

"None of your business," I told him. It was not entirely true, I suppose. I was still steering him, but he was starting to drag his feet as we got closer to the door.

"I have to see Close right now!" he said, coming to a full stop.

He started to get energized again. I firmed up my grip and shoved him through the kitchen door. I used my back to close the door. He was in pretty good shape for his age, but he had a lot of years on the odometer..

Rodd and I shared a beer in the kitchen. We didn't say much and I didn't take any notes. Dickie joined us for a bit and gushed over the concert, but I could tell that Dickie was just blowing smoke and Rodd thought so as well. No one really wanted to talk about the concert. Then Dickie got a cell phone call, and started whispering and then he took it outside. I would have to look into Dickie's affairs when I got some free time. Dickie was up to something.

We heard a commotion at the front door and then LT breezed into the kitchen. He was startled to see Rodd, but he handled it well.

"What's going on?" said Rodd. 'What are her parents doing here?"

"Rodd," said LT. "We need to have a little chat."

"Damned right we do."

We stood up and started for the summer office. LT turned around, saw me and said, "Max. could you please go pick up Teddy at Scott Aveda's?"

"Do you need me to take notes? Dickie can get Teddy."

"No. Dickie has to pick up some food for tonight. You can take the Caddy."

"What's tonight?"

"We are having some people in."

"Tonight?"

"Teddy's waiting."

She was, too.

12

THE NEXT DAY I GOT up late, real late. I was sore and angry and confused. It wasn't just the two different attacks I had survived (barely), it was that Teddy and LT had been at their most obnoxious. On top of everything else, Rodd's world had started to crack apart. Metaphorically speaking his California had already slid into the sea, his Rockies were tumbling and his Gibraltar was about to crumble. They're only made of clay, like his feet.

And poor Teddy; it was all getting to be too much for Teddy.

She has been an industrial designer, an editor, an interior designer and she has had designs on LT since they were in summer camp together. Teddy Martin-Smyth is not someone to be trifled with, although you wouldn't know that to look at her. To look at her, you would think she was just another dark-haired pretty New Yorker who has been on a diet too long, been unmarried too long, been too long in the fluorescent halls of corporate offices and is too long for her shape. I didn't say bony. Teddy is all about the legs. Above the waist, the biggest attraction is the eyes. They are big and quick and they catch the light. If she had wings, she could hunt the Amazon rain forest at night, and believe me, you would never hear her coming.

She had a rough night. We all did.

The evening started nicely enough when the Maxwells joined us for dinner. He is an old friend of LT's mother. LT invites both of them to the house because they don't get out much. I had to go pick them up and drop them back at their place on the ocean. He's a nice old guy, but he repeats himself and he is a little hard of hearing.

"Stop me if I've told you about the time Lawton was at summer camp and his mother and I were on Cape Cod together …" he said from the back seat.

"I've heard it!" I said. I was taking him at his word. "Lawton got stung by a jelly fish and he wanted the doctor to put peanut butter on it."

"What?" came from the back seat.

"Skip it," I said.

"Lawton was learning to swim that summer and he hated it. His mother, good lord she was a looker, was interested in some property on Cape Cod. She wanted me to go with her because she always said she valued my advice. You know they say that she and Kennedy were …"

I drove and let him talk. I nodded a lot.

Dinner was late because we all had to crowd into the little den to watch the six o'clock news and then the celebrity channel gossips to see how the media was playing the story of the disappearance.

It was bad. All of them made the connection between the money and the disappearance. Everyone was running old file footage from the Grammies when Rodd and Arlene had posed a lot as a couple. She was wearing a black dress with a lot of hand sewn beads that sparkled. She looked heavy, but very nice. He looked a little tired and a little distracted.

"What are they setting up?" I said to LT.

"Shhhhh. They are trying to establish a motive."

"The money," said Teddy.

"Of course," he answered.

"Look at her mug shot!" said Teddy excitedly. "That's a mug shot."

"What?" said Mr. Maxwell. "Isn't she married to that singer, Rocky something?" His wife patted his arm softly. He turned to her and said "What?" more softly. She smiled and nodded to him and he went quiet.

Over the head of the new presenter on Channel Five, was a full face head shot of Arlene. Underneath her face at a slight angle was the word "missing" in a dramatic typeface that looked like something from a wild west wanted poster. Arlene's face had a kind of cherubic benevolence. The camera had caught her in the middle of a smile that hadn't fully developed into something expressive. It made her look vacant.

"That's a funny picture to use," I said.

"That's the victim look," said LT.

"It's perfect," said Teddy.

"They can't find that woman," said Mr. Maxwell.

"They know dear," said Mrs. Maxwell.

"What?"

She patted his arm.

As the presenter spoke, a new face appeared above his head. It was a shot from the waist up of Rodd Rock with no shirt on. His face was distorted by either pain or passion. His body was covered with drops of what was supposed to look like sweat and probably was. The shot was taken when he was performing in his stage persona. He appeared to be screaming.

"OK," said LT. "The demonization has begun. The narrative has been established. They will continue to build on this. She will be portrayed as the perfect victim and his publicity shots from the Lobes will be used to establish him as a monster. I've seen enough. Please turn off the television."

"That's him! The singer! It's that Rocky fellow!" said Mr. Maxwell.

LT rose up and said, "Shall we adjourn to the dining room?"

Everyone stood. We filed out like school children after a classmate had been yelled at by a teacher. Shoulders and heads were down. The mood carried over into the dinning room. Things were quiet for a while until Teddy said to LT, "This is the end of his career."

"It's too early to tell," he said thoughtfully.

"Do you think they will ever find Arlene?" I said.

"I doubt it. This thing has not been done by amateurs," said LT.

"You know," said Mr. Maxwell, "that singer's wife is missing. They think she might have been kidnapped."

His wife patted his arm and smiled and nodded to him.

"What?" He said to her.

"Yes," she mouthed, but did not make a sound. "That man is a client of Lawton's,"

"Who?"

"The singer," she said softly. "That's Lawton's client."

"Our Lawton?" he said to his wife. Then he turned his face to LT. "You represent this fellow whose wife is missing?"

LT just nodded broadly.

"He's bad business. I wouldn't get involved with someone like that. He'll make trouble wherever he goes. Can you get out of it, Lawton?"

Lawton just waved his face from side to side.

"There was a thing about him in the *Times*," said Maxwell. He was getting excited by the subject. "He's trouble. I'd give him his retainer back if I were you and say, 'See ya.' I'd do it in a heart beat. Don't tell me you need his money. Money from people like that … isn't worth it. It's dirty money, blood money."

He felt the pat on his sleeve. He didn't look down at his wife's soft hand. "That's what I have to say." And then he fell silent.

The silence in the room lasted for a long time. We ate. I didn't do much tasting. It was the lowest I had been in a long time.

Suddenly Dickie appeared by my side. I hadn't noticed him coming in. He bent low and said into my ear, "Mr. Kelly. Carrie would like to speak to you on the phone." He backed, turned and was gone without waiting for a reply.

I stood. "Excuse me, please, for a moment."

"We don't take calls at dinner," said LT, in a matter of fact tone.

"This will only take a moment. It's Carrie."

I went around the corner and up the stairs to my room. I picked up the hand set and said, "It's OK Dickie, I've got it."

"Max!"

"What's the matter, Carrie?"

"I can't deal with this. I have to get out of here."

"What's going on?"

"Rodd is crazy. He has locked himself in his room. He told me to get him on a plane to Europe! I told him he can't leave. It would look terrible, but he says he has to get away from the press and they have been just awful. There's a crowd of them outside the gates and they have those horrible trucks with the satellite dishes all over the street. I told him that if he runs away I'm going to quit and he said suit yourself! Max, I don't know what to do!"

"I'll be right there."

"Be careful, the grounds are full of media people."

I changed into my jeans and put on my Topsiders. They were comfort choices, not for style. I went down the stairs to the dining room and went in. No one was saying anything.

"LT, Carrie wants out," I said to all, but I was looking at LT. "I said I would go pick her up. Can I use the car?"

"If you must," said LT, grumpily. His dinner party was off to a bad start. He didn't know that it was going to get a lot worse. "She doesn't want to stay at Rodd's?"

"No. She sounded pretty bad. She's been having a tough time over there for a while now and I think this media stuff has pushed her to the breaking point."

"Bring her here," said Teddy.

"Here?" said LT

"She's Rodd Rock's personal assistant. If you leave her out there anywhere, they are going to track her down and try to get information out of her. Do you want that?"

"No," said LT, emphatically.

"Then let Max bring her here."

"But Max and she were … ah … they have had a relationship," said LT.

"That's over," I said.

"You may feel that way now," said LT, "but you are susceptible. Don't try to tell me otherwise." He was compressing his lips in displeasure.

"Susceptible? I am susceptible? To what?"

"To a raised eyebrow, a soft voice, a fluttering of moonlight, an aperitif, the waft of en peu de parfum, an evening breeze, a whispered sigh …"

"Listen to yourself!" I said. "You need counseling. This whole project has made you whacky doodle all day!"

"But sweetie," said Teddy, flashing her blinkers at me, "this is an argument you lost years ago. Remember when Donna Schnell moved in? All one has to do is make a feint in your direction … you will swing at a balked pitch."

"Ah …" I actually didn't know what to say. Teddy was just teasing and I wasn't in the mood for teasing.

"Bring her here. I'll watch out after her," said Teddy. "She can stay in my room."

"I will not have padding about in the middle of the night. Do you understand me?" from LT.

"Don't worry about it. I'll be back in a half hour. Tell Dickie to hold my dessert for me … oh … and tell him to leave out two spoons."

As I turned to go, LT was starting a frown. I didn't wait to see if it would have developed into further verbiage. I left.

The Montauk Highway was stuffed up. It always is in the season. The Caddy and I crawled along until I made the turn to the right, toward the ocean. I hadn't gone fifty yards down Rodd's street when I saw the first of the news trucks. It was all white with no identification and it had its satellite dish pole fully extended. Wire wrapped down around the pole making it look as if it had some giant spring attached.

The closer I got, the more I saw. When I got within fifty yards of Rodd's gates, the crowd of people and equipment was choking the road down to slightly less than a car width. I saw two different people being illuminated as they spoke into video cameras while holding a microphone. They were posed to put Rodd's gates and a little glimpse of the house in the back ground. Other news people had cameras stuck on tripods raised up to see over the wall, keeping an electronic vigil on the house in case anything should happen. I couldn't imagine what that might be. The house would suddenly explode? Levitate up to the mother ship? The hall light by the bathroom would turn on?

It looked a little like a Hogarth painting that LT had showed me in London. The costumes were different, but the attitudes were similar. Some in the crowd held paper coffee cups, some were joking around, some were fussing with equipment and running wires from the equipment van to lights, cameras and action in the street. Men had paired off with women. Pairs were engaged in conversation. One man was leaning his hand against Rodd's rock wall so that he had a woman in a kind of arm prison and you could tell from his body language that he was trying to break her down for an evening's relationship. From her body language it looked promising for him if he didn't overdo the sales pitch.

Somebody in blue jeans was hanging on the gate by standing on the mask of tragedy and he was holding a large camera with a six inch wide telephoto lens over the top of the ironwork to snap a picture of … I don't know … Rodd Rock's driveway maybe.

Somebody was handing out coffee from the back of one of the vans. Generators were running. It was like a gypsy encampment, a small temporary village of info gypsies. Their campfires were halogen. Their instruments were video cameras. Their song was alarm and complaint. "Rodd Rock, lead singer of the Lobes and the former husband of super-model Karin Shane, remains in seclusion in his Hamptons mansion. His current wife has been missing since Friday. She had recently begun proceedings for a legal separation from the colorful rock star, who has been married twice before and has three children by Ms. Shane. There were no children with his first wife, who lives in England. Millions of dollars are at stake in the event of a divorce and a police spokesman has informed Channel Five that foul play has not been ruled out.

"The missing woman was last seen at a sold-out concert at Jones Beach. A tote bag belonging to the missing woman was found on the grounds in the VIP parking area of the popular concert venue. It contained her purse with money and identification, her cell phone, some jewelry, and items of clothing. There have been reports by witnesses of a car seen leaving the VIP parking area at a high rate of speed. Police are looking for a black Lincoln town car. They also would like to question the driver of a black GMC Denali seen leaving the lot at the same time. Search teams fanned out over the shoreline adjacent to the outdoor theater looking for any sign of the missing woman. Her parents have offered a reward for information about their missing daughter. Sources close to Rodd Rock have stated that he is being treated for depression. This is Connie Wendy for Channel Five News, reporting live in the Hamptons."

Back to you, Todd, or Chuck or Bill or Chandra in the studio.

Hurricanes, burned-out tenements, chemical spills, hit and run deaths, murder-suicides, vans run down at railroad crossings by speeding trains, and drowned children all receive the exact same tone of voice, the same urgency, the same knowing glare into the camera. And now Arlene was a lead item in the news and Rodd Rock was revolving up into firing position. Rodd was about to feel the media hammer.

I didn't pull into the apron in front of the closed gates. I didn't want to get stuck there. I drove past. There was no place to pull over until I gone 200 yards past the next driveway. I found a space and pulled in. I flipped open my phone and pushed the numbers for Carrie. She answered on the second ring.

"Where are you?" she said.

"I'm on the street, in front of the neighbor's. I can't get near the place."

"Pull in the next driveway south and I will meet you in their yard. They're away. The caretaker is a friend of Rodd's. I'll sneak through the hedges."

I fired up the Caddy, made a many pointed U-turn and then drifted on idle up to the neighbor's driveway and pulled in. There was no gate. By the time I got to the house Carrie was coming out of the hedges carrying a backpack with one hand. I barely slowed down and she was in and the door was slammed. She threw her pack onto the rear seat.

I pointed the Caddy's nose toward the street and we moved. Carrie ducked below the glass. The Caddy provides a virtual cockpit of carpet and leather below the level of the glass. If you have to duck down from the media, it is nicer in a Caddy. Everything is nicer in a Caddy. I pulled onto the street and turned toward the ocean, away from the reporters.

"You can come up now," I said

"Tell me when we are clear."

"We are clear."

She came up slowly and peeked over the door to make sure I wasn't fibbing. Then she squirmed up into her seat, but she didn't stay there long. She didn't reach for her seat belt, she reached for my neck and then she was on me and she was trembling. Little sounds came out of her. It sounded like a bad night at the puppy mill. She wasn't trying to talk, she was trying to get control of her emotions.

"Hey!" I said. The car swerved violently as she rubbed against my driving hand.

She grabbed on tighter. I let go of the wheel with my now useless right hand because it was being crushed by trembling woman parts. I drove with my left.

"Hey ..."

That is how we drove for a block or two until I pulled into the beach parking lot. We were nearly alone and I found a place where there were no other cars around if she wanted to have a good cry and maybe some shouting, but that was not what she had in mind.

No sooner had I killed the ignition than her face was in mine and her lips were on mine and hands ... well...

I swear, I will never understand women.

13

THINGS WERE QUIET IN THE Caddy. They had been quiet for about eight minutes. Carrie was resting her head on my shoulder. She had both of her hands wrapped firmly around my upper arm. I was as dopey as a fighter who had just gone four rounds with Mike Tyson. She didn't bite my ear off, but she had had her teeth on it and she was using them.

I wasn't about to speak first. It was one of those situations where whatever you say is going to be wrong; is not going to have the correct tone. The truth is, in a situation like that, there is no correct tone. You have to be emotionally cool and together, but you have to be warm and mushy at the exact same time. It can't be done. LT could do it, but he's a hired mouthpiece often hired to do the impossible. I'm sure he knows just how to speak to Teddy except when they are fighting and then everything he says is held against him, for months.

I'm a man-of-action and now that the action was over, I was on uneven ground in the dark, in a fog, and quicksand was all around.

I don't remember whose idea it was to turn on the car radio. The car doesn't have a CD player because they weren't available when the car was made, way back in the old century. The music was low and it was nice. I think Melissa Etheridge and a new Van Morrison and then an old Lobe hit, "The World is My Home" from their hippy-dippy phase. I didn't feel like clapping along. I wouldn't have even remembered that the song was played except that the DJ decided to break in at the end of it right in the middle of a solid Power Hour set of hot adult contemporary format, "That was of course Rodd Rock and the Lobes back in 1973 from the green album that went double platinum. Rodd Rock was in the news again tonight. CNN is reporting that the head of security at Rodd Rock's palatial Hamptons mansion is a convicted felon with ties to organized crime, who was once questioned about the murder of a Baldwin, Long Island couple. Although described by the district attorney as a person of interest in the double homicide, there was insufficient evidence at the time to bring him to trial. Rodd Rock's wife, whom sources say was planning to divorce the rock star in what could have been a multi-million dollar settlemen, was reported missing earlier in the week. Next we have something new from Bonnie Rait …" I had heard enough. I killed the radio.

"Did you turn off your cell phone?" I said to Carrie.

"Of course."

"Maybe you better turn it on. Mine needs to be recharged."

She fumbled around for a moment and came up with a little silver phone. She flipped it open and pointed it at me.

"No pictures!" I said.

"I have to have one."

"Not now. Someone mussed my hair."

"Oh! It's cute. Want to see?"

"No. Have you checked your messages?"

"Uh oh. And here's one from your boss. It's a voice mail … ah … hold on … mm … I think he wants you back home and he sounds kind of worked up."

"Crap! We have to go."

"What about me?"

"You are staying at LT's with me."

"Ooooooh."

"LT made me promise there would be no funny business. I didn't think there would be …"

"And now?"

"Now … I'm not so sure. Buckle up. We have to get going."

"Wait! There's a message from Rodd."

"I have to get back," I said. She fiddled with her phone. I swung the Caddy around toward civilization and lit the lights. Then I hit the high beams and put my foot down.

"Rodd still says he's going to Europe," she said. "Europe? We've discussed this! He can't go anywhere with his wife missing. What's that about?"

"He would be nuts to try something like that," I said. "The cops would never let him leave the country. What can he be thinking?"

"I don't know anything anymore. I don't know why people do what they do. You think you know somebody and then …"

"You don't think he had her … you know … taken out, do you?"

"Rodd? I have seen Rodd in a murderous rage, more than once. He went after me when he was drunk a couple of times … Could he kill someone? I don't know. When you and I worked for Mr. Taylor, I thought I knew something about life. Remember when the biggest goal of my life was to get transferred to Albany? Then it turned out that Taylor was mixed up with people who wanted to create mass murder. That shook me. I mean I went out with him! But see, I thought I knew about people. It's very strange. I thought I knew you. Ha!"

"You knew me. That was me."

"I didn't know about you and what I thought I did know turned out to be completely wrong, phony. You will never know how devastated I was when I found out you had a whole other life. I thought I knew how to handle you. I thought I had the steering wheel in my hand. Then I find out it went to another set of wheels on a different car! And you weren't even in it."

"I never made up anything about me," I said.

"No. It's what you left out. Nobody knew you."

"It wasn't because I didn't want to be known," I said.

"You don't know what you want," she answered. She had put her head down and was looking at the old, sandy carpet. Living near the beaches makes for sandy car carpet.

"Why do you say that?" I said.

"Because I have eyes and I can see," she said, not looking at me.

"See what?" I asked.

"Stuff," she said. She was still looking down. My eyes were suddenly on the rearview mirror. My heart rate picked up the tempo.

"How many people do you know that own a Viper?" I said.

"I don't know, why?" she said, looking at me.

"One just pulled in behind us, two cars back … don't look."

"Why not?" she said, turning her head around.

"You don't want them to know you know they're back there," I said. My hands shrugged for me. They lifted themselves up from the steering wheel and turned over.

"Why not? What are you going to do? Lose them?" she said.

"Well … I'd like to keep my options open."

"Get real. This ancient old honker is the size of a moving van. Men! You just like to play at being a man-of-action. You should at least try something halfway original. I mean, stop the car and go back and challenge the driver to a game of quoits or something."

"Quoits? What is that?" I asked.
"I don't know. I read it someplace."
"How do you play it?" I said.
"I don't know. I didn't read that far."
"Hold on to your seat belt, here he comes."

The Viper had pulled out and passed across two yellow lines. He had pulled in behind, close behind.

"So what?" she said.

"What do you mean, so what? That was a very aggressive move. It looks like your buddy Paul Williams also known as Dominic Pancetta. Hey! What are you doing?"

"I'm giving him the finger," She said. She was, too, with motion.

"Put that down! Are you insane?" I yelled.

"He's a jerk!" she said. She said it with finality. The case was closed.

"Oh, crap, you've fired him up now."

The Viper was dropping back and making runs at our rear bumper. After each run, the driver would disengage the clutch and race the engine. I was surfing on adrenaline, but not in panic at that time. That came later.

"Now what are you doing?" I said.

"I'm showing him my cell phone and I am dialing my cell phone with great big and slow movements that even a moron can see, nine…one…one…now I'm holding the phone up to my face, as if I am really talking to…hello?"

"That's not 911, is it?"

"How late is your kitchen open tonight? Uh huh. Do you think we need reservations? OK. We'll see you later."

"What was that?" I asked. I didn't look at her. I was watching the rear view mirror closely.

"I'm hungry. You're going to take me out."

"Son of a bitch, he's pulled off." The Viper turned into a parking lot for a glass business that had shut off its showroom lights hours before.

"Men!"

"Where am I taking you later?'

"Out to get a decent meal. And then … and then … we'll see."

"And you've picked the place?"

"Damned right. After what you put me through at the beach, it's not going to be any roadside diner."

"*Put you through*?" I said.

"I've had a trying day and you took advantage of my insecurities."

"Lady, I was mugged!"

"And you must be made to pay and pay plenty. I have other appetites, you know."

"Taylor had a crush on you, but he never knew what he was dealing with. This is our turnoff."

I followed the road to LT's driveway. As I signaled to turn in, a pair of car headlights flashed on just fifty yards ahead. They were set low and wide.

"Uh oh!" I said.

"What?"

"The Viper!"

Instead of slowing down to make the turn, I pulled in the driveway a little sideways and fed in enough throttle to keep it sideways on the loose gravel. Then I laid on the horn and I kept it mashed down as I wheeled around the damned Peugeot and slid to a stop under the big cherry tree.

The headlights of the Viper were slewing crazily. He was all over the driveway. The car appeared to be completely out of control, but he hadn't let up on the gas. The rear end swung sideways, this way and that. His tires were spinning up a shower of stones and he had a lot of momentum.. Carrie had her door open and was halfway out of the car. I threw myself across the seat and grabbed her shirt. She was safer in the old Caddy than out there with a maniac in a Viper. With my other hand I kept the horn down. Lights were going on in the house. Someone had punched the panic button on the security panel. The front door was just beginning to open when there was a terrible, terrible sound as Viper and Peugeot were instantly fused in a burly ball of macho and French sheet metal. The headlights went out with the bang.

"Now! Run!" I yelled.

She didn't need a push. She started for the house. Dickie came out of the front door at the exact moment that Dominic came out of the Viper. Dom had a baseball bat in his hands and he was waving it above his head. He was coming right for me and he was screaming.

The words he was screaming don't matter. There is no point in recording them,. He was screaming and he meant trouble. His words were as vulgar as he could make them and he had had a lifetime of practice. I was a this and a that and LT was worse and his mother was … a lot of things. We were all going to get it because we had cost him his business and he was going to lose his house and of course his girl because we had messed everything up by sticking our noses in places that they shouldn't be stuck …

I was out of the Caddy and backing toward the house. I didn't turn and run because I had to gauge his every movement. He had begun swinging with the bat in a kind of figure eight pattern. He was trying to connect with my head about halfway through the top of the eight, but he was so out of control he wasn't connecting with much of anything. I was dancing backwards and timing my moves with his swings. I was looking for any kind of opening. Good old Dickie was creeping up behind. He would have looked a lot more menacing (all five foot six of him) if he had snatched off his apron before racing from the foyer … still … four hands are better than two. To my knowledge, Dickie had never actually tried out any of his long studied martial arts on a living human being. This was his big chance to see what eight and a half years of martial arts training had produced. I'll say one thing, Dickie was creeping up so quietly that Dom had no idea he was in the picture.

Dickie was trying to time the back swings. It was taking all of his attention and brain power. His deadly weapons, his hands, were starting to flail some humid summer air. He ducked low, in close, as Dominic swung way back for a head basher. The bat passed close enough that I felt the breeze and that was my cue. I didn't want the bat cocked again. I was running out of back-up room. When the bat came all the way down, I lunged. Dickie was still low in back of Dom. It was a classic bully topple. I went high. Dickie stayed low and the bully went down hard, tripped up by the celibate houseboy.

As Dom hit the grass, Dickie came up, lifting Dom's beefy legs and pinning his back. I piled on like a late-hitting corner back. I wanted to tie up the bat. We started to scuffle. Dom would have given a better account of himself if he had just shut up and taken care of business, but he had to run his mouth about all the terrible things that awaited us. Dickie wrenched the bat away after I elbowed one of Dom's hands. It hurt and he bellowed even louder. With the bat gone to one side I was free to smother his forearms. The feet were working, but Dickie was doing something with them. I couldn't turn around to look.

Dom was powerful and overcooked on adrenaline. We could have scuffled like that for another ten minutes or so and one of us was going to get a bloody nose, except there was a mighty cry of "*Stop it at once!*" The voice was so commanding that my hair stood up. LT had arrived. The voice seemed to come from some deep and scary place inside the baby-faced consultant. It was if some long-dormant, whisky-voiced demon had awoken from millennial slumbers to announce that a time of tribulations was nigh. I thought for a moment we might need an exorcist.

At LT's command, Dom gave up about half the fight. He was still twisting his body, feeling for a weakness, but the fight had gone out of him. Then LT was right in his face and LT literally brushed me to one side. I was so shocked, I went with it and rolled over once before regaining my feet. What I saw still bothers me to this day. This is how it happened. LT was glaring down at Dominic (Dickie was doing something to Dom's feet while sitting on them). Then LT turned his left hand over and he was holding a little yellow Post-It pad. With his right hand he reached into his jacket and pulled out one of his good fountain pens (he collects) and he bit off the cap with his teeth and then (he had never taken his eyes off Dom who went very still in the face of this strange ritual) LT wrote something on the Post-It pad and then he shoved it in Dom's face.

Dom focused on the pad. His lips began to form words as he read the words, then his eyes got big and his mouth opened and his lips drew back and he suddenly appeared to be paralyzed.

"Dickie, get off of him," said LT. Dickie stood silently and backed off ten feet.

"Dickie, I need a lighter," said LT.

I almost said, "Dickie doesn't have a lighter…" but Dickie started fishing for one in his pants underneath the apron. By golly, he found one. I had no idea what was going to happen next.

LT ripped off the top sheet of the post-it pad and flicked the lighter and then held the Post-It with whatever was written there up to the little squirrelly flame and he held it there until the paper caught. Then he backed his hand away from the lighter about ten inches and we all watched as the page was consumed while LT rotated it so that the flames could reach all of it except the little corner by which it was held between thumb and finger.

When it was ashes, LT leaned way down again into Dom's face and said very quietly, "I want you off of my property within fifteen seconds."

"Shit," said Dom but he levered himself backwards away from LT's leering face. After slithering back out of range, he began to get up. Whatever he had been running on, was used up. The rage in his face had been replaced with something that looked like fear.

He walked back to his car and damned if he didn't push the airbag to one side and try to start it. It wasn't going anywhere under its own power. LT leaned in next to me and said in a forcible whisper, if there is such a thing, "Call the car carrier. Flatbed them both out of here. Have the Peugeot dropped off at Gunter's. Make Dominic wait out in the street. Watch him." With that, LT turned his back and started for the house.

"Dickie," I said, "go in the house and call Albert at the garage. Try his cell phone or call the emergency number. It's in the book. Tell him we have two to transport. I'll walk Dom to the edge of the property."

"Roger."

"Dickie?"

"Yes?"

"Please don't ever say "roger" again."

"Sorry."

"And Dickie?"

"Yes?"

"Thanks. You did real good."

"Thank you, Mr. Kelly."

Then Dickie started walking slowly back to the house. Mr. Maxwell appeared at the open front door. He was still holding his napkin. LT walked to him, took his arm and led him back into the inner light. The night sounds resumed and it was just me and Dom and the cicadas or crickets or whatever was making the racket in the early Hamptons evening.

"OK. You heard him. Let's wait over by the other side of the hedge."

"Do you know what I paid for that freaking car?" [He actually said "fucking," but I am trying to find a way to write nice and still capture the tone of his conversation.]

"I know what they retail for," I said.

"It was a repo, but still. You could buy a house for what that car set me back."

"A house? Where? East New York?" I asked him.

"Well, you used to be able to. Look at it! Oh man … oh man…"

"Dom. You were trying kill somebody."

"I was angry."

"You ever tried anger management?" I asked.

"Yeah. They made me take counseling in … you know … when I was incarcerated."

"You wrecked LT's car!"

"Yeah, I lost control on the gravel. It was an accident."

"Accident? You were doing fifty in a driveway zone, for god's sake. You were trying to kill someone."

"I was real angry. I lost everything! Everything's gone. People are saying I had something to do with Arlene's disappearance! What the hell? Oh man … I only had that car seven months. You think they can fix it?'

"What do I look like? An insurance adjuster? I'll tell you one thing," I said.

"What?"

"The Peugeot has had it. It ain't coming back. Not this time. I owe you one."

"You think Mr. Close has called the cops?" he asked. For the second time that evening he looked genuinely worried.

"I don't know. I don't think so. He would have told Dickie to call them, if he wanted them in on this. I think you got lucky this time."

"I can pay him for the old car. What do you think the blue book on that is, a grand or less?"

"Blue book? History book, maybe," I said.

"I could pay him a grand or two, not in the next couple of days…I have to see a guy, but I can pay for the car. I know a guy that can get parts for imports … see … if my PO hears about this I will have no end of hassles …"

"Dom, you tried to kill somebody," I said.

"Road rage is a sickness …"

"Ha!"

"No!" he said. He was serious. "It was on the news, Sudden Anger Syndrome or something like that. I should be on some meds. I don't know what comes over me."

We talked a little about life in Brooklyn and Italian food while we waited for the wrecker. It wasn't more than 15 minutes. The operator was good. He managed to get both cars on the flatbed. It helped that there wasn't much left of the Peugeot. I asked the driver to drop Dom off anywhere he wanted to go and I slipped him a hundred dollar bill. It took a big argument with the lawyer to get reimbursed. I tell the lawyer that you don't get a receipt when you tip someone. He says without a receipt, no reimbursement and how does he know I am not scamming him by rounding up the amount of the alleged gratuity? And so on.

I was walking back to the house when Teddy came out of it. She didn't come far when she turned and yelled back at the door, "That's not the way I was raised! I don't have to take this shit from you or anybody!"

Teddy has a mouth on her when she is angry.

There was a mumble of something from the open door. I couldn't hear any words, and I had slowed way down not wanting to wind up in the middle of anything. I was still out in the night; just another shadow under the old cherry tree. Then a mumble came from LT in the lighted doorway. Whatever he said, didn't help. Teddy stamped her foot and yelled, "You leave my father out of this, or by God I will say things about your mother that you and I and all the readers of the *Post* will regret for many years to come! You want to talk about dysfunction? Huh?"

Teddy was warming to one of her subjects and she was now advancing on the door she had recently come out of. Something was said. I'll never know what, but it caused Teddy to reach down, grab off one of her shoes and throw it hard. I don't know if it connected, but a second later the door was slammed with plenty of emphasis.

She had walked about five or six paces, hobbling on a single shoe in the gravel, when she saw me. I was standing very quietly not knowing what else to do.

"He's a pig," she said to me.

"He can be," I said.

"Piggy piggy piggy piggy piggy! He's a child."

"At times," I agreed.

"He's like a little boy playing at cops and robbers. Some day he is going to annoy the wrong person and he will be stepped on the way you step on an ant or a cockroach. You know what's really scary?" I shook my head. She didn't pause long enough to notice. "He doesn't know when he is in over his head. He's a controlling type."

"Tell me about it ..."

"And he thinks he can manage and manipulate and control, but nothing, ever, not once, goes the way he thinks it's supposed to go ... ever ... Why am I talking to you? You're the great enabler. If he didn't have you, there would be no cars crashing in his driveway, no fist fights with bat-wielding sociopaths who have been implicated in at least two murders ... *that we know of* ... no death threats from operatic loonies with nicknames out of a bad Sopranos re-run. My father offered Lawton a very nice position." She hadn't slowed down any. I was keeping up out of politeness. I didn't think she was done venting. She wasn't.

"I wasn't brought up this way. I didn't sign on for this ... this ... turmoil. Tell your boss ... tell him ... if he wants me, I'll be at Rodd Rock's mansion."

"Wait a minute, why would you go there? That would be like jumping from the frying pan into the pressure cooker, That is, if you could get the top unscrewed."

"He needs me," she said. The lower lip came out.

"Who?"

"Sidney Porkhouse," she said, looking as if she might cry.

With that, we had reached the Cadillac and she was getting in it. She had her keys in her hand. As she started to move the fist full of keys toward the ignition, I reached through the open door and grabbed her wrist, the one connected to the hand with the keys. They jingled.

"Hey! Let go!"

"How much have you had to drink?" I asked.

"Let go."

"Teddy. How much have you had to drink?"

"Not enough, apparently. I haven't scratched your eyes out yet."

"You want me to drive you?"

"What is it with you men? I'm a better driver than you."

"If you take the Caddy, you will leave us without a car. I have to drive the Maxwells home."

"Oh. OK. Do you have your cell phone?" she said in a new tone. It was much softer.

"Not on me."

"I'll call Rodd from the house and have him send a car," she said.

I will never know what would have happened if she had showed up at Rodd's in that mood with her judgment impaired to that extent. I will always wonder. What if I had not been there to grab her wrist? But I was and I did. The mood and the moment collapsed. I walked with her back to the house. She limped along with one shoe on and one shoe off, but it didn't slow her down very much. She was still angry enough that pea gravel underfoot didn't mean anything. I was worried that there would be a blow up when she and LT crossed paths again, but he wasn't visible in the front hall. At the stairs she said to me, "I'm going to go change my shoes. I'll call from my room." She ascended.

I followed the sound of a television to the kitchen. The lights had all been dimmed; one of the "scenes" Dickie has programmed into the computerized lighting system. There was the terrible blue glow of the TV screen reflecting on the far wall, the ceiling and on five pairs of shining eyes. One pair belonged to LT. The TV is something Dickie keeps hidden in the island cabinet below the granite counter top. He is not supposed to have it. He sneaks in some furtive viewing whenever he thinks he can get away with it. From the look of things, Dickie must have seen something on his illicit TV set and yelled out to the others in the sitting room.

"Hey!" I said. I walked behind the little group and put my arms around Carrie's middle. She leaned her head against me.

"24/7 has a segment on the disappearance," said Dickie.

LT looked at me briefly, looked down at my hands, frowned with closed eyes, and then looked back at the screen.

One of the 24/7 presenters was speaking, "... and we agreed to disguise his voice. What you are about to hear may be upsetting to some of our viewers. Viewer discretion is advised. We asked our informant about the man Rodd Rock describes as his security contractor."

Cut to a heavyset man in silhouette. You couldn't tell much about him except that he was a hundred pounds overweight, he liked large shirt collars, he was balding on top and he slumped in his chair. When he spoke, his voice was digitally altered so that he sounded like Darth Vader doing a bad imitation of Joe Pesci.

"Dominic Pancetta was a soldier in the Gnotto Brother's crime family. He worked under Johnny Buonapessi as a low level enforcer and stooge ..."

"That's Johnny Buonapessi speaking!" said LT.

"Shhhhh", said Dickie.

"Who is?" I said.

"The informant! He has a book coming out. Teddy heard from one of her editor friends. He's shilling for his book!"

"I can't hear what he's saying," said Dickie.

"… twice on drug trafficking charges and once for two counts of murder …" said Darth Pesci.

"How do you know it's him?" I said.

"Shhhhhhh," said LT

At about that time a waif-like shadow glided across the kitchen floor on little cat feet. Teddy was with us. A moment later I could feel her hot breath on my neck and then a moment after that, a soft hand on my upper back.

The presenter's voice was heard, but the camera remained locked on the informant, "So, if you wanted to make someone disappear and make sure there was no evidence … could that be done?"

"Easy. There are things you can do, ways of handling it. A professional knows these things. Dominic Pancetta was charged with murder, but it never came to trial because of lack of evidence. He's been on the street a long time. He knows how it's done."

The presenter spoke, his voice was soothing, "So if someone wanted a specific person to disappear and had the money and was willing to pay for it, there are people that would take care of it just like it was cleaning the pool or putting on an addition?"

"Sure, That's why the old guys called it putting out a contract. It's not personal. It's business."

"Now, they never found Jimmy Hoffa, did they? In spite of stories and searches and tips and they dug up that whole field in Michigan …"

"No. If a guy knows what he's doing. You don't find anything."

"In your opinion, with your experiences in the underground world of murder for hire, where do you think Arlene Rock is tonight?"

"In a lime pit in the Catskills."

"Do you think it's odd that her husband, who stood to lose millions if she had been allowed to go forward with her planned divorce petition, employed a known felon, connected with two murders and having served time for a major felony and is known to associate with organized crime as his …" the presenter paused slightly, but enough to give emphasis to what came next, "security contractor?"

"Odd? No. It pays to have the right man for the right job. He wanted a professional. That's what he paid for. That's what he got."

The camera shifted back to the presenter. The presenter had both eyebrows up. It was nothing more than that. But he was letting the audience know with his eyebrows what he thought of Rodd Rock and where he thought Arlene ended her days. If you brought a transcript of the show into a courtroom to try to prove slander, the words on paper would get the case thrown out of court. It was all done with the eyebrows and a little twist in the tone of voice and a significant little pause.

The presenter wrapped it up. "We will be following this ongoing story. Tomorrow, 24/7 looks into allegations of fraud and high level drug connections when we investigate the millions of dollars Rodd Rock accuses his agent of stealing from him in a segment called Pot of Gold. On Thursday's show, famed psychic Orestes talks to us about where she believes the authorities should look next to find the remains of the missing wife of the former Lobe. For additional information and a schedule of all of our segments log on to …"

LT pushed the little power button on Dickie's old TV and it went dark. Everyone was quiet. No one moved.

"Well!" said LT.

"This looks bad for Rodd," said Teddy.

"Yes," said LT. Dickie and I were staying out of it. Carrie tensed up, but said nothing.

"It's not really fair," said Teddy. "That whole piece was nothing but innuendo."

"It isn't fair. It's not about fair. They have a narrative established and they are proceeding. I thought you were going out?" said LT.

"Hmm, I was. Is there any of that caviar left that Dickie got from the Russians in Brighton Beach?"

"Yes. It's vile, but … it's caviar. Would you like some?"

"I think I would. Dickie? Would you be a lamb and make some toast points?"

Dickie nodded.

"Carrie?" said Teddy. "A little bubbly and some fish eggs?"

"Thank you. Please. Max?"

"I'll have a beer and some rice pudding." I said.

"If you do," said LT, "you will eat it in the kitchen unobserved by civilized people."

"That suits me fine," I said. It did, too.

Carrie pouted and said, "I'll be with the fish eggs. See me when you are done."

Teddy took her hand, and drew Carrie to her side. Then she looked at me with one eyebrow raised.

"You know," said Mr. Maxwell, "the Missus and I made a pact when we were married. We never go to bed angry. Isn't that right?" He looked to his wife. She patted his hand and smiled and nodded.

"What?" he said.

"We really should go home now," said Mrs. Maxwell. "We are not used to all this drama. This has been a very exciting evening for us." .

"Nonsense!" said Teddy. "You will have some caviar and a little champagne maybe a scotch for your husband and then Max and Carrie will drive you home."

"Maybe just a taste. Come on, dear. Would you like a little scotch?" She pantomimed the act of drinking.

"Do you have any scotch, Lawton?" said Mr. Maxwell

"We'll be in the sitting room," said LT to me. He pulled down a bottle of Glenfidich from the drinks cabinet. Then he turned to Dickie and said, "There is an old bottle of Tatinger that somebody left here one night last winter. It's in the cellar wine cooler. Could you bring that when you bring the caviar?"

"Certainly," said Dickie.

They all left the kitchen. Teddy and Carrie were enjoying some whispered amusement and I suspect that my name had some small supporting role in the comedy. LT had Mrs. Maxwell's arm and she was looking at him, with eyes of wonder. She was saying something I didn't catch, but whatever it was made LT smile happily. Mr. Maxwell ambled along behind looking around, as if he had never seen the place before. As the others went through the doorway, he reached out to play with the dimmer panel. His finger poked around and the lights went through their various settings. Then he turned back to Dickie and me and made a funny "oops" smile and shrugged.

When they were out of sight, Dickie went to the light panel and pushed one of the buttons. The overhead pendant lights dimmed down to an orange glow. The sconces dimmed slightly. The under counter lights dimmed down, and the big lamp over the breakfast table switched from ambient glow to down-light spot, making a warm spill of incandescence where my rice pudding would soon sit.

Dickie and I were alone in his kitchen.

"What do you call this scene, Dickie?"

"You don't call it anything. You just push the sixth button from the top on the keypad."

"What would you call it, if the scene had a name?"

"After hours. Closing time." Dickie then sighed, one big, long, in-breath and a slumped out-breath. Then he opened the big refrigerator door and took out two eggs, an onion, and the rest.

My heart went out to him. It really did.

14

I was a little sore the next morning after my workout with Dom (Paul Williams) Pancetta. It wasn't anything serious, just little hints and allegations in the joints and leg muscles. We were all a little slow getting up. Carrie slept in the guest room till almost ten o'clock. I found out later that there was a little padding around in the night, but Carrie had run into Teddy in the hall (Teddy heard noises and thought it might be me) and the two women had descended (in every sense of the word) to the kitchen to talk about you know who. I was so asleep I would have needed an injection of caffeine to wake up enough to smell the coffee.

When I did wake up and had the dentals scrubbed and polished using the weird dentifrice that Teddy gets in bulk at Price Club, and had reached the kitchen, I found that Dickie had already appropriated the newspaper. He did make some good French press coffee, however, and I was still impressed by his performance the night before so I cut him some slack. It may have been deli thin slices, but it was still slack.

It was weird. There was something different about Dickie. Something was simmering in his crock pot. I suspected that something was a miss and I intended to find out who.

"Good morning Dickie."

"Oh. Hi, Max. Did you get anything to eat last night?"

"We had leftover steak and scalloped potatoes. We polished off the rest of the German cookies. You may want to put those on your list. What's in the paper?"

"I'm doing my puzzle."

"Ah!" I said. "What's a six-letter word for not heavier but ..."

"I don't know; lighter? Where do you see that?"

"In your pants, Dickie. What's the deal?"

"Nothing," he said sullenly.

"Why are you carrying a lighter?"

"Sometimes I need one. I'm trying to concentrate on this puzzle."

"Dickie, what do you light up?" I pressed him.

"I don't know."

"Dickie, three days ago I found a butt out by the garage. It was a cigarette butt. It was the brand you used to smoke before you became a pain in the ass. Was that your butt, Dickie?"

"I'm trying to think."

"So am I. You are smoking again, aren't you?"

"Once in a while. What of it?"

"I found an empty bottle of Tequila in the recycle bin two days ago."

"So?" he said. He looked up at me. His eyes were challenging me. I was getting warmer.

"LT hates the stuff and Teddy only drinks the good stuff, one hundred percent agave."

"So?"

"This was cheap mouthwash tequila made for the mass market, for making frozen margaritas where your taste buds slam shut and you freeze your brain."

"So?"

"The top of the blender was in the prep sink the other night and I stuck my finger in it, to the residue and I licked my finger and you know what it tasted like?"

"What?"

"That frozen concoction that helps you hang on."

"So?"

"You left your Jimmy Buffet CD next to the wave radio with all of Teddy's world music and reggae CDs."

"So?"

"What's her name, Dickie? Who got you smoking and drinking again and listening to Jimmy Buffet? Who is it, Dickie?"

"If I tell you will you leave me alone?"

"I promise; at least until the next time."

"I got an e-mail a couple of weeks ago from someone I knew back then …"

"A girl?"

"Yes. Mindy Minder," he said.

"You made that name up," I said.

"No. I wish I had. Mindy was … she taught me … ah … I had lost track of her."

"No one has a name like Mindy Minder."

"Her sister is Mandy," he said solemnly.

"Dickie. I was all prepared to be nice to you. I came down here with a little brand new shiny respect for the way you acquitted yourself with Dominic last night and now you go and key the paint job with this fantasy you are trying to get me hooked on, so you can laugh at me and say 'Ha! Made you believe it'. I've been around, Dickie."

"They were twins. Swear to god!"

"I'm not prepared to believe you, but I am intrigued. She sent an e-mail?"

"Yes and she said …"

I never got to hear. There was a scream from the summer office. It sounded as if someone was being dipped heel first into an industrial shredder. We ran.

We didn't run far, maybe twelve large steps, I never paced it out, but that brought us to the doorway of the summer office. LT was there and he was still on his feet. Whatever had attacked him was nowhere to be seen, unless it was the piece of paper he held in front of him as if it had teeth and claws.

"What's happened?" I said. Dickie merely looked on with goggle eyes. There were footsteps on the stairs. Teddy called out before she was in visual range, "Lawton sweetie? Are you all right?"

At the top of the stairs I could hear Carrie calling down, "Is everything OK down there?"

LT looked as if he was trembling and maybe he was. He sucked in a big wind and I knew when he started using it, no one would get in a word so I yelled out the doorway to Carrie, "It's OK. LT was clearing his throat."

"This is not to be borne!" he said. He slowly shook the paper for emphasis. I shuffled close enough to see that he was holding a fax. It looked like a proposal or an estimate.

"What, sweetie?" said Teddy. "Is it your ex-wife again?" she had arrived at the doorway. She didn't enter. I think she wanted to make sure it was safe, first.

"No. As bloodthirsty as she is, and she has exceeded the bounds of taste on many grim occasions with her overweening, one might almost say heroic, greed, but even she has remained within the confines of reality as we know it. This is from another dimension entirely."

"What is, sweetie?"

"I asked Carl at the garage to give me a good faith estimate for putting the Peugeot back in shape. I expected the estimate to be higher than (perhaps double) the official value of the car , but ... this ..."

Teddy got in closer than I was prepared to do. When a wild animal has been wounded the last thing you want to do is crowd it. Teddy gently took the paper from LT's hand. She scanned down to the bottom line. Her face showed bland concentration. After a couple of beats of silence, she said, "Yes. That's about right."

"Twenty eight thousand dollars?" said LT.

"Sweetie, he's itemized it. Look at the line items. You are going to need the frame straightened, new quarter panels, steering box assembly, front suspension members, glass, seats, engine mounts, drive shaft, shocks...you saw the car. You need all these things."

"It isn't worth it."

"Of course not, sweetie. It never was."

"You didn't like the Peugeot?" asked LT, with a kind of wonder in his voice.

"Years ago I thought it was -- I don't know -- eccentric. That was years ago. Sweetie, it smells."

"Like what?"

"Like rotting headliner, like storage mold, like brake fluid, like decaying rubber. It's an old car."

"I loved that car."

"And you treated it very well. You gave it a good life. It's had a longer life than any other French car in the country. And now the nicest thing you can do for that car is to have it put down."

LT made a sound like a whimper. I realize that high-powered consultants don't whimper, so I am not prepared to say it was a whimper, it just sounded like one.

Teddy put her arm around his shoulder and he pushed it off. Then he spoke.

"Everyone out! Out! I want to be alone with my thoughts."

"Lawton, sweetie, come into the kitchen and have some breakfast."

"Get out! Close the door."

She didn't argue. She turned on her slipper and shook her hair once and set her jaw and she was gone. Dickie and I fought each other for the doorway. He squeaked by first because he's a wiry little houseboy and he had a step and a half on me. I closed the door behind me. Teddy ascended the stairs to join Carrie as they began re-pointing their facades and slipping into something more appropriate. Dickie and I ended up in the kitchen with the food and the boiling coffee water.

Things were just settling down in the kitchen when the phone rang. It's Dickie's job to answer it, but Dickie had his laptop out surfing the web and I was looking for something solid to grab onto. The phone was just begging to be held.

"Hello? Lawton's Close's residence, this is Max speaking. May I help you?"

"Max?"

"Mel?"

"I just got a call," said Mel Viktor in my ear.

"Yeah?"

"It was from the people that have something everyone is looking for. Is your phone secure?"

"This phone? Yes. Are you on your cell phone?"

"Yes. You know what I'm talking about. These people want money and they don't want any fuss. You know?"

"What people?" I said. I was signaling Dickie to tell LT to pick up. Dickie wasn't getting it. I was trying to stall Viktor and communicate with Dickie in sign language.

"People," said Viktor. "They have the thing that everyone is looking for and they want to keep this just between the people involved. They were very, very emphatic about that. You understand?"

"Why did they call you?"

"I don't know. Why don't you ask them? Maybe because I handle the money."

There was a little shopping list pad on the island. I stretched the phone over to the island and wrote, "Tell LT to pick up!!!" on the pad. Dickie nodded and left the kitchen.

"So what do they want?" I asked Mel.

"Money. If we do what they say and give them what they want, nobody is going to get hurt."

There was a click and LT's voice said, "Mel?"

"They've made contact," said Mel.

"Who?" asked LT.

"They just want money."

"Who wants money?" asked LT.

"The people that have the thing everyone is looking for," said Mel.

"What's that?" asked LT.

"The thing!" said Mel. "They don't want anyone else involved. They are watching me. They just want the money. You have to call the bank. I have to arrange for the money."

"Kidnappers?" asked LT.

"Not on the phone!" said Mel. "They don't want anyone else involved. They are watching me. I don't want anything to happen to the thing. I need you to call the bank and clear it with them."

"How much do they want for the safe return of the thing?" asked LT.

"Not on the phone. There's plenty of money in the bank. I need you to release the money. Please call the bank. People's lives are on the line."

"I have to talk to Rodd," said LT.

"These people aren't playing games. We are running out of time here. I need you to call the bank. Rodd's going to tell you the same thing. Don't get anyone else involved. They are watching me. You got to do what they say. You got to do it right now. Call the bank."

"I'll see what I can do," said LT, and then he hung up.

"Hello?" said Mel.

"He's gone," I said.

"Tell him to call the bank. These people are serious."

Then Mel hung up.

I turned toward the office when the phone rang again. I thought it might be Mel. I picked it up.

"Yes?"

"Hi. This is Rachelle Huggly from NBC nightly news. Is this Lawton Close?"

"No. "

"I would like to speak with Lawton Close. Could you put him on, please?"

"No. He can't come to the phone right now. Can I take a message?"

"What's he doing?" she said.

"He can't come to the phone right now. He's away from his desk. Would you care to leave a message?"

"Tell him it's NBC," she said.

"I would like to do that, honestly I would, but he is not available at the moment. You can leave a message if you like and I will make sure he sees it."

"Is he in a meeting?" she asked.

"Maybe you would have better luck another time."

I hung up the phone.

"Who was that?" said Dickie, coming back in to the kitchen.

"NBC news."

"Who was it really?" he asked.

The phone rang. Dickie's hand shot out for it, but mine was faster.

"Hello?"

"Did you hang up on me?" said Ms. Huggly.

"Yes." I hung up again.

"When the phone rings, please allow me to get it," I said.

The phone rang. Dickie remained motionless. I let it go to the third tone and then I picked it up.

"Yes?"

"Listen! Whoever the hell you are. This is NBC news and I am calling to get a confirmation or we are going to run ..."

"Hello?" there was a third person on the line. He couldn't be alone with his thoughts for three minutes. "Who is this in the phone? Dickie? Are you on the line? Who keeps calling?"

"Mr. Close? This is Rachelle Huggly. I'm with NBC nightly news. I am calling to get a confirmation of certain ... there have been allegations. I was telling the idiot who answers your phone."

"Dickie?"

"No. It's me," I said.

"Hang up. I'll handle this."

"But ..."

"Hang up."

I did.

Teddy strode into the kitchen holding a folded up newspaper. Her sandal heels banged on the floor like firecrackers. Judging by the typeface, she had the *Times* cradled under one arm. The Herald uses a more modern typeface. She looked at me and saw something in my face.

"What's happened?" she asked.

"Mel Viktor just called to say that Arlene has been kidnapped and the people who have her called him to arrange for the ransom."

"He said what?" she asked.

"The kidnappers called him because he controls the money. He used to. I guess the kidnappers don't know about LT yet. They told Mel he better put up the money or Arlene is ... you know."

"Who?" she asked scrunching up her face.

"Mel Viktor," I said.

"He said Arlene had been kidnapped?" she asked again.

"That's right."

"This morning?" she asked. She was acting as if she had not had her coffee yet.

"He *called* this morning, but of course she would have been taken at the concert."

"Mel Viktor is a snake," she said. "Have you seen this?" She took the *Times* out from under her arm and shook it. "We can't let Lawton see this. He'll lose it entirely." She slapped the magazine down in front of Dickie. I looked over their shoulders.

There was a picture of LT in his dinner jacket that I recognized from the HIMCA gala the night I crashed into the tent. The picture was taken as he and Teddy were making their entrance. The cameras had been focused on Teddy that night, but she had been edited out of the magazine image leaving LT standing alone in his tux. He had a slightly aggravated expression on his face and the strobe lighting and white background, and his hair brushed straight back, made him look a little like an Anne Rice character surprised on his way back to the crypt before sunup.

There was a headline, of course. It read, "Life in the Shadows." There was a longer subheading; "Rodd Rock's Mysterious Counsel Has Ties To The Mob and the Washington Power Elite."

Under LT's picture was a caption, "Lawton Close at play in the Hamptons, the power behind the overlord's throne."

"What does it say?" I asked.

"Read it for yourself," she said as she spun it in front of me.

"I don't have time to read it. LT is going to have to go to the bank to arrange for money for Arlene's kidnappers. There's a lot going on right now."

"Lawton is going to call the cops and let them deal with Mel Viktor and the kidnappers," said Teddy.

"They told Mel they were watching him. If he calls the cops, we'll never see Arlene again."

"They always say that," she said.

"I know," I said.

"Do you know the kidnappers?" she said to me. "Are you willing to personally vouch for them that they will honor their word?"

"Me?"

"Yes, you."

"I don't know them. What do I have to do with the kidnappers?"

"What's to stop them from taking the money and then killing Arlene anyway?"

"I don't know."

"That's why it's better to let the police handle this. They have people trained specifically for kidnapping."

"What's that, dear?" said LT, as he entered the kitchen. He was holding a few sheets of paper printed on one side.

"I was telling Max that one can not negotiate with kidnappers and that the only logical thing to do would be to call the authorities and you are nothing if not logical. Ergo..."

"Please don't say "ergo,." he said.

"You have called the police, haven't you?" asked Teddy.

"I was just about to do so," he said. "Look what NBC just sent over!"

"What is it, sweetie?" asked Teddy brightly, as she turned the *Times* upside down, slowly.

"I'm the power behind the overlord's throne!" he said glancing, down at the top sheet.

We waited for it. No one said anything. He looked up.

"Isn't that funny?" he said.

"Lawton dear, people say crazy things in print these days. It doesn't mean anything."

"Mean anything? Do you know what this publicity would cost if I had to pay for it?"

Apparently he wasn't going to blow. He was going to gloat.

"You should call the police about the kidnappers," said Teddy.

"I will, I will. One thing at a time. I think Mel Viktor has become unhinged."

"He is not alone," said Teddy, with one eyebrow up. The eye beneath the arched brow regarded her lover (and my boss) coldly. Do you know what you are doing? Sweetie?"

"I'm not entirely sure. Things seem to be more complicated at the moment than expected."

"Has anyone told Rodd about the ransom demand?" I asked.

"I believe Mel has stirred that particular pot," said LT.

The phone began to sound. Dickie, who had been hanging back from the group and staying silent, reached for the wall phone.

"Mr. Close, it's Rodd Rock," said Dickie, holding the phone out as if it was about to explode.

"Ah yes!" said LT. "A stirred pot never rests." He grabbed the phone from Dickie, who stepped back suddenly, as if he thought he might be swatted.

"Rodd!" said LT cheerily. Then LT listened and nodded silently and somewhat impatiently. "I know, I know. I was just about to call the police." Then LT listened again for a moment before saying, "All right! I understand. I will give it 24 hours before I call them, but my professional opinion, for what it may be worth, is that we should call immediately."

LT listened for another fifteen seconds and then said, "OK. I'll be there in a few minutes." LT held the phone out until Dickie figured out what he wanted and took the phone from him to hang it up.

"What did he say?" asked Teddy.

"He said no cops for 24 hours," said LT. "He wants me there for a strategy session. I want the lid on this until I say differently. Do you understand that, Dickie?"

"Yes, Mr. Close."

"You want me to go to Mel's and take the equipment?" I asked. We have handled kidnappings in the past, but usually with groups outside of the country.

"Not yet," said LT. "Wait for my signal. I'll be at Rodd's for the next hour or so. I want to keep Mel on a short leash until I know a little more about what we are up against. Max, I want you to go over to the castle and hang around."

"What if Mel won't see me?" I asked.

"Tell him I'm working on the money. That should calm him down. Tell him I want you there to act as intermediary."

"To what?" I asked.

"I don't know. Don't be so literal minded. Kidnappings always involve intermediaries. Tell him you are acting as one."

"You are making this up as you go along, aren't you?" I said.

"Do you have a better plan?" he said.

"No."

"Then why are you still standing here? Please go at once to the castle and keep an eye on Mel Viktor. He is unstable, unscrupulous and intemperate. He is going to be no end of trouble, I just know it."

LT's predictions never work out properly and this one was no exception

15

When the flashing started in my rearview mirror, I looked down at the speedo and saw that I was twenty over the posted thirty five. I pulled over.

I waited. He came to my window. I looked up. It was the chief himself, the alpha male in the constabulatory wolf-pack.

"It's you," he said.

"Who else would drive this antique?" I said.

"She does sometimes. She likes to speed, too. Where are you off to?"

"Errands," I said. I opened my wallet and showed him the card that entitles the bearer to respect and understanding in matters of traffic deportment. It should. It cost a bundle. He nodded solemnly.

"Keep it down, will you?"

"I try." I said.

"You are going to have to do better than that. Remember when you took your boss's car and made a mess of the big Taste of the Hamptons Gala?"

"Yeah? I was chasing some bad guys," I said.

"Uh huh. Well, that's what I'm talking about. You see, that's my job. That's not your job. You can't find me a job description anywhere that says you have to destroy a tent full of summer people who paid thousands of dollars *each* to be in that tent. You see?"

"OK. Where are we going with this?" I said.

"Do you have any idea of the position you put me in after the tent incident? Do you?"

"Let me guess," I said. "A shit tornado?"

"Funny. More like a shit hurricane because it made a wider swath and went on a lot longer, a lot, lot longer. Your boss asked me to have some consideration for the fact that you are ... I can't remember the words he used because I don't use them myself, but he wanted me to take it easy on you because you are enthusiastic sometimes."

"LT was working behind the scenes? For me?" I asked.

"You better believe it. Didn't you think it was odd that you are not still in jail?"

"It is?"

"But you see the rich people in the tent, they were putting pressure on me to have you suitably punished."

"Drawn and quartered on little toast points with beurre blanc?" I said. He looked at me for a beat and then I saw the smile. He couldn't help it. His smile ratted him out.

"Yeah. Something like that. Let me tell you, the pressure was intense. You gave me one tough year. But things cooled down and things were forgotten, for a while. And then your Lawyer Boss started representing Scott Boucher when he was building that 60,000 square foot house. I'm telling you it opened up all the old wounds. A certain homeowner's association wanted me to press charges against you before the statute of limitations ran out as a way to get your boss to back away from the Boucher deal. These money brokers play rough. I told your boss it would be better if you weren't around because I didn't think I could I could get the association to drop it. He said he would arrange for you to spend some time in the Catskills."

"*What?*"

"He said not to worry. He would make sure you were out of town until the statute of limitations was no longer an issue."

"Is that why?" I asked.

"Why what?" he said. I had upset his carefully built introduction to something.

"He maneuvered me into taking a job in a crap-hole hotel working for a crazy guy from the Middle East! I just never knew why."

"Well, you didn't hear this from me, but he mentioned that he wanted to see what you could stimulate in the Catskills. He was sure there would be a response. There was, but not the one he was expecting. A guy from the FBI said that you broke up a very nasty operation, just by being on the scene. You didn't even know what was going on."

"Son of a bitch!" I said. Pieces were falling into a place that I didn't even know was missing pieces. "Son of a bitch!" I repeated..

"You didn't hear this from me," he said.

"I have to find some way to get back at him. This is way over the line. You want a laugh? Do you know what my salary was for those twelve months I was in the mountains?"

"This isn't a laughing matter. This was all deadly serious. My job was at stake. You have no idea what summer people can be like …"

"We had a fight. I resigned. I looked around for a job and I have a degree in hotel restaurant management and I got this tip from a guy in New Jersey."

"The guy in New Jersey worked for the same hotel chain, right?"

"Yeah."

"That's the guy who told your boss that there might be something funny going on in the Catskills."

"So he sent me in blind, dumb and stupid to see if there was a reaction! I could have been killed!"

"He had one of the local guys keeping an eye out for you."

"In Barterville?" I asked.

"Yeah. Why do you think you never got a speeding ticket? You are going to have to learn to drive at the legal limit. Now look. This Rodd Rock thing has turned into another big headache. There you are, right in the middle of it. You know what high blood pressure is?"

"I have an idea. The pressure of your blood gets … ah … elevated?"

"You don't want it. They call it the silent killer because you don't know you have it. You can't feel it, you can't see it, but it can kill you just the same. You see, there's a lot you don't know. And what you don't know can not only hurt you, it can kill you."

"Are we talking about something else here? Because the hair on the back of my neck just stood up. Are we talking about high blood pressure?"

"Look. I like you. I don't know why, because whenever I have a pain in my ass I turn around and you are somewhere close by with a pin in your hand and a dumb innocent look on your face, but I like what you did on the deal where that guy got his head chopped off. Still, I have to watch out for my community. And I tell you what, my heart is with the little people who are being bought out and taxed out of their homes and lives. If push comes to shove … I'm going to do everything I can for my friends and relations. You would do the same. I know you."

"So what's the bottom line?"

"Just this. I pulled a lot of strings to keep you out of trouble in the past. I put my job on the line and because of that, my house and my kid's college education. That was then. This is now. This Rodd Rock thing is all over the world. I had two calls from London this morning. You know what time it is over there right now? I've been on three different TV shows and I don't like being on TV shows. Some jerk in the *Herald* wrote that I was a pinheaded Mayberry second stringer. You see what I mean? I don't want to be in the *Herald*. I don't want my face on the Channel 7 News. I don't want my kid seeing some guy on TV saying that I don't know my job; some expert from Los Angeles who doesn't know what I do or how I do it. I've got a gut full of resentment right now and I'm looking for someone to unload it on. You understand?"

"Hey. I'm not talking to the press."

"No, but I didn't major in communication. I majored in criminology. I am not comfortable as a spokesperson for anybody or any thing. I'm a cop. I know human nature. I want this whole thing ended so we can all go back to real life. I want you and your boss to keep your heads down and your mouths shut. Someone is leaking official information to the media and if I find out that you or your boss is involved … ah … I don't know. I just don't know. So I'm going to let you off with a warning this time."

"For what?"

"For everything. A word to the wise is sufficient. My Aunt Mary always told me that. I'm telling you."

"OK. I hear you. I don't know what I can do about it, but I hear you. You don't talk to LT this way, do you?"

"He's a lawyer," said the chief. Then he wagged his head slowly.

"Yeah. What does that make me?"

"You and me are stuck in the middle between Rock and a hard place."

"Did you just make that up?" I asked.

"I did. Have a nice day."

He started to walk back to his car, then he stopped. He didn't do anything for a second, his back was still to me, then he turned slowly in my rearview mirror (objects are closer than they appear) and came back to my window.

"Oh," he said, "by the way. You know there's a stalker?"

"Yeah. Thomas Valderben."

"I guess everyone knows about the stalker. Who told you?"

"Rodd Rock. He had us and his security people looking for him when someone saw him at the concert in Jones Beach. That was the night Arlene disappeared."

"Uh huh. He's a sick guy. So you know about the stalker."

"I know there is a guy who stalks. I know there was a court order of protection."

"That's right. He lives in the city or did. He got to be a real problem for Rodd Rock: break ins, harassment, petty theft. Then there was an incident with a knife. Valderben spent some time in the courts and jail, but he was judged to be a nut job, who couldn't be held accountable for his actions. So of course they let him go. You tell me how that makes sense? He's managed to stay out of our computer for the past twelve months, but people in New York were concerned because he walked out on his lease and disappeared."

"So?" I said.

"So he turns up in a routine traffic stop in Southampton three weeks ago. They write him up for driving with a suspended license and set a court date. He fails to show. But he's been around and I think he's still in the area. In fact, I'm told that he was spotted at the High Dune Motor Lodge in Hampton Bays, You know where that is?"

"On the old road," I said. I was getting the tingle.

"That's the place."

"What if I wandered over that way?"

"I wouldn't bother. The Southampton guys told me that he checked out of the Motor Lodge and they don't know where he went."

"I didn't get a good look at him at the concert. It was dark," I said. "We had an old photo, but the quality wasn't good."

"Short dark hair, fuzz cut, slightly balding, heavy hips, five eight, 225 pounds, he likes short pants and checked shirts and he always wears red running shoes."

"I saw the shoes; they were hard to miss," I said.

"He stands out. It may not be anything. I just wondered if you or your boss was aware that he had been in the area. You know, there's a bench warrant, but I don't think anyone is actually looking for the guy. What I'm telling you came to me as a tip. I don't think there's anything to it, but if Rodd Rock's wife goes missing and a stalker with a history shows up about the same time … let's just say I don't like coincidences."

"I hate 'em. Speaking of which, he drives a light blue Saturn, right?"

"That's his car. It's not legal."

"If I see him on the road, can I call it in?"

"Please do. Well, there you have it. It didn't come from me, but I'm an interested party. Can I depend on you to let me know if you find something?"

"Like what?" I asked.

"Anything," he said, deepening his voice. He sounded serious.

"OK. I'll keep my eyes open."

"And Max."

"Yeah?'

"Don't go on any high speed chases. Drive safely and buckle up. It's the law."

"Yeah, the law."

He turned his back and walked slowly to his cruiser. He settled into the driver's seat slowly like he had a bad back. He caught my eye in the mirror and waved me on. I started the engine and selected Drive from the choices offered to me by Cadillac engineers. I checked the mirror and swiveled my head just like they tell you in Driver's Ed. I used my signal. I cranked the wheel, fed in the gas and merged nicely into the traffic stream. Mr. Poddinghurst would have been pleased. He told me I would probably fail driver's ed because of my lousy attitude.

So, Rodd's stalker was summering in the Hamptons. Maybe he just wanted to recreate in the playground for the rich, or maybe …

16

MEL WAS NOT AT HIS castle. The new receptionist (she might have weighed 80 pounds in a soaking wet tee-shirt) said that he had gone to his apartment in the city. I called LT's cell phone from the castle parking area and told him that Mel was gone. He said he was just a mile from home. The meeting with Rodd had been unproductive. He told Rodd that time was critical and that he thought waiting 24 hours before calling the cops was a mistake. Rodd had become quite stubborn, and he was, after all, the client. So there would be no call today.

LT told me to hang out near the castle for a couple of hours to make sure that Mel did not return.

Before ending the call, I mentioned getting pulled over and that the chief was concerned about the stalker. LT had an odd reaction.

"The stalker, here?"

"That's what I'm told," I said. "Remember, I said I saw a blue car at Rodd's the night of the incident with Dom Pancetta?"

"So he's here?" he said again.

"Last seen in Southampton, but he's probably moved on. The chief thinks he might still be around and wants us to tell him if we see him."

"That's just what we need.," said LT. He sounded angry and frustrated. It surprised me.

"What's the matter?" I asked him. His reaction was out of scale with my understanding of the threats on our horizon.

"It's a complication for which I have no preparation," he said.

"A complication? Maybe it's the answer," I said.

"To what?" he said.

"Maybe the stalker kidnapped Arlene."

"Why?"

"How would I know? Why does a crazy guy do anything?"

"Deluded souls are often compulsively logical. It's just the premise that's insane."

"OK, so he is compulsive about Rodd and she is his wife and she's going to try to soak him for a couple hundred million and …"

"I suppose that is the kind of thing that would have to be considered. It would be unprofessional of me not to consider it. Hmmm. And the Chief said that he is still around?"

"I told you I saw his car in front of Rodd's house the night Dom was in the basement. The cops popped him for an out-of-date inspection sticker and a suspended license. He never showed up to pay his fine. When they ran the computer on him, the bells went off. I think he's in full stalking mode."

"I suppose we have to look into it," said LT. "What a bother."

"If he did it, he would be crazy to stay in the area," I said. I was thinking aloud.

"Did what?" said LT. He was acting distracted. He is usually right on top of the conversation like a mongoose on a cobra.

"Anything! Kidnapped Arlene."

"I have to make a call to Carlton," said LT, as he sighed. You stay there until call you back. Is your cell phone fully charged?"

"Yes," I said. We have had some problems in the past when my cell phone went dead at a critical moment. I would feel more defensive about it except that he hardly ever carries his because he says it cooks the bone marrow with microwaves. At critical moments when my cell phone has been dead, he hasn't had his, so it wouldn't have done any good anyway.

I was still at Mel's an hour later waiting for him to return when the cell phone vibrated in my pocket.

"I'm here," I said into it.

"Good. Here's the latest address on Thomas Valderben," said LT in my ear. He gave an address in Montauk, a converted motel called the Ocean Way Mews.

"What do you want me to do? Mel hasn't showed here."

"I want you to go to Montauk and check this out. Mel Viktor's EZ Pass was used at the Midtown Tunnel earlier today."

"How did you find that out?" I asked.

"There are things you would prefer not to know," he said.

"Like the fact that the chief told me that you had someone watching me in the Catskills. He said that our friend down in Atlantic City thought there was some funny business at the hotel …"

"Are you going to start being difficult?" he said after a pause.

"The chief was very informative," I said.

"Stop!" he said. "This is not the time. We have a tough situation in front of us. What is done is done. Get over it. I need your attention fully engaged in the present. We can't afford resentment-induced sloppiness in this project. We are under the scrutiny of big media. Everything you do and say is magnified by a giant eye connected to a tiny brain. Perception is everything. Pay attention!"

"I don't like this project," I said. "I am beginning not to like Rodd Rock. This is the messiest project we have ever had. There's too much gray. I need some black and white. I like action, not posing for the big eye."

"Find our stalker. That should give you something to do."

"And if I find him?"

"Do not stimulate. Do not interact. Verify his location. Call me immediately. I will have a word with the chief and we will see if we can get Mr. Valderben put on ice."

"What if he has Arlene? Or what if he tries something with me?" I asked.

"Listen to me! I don't want you to engage. He is not keeping Arlene prisoner at a motel in Montauk. Let the authorities handle this. Let them discover what, if anything, he has been perpetrating."

"I have my gun," I said.

"I very much doubt you will need it. I must ask you to remain professional and disinterested."

"Arlene is out there somewhere!" I said. I might have shouted it.

"Yes," he said. I waited for more. It didn't come.

"So?" I said.

"So, find Valderben. If you spot him, phone it in and do *not* engage."

"Should I stop there and get the camera?" I asked.

"I don't see why. This should be a simple visual verification."

Nothing is ever simple when LT is involved.

I took the Caddy. There was no other choice. I drove out to Montauk. Where the road forks I took the road that runs along the ocean. The road reminds me of the Cyclone at Coney Island. It has the same ups and downs, but stretched out into a straight line.

Ocean Way Mews sounds better than it looks. I guess they named it Ocean Way because it is on the Way to the Ocean. You can't see the ocean from the Mews. It would take a few minutes to walk to any salt water. The sad collection of wood-sided buildings used to be a motel complex, back in the fifties I would guess. The buildings had been recently repainted and cleaned up. The motel was now something like a condominium for transients. I parked next to an overflowing dumpster. The parking lot had once been a thin crust of black top, but it was now mostly sand and weeds. The blacktop was slowly crumbling and bleaching in the sun and salt to a dull gray.

The housing units, some of which had been individual cabins, were all painted white. Everything that wasn't glass or asphalt shingle was painted white and even some of the glass and asphalt had felt the lash of the paint brush.

The cars in the lot were a sad bunch and some were almost as old as the Caddy. One, a '55 Chevy, was a lot older, but it had been rodded out with air scoops and funny suspension parts and a paint job that must have looked pretty smart when it was applied a decade or so in the past.

43G was in the old center building around which the little cabins squatted down like ducklings next to their mama. There was a rickety stair at the front of the building and a long wooden corridor that was still hanging on to the front of the building by the tips of its toe nails.

I walked along as quietly as I could till I came to 43G. I didn't knock. I looked through the window. The blinds were closed, but they didn't close all the way. I couldn't see much, but there were posters on the walls.

Below me a voice said, "Can I help you?"

I looked down and there he was; the stalker. He had the red running shoes, baggy cotton pants, a weird checked, short-sleeved shirt of a pattern and color that I have never seen offered for sale in this part of the solar system. His hair was mid-length and looked like it hadn't been washed for a couple of weeks, or maybe he just used grease on it. His eyes were bugged out. It was hard to look at them.

LT said not to engage.

"I'm looking for someone."

"What's the name?" he asked.

"Eric Johnson," I said.

"Nobody by that name around here."

I started walking back down the corridor until I came to the steps. He matched my movements below so that when I got to the top of the steps he arrived at the bottom. He was staring at me. I started down. He waited.

When I was three steps from the bottom and moving slowly he said, "What are you doing here?"

"Like I said, I'm looking for a friend. What's it to you?"

"I've seen you before," he said.

"Really? I get around." I said and stopped. I think we were already engaged. Sometimes LT tells me to use my initiative. When I got down almost to his level, I could see that he was pear shaped. His body stored fat in an unusual pattern. Most of his weight was in his rear end and upper thighs. He was wearing a purple little button, crudely made, that read, "I am only visiting this planet." Oh, great. A transient's transient.

"I saw you at the concert. I saw you going into Rodd Rock's house." He said. The way it said it, it sounded like an accusation.

"You did? What were you doing there?" I made it sound like an accusation. He was the one with the protection order.

"It was on TV." He was lying about how he saw me. It wasn't hard to tell. He didn't care if I knew.

"I've seen you before." I said. I wanted him back on the defensive.

"So?"

"So what are you doing here?"

"I'm on vacation," he said.

"From what?"

He paused for a moment before answering. Then he leaned in close and his eyes got even bigger and he said in the kind of voice they send the exorcist to correct, "From the assholes."

I got the tingle. I also realized that he was not available for a conversation in the sense of a free exchange of ideas. Still ... there were things I was curious about. This was my first stalker.

"Why are you always wanting to bother Rodd Rock?" I asked him.

"Bother?"

"Yeah. Why did he have to get a court order to keep you away from him?"

"He didn't do that. The people around him did that."

"Why would they try to keep you away from him?" I asked.

He paused before speaking. He was watching me very closely, as if he were calculating something to the third decimal place. "I don't know."

"What reasons could they have?" I prodded.

"Jealousy. I don't know. They don't want anyone to get to Rodd to tell him what is going on."

"Do you know what is going on?"

He didn't answer. He compressed his lips and just stared at me. I had gone too far. I could have broken it off right there; maybe I should have.

"I can get a message to him for you," I said. "What would you want me to say to him?"

"He's getting bad advice," said the stalker.

"Who from?"

"From … them," he said.

"Who is them?" I asked.

"All of them, the record company, the corporations, the suits, the lawyers, the sycophants."

"What are they telling him?"

"He's lost his way. He's caught up with all the bullshit. He's selling out. There isn't much time."

"Time for what?"

He didn't answer. He scanned my face again.

"Time for what?" I asked again.

"I don't have to talk to you."

"Time for what?"

"Look around you."

"Yeah? What do I see?"

"The machine," he said.

"What machine?"

"The everything machine. It always wins."

"What about Rodd Rock?" I asked him. His eyes had narrowed to miniature black holes. No light escaped from them.

"He stood up to it. He held out … as long as he could. But he's inside the machine now."

"Do you stand up to the machine?" I asked him.

"Every day."

"You think you could save Rodd Rock?"

"Of course," he said. He was sure of it.

"Why? What do you know that he doesn't?"

"It's what he's forgotten. He used to know. We were the same. I was in his heart and his soul and he was in mine. Then they put him to sleep and he began to forget. But they didn't put me to sleep because … because … I can see things."

"You identify with Rodd?" I asked.

"Identify? I am Rodd Rock. He has become an imposter."

"You probably don't like Arlene very much, do you?"

"She's a fool. Fools can be dangerous."

"I can see that. Why is she a fool?" I prodded.

"She wanted to own Rodd Rock. She wanted to control him. She wanted to take his life and live it, but she didn't know what his life was. She didn't fit in."

"So she had to go?" I asked.

"She's gone," he said and then he stared at me so hard I almost had to look away.

"Do you know where she is?" I asked, after a pause to call up the will to continue.

"I don't have to talk to you. You should leave. I want you to leave. I don't have to talk to you."

"Do you know what happened to Arlene?"

"Of course!" he said. He was very excited about something.

"What happened?"

"It's the machine," he said. His tone of voice hinted at barely contained rages.

"What's the machine?" I asked.

"She is caught up in the machine."

"Where?"

"It's everywhere." He kept his weird eyes on me the whole time. Most people look around when they speak. Being in his line of sight was like being targeted by a laser sight.

"Where is Arlene?" I asked.

"Wouldn't you like to know," he said.

"Could you tell me?"

He leaned in close. His eyes were focused hard on me, but he narrowed them to little slits. I found myself leaning toward him. I became aware of his breath. It was reminded me of the sludge at the bottom of a storm culvert. He got very close to my face and said, "Fuck you."

I don't know why I was startled, but it wasn't what I thought was coming. I don't know what I thought was coming. I guess I thought he would say something weird about being tracked by a mother ship, or all in all we're just another brick in the wall, or make some allegation about the grand conspiracy behind everything.

It was the hatred in his voice that gave me the tingle. He was mad as hell and I mean hell with fires and pitchforks and endless, screaming torment, gnashing of teeth and hideous corrupted faces appearing suddenly out of the billowing smoke. I felt like I wanted to take a long Hollywood shower with a new bar of antibacterial soap.

"Right back atcha." I said. It was lame, but I was scrambling for thoughts.

"I don't like you," he said.

"I don't like you either, a lot. If I find out you had anything to do with Arlene's disappearance, I'm going to find you."

"You better keep your eyes on Carrie," he said. The tingle became a slight shaking in my right fist. My face felt hot. I must have been blushing.

"What does that mean? What are you talking about?"

"She lives there," he said. "Doesn't she? She's in that house at night when the lights go out. She's in there with Rodd. Isn't she? She brought this on him. She is trying to bring him down. Carrie is part of the machine."

He had touched a button, a nerve, a trigger. He was watching intently for my reaction and I'm sure he got everything. LT always says I don't have a Poker face. I know I suddenly realized that I had rounded up a fist and compacted it until it hurt.

"Listen, you little creep …"

"No! You listen! You better watch out! That's all I'm going to say. You better watch out. I don't have to talk to you. You're nothing. You don't even know what's going on. Leave me alone. I don't have to talk to you."

"Would you rather talk to the cops?"

"Bring 'em! I don't care. Bring on the whole machine! They can't see me because I'm not inside."

He didn't say anything else. He just stared. The guy knew how to stare. He didn't just open his lids all the way. That would have been too comic. He didn't squint. That would have made him look weak. He just used his eyes to send me a frightening message that the lights were on and somebody was home and maybe there was a small crowd at home and they were watching me out of the window.

I didn't say anything else because I had run through all my initiative. I'm sure LT could have thought of something to say and he would have cracked the case (project) wide open, but he likes to talk and I like to act. I wanted to start to act on the guy with the purple button and the beady eyes. I had one fist ready, but I couldn't bring it up and cock it. Maybe I should have. Maybe what happened later might not have. Maybe someone else didn't have to die, or maybe it would have been worse. A crazy stalker doesn't follow the rules. Logic is for small minded people who lack vision and can't see that they are in the shadow of the machine, like me. I backed off and walked to the Caddy. Funny thing; It had a flat tire.

I drove the car out onto the old road and then another couple of hundred yards along it before pulling over. I got out of the car, opened the trunk and moved LT and Teddy's shotgun cases so I could pull back the carpet to expose the spare. Then I had to find the jack. It took a couple of minutes. Before pulling the spare out, I called in. Dickie answered.

"Where is he now?" I asked.

"I had to drive him and Teddy to the Home and Garden Show in the rental car. I was just about to go do some shopping and pick them up."

"Did he take his cell phone?"

"No. It's on his desk."

"I'll call her cell phone," I said.

"It's on his desk too," he said.

"What is it with these people?" I said.

"Teddy didn't want it to go off when she was talking to someone at the show. She says that it's rude. And people have been calling her about the Rodd Rock thing. She's used up all her minutes."

"When you pick them up, tell LT that I found Valderben at the motel."

"How do you spell it?" said Dickie.

"I have no idea. Sound it out. Just tell him I saw the stalker. He will want to tell the police chief."

"OK. Are you coming home?"

"I'll be a little late. I have to change a tire."

"You got a flat?"

"Yes."

I was trying to get the wheel to slide onto the mounting studs when I heard a car coming. We once had a project where someone gave a guy a flat and then hit him with a car when he was trying to change the tire. I dropped the tire, stood up and got behind the front of the car to give the passing car plenty of room. It was a light blue Saturn and when it got close enough I could see Valderben at the wheel. The car was filled with junk. It looked like our stalker was moving to a new location.

He wouldn't look at me. I stared at him until he was gone. Then I flipped out my phone and dialed Sag Harbor Police. Of course the chief was out. Maybe he was at the Home and Garden Show. I left a message that I had found Thomas Valderben, added the address of the motel and mentioned that he looked as if he was moving out. Then I walked back to the motel and verified that his room was now empty.

Great.

17

LT's summer house and office has a low table in the hall to the kitchen. It is so narrow that I always thought it might have once been a larger table that was cut in half and attached to the wall. Teddy uses the little table to display her flower arrangements from the cutting garden. As a man-of-action, I like to walk fast and I never bother to stop and smell the roses or whatever Teddy has set out in one of her weird vases. There are usually two vases full of whatever is in bloom in the back of the house. This time I did stop. I didn't stop for the roses. I stopped because there was a skewed stack of car pornography between the flowers. You wouldn't believe the layouts. Some of them had their hoods open and you could see the actual plumbing. Some had their tops down. Some had their doors wide open and you could see their seats. They were all pulse racing fantasies; "drive ME!" they said "I will make you feel like a real man. I like to be driven hard!"

I whistled. I don't whistle often; maybe once every three or four years.

The top brochure in the pile was for a Maybach. That was way over LT's head. The brochure was circumstantial evidence of the hand of Teddy. Teddy had been busy. I went down through the stack until I hit the thickest layer, the one that showed genuine interest. Below the single brochures for Jags and Mercedes hard top convertibles and Lexus SUVs and the Escalade was a thick band of Mini-Cooper brochures showing every possible color combination and interior package. I groaned. It put me in a bad mood. I passed into the kitchen on a slow-foot glide. I was in a mood for trouble. I was looking for trouble and I found him.

Dickie was at his island and he had his lap top out. He was typing furiously and concentrating real hard. Something was up.

"Recipes?" I said. He jumped.

"Huh? Oh, hi, Max. No. I was just doing a search." He pulled the top half of the lap top down slightly. He was hiding something. I knew what I had to do.

"Do we have any fruit?"

"I got in some nice cherries. There's a couple of pears, but they're not ripe yet. There's half of Teddy's cantaloupe. I think there are some seedless grapes left."

"I can't find the cherries," I said from the refrigerator.

"They're right there on the top shelf."

"I don't think so."

"They are right ..." he sighed and got up from his chair. It made a scraping sound as he pushed back from the island. He turned around and poked his head into the fridge. I backed up to give him room and just happened to flip the lap top monitor fully upright so I could read it.

"Hey! Dickie! You have an instant message from Mandy!"

"That's none of your business!" he said as he backed out of the appliance with a plastic tray of bing cherries in his hand. "The cherries were on the second shelf in the back. Somebody must have moved them." He said 'somebody' in a pointed way, as if he suspected me. He shoved the cherries at me with his left hand and using martial arts quickness, he flipped his computer screen down with his right hand. I took the cherries to the office. I needed to do something. I decided to straighten up the books in the office. LT takes books down and leaves them about. So does Teddy. It annoys me to see them pile up unread. I don't know why.

The phone went off just as I was balancing a stack of books with my chin and there was a slight reflexive wobble of the stack. I was trying to move them from LT's desk to the lip of the book case. I looked at the phone and froze.

"Come on Dickie...pick up." The words came out funny because my mouth was helping my chin keep the stack from falling, but I was only talking to myself anyway.

"Toootle oootle ootle..."

"Where is he?" I said to myself.

Then a book started to slip and I did a head fake, but the book wasn't buying it and went around me to the basket. The rest followed as my hands came up to stop them. They knocked the waste basket over. Crap!

"Toootle toootle tootle…" It was the business line; line one.

"Hello? Lawton Close and associates. This is Max speaking. How may I help you?"

"Dickie?"

"No, this is Max. May I help you?"

"Is Dickie there?" said a girlish voice.

"No."

"Where's Dickie?" This was followed by a rolling torrent of giggles. Adults don't giggle, at least the ones I know. This sounded like the squeals of piglets.

"No one knows. He may be having an out of body experience. His husk is here, but unresponsive."

"Who is this really?"

At about this time I heard the powder room door open and the sound of flushing. "Dickie?" I called out.

"What?" came from the hall.

"You have a call on line one. That's the business line so it must be business."

"Who is it?"

"Sounds female."

"What?" he said.

"Dickie has just returned to his husk," I said into the phone. "Whom may I say is calling?"

"Tell him it's Mandy and Mindy…no! Wait! Tell him it's Gloria Gundergelder!" There was a lot more giggling. Dickie was now at the doorway. His eyes were open as wide as they get. He was wide-eyed and stupefied.

"Do you know a Gloria Gundergelder?"

"Oh…my…god!" said Dickie. His eyes opened even wider. He was exceeding their design limits.

"I sense a story," I said.

"Is … she … on the phone?"

"No. Mandy or Mindy wanted me to tell you she was on the phone. They are a couple of real queens of comedy."

"Dude!"

"Yes Dickie?"

"Don't do that! You could mess a guy up. I'll take it in the kitchen."

"Where's the boss?" I asked him.

"They went to pick up the new Mini and drop off the rental."

"They got a Mini?'

"Oh, yes," he said. I couldn't read his opinion through his tone.

I turned my attention to the phone and had to break in on the giggles. "Mr. Douglas is preparing to pick up the phone. He'll be with you in a moment."

Dickie turned and shuffled to the kitchen. I waited.

"Hello?" said the celibate houseboy after a moment in transit. Dickie was on the line. You can take that any way you want.

"Scoobie!" said the girls in unison, followed by a lot of giggles and chatter. I put the phone down and without thinking, found myself wiping my phone hand on my pants.

I was bent over the fallen books when I heard the front door open. A few seconds later, LT entered quietly. Only his shadow let me know he was in the room. I had most of the trash back in the basket, except for some cigar ashes when he spoke, "What's going on here?"

"Huh? Oh! Hi. Did Dickie tell you that I engaged the stalker?"

"Why did you do that? I thought I told you not to engage the subject. And speaking of Dickie, what's going on in the kitchen?"

"Dickie got a call from some old classmates of the gender to which he does not subscribe."

"A woman? Women?"

"Judging by pitch and giggles, yes."

"Don't ever say things like that around Teddy."

"I won't" I said, firmly.

"Do they know he's celibate?"

"I doubt it, too many giggles."

"What do they want with Dickie?" he asked me. He genuinely didn't know.

"I didn't ask. I can guess. You care to hear my speculations?"

"No! Where is the stalker now?"

"I don't know," I said. I stood holding a couple of books. He eyed the books and would have asked what they were doing on the floor except that there were more important things to worry about.

"What do you mean, you don't know?" asked LT.

"He moved out of his rented room," I said.

"Where did he go?"

"I don't know," I said.

"Why didn't you follow him?"

"Someone cut the valve stem off the left front tire."

"What does that mean?" he asked. He doesn't know anything about cars.

"It means the car had a flat, on purpose."

"Did he do that?"

"I didn't *see* him do it, but what do you think?"

"Did you tell the police?"

"I left a message for the chief, but he was out. As long as Valderben stayed in Montauk, he was within the terms of the restraining order. There isn't much the police could do except stop him for driving with a suspended license and maybe give him some trouble for the failure to appear."

"And vandalizing automobiles!" said LT.

"Yeah. Hard to prove."

Line two lit up and the phone tootled. I picked it up.

"Max?"

"Carrie? What's up?"

"I'm at the house."

"Is everything OK?"

"The real estate brokers have just left. The house is for sale."

"LT, Carrie says that Rodd's house is for sale. The real estate people were just there."

LT looked serious and nodded.

"Max…" said Carrie.

"Yeah?"

"They are asking forty five."

"Forty five what?"

"Forty Five million."

"Wow."

"I have to go. I'm being called. Can you take me to dinner later?"

"I'd love to."

"I have to run. Later." She hung up.

"Where do we stand with the kidnappers?" I said.

"We don't stand anywhere," was his answer.

"Did you call the cops yet?" I asked.

"No. What would I say? Unknown kidnappers have made unknown demands through Mel Viktor who has disappeared? They don't seem very anxious for their money, but Mel certainly did. Until the kidnappers call me or Rodd, I am going to put the idea of a kidnapping on hold. Why?"

"Can I have the night off?" I said to LT.

"You know it's scallop night. Dickie has found some rather nice sea scallops,"

"Carrie sounds like she needs a little hand holding."

"If only that would suffice."

"Can I?" I asked. The tone of my voice was more like pleading.

"I suppose you will want the new car."

"It would be helpful."

He sighed. He compressed his lips. He looked me over the way you might look over a piece of suspect pottery in a yard sale. "If you must." He then handed me a key that was still attached to a large promotional plastic disk printed to look like a golf ball. It had the name of the car dealer and the slogan "Parr Motors where you always swing a great deal."

"I appreciate it."

I ran up the stairs to prepare my husk. I ran it through the shower, re-shaved the visage and adorned it with expensive pants and a polo shirt. I killed some time with a book that Carrie wanted me to read – a mystery about Plum Island written by a local guy. Then I left the house without seeing anyone and folded the husk into the driver's seat of a shiny new automobile. It was my first time in a Mini-Cooper. It was also my last.

Carrie was outside the gates when I got there. She actually waved when she saw me, as if I might miss her standing in front of the overly wrought iron gates of the Rock Pile "Rodd Rock's Palatial Hamptons Estate". There were still some media types around, but not many. The neighbors had made a big effort to force them off the road. It turned into a mess that people still sometimes write letters about in the local papers. Some heavy hitters were involved. One of the funniest was the guy that owns a certain cable network complaining about the uplink trucks and their generators and all the rest and some of them were his own.

I pulled up. She jumped in.

"Ooooh! This is cute!" she said, looking about with enthusiasm at every detail.

"I don't care much for cute. This is like a girly man's car."

"Did you ever see *the Italian Job*?" she asked.

"Yes. Both versions. This isn't a British car. I mean British cars never run, but they look so good. This is as close as LT got to a German car. I was hoping for something with a little more heft."

"Boys and their toys. It's comfortable," she said, moving her shoulders and butt around like a bear getting ready for a long winter's nap.

"Whatever," I said. I was negotiating the controls. We had begun to move.

"Rodd has had nothing but trouble with his TVR," she said. "It's in the shop constantly."

"That's the British car experience," I said.

"Where are you taking me this evening?"

"Where would you like to be taken?"

"For dinner," she said firmly.

"I thought we should try Della Lupo. It's hot right now. Do you like Italian?"

"I'm not big on pasta," she said.

"You didn't grow up in an Italian neighborhood."

"I don't think so. You did?"

"Well, there were a lot of Italians in Sheepshead Bay," I said.

"Uh, huh."

"You want to try some other place? Except, I made reservations."

"You have the wheel. You're driving. You decide," she said brightly. She then leaned back into the seat and looked out over what would have been a hood on a normal car. She was looking forward to a nice night out.

I decided that we weren't going to try to get reservations someplace else and we went to Della Lupo. We thought it was going to be a quiet break from all the tensions of a high profile disappearance. The problem with being in the middle of a project (rather than at the end or the beginning) is that trouble is still in a growth spurt. It sends out little runners to trip up the unwary. Carrie and I were the very picture of unwary as I wheeled the little car along the Montauk Highway with the rest of the summer crowd. I listened for a moment to the tiny little engine whispering of Teutonic competence, and then sat back and relaxed. We were on our way into the rapidly darkening Hampton night where passions, like objects in your rearview mirror, are closer than they appear.

I was told that Della Lupo was the real thing, specializing in the cuisine of Northern Italy. The owner, Mr. Lupo, had a successful restaurant in Brooklyn, not far from where I grew up, that got two stars or three chef's hats depending on who you read. He opened up in Southampton to try to cash in on his reputation. I made the reservation under my name. Kelly is not an uncommon name. A Kelly could be anybody.

We walked through some big glass and aluminum doors into a little glassed vestibule that was closed off from the restaurant proper by a partial wall of red drapery. The drapes were the dividing line between the new world and the old. As we passed through a small opening in the fabric, the light changed to intimate. The noise level dropped out entirely. Our first obstacle was a small mahogany podium manned, if that is the proper term, by a thin swarthy fellow with a permanently raised left eyebrow.

"Yessss?" he hissed.

"We have reservations?" I said in an asking tone.

"And you are?"

"Kelly, for two at eight-thirty?"

"Yes," he said. I was in the good book. He nodded to himself. Then he looked me over with a raking glance and practically memorized Carrie's physical person while he felt around for two menus from his pile. He was looking at her so hard, she reflexively straightened her skirt. "This way," he said and turned his back on us. He led us into a large, dimly lit and heavily upholstered chamber. It was as if a Tuscan farmhouse from the 1300s had been decorated by a Hollywood set designer's idea of a suitable environment in which to shoot a Wagnerian opera entitled "Twilight of the Call Girls." The design philosophy seemed to be something like, if it moves make it red, otherwise gild it.

We sat. No, we assumed our thrones.

"Can I get you something from the bar?" said our greeter-and-seater as he passed a menu to Carrie and then one to me. They had the weight and gravitas of stone tablets.

"She'll have a cosmo and I'll have a glass of Chianti."

"Would you like to look at our list?" he said with deep-down serious tones.

"Chianti? List?"

"Perhaps you would care to choose," he said as he flipped open a small fat book of a wine list to the red by the glass pages. It was all in Italian and I didn't recognize any of the names. I recognized some of the prices though because I had just seen them when I was looking for a new jacket at Brooks Brothers in Riverhead.

I ran my finger down the double digits until I came to something that didn't make my blood race. "This looks ... doable."

"Very good, sir. An excellent choice," he said, but his heart wasn't in it. He had me pegged. Back in Brooklyn we used to think Rufino was something special and you could take the bottle home and put a candle in it when you wanted some atmosphere.

Carrie and I had a moment to consult the tablets unmolested. Pasta primavera was thirty five bucks a la carte. I got the tingle. The five course Chef's Special which included World Famous Gnocchi a la Lupo was more than Knicks tickets to the Garden for two.

"What looks good?" I said to Carrie. I hoped she couldn't detect any despair in my voice.

"You like calamari? You want to split an order?" she said.

Then a shadow fell across our flickering table lamp, darkening slightly the white linen cloth and stealing the highlights from our flatware.

"Hello. I'm Justin and I'll be your server this evening. First I'd like to tell you about our specials. The fish of the day is striped bass. It is rubbed with extra virgin olive oil, wrapped in ..."

I didn't listen to the rest of it. I was looking at Carrie's face and she was resting her chin on her hands and looking at Justin and she had that smile she gets that gives nothing away, but I knew she was back there at Taylor's in the Catskills and she was in a heat blasted and steamy, yellow-lit room filled with dented and dull stainless steel. Someone was calling out the orders and on a big blackboard someone had written "Push Veal Special!!" She had a knife in her hand and she was using it. The soundtrack, rising above the powered-vent roar came from the Mexican dishwasher's radio that was always tuned to classic rock. He often tried to sing along. The memory-vision took me back there with her. Every time we think we know what's coming next in life, everything changes -- everything.

Carrie had the medallions of veal covered with a white wine reduction over polenta. I can't eat veal, not since I was a little kid. I had the scampi. There was nothing better on a Catholic Friday night, when I was growing up, than the scampi at Baron Nellos on Oriental Avenue. Lupo's was as good or better. I had a side of pasta that was perfection in a monkey dish.

We were halfway through our entrées when the Lupo came out of his den. I didn't pay any attention to the red-faced, chubby little man in his spotless Bragard kitchen jacket as he slammed out of the kitchen doors and headed through a crowded dining room in our direction. My eyes registered the commotion, because they register everything that moves, but my brain was neck deep in the essence of fresh basil, peeled and seeded plum tomatoes, a strong garlic back beat and pasta that felt almost bread-like on the tongue. It was made from the soft wheat that grows only in the Po valley. Soft wheat pasta has to be made fresh, it doesn't dry well like semolina pasta. It was simply the best pasta I ever ate in the Hamptons.

Even when the strange little man in whites stopped in front of our table breathing hard I wasn't prepared to be alarmed. He had obviously stopped at the wrong table.

But he hadn't.

"I don't want your business," he said loudly, as he bent over us. His chubby little hands snapped out and gained control of the four corners of our white table cloth. My brain still wasn't up to speed. I noted his action, but didn't push it to the logical outcome. He did. He yanked his hands toward the ceiling and the white tablecloth trap slammed shut over our tumbling water glasses, our sputtering table lamp, our pasta, our breads, our butter, veal medallions, bread plates, her second cosmo, my first Chianti. Everything flickered out and flooded and smashed into that snapping white mouth. Dinner, for us, was over.

"Get out! I don't want your business! Don't come back! Tell your Rodd Rock that he has brought dishonor on my cousin! He has made big trouble for everyone. He is not allowed here nor any of his associates. I want you out. Pepe!"

He was holding the bulging table cloth over our table. It looked like a elephant's diaper, and it was showing wet and would soon be dripping.

Carrie was already on her feet. I joined her at an altitude where both of us were looking down on Mr. Lupo.

We were joined by a sullen busboy. We didn't need Pepe to get the message. It wasn't subtle. I didn't know what to say, so I said nothing. I reached into my wallet and threw a fifty on the bare table.

"Keep your money!" said Lupo with a spitting motion.

"It's for the drinks and Pepe. I don't want to owe you or anyone you hang around with, anything. By the way, that's pretty good pasta and you know what? Joody Bells once made me pasta in his house in Teaneck and it wasn't half that good."

"Get out!"

We did. The other diners were paying close attention to us as we walked the walk toward the opening in the red drapes. As we passed the bar, I noticed a little semi-private room beyond it. It was dimly lit and the walls were covered with murals of Italy. They were almost like photographs. Everything else in the room was covered with expensive fabrics. Only one table was occupied. There were four bodies at the table, two looked like working girls. I knew the men. One of them turned to us and made a gesture like a gun with his pointing finger and cocked thumb. He smiled happily. It was John Gnotto. I made the gun sign right back to him. He shook his head and smiled even more. The other guy just smiled, but there was nothing happy about it. It was more of a wide smirk.

We didn't talk the talk until we got outside. I liked that about Carrie that she didn't try to talk. She didn't try to put her mark on the proceedings. But when we cleared the big door and turned for the back parking lot, she spoke. "Who was the guy with Paul Williams?"

"John Gnotto. Apparently he is showing us that we can't touch Dom Pancetta who you know as Paul Williams. Dom is under his wing."

"Is he a big deal?" asked Carrie. She isn't from New York. The name of a local alleged crime lord wouldn't mean much.

"He can pull strings," I said.

"What was the Judy Bells remark?"

"A guy I knew. It would mean something to Mr. Lupo. It's a name."

"Who is his cousin?"

"I'm guessing Paul Williams, AKA Dom Pancetta."

"He was really steamed," she said.

"Yeah. I should have seen it coming, your horoscope for this morning said, 'tensions run high'."

"You read my horoscope this morning?" she asked.

"I did. I wanted to see what was in the stars for us."

She took my elbow with her hand, then slipped her hand around it for better purchase.

"Hmmmmmm. I didn't know you believed in that stuff."

"I don't."

"What is it with you and restaurants?" she asked. "When other men take me out to dinner, it usually stays on the table. Not with you."

"What can I tell you. I'm a man of action. Where would you like to go next for dinner?"

"I don't need anything but a drink. I had enough of Della Lupo's bread and fried calamari."

"I know a place," I said. I did, too.

"Every time you take me out to a nice place…" she started and then stopped.

"Yeah, well. I know a lot of …" I said.

"Yes?"

"Interesting people."

"It's never dull," she said and tightened her grip.

"Dull, it isn't," I said.

My second choice was out on the highway. It used to be an old house. Now it was the place to go if you wanted to spend a normal week's salary for dinner and a couple of mixed drinks. I honestly don't know why I picked it that night, maybe hurt pride. I was trying to impress the lady and that's tough in the Hamptons. It takes brute spending power. I can pretend for a night and pay down my card for a couple of months, but I have a credit limit. Chemin De Fer could easily make me exceed it if we went for the full four course treatment with bubbly, It was bad enough with just the bubbly.

Of course the place was filled up. It was also noisy. In comparison, Della Lupo was dead quiet. New Yorkers like it noisy. It makes the air seem to be filled with energy. I don't always like noisy, but I wanted it that night. We went to the bar and stood. She had another Cosmopolitan. I had a beer; to start. While we were standing, three people in front of us at the bar got up to go to their table.

"Grab it!" I said shoving Carrie toward the opening. I didn't have to say anything more. She was already sideways and forcing the issue with elbows and body pressure. She's good that way.

We sat. The third empty seat was taken up by a slim blonde. Her date hovered behind her. When she smiled shyly at us, he put a beefy hand on the back of her neck and began to massage it in a possessive manner. Whatever.

I was about to try to think of something to say. I didn't really want to say anything. I really wanted to shut down the whole failed date and try again the next night. I was embarrassed a little, tired a little and I needed to get to an ATM. I was about to start thinking of something witty to say just to keep the evening from suffocating when a sharp edged note of middle-aged girlish laughter pierced the echoing babble of loud New York chatter.

At first I didn't think anything of it. New Yorkers are often loud, especially out on the town. Then it happened again and I saw a couple of arms in the air. There was something about the laughter. There was something almost familiar about it. I stood up and looked toward the sound. Diners were doing the same thing. I just had to scan to the center of the ring of turned heads. What I saw there made me jump slightly on my bar seat. I could see just a teeny patch of silvery, shiny, silk dragon jacket. The good one he only wears "out".

"Come on!" I said and grabbed Carrie's hand. Her other hand latched on to her Cosmo in a reflexive motion. She was protecting her treasure from the shocks that flesh is heir to.

"What are you doing?" she said.

I was already on my feet. "Come on. I want to show you something that hasn't been seen in fifteen years."

She snatched her hand back from my grip and used it to protect her drink, but she was up and moving. It took a little pushing to get away from the bar. My seat was already being filled before I had properly cleared the privacy zone that in my mind extends eight inches, minimum, beyond the actual dimensions of the stool.

There were three lines of bar patrons and we broke through them and were in the relative clear of a crowded restaurant on a Hamptons boogie night in high season.

"What is it?" said Carrie, as we put some moves on a couple of busboys and one older guy who was looking for a restroom, any restroom.

And suddenly, as bodies parted and things were revealed, we were upon them. We were above them. They were so busted.

"Dickie!" I cried out.

He gulped. People hardly gulp anymore, but Dickie is a Darwinian backtrack.

"Dickie!" said Carrie. She took in the whole scene in an instant, the empty glasses, the smeared dishes, the gnawed bones, the crumbs, the dilated pupils, the weird lipstick colors, the massive costume jewelry, the décolletage that would house a family of prairie dogs and their guests. "You've tasted meat!"

Dickie was in the act of standing. Some dimmed-out conditioning from his early manhood came online and he was standing because a lady had joined his table. These things appeared on Dickie's face like a news crawl on a 42nd Street jumbotron: guilt; confusion; irritation; and excitement. Dickie had tasted meat.

He began to wave a flattened hand between the two women at his table and he spoke like a booth announcer for a quiz show. "These are the Minder sisters, Mandy and Mindy. I believe you have spoken with them on the phone. That's Carrie Strudell, and this is my associate, Max Kelly "

"Hi!" I said. I hope it sounded cheery, "I think I've just been promoted to associate."

"Hello," said Carrie. She didn't bother with cheery.

"You know," said either Mandy or Mindy, but the one who put her bangled and tawny hand on Dickie's skinny thigh when he resumed his seat (and after his pretension to antique formalities, he didn't just sit back down, he resumed his seat) "the waiter asked how the two of us got along with just one guy!" She spoke in a voice that wasn't as loud as it was cutting. I'm sure you could hear every word out by the dumpsters even as the debris of another Hamptons evening was being poured out where the grape skins of wrath are stored for early collection. "I think he was trying to put the *moves* on my sister! And I just said, 'Oh, we ménage! Get it?"

This set off an explosion of giggles and laughter, not from me and not from Carrie, and not really from Dickie who fixed his face like it was laughing, but no sound came out.

"Sit down!" said the other sister. The fourth chair was empty. There wasn't a fifth.

"Mind if I …" I said to the two overly handsome men at the next table. They were looking pained, but the closer of the two waved away the empty chair, as if it were something he had been meaning to donate to charity.

Carrie tugged on my jacket where the others couldn't see. She wanted no part of what was about to go down. I ignored the tug. Moments like that one don't come around every day. We sat.

"Isn't it exciting?" said one of the twins. I never did learn to keep them straight.

"Isn't what exciting?" I said, walking right into whatever it was she was setting up.

"A famous murder with a really famous celebrity and Dickie is right in the middle of it!" she said. Her head was going like a bobble head doll on the rear deck of a big car with bad shocks going over railroad tracks.

"We were watching the news one night," said the other twin, "and there was this shot of Rodd Rock and there were some people around him and Mindy said to me isn't that Dickie Douglas?"

"We called him Dickula in school," said Mindy. This set off another tremor of giggles and bobbles.

174

"It's like a take off on like Dracula, but he's a Dick. Get it?" More laughter, big laughter. Dickula was looking like he was sitting on a steam pipe. He was beginning to perspire on his forehead, which he never does, and he was red in the face. We made eye contact. He knew I was storing all of this up, for future use. Dickula was in for a mauling at my convenience.

"Yeah. He was so strange in school. He always fell asleep in first period," said one of the twins, probably Mandy. "We always joked that he was up all night sneaking into girl's rooms to suck their blood. He never went to the beach. He was so white it was like he slept in a coffin or something. But he was kind of cute and really, really shy. He was the absolute last person you would ever think would be on TV! And there he was! On CNN!"

"I said it can't be Dickula," from the other sister. "But we looked real close and it *was*! He was in the Hamptons. Then we heard the name Lawton Close and Mandy said we should Google him. There were hundreds of hits and one of them mentioned Dickie Douglas from West Palm and we were like oh my god! It's Dickula!"

"So I said try the white pages on line," said Mandy. "But it's unlisted! How can a lawyer have an unlisted number? How does that work?"

"So I said try the alumni office," from Mindy. "And they had his information, but they wouldn't give it to us."

"No! They said they had to ask Dickie if he wanted to get an e-mail from us and he did! He sent back the cutest e-mail didn't you Dickie? It had an animated smiley face and everything!"

"An animated smiley face?" I said, "Dickie! You dirty dog!"

"So we started writing! And Mandy said we have to go to him! He's like all caught up in the biggest murder in ever! Dickula is a *celebrity!* Uncle Jerry has a place in Westhampton, so we just loaded up the Lexus and here we are! We even brought the year book."

"You brought the year book?" I said.

"Of course! You want to see it?"

"Are you kidding? You have it here?" I said.

Mandy's head went down below the rim of the table like a Key West sunset at the exact moment the waiter arrived at our table. His face was set in a grim mask of pleasantry. The little eyes behind the mask were the eyes of panic.

"Another round?" he said.

Mindy nodded like a trained horse and dipped her forefinger down like a dowsing stick and whirled it around the table three times. The waiter turned to Carrie and said "Is that a Cosmopolitan?"

"Uh huh."

"Another beer?" he said to me.

"Sure. I think I'll switch to whatever light beer you have on tap."

"What are you having, Dickie?" I said as I grabbed his nearly empty glass and sniffed it.

"He's having a Sprite," said one of the twins. "Dickula is a party pooper."

It smelled like Sprite. "OK then," I said.

Dickie frowned and said "Dude!" I was only looking out for his best interests. Meat is one thing. Cheap costume jewelry on deep dish apple décolletage is another, but someone had to draw the line at booze and I was the only man-of-action at the table.

The waiter turned his back just as Mandy rose above the rim of the table like a Samoan sunrise. She had one hand on the handle of a large natural fiber (it looked like dried grass) tote bag or giant purse and the other hand was down inside. That hand soon emerged with a scratched old yearbook that had a fake leather cover in dark maroon. The sight of it set more giggles off. It came down on the table flat and eager hands tore at it like crow claws on road kill. Pages were brushed aside like dried skin and hair to get to the meat of the thing.

"That's me!" Mandy spun the book around and pointed with her finger.

"Oh …" I started to say more when a foot mashed down on my own. Carrie didn't like the tone of voice I was setting up.

"That's me!" said her sister pointing to the black and white face in the next square. They were so similar looking they could have saved some money and used the same picture twice. Maybe they did. You could tell it was the twins. They hadn't changed very much. I looked at Carrie, a little quick glance just to see if there were bogies at my three o'clock. There were two of them; her eyes. They were locked on. Evasion was useless. Her foot had retreated upward, under the table to the kill position. It had the height advantage. She must have learned that trick from Teddy, or else it's instinctive.

Dickula was leaning forward and staring intently at the two-inch by inch and a half graven images. Both sisters had an identical haircut; black bubbles of hair with bangs. The hair made the most of their sharp little fox faces. They must have been very popular in school.

It was apparent that they had both had some minor cosmetic surgery since the pictures were taken. They were striking looking with and without the surgery. They would have stood out in any crowd then and now, even before speaking.

Dickula was staring at them, as if he had never seen a picture before. I think he was back there in his own wasted youth. It was some kind of memory trance. I believe I could have stuck him with a pin and he wouldn't have felt it. I was wondering where I could find a pin when one of the twins said, "I want to see Dickie."

"He's more toward the front," said the other.

Busy hands began ruffling pages to the rippling of expectant giggles. The pages stopped at some faces with D names below, but there was no one that resembled Dickie. One more page was turned. I scanned both new pages and I missed him in the first pass. But a gaily painted finger nail flew down like a smart bomb and tapped him right on his photographic chest.

"Dickula!"

Good god. It was Dickie, if you squinted. He had long hair falling over both sides of his face. The hair was blond, almost white. He looked scrawny and sullen and he was wearing a white sports jacket with some dark colored shirt, open about three buttons. He looked like a surfer dude in the night of the living dead.

"Dickie!" I said, "I'm glad you lost the mustache. You look like …"

I don't know what I was going to say. I never got to form up a fitting analogy because at that moment the drinks arrived. It took a little commotion to distribute the medicine. The girls were both having white Russians. Bartenders hate them because the milk ruins their detergent bath and they have to drain the sink and start over. You know stupid trivia like that when you use your associate's degree in hotel restaurant management to actually work in a hotel. I would advise against it.

While drinks were being handed down and passed right and left, Dickie drew the yearbook to his chest and peered down at it. He began to turn pages slowly. I was starting to feel sorry for him and I don't know why. He looked a lot cooler in his yearbook than I did in mine. I went to a parochial school. We were a mess.

When the waiter had gone off to attend to other needs in other places, Mandy said quite seriously, "So do you think he'll get away with it?"

"Oh, sure," said her sister. "They'll never find the body."

"So you think he did it?" said Carrie. Her voice was completely neutral as far as I could tell.

"Of course," said Mandy. She said it impatiently. I found that her self assurance about Rodd was annoying for some reason. It made me want to defend him.

"What about evidence?" I said.

"He hired a killer to run security?" she said to me. Then she offered to the table, "It's all about the money. He didn't want to split the money. He's just like my first husband. I call him my starter husband." Then she turned to Dickie and said, "Do you remember Joel DeShaw?"

Dickie made a face.

"He wasn't that bad!" she said.

Dickie made a bigger face, as if he had just bitten into a rotten habanero pepper that was rancid, but still burned.

"His father had a car dealership," she said to the rest of us. "He was a little dorky, but he had a great car."

"First husband?" I said, just to stir the pot.

"When the training wheels fell off, I couldn't ride him anymore!" she said. This started up the giggles again. She led them. I was sure from her delivery, that the line had been used before. She had the timing of a professional comic. "Then I met Dug-glass."

"His name was Doug Glass?" I asked.

"No. His name was Douglas Chesterton Cartweal the fourth. He had a Harley and a Donzi."

"Should I ask what happened to him?" I said.

"No," said Carrie, smiling brightly.

The twin pouted and said, "He was fooling around with Jennifer Ventana. You remember Jen, Dickie?"

Dickie had a sudden and involuntary general muscular contraction. I would have to ask him about Jen Ventana at a later date. The twin didn't notice his reaction. She was panning her audience to make sure she was still at the epicenter of attention. I'll never know what aftershocks she was preparing because Carrie said, "I'm a little tired."

I looked over at Dickie. He caught my eye. Then he silently and hugely mouthed the words "Help me!" He got that from some cartoon cat that was voiced by Nathan Lane. I almost laughed out coffee through my nose.

Carrie had had enough. She stood up.

"I'm ready for bed," she said with a yawn.

"Oh! Max! She's ready!" said one of the twins, setting off a round of titters.

"No!" said the other one. "It's too early. I want to go dancing. Why don't you guys come with us to the Dragger? There's a live band!"

"You go," said Carrie to me with a straight face. "There's a free twin. I'll take the Mini back to LT's. You can get a ride with them."

"Naw. I've had a long day," I said. "I'll drive the Mini."

"Awwwwwwwwwwww," said one of the twins, pouting.

"Does Dickie dance?" I said to the other one.

"Dickie was famous for doing the cosmic robot. He could do the moon walk and everything!"

"I'm almost tempted. It would mean a lot to see Dickie do the cosmic robot, but …" I stood up.

"Awwwwwwwwwww, you're no fun."

I opened my wallet and flipped Dickie more than enough to cover what we ordered and a fat tip. He raked it in like a guy who had bluffed on a pair of deuces and didn't want to be found out.

As we went out the door and turned to walk into the back parking lot where I had been lucky to find a space even driving a Mini-Cooper, I scanned the parked cars as I always do. The cars were what you would expect to be gathered up alongside one of the most expensive night spots in the Hamptons. All except one. The faded baby blue Saturn was way out of its element. So was the guy sitting darkly behind the wheel. He was pretending he wasn't seeing us.

"Stay here," I said to Carrie.

"Why?"

"I have to see a guy. Stay here."

"Who?"

"Thomas Valderben. Stay here. I won't be a moment."

"The stalker?"

"Yes. Wait for me right here."

I started walking slowly toward the car. She followed two steps back. I was concentrating on Valdeben. I didn't know she was behind me until I reached the car. He stared straight ahead, refusing to acknowledge us. I knocked on the driver's side window, which was up all the way on a hot night. Nothing happened. I tried the door handle. It was locked.

I knocked on the window a little harder. It came down a crack. It must have been electric. I didn't see him move. He would not look at us.

"What are you doing here, Thomas?"

He made a vulgar expression.

"The police are looking for you. You shouldn't be here."

He made a slightly more colorful vulgar expression, but then he said, "She's next."

"Who is next, Thomas?"

"The bitch you had dinner with. She's behind all the craziness. She's a traitor, a mole. She forced Arlene out. She hates Rodd Rock because he wouldn't give her what she wants," he said.

"What does she want Thomas?"

"She wants everything."

"What is everything?"

"She wants his mind. She wants his money. She wants to be inside of him. She wants to make him safe for the machine."

"What are you talking about, Thomas?"

"Her," he said and he turned his face to the two of us. It was the kind of face you see in a fun house with a blast of air and a recorded scream. I got the tingle so violently, I think I may have had a spasm. Carrie grabbed onto my arm, but said nothing. "She's fucked everything up. She's trying to destroy Rodd Rock. I hate her."

"What are you talking about? What did she do?" I asked him.

"Somebody is telling things to the media. Somebody is trying to destroy Rodd Rock's career and his place in history. It has to be somebody close to him, *somebody who lives in his house!* I've been watching. She wants Rodd Rock all to herself and if she can't have him, she is trying to ruin him and his legacy. She's part of the machine. I found out some things about her! I found out that her father was in Naval Intelligence. She's a plant. She's a user and a snitch. She is out to destroy Rodd Rock! It's almost too late now. There's almost no time! She has to be stopped! If I have to, I will stop her."

"Are you talking about me, you little rat shit pus ball?" said Carrie, shoving me to one side and stepping up to the plate. The window closed like a startled scallop's shell. He turned his face to the front and twisted the keys to start the motor.

I shoved Carrie back away from where the wheels would roll if he tried something dumb, but I didn't want to end the interview. I wanted to keep stimulating him. She didn't want to be shoved out of the way in mid challenge. She tried to shove *me* out of the way. I think she scared him off.

"Thomas!" I yelled.

He put the Saturn in drive. I shoved Carrie back while she was trying to shove me to one side. Thomas flipped us off and then tromped on the accelerator. He didn't exactly light up the Saturn's tires, but he moved some loose gravel around. He managed to scuff my toe with the rear tire. I banged on the trunk lid as it went by. I was angry, frustrated and something else that I couldn't identify.

We were both thoughtful on the way back to the house. Carrie said a couple of things to Thomas Valderben in abstentia. If he had heard them, he might have kept driving. It would have been better for all concerned if he had, but fate is fate and character is fate's stooge.

I called the house.

Dickie answered and directed my call to the man who pays the phone bills.

"You drove on that tire!" he said by way of an opening pleasantry. It put me immediately on the defensive.

"What tire?" I said.

"The flat tire! You drove on a flat tire!" he said angrily.

"I wasn't going to hang around," I told him.

"Gunter says it is ruined because you drove on it. He had to replace all four. Do you know what that cost?"

"I only drove a couple of hundred yards; just to the main road."

"Well, that was enough to break down the sidewall, according to Gunter."

"I wasn't going to wait there. You didn't see the look in his eye," I said.

"I told you not to engage. I just wanted you to reconnoiter."

"He engaged. We've been through this already. He found me. And we just had another run-in with him tonight which is why I am calling in."

"A run-in with whom?"

"The stalker! Thomas Valderben. I took Carrie to Chemin de Fer for a drink and Valderben was sitting in his car in the parking lot. He must have followed us. I saw him when we came out and I went to have a word with him."

"What was *he* doing there?"

"How do I know?" I said. "When he saw Carrie, he said she was responsible for all of Rodd Rock's troubles and that he might have to stop her."

"What did he mean by that?" asked LT.

"You want me to interpret the motives of a whacko stalker?"

"No! Why did you speak to him? Why couldn't you leave him alone?"

"LT! He's following Carrie! He's stalking her! He threatened her."

"With what exactly?"

"The threat wasn't in the words so much as the way he said it. This guy is capable of anything."

"All the more reason to stay away from him."

"He followed *us*!"

"Did you call the police?" said LT.

"No, I called you. Do you want me to call the police?"

"No. I'll call the chief. He wanted me to let him know. Which way did he go?" asked LT.

"East on the Montauk Highway. Make sure you lock up good tonight. You might want to call Rodd and tell him to have somebody patrol the grounds. This guy is highly motivated and needs a lot of heavy medication or a straight jacket."

"Why did you insist on stirring him up! I don't need this now!" said LT.

"Tonight?"

"No, the other day at the motel."

"I didn't stir him up! I didn't even know he was there."

"And I specifically told you not to engage," said LT.

"He engaged me! This guy is capable of *anything*. He scares me. He disabled the car! Maybe he was trying to keep me there to add to his collection?"

"Collection of what?"

"Whatever! You've seen the movies and so have I: skins; pinky rings with the pinky still in them; lady parts."

"What would he want with you?" said LT, with an audible harrumph.

"How do I know? You didn't see the look in his eye. He just told me that he might have to stop Carrie because Carrie is destroying Rodd Rock."

"He said that?"

"Those were his exact words. What do I have to say to get you take this thing seriously?"

"All right. I'll call the chief. I'll alert Rodd and make sure he has coverage on the grounds. I'll call Carol and get some people. I don't want Dominic anywhere near Rodd. I will call Carol and have her tell Bobby Dunton to drive out. I will have him track down and surveill our stalker."

"Good. Somebody should be tailing this guy. Where is Tyrell? I wish Tyrell was there. The stalker has crazy guy smarts. He's going to give Bobby Dunton the slip."

"He's a compulsive fan, not a mastermind," said LT

"He's crazy and dangerous and paranoid and highly motivated," I said.

"Don't make this any more dramatic than it is," said LT.

"I couldn't. This guy is going to keep pushing the situation until someone or something stops him."

"Let the authorities earn their keep on this one. He is not our concern."

"What if he did something to Arlene?" I asked.

"Like what?" he said.

"You know like what, like murdered her," I said.

"You are letting your anxiety and your imagination run away with your good sense. You are being cuckolded by unworthy feelings."

"I don't know what you just said, and I don't think you do either, but if you want to talk about anxiety, we saw Dom Pancetta sitting with John Gnotto at Della Lupo's just before we were thrown out. John made sure I saw them together. I think he is telling us that Dom is off limits."

"I've expected something of the kind. There are fences going up all over the place. We are in the critical phase of a difficult project. I must retain freedom of thought and movement as long as possible. I hope you didn't do anything to annoy John Gnotto!"

"No! He had us thrown out of the restaurant. It turns out that Lupo is a cousin of Dom's," I said.

His reaction was completely unexpected. "What are you playing at? Why did you barge in on John Gnotto and Dominic Pancetta in his cousin's restaurant? Are you trying to start a turf war?"

"I didn't *know* it was Dom's cousin and I sure as hell didn't know that Gnotto would be there. Believe me, I wouldn't have gone. I just wanted to take Carrie out for a nice meal to get away from all of the insanity. How was I supposed to know that the inmates had taken over a Hamptons eatery?"

"I must insist that you begin to lower your profile until we have sorted out some things."

"What does that mean?" I asked.

"I want you both to stay inside and out of trouble. Every time you leave the property lately, I get an upsetting phone call."

I had to lob the conversation back to his side of the net. "Has anyone heard from the kidnappers?"

"Not a word."

"From Mel?"

"Only silence," he said. "We need a break. I am having difficulty sleeping. I have tasted anxiety and I don't like it one bit. I want the two of you home and under my roof as soon as you can get here. I forbid you to go to an Italian restaurant until this thing is settled one way or the other."

"What did you just say?"

"You heard me."

"Yes. I heard you, but did you hear yourself? The insanity is catching! I'm going to start wearing a surgical mask."

"That will certainly set the proper tone. By the way, I called out for Dickie and Dickie is not here."

"Last I saw, he was at a bar with those two giggly, whatever they are, from his haunted past."

"Socializing?"

"You could call it that, I guess," I said.

"At a bar? Dickie has been sober for more than a decade," said LT.

"He may still be sober, but I'll tell you one thing."

"What's that?"

"He has tasted meat," I said.

"You aren't attempting one of your metaphorical excesses, are you?"

"Maybe. He's in there with the Minder twins. He's overmatched. They will tear him to toothpicks metaphorically speaking."

"You must save him."

"I can't. He's an adult."

"In what sense?"

"In legal years."

"If anything happens to Dickie, I'm holding you personally responsible."

"Whatever. Carrie and I are coming home to bed."

"In separate rooms! No funny business! I won't be up when you get here. See me first thing in the morning. And tell Dickie to come home immediately."

"Dickie is on his own. I'll see you in the morning."

The connection went dead. Carrie looked at me funny. "What did he say?" she asked.

"I am supposed to save Dickie."

"From what?" she asked.

"Exactly," I said. "Your Mini awaits you."

18

THE NEXT MORNING, WAS THE morning we first saw the *Rumeur Monde* story. LT does not have a sympathetic persona for the tabloid sensibility. For one thing, he is not, in any sense that might be meaningful to the popular culture, a good sport. He is also not entirely able to cloak his disdain for a lot of what passes for culture in the post modern era. Even in a furry hipster hat, he is able to give the impression that he suspects that the emperor's clothes are not as advertised. His general seriousness, reticence and Ivy League vocabulary, not to mention his high profile (and rich) clients, make him an easy target for crusading journalism students who are looking to ride envy into the winner's circle. He has been called a lot of names in print and on camera. This time, however, the scribblers at *Rumeur Monde* had managed an out and out smear job. Somebody in the editorial office wanted LT's scalp and the young braves were only to happy to strap on their breech cloths and paint their faces for battle.

I could tell Dickie was upset when I ambled into the kitchen. I was trying to get my eyes to focus. He looked furious. Dickie doesn't ever look furious because he meditates and medicates and mediates his troubles away.

"What's the matter?" I said to him. He looked up at me from a magazine that he had opened on top of his morning paper. He looked up with something like hatred in his eyes. "Are you angry about me and Carrie catching you out last night?"

He didn't say anything. He merely swiveled the magazine around so I could read it. He then pointed a bony finger at an article with pictures. The finger reminded me of the Ghost of Christmas Future. I walked closer and worked my eyes until the text came into focus. I recognized the picture even in a blur.

"Dickie! That's you! What are you doing in *Rumeur Monde*? Why do you look so ... Dickie! This is a picture of you in rehab. The caption says that Richard Douglas spent time in rehab for alcoholism and drug addiction.'

"That's the jump page," said Dickie grimly. "Wait till you see what they say about you."

"Who?" I said, thumbing forward to page 34.

"Roger Playless wrote the article. It's a hit piece," said Dickie.

By then I had page 34 opened and flattened out. Holy shit! There was a terrible picture of LT taken at some party that made him look unearthly. His skin was so white from the strobe flash that Casper the Ghost would look like he just came back from Florida in comparison. LT's whited face was startled and angry in the shot. It's not a good look for him. The caption read, "Lawton Close prefers to work in back rooms filled with his own smoke." Below his picture was a shot of Teddy standing next to Margaret Biltmore. They were both in sparkly party gear. It was another night shot with too much strobe. Her caption read, "Society designer and heiress Theodora Martyn-Smyth has her own room at the Close mansion."

Below her and almost at the bottom of the page was a picture of me and Lyon Biltmore taken during a Rodd Rock event at the Rock and Roll Hall of Fame in Cleveland. It looked like I was attacking Ms. Biltmore and she looked like she had had way too many mojitos, which she had. I focused even harder and read my caption, "Max Kelly, the enforcer, was lucky to escape manslaughter charges when he drove his car into a tent full of Hamptons Glitterati."

"*What?*" I said.

Dickie was watching my face.

"What is this?" I flipped the magazine closed to see the cover. One of the headlines read, "Rodd Rock's Mouthpiece in Close Quarters – Roger Playless turns over a slimy Rock in the Hamptons.".

"I told you," said Dickie. "It's a hit piece."

"I didn't go out with Lyon Biltmore!" I protested. "That was a professional operation."

"She still writes," said Dickie. He has a thing about Lyon Biltmore.

"That's because I was polite and answered her first post card because I didn't want to hurt her feelings." I turned back to the page with Dickie's picture. I read a couple of lines. "Richard! It says you were once arrested for conspiracy to distribute schedule one narcotics?" I said.

"Marijuana is a schedule one substance. So are peyote buttons. It's all bullshit and my father got the thing quashed."

"But you had the stuff on you?" I said. I was dividing my attention between Dickie and the text.

"Well ... duh," said Dickie, with a little childish inflection on the duh. "It was for my own use."

"This makes you sound like the regional sales rep for a Cartegena Cartel. They say you were with Belle Crank, just before she died? They are implying that you were involved in her death!"

"It's a hit piece. They even quote LT's ex-wife."

"They do?" I said. I started riffling pages back to the beginning of the article. "What did she say?"

"That LT is compulsive something, I can't even pronounce it, and that he is an emotional batterer."

"What's that?" I said.

"I don't know," said Dickie, "they make it sound like he flies off the handle."

"All the time," I said. "He gets excited."

"They call it abusive."

"Here it is," I said and I read just a little bit of the third paragraph. "Geeeze! We can't let LT see this."

"Too late. Somebody left a stack of these down at the end of the driveway last night while you were out with Carrie. Mindy and Mandy found them when they came to pick me up and I put them in the recycle bin, but LT saw me and asked me what they were. I hadn't read them, so I just said somebody left a bunch of magazines on the driveway and I was throwing them out. LT and Teddy each took one. I wasn't here when they read the stuff about themselves. I didn't know about the hit piece until I came down to make the morning coffee."

"This makes him out to be some powerful Washington fixer with hired muscle," I said. "That would be us, Richard."

"I have a black belt," he said. You should have seen the look on his face. He was pleased to consider himself as hired muscle. It was touching. I almost said something to straighten him out, but the phone rang.

I was standing and he was sitting. I grabbed the phone to shut it up before it awakened the fixer. It was line two, not the business line.

"Lawton Close residence," I said.

"Is Dickie Douglas there?" said a male voice.

"I believe he may be," I said. "May I tell him who is calling?"

"Yes. It is his father."

"One moment, please." I pushed the hold button and showed Richard the hand set and said, "It's your dad."

He looked startled. It took him a moment to take it all in; father, phone, early morning, would like to speak to his son, Richard was that son, therefore ...

I never got to hear what was said because line one went off. Since Dickie had his paws wrapped around the kitchen phone, I sprinted for the office. I made it on the second ring.

"Lawton Close's office, may I help you?"

"Did you get the little stack of party favors I left on your driveway?"

"Dominic?"

"Yeah. Did you read about yourself?" said Dom Pancetta AKA Paul Williams.

"Aren't you supposed to just breathe hard or ask me what I'm wearing?" I said.

"I know what you are wearing," said Dom. "You are covered in shit."

"Did you talk to Roger Playless?" I asked him.

"He bought me lunch," said Mr. Pancetta. Then he made a rude remark and hung up at his end. I put the phone in its holder and I was just looking at it, waiting for a thought to come. I could feel it coming. It was making my face scrunch up with effort. It was a big thought and dark, like the first clouds of a dangerous frontal storm, but I never got to have it because line one on the phone went off again. Line two was still lit. Dickie was on with his dad. I had to answer it and risk one of LT's comments. I grabbed as the third ring was just starting,

"Yes?" I said into the phone. I wasn't in the right mood for phone manners.

"Is this Lawton Close's office?" said a deep voice I had never heard before.

"Yes, it is. How may I help you?"

"I am calling for Joseph K Larimee. I would like to set up a meeting with Mr. Close to discuss the possibility of his consulting on an extremely difficult matter."

"May I ask you how you heard about Mr. Close?" I asked.

"He seems to be getting quite a bit of publicity lately," said the unidentified caller.

"Most of it bad," I said.

"Yes. We need someone who will be ruthless on our behalf."

"You want a son-of-a-bitch," I said.

"Exactly," said the caller.

"Max! What are you doing to the phones!" said the son-of-a-bitch from the top of the stairs. "We are trying to *sleep!*"

19

BACK IN THE KITCHEN, DICKIE was still on the phone with his father. He was doing a lot of listening and very little speaking. When he saw me, he started wagging his finger at the refrigerator door. Someone had stuck a note on it with a piece of transparent tape. That was a novelty. LT doesn't allow items of any kind to "Mar the surface of the Frigidaire!" Such occurrences put him in such a bad frame of mind that it is never the time to remind him that the appliance is a SubZero. I plucked the note from the door and raised it into my limited field of focus. It was from Carrie.

"Dearest Enforcer," it read, "Rodd called – I have to go to the mansion.. Call me. Maybe I can hire your muscle later if it is free."

"If it is free," I muttered to myself, "you don't have to pay for it." I tore the incriminating evidence into little pieces and I put half of the pieces in the garbage can under the sink and the others in the garbage can in the pantry. If Teddy had seen the note, I would get a ration of teasing. I was thinking about Teddy when she padded into the room holding some cut flowers and she was humming. Her little brocaded bedroom slippers were leaving wet footprints across the stone tile. The hem of her bathrobe was wet. Teddy had been out to the cutting garden in the dew. She had taken LT's good scissors from his desk to cut flowers. There would be comments about that. I didn't want to be around when they were made.

"Maxine!" she said brightly. She calls me that every now and then. It goes back a couple of years. Someday I may tell you about it.

"Teddy," I answered. I kept it neutral, not like I was inviting conversation.

"Ooooh. Is the man of action testy today?" She was speaking in the baby talk voice she uses when she wishes to annoy her prey.

"You seem to be in a pretty good mood ... considering."

"I am. The sun is up. The sky is clear. And you know what?"

"What?" I waited.

She put down the flowers on the countertop, used her right hand to scrunch up my cheeks until my lips looked like blow fish lips. I let her play. "All the men in this house are having a kind of PMS. I think we eat too much chicken. It's full of female hormones. Did you know that?"

"I don't eat a lot of chicken," I said.

"Then I don't know what your excuse is. Where is Carrie? She was not in her room."

"Carrie has gone to work at the mansion."

"I would feel better if she got out of there," said Teddy."

"I have been trying to tell her to just quit," I said, "but you don't tell Carrie anything. You maybe suggest."

"Did you and Carrie have a fight last night?" she asked.

"I didn't think so. We ran into Dickie and his dates at ..."

"His dates?"

"The Minder twins. He went to school with them."

"That's why he stayed out all night?" she asked. Her eyebrows went up two notches. Both of us turned to Dickie, who stuck a finger in his free ear, frowned and turned his back on us. He then said "Uh huh," into the phone.

"Dickie stayed out all night?" I whispered. My brows rose as well.

Something buzzed in Teddy's robe pocket. She drew forth her cell phone and flopped it open, peered at the caller ID and then lifted the instrument to her ear. He robe fell open with the effort and I looked away. Sometimes Teddy is not completely and thoroughly covered with fabric under her robe. You never know.

I have never put my cell phone in my bathrobe pocket. For one thing, while I do own a bathrobe that Teddy gave me for Christmas, I have never worn it. For another thing, I don't even look for my cell phone until I have to leave the house, and even then, sometimes I don't bother.

"Hello?" she said,

There was a moment of silence while she received information and in that moment I heard Dickie say (keeping it low) "But I like it here."

Then Teddy said, "A full price offer? And has he accepted?" She listened to the answer and then continued, "Thanks! Maybe Lawton will get paid after all. See you at the club!"

She hung up. Then she looked off into nothing for a moment. Then she said, in a thoughtful voice, as if she might be considering if the loveseat would look better on the other side of the couch, "I am not speaking to Lawton just now." Then, as if a small cloud had moved on, she brightened up, turned her eyes to mine and said, "There is an O and A for Rodd's house. He came down to thirty eight. Did you speak with Lawton when you came in last night? Did he tell you about what the police found?"

"No. What did they find?"

"They found pornography on one of Rodd's computers that they took to search for evidence about Arlene."

"What kind of pornography? Weird stuff?"

"I think it's the normal male fantasy of earth mother chesticles and a free quick-lube with every fill up."

"So?" I said.

"I know. So what? But they are trying to make some kind of case about it. It would be odd if the sex and drug overlord didn't have pornography on his computer. Still, Rodd called while you were out and he was quite upset about it. He thinks Dominic Pancetta was using his computer to visit pornographic web sites."

"That makes sense," I said. "That may be one of the reasons Dom was in the security room when I drove Carrie home that night. The big server is in that room, or was until the cops hauled it out of there. But why does anyone care? It's not illegal. So what if the overlord of sex and drugs has dirty pictures on his home computer? Wouldn't it be a bigger deal if he didn't?"

"The fact that his wife is missing changes everything. This is going to hit the news cycle like a marinated steak on a hot grill. There will be a flare-up," said Teddy. "Anyway, Rodd Rock has given up the protections he enjoyed when he was part of the business. He's an outsider now. Since his wife went missing, he is off the reservation. He is the bear that has wandered down a suburban street in New Jersey just when school has let out. We all know what happens to them."

"LT is an outsider," I said.

"Not really. LT is all that is left of what used to be the crowd that ran things."

"You are part of that, too," I said.

"I guess you could say that. My grandfather on the Martin side owned the Cincinnati and Kentucky Railroad. My father went to Yale and had a law degree, but he never practiced after he got caught up in Wall Street. The Martins and the Smyths certainly had their innings."

"Your father was a Martin?"

"Yes. My mother was a Smyth; one of the Chicago Smyths, but she moved to New York to study art. That's where she met my father. She was still in school. I'm afraid he was a bit older."

"So you hyphenated."

"Yes. It was the fashion at the time, or a decade previous. I was in publishing for a while before I worked as an industrial designer. I thought hyphenated looked better on the masthead."

"You never got married?" I asked.

"I was engaged a lot."

"Who broke it off?"

"Usually me," she said. She shrugged.

"Why?"

"I don't know, claustrophobia. I grew up a little wild and very free and that puts some men off."

"How did you break up with your fiancés?"

"It depended on the schlump," she said.

"They can't all have been schlumps?"

"Oh, yes; they could have been and very likely, they were. But I was young and I am probably remembering it through what Lawton calls my myth system."

"Did you ever just disappear?" I asked.

"You mean to break it off with a schlump?"

"Yes. Did you ever seem to be having a good time and then just disappear?"

"Only once. I was moving anyway. He was a sad little schlump. He was nice, but needy. Believe me, a needy schlump is a full time occupation. No amount of assurance in the world is enough. I found I wanted to do other things than stoke his boilers to keep his steam up."

"Is Rodd Rock needy?" I asked.

"Terribly so," she said. "Worse than you."

"You think I'm needy?" I asked her. She was setting something up.

"Oh, god yes," she said, with entirely too much emphasis.

"I'm needy?" I said.

"Not as bad as Dickie."

"What do I need?"

"Some mothering, a little attention and a swift kick in the ass."

"Is Carrie needy?" I asked.

"No. She is a little unsure of herself at times, but that is not the same as needy."

"What about LT?" I said.

"What about him?"

"Is he a schlump?"

"LT? No. He's an eccentric."

"You knew him growing up, didn't you? You went to camp together?"

"Yes...camp...That's probably it."

"What's it?" I said.

"I loved camp. It got me out of my crazy household. It let me be me. At camp I was the best there was in sailing, and archery. I was a good runner in track. Lawton was there. He was runner-up in the biggest regatta of the summer. He understood better than anyone else how well I sailed to win. It was as if we could read each other's mind. He tried to cover a certain move I made, but I was too quick for him. He said something naughty that carried across the water to the whole camp. While I was basking in adulation, he was assigned KP. I believe he was peeling potatoes that would be mashed later for the victory dinner. Isn't that delicious?

"I had to stand on my chair in the dining hall while the entire camp applauded. My eyes searched him out while I was standing there. He made a face. I lost my heart.

"He was different even then. Maybe I stay with him because he is the last piece of my childhood and that happy time … hmmm …. maybe it is all just an association. Wouldn't that be funny?"

"Was he good at archery?" I said. I was trying to picture LT with taut bow string clawed to his cheek and his feet apart, pointing his arrow at a distant bull's-eye.

"Hopeless."

"Track?"

"Beyond hopeless."

"Arts and crafts?"

"All thumbs."

"Sailing?"

"He was a good sailor," she said. "If I had stayed home, he would have been the best. That may be part of the attraction. I beat him at his own game. I still can."

"Still can what?" said LT, as he entered through the archway.

"Beat the pants off of you sailing," said Teddy.

"I stand ready to make you regret that remark at a time and place of your choosing," he intoned.

"I shouldn't be speaking to you. We are not on speaking terms. But if you want to try me, how about now?"

"Now isn't good for me. Max? I need to see you for a moment in the summer office. Please bring your coffee."

"I don't have any," I said.

"Well, why don't you make some and bring me a cup," he said as he turned away and began to walk down the hall to the office.

"He couldn't just ask me to get him a cup of coffee," I said.

"No. He couldn't," said Teddy.

Dickie was still on the phone, so I got out the French press and a bag of LT's favorite beans. When I ground them up, Dickie turned around with the phone still stuck to his ear and made a face. What was I going to do about the noise? The boss-man-son-of-a-bitch needed his java. Beans would be ground into powder. Water would boil.

It took about eight minutes to get the tray ready. I carried our cups and the French press carafe to the office where I was greeted with a bleary eyed nod and a grunt of approval. When the boss man had his first mouthful of coffee, and had considered it for a moment and found it passable, he allowed it to trickle down into his gut. Then he was ready for business.

"I want you to go see Dom Pancetta at his office," he said.

"Why?"

"I want you to stimulate him."

"What for?"

"I want him to feel pressured," said LT.

"Why?" I asked him.

"It's a carom shot. I want to get at Mel Viktor. I want to flush him into the open. I want you to tell Dom that I intend to have him arrested for assault."

"Is that true?" I asked him.

"No. It's too late for that now, but he needn't know that. My sense of Dom is that he is a hothead. He will respond to the threat without thinking it through. He will imagine that I am just getting even with him for his childish escapade with Roger Playless. A cynical man is always looking for an excuse to enjoy his anxieties."

"You know you are playing with fire," I said.

"We control the match. It is his volatility that makes him vulnerable. I would like you to apply the lit match for me as I have other things to which I must attend," he said.

"What if he goes off while I'm next to him?"

"That's your call. I pay you to be the man-of-action. But I would caution you against standing too closely to Mr. Pancetta when you apply the match."

"What about John Gnotto? If he goes off, we are all in trouble."

"I'll take care of Mr. Gnotto. I have already spoken to him about Dominic Pancetta. I have got him to agree that Dom is a public relations catastrophe for the various Gnotto enterprises. I have made a little deal with Mr. Gnotto.

"I hope you know what you are doing."

"So do I," he said and then looked at his watch. I wish I had been more assured.

It didn't take me long to get to the parking lot in East Hampton. It took longer to find an available space. Walking up to the Paul Williams Security Group store front, I got the feeling that something was odd. It just didn't look right. For one thing, the front door was wide open and that is not a good look for a high end Hamptons security operation. Also there were a couple of cardboard boxes thrown down haphazardly in front of the open door and brochures were lying on the ground. As I got close enough to look in, I could see the receptionist coming out in the office.

"Hey!" I said to her. "What's going on?"

"I've lost my job, that's what's going on," she said. I would characterize her voice and body language as angry. "Paul has skipped out. You wouldn't believe the phone calls."

"Paul isn't here?" I asked. I heard her the first time; I just wanted it confirmed.

"I don't think so," she said with plenty of sarcasm.

"Where did he go? I have to meet with him."

"You think I know? Nobody knows. He *skip*...d out. You know? Like *not* here?"

"When did he first not show up?" I asked.

"Huh?" she said. She had come to a stop on the little sidewalk in front of the store front holding a box of personal effects. One of them was a photograph of her and Rodd Rock.

"When did you first realize that he had skipped out?"

"I don't know," she said. "When he didn't show up and the whole world was calling trying to talk to him and his voice mail filled up and I didn't know what to do with his messages."

"When was that?"

"He didn't come into the office yesterday at all."

"Did he call in?"

"Once, he told me he was going to be late and then he never came in,"

"How do you know he's gone?" I asked. "It's only been a day. Maybe he'll be in later."

"I don't think so," she said. "This morning the landlord and the sheriff came in to tell me I had to be out of here by the end of the business day. Paul hadn't paid his rent in three months."

"So you are taking everything out of here?" I asked.

"What I can fit in my car," she said.

"Are those boxes of customer records?" I asked, looking down at the sidewalk. One of the visible folders was marked "Receivables".

"Yeah," she said and started to walk around me to get to her car. I picked up a couple of boxes and began to follow her. "I'm keeping those until he makes good on my last paycheck. It bounced on me and the bank told me he closed out the business account."

"Where's your car?" I said.

"The white Civic," she said, pointing with her chin.

"Does he have a cell phone number?" I asked her.

"No answer, no message, I tried that," she said.

"What's going to happen to his customers?" I asked aloud, not expecting an answer.

"I don't know. Some of them are ready to kill him, especially his business partner."

"What's his name?" I asked.

"John Gnotto," she said.

That brought me up short. We both stopped. She looked at my face, as if there was something on it. I'm sure there was.

"Do you know Mr. Gnotto?" she asked.

"Yes," I said.

"It's funny about him," she said. "Paul would never let me mention his name. Whenever they had a meeting, Paul had to go into the city on the Jitney. He must be a very busy man, and important."

"Oh yeah. He's both," I said.

"Maybe I'll call him and tell him he better make good on my paycheck, or I will raise hell."

"You could do that if you wanted," I said, "but I wouldn't."

"Why not?"

"Have you ever heard of the Gnotto alleged crime family?" I said.

"I don't know, maybe. Does he have something to do with that?"

"He's the head of it…allegedly," I said.

"Why does everyone always say allegedly?" she said. "What does that really mean?"

"In this country a man is innocent until proven guilty especially if the man will kill you for saying otherwise."

"So I shouldn't ask him for my money?"

"Ask him whatever you want," I said, "But be nice and don't expect to get it. And say thank you when you don't."

We were at her car. I handed over the boxes. She said "Thanks for the help." That was the end of Paul Williams Security Group.

There were more endings to come.

My cell phone went off just as I was turning around to back out of my parking spot. I put the car in Park and flipped out the phone.

"Yeah?"

"It's me," said LT.

"I was just going to call you. Paul Williams has disappeared. His store front is abandoned and he had a silent partner, guess who?"

"I don't care. I have to tell you something."

"John Gnotto," I told him.

"What about him?" he asked.

"He's the silent partner."

"I see," he said. He did, too. Things were coming together quickly. "I can't say I am surprised. But listen to me,"

What's up?" I asked.

"I would like you to drive to Atlantic City," he said.

"When?"

"Now," he said, "while they are still on the scene."

"Who?" I asked him. "What scene?"

"Tyrell just called. He has heard from one of his friends at the precinct house that the body of Mel Viktor has been discovered in a parking lot near the airport in Atlantic City. The investigators haven't arrived yet. I want you there before they move the body if you can do it."

"LT! If I drive at a hundred, that's still three hours."

"See what you can do. I've spoken to a sergeant Quinlan. He knows you are coming."

"What if I get popped for speeding?" I asked. I really didn't want to go to AC.

"Use your card. It cost me enough," he said.

"What if I burn up the Caddy?" I asked.

"What are you still doing there?" was his answer. "Call me from the scene," he said and then the phone connection ended.

Poop and turds.

I backed, pointed the big midnight blue snout of the Caddy towards the Montauk Highway and stepped on the gas, a lot of it.

20

I ONLY GOT PULLED OVER once. It was in New Jersey. I showed him the get-out-of-jail-free card and he frowned. Of course he had to let me go, but he asked the name of the chief who issued it. I told him. Then he nodded to himself, bit his lip and kept the card. They do that sometimes. They must have their reasons. "Drive safely and have a nice day," was all he said as he turned his back and walked slowly back to his police car. I was free to go, but without LT's magic card. I kept the speed at 85 the rest of the way.

I didn't have any trouble finding the parking lot near the airport because of the number of official vehicles. Only a few of them had their flashers going, They must have been among the first on the scene. It wasn't much of a scene. It was just a large unused parking area near an abandoned factory of some kind. Nature had begun her slow rehabilitation of the premises for her own purposes. She put up weeds and creeping vines as a construction fence while she began the demolition of the pavement with grass and weeds. It was going slow, but she didn't seem to care. Time, she had.

There was a lot of bother getting in to the scene because the uniformed officer in charge of keeping out the public had been given a task that suited his intelligence. The smart people were poking around the crime scene trying to find out what had happened. I wouldn't call the gate keeper a stooge, but he was no Marx Brother, either. It took a cell phone call to LT, who called someone in New York, who called someone in A.C., who called someone at the scene who could make decisions, who delegated someone to go over to the entrance and tell the task master to let me through – and he argued about it! I didn't see a promotion in his future. Still, I gave him a good natured nod as I passed by him. He looked sideways at my nod, as if he suspected my motives.

I've seen some bodies. Some bodies look like they had just gone to sleep for a moment. Other bodies are so damaged that it is hard to tell what they had been. Sometimes clothing is the best indication that the thing, or pile of things, had once been a human being who could have liked a beer and maybe watched Wheel of Fortune.

About the only way you could tell it was Viktor was the boots. The last time I had seen them, they were on a desk and Viktor was full of emotions and schemes and himself. Now all of those things had been drained out of him and what was left was rotten. They were just about to put him in the bag when I got there. The guy at the head nodded down, indicating I should follow where his eyes were pointing so I could see what was left of Mel's face.

"Geeeze!" I said with a shudder, "what did that?"

"It looks like he was shot in the face at close range, probably twenty or so times, maybe more," said a guy in a badly fitting suit next to me.

"Why?" I asked.

"How the hell should I know?" said the guy in the suit. "Ask the guy who did it." I have cleaned up his expressions. The same old four letter words have lost their shock value and I'm getting tired of hearing them (and writing them) all the time.

"Who is that?" I asked.

"How the hell should I know! We just got here!"

"Who discovered the body?" I asked.

"What hell are you? A reporter?" said the guy in the suit.

"I'm from New York," I said.

"Oh! Hey! Everybody! Listen up here! We got a guy from Nu Yawk here, so …" he shouted it out. Nobody paid him much attention. I decided not to ask any more questions until I could find a human being.

They wrapped up the body and slid it into the back of the morgue van. I didn't watch it leave. A number of officials left soon after Mel. The rest stayed behind to write things and look for shell casings and mark out possible items of interest. They had marked quite a few items, but I didn't see anything that interested me. I found a young guy with a nice face and approached him. He was drinking coffee.

"How ya doing?" I said.

"OK," he said. There was no smile, but a pleasant tone.

"Where'd you get the coffee?" I asked.

"You want some?" he said pushing the cup at me. "It's cold."

"No, thanks," I said.

"There's a Dunkin down the street," he said with his thumb pointing the way. For a brief moment, I thought he was talking about an incident of some kind.

"Thanks," I said. If he was willing to share his cold coffee, maybe he would share some information.

"What have they got here?" I asked.

"The victim is some guy from New York named Mel Viktor. Viktor the vic. To the Viktor belongs the spoils, but this Vic is spoiled and no one belongs to him no more. He had a nice girlfriend and then somebody beat him and then put some rounds in his face. They dumped him here."

"How did you identify the vic?" I asked. I used his term because I was on his turf.

"His girlfriend reported him missing. He never came back to his room."

"How did they make the ID?"

"The girlfriend. We had a hell of a time tracking her down. Her boyfriend is laid out in a parking lot with his face shot off and she's in Trump's at the blackjack table."

"How did she take it?"

"She was pretty upset."

"Like she was shocked upset?" I asked him.

"You know, upset. But she had had a few drinks."

"Starting pretty early," I said.

"Yeah. Well. This is Atlantic City. Nice looking, though. I wouldn't mind buying her a drink."

"Did he have ID?"

"No he was clean before they dumped him. No money, no cards, no ID."

"Robbery?" I asked.

"That would be one hell of a robbery. They shot his face off."

"They? More than one?" I asked.

"Who knows?" he said.

"What if it isn't Mel Viktor?" I asked. I was just thinking aloud.

"What if it isn't?" he said. "Then it would somebody else."

"What I mean is, why shoot someone's face off unless you want to make it hard to ID the body?"

"Anything is possible," he said.

"You live here?" I asked him.

"I got a condo unit in Brigantine," he said.

"Have you ever heard of Mel Viktor?" I asked.

Two Masks

"He was some guy from New York. I hear he was a player."

"How do you mean that?" I asked him. Some people use the term to mean somebody who can pull strings, but we were standing in Atlantic City.

"He liked gaming," said the cop.

"Did he win or lose?" I asked.

"Does this look like winning?" he said to me and then raised his eyebrows.

"Naw," I said. "But did he have a reputation for losing big?"

"What they tell me is that Mel Viktor liked to drop a couple of hundred gees just to get the blood flowing. Then he could concentrate on losing some real money."

"So his room and meals were comped?" I wondered aloud.

"This guy was a player. They probably paid for his plane ticket."

I thanked him and walked off a couple of paces to call LT.

"Yes?" he said.

"Is that any way to answer a phone?" I asked.

"What did you find?"

"It's probably Mel Viktor. His face was obliterated. He's been dead for 8 or 9 hours, maybe more. There were no shell casings at the scene, no muss, no fuss so the speculation here is that he was killed elsewhere and dumped here. His girlfriend got tired of waiting for him to come back to their room, so she called in a missing person report. When they tracked her down to ID the body, she was having drinks at the blackjack table before noon. Apparently Mel was a problem gambler. He liked to lose big numbers. Maybe he lost more than he could afford this time?"

"Well, of course he did," said LT.

"Why do you say that?" I asked.

"Because this time he lost his life."

"Oh, yeah. There's nothing much to see down here. I don't know why I came."

"If you had to guess," said LT (and he never asks me to guess because he doesn't believe in guessing) "what are we dealing with here?"

"It sure looks like Mel ran into some trouble in Atlantic City."

"I'm being serious," said LT. "What is your impression?"

"My impression? This looks like Mel lost some money to the wrong people. Whoever they were, they didn't act like professionals. But maybe that's the point? Dickie talks a lot about disinformation. Why would you shoot a guy in the face twenty times?"

"To conceal his identity?" said LT. "To make it impossible to match dental records?"

"Yeah, OK. I get that. But then why leave his boots on? They were handmade, one of a kind and easily traced. That makes it look like amateurs."

"What's your point?" said LT.

"Either it was done by amateurs or by professionals wanting to look like amateurs," I said,

"Which leaves it open in your mind to anyone and everyone. That's not helpful."

"I'm just saying … You don't think this is about Rodd's missing twenty million, do you?"

"I am sure it is in some way related," said LT.

"You don't think Rodd had someone …" I started to say. He cut me off.

"Stop it! I forbid you to indulge in idle speculation! Get me facts!"

"There's nothing else to see here. I'm just wasting my time and your money."

"Hang around until at least dinnertime. See if you can get to the girl friend. Find out anything you can about Mr. Viktor's last hours."

"All right. I'll do what I can, but don't expect me to find much."

"Anything is better than nothing."

The girl friend was depressingly easy to find. I got her name from my new buddy with the cold coffee. I got her picture from the Internet at the Tropicana Hotel online room where I paid way too much money per minute to prowl the net. She showed up in a number of pictures relating to the separation of Mel Viktor and his wife. I knew she was staying at Trump's Casino and I found her back at the blackjack table with a fresh drink and a nice pile of chips.

"Are you winning?" I asked.

She turned her face to me and I could see she had been crying. She was no knockout, but her body was worth a head turn. She knew how to show it off. When she turned her face to me, she was going to tell me to screw off, you could see it coming. But then she saw me, her face changed and she said, "I'm up on the table, but I've just lost my boyfriend."

"Oh," I said. But then I remembered, I was not supposed to know, so I said, "You have a fight?"

"No. He passed," she said. Then she peeked at her down card. It was an 8. She had a 10 showing.

"He's no longer with us?" I asked.

"No."

"Was he sick?" I asked.

"No. I don't want to talk about it."

The dealer had nineteen. She didn't watch the chips go. She was fingering the chips she had left.

"You staying here?" I asked.

"No. I'm booked on a flight to Islip at six. I'm just killing some time."

"Really? I'm staying in East Hampton for the summer."

"I have a place in Southampton," she said.

"Hey, I have a car here. I'm driving back in a few minutes, you want a ride?"

"I don't know you," she said. She wasn't being coy. She wasn't about to accept a ride from a stranger. I thought maybe I could make myself less strange.

"My name is Max Kelly. I'm working for Rodd Rock, he was the lead singer of the Lobes. Remember him?"

"You're kidding! My boyfriend was his manager!"

"Mel? Your boyfriend is Mel Viktor? You don't mean that something has happened to Mel? I saw him last week at the castle. He was in great shape!"

"He's passed."

"Oh! What happened?"

"I don't want to talk about it. OK?"

"Oh, man! This is terrible. Mel is gone! Does Rodd know?"

"It just happened, I mean, I just found out. They don't know when it happened. He left the room while I was getting dressed last night for dinner. He was taking me to some expensive place, but he said he had to see a guy and then …."

"Then what?" I asked.

There was a long pause. She shrugged but didn't say anything. I moved my head around to see her face. The tears were coming. I backed off. The dealer gave her a down card and then an ace. She didn't look at her hole card. The dealer asked her what she wanted to do. She lifted the hidden card and saw that it was a jack. "Blackjack." She said and flipped the cards over. Then she started crying.

"Come on," I said. I took her hand and lifted her up. "You shouldn't be traveling alone. I'll give you a ride."

She didn't resist. I took her chips and flipped a couple at the dealer who rolled her eyes at me. I don't know what she meant by that. I just smiled.

While she got her things from her room, I called LT and told him I was on the way home with Mel Viktor's girl friend Charlynne. He grunted. He started to tell me that it was more important to stay near the cops and find out what they were finding out about the shooting, but he could find out anything he wanted with a single phone call to Tyrell's contact Quinlan. Then he said "Do what you think best, but be very careful of a needy woman in shock. I don't need any complications at the moment and neither do you. Call Carrie."

I called her next and just said I was driving home. I said I would miss dinner. She said she would wait up.

Mel's girlfriend's name was Charlynne Yost. She was from Astoria, Queens, originally, but had moved to Manhattan where she worked as a secretary for a European bank. She met Mel at a party in the Hamptons. She and some friends had rented a group home in Hampton Bays to be close to the action, Apparently she found some. She got her first tattoo and met Mel the same day. The tattoo was small and in good taste, she assured me. I couldn't say the same about Mel.

A month later, he set her up with a little place of her own in Shinnecock Hills overlooking the bay. It was small, but private. He talked about marriage when the thing with his wife was settled. She wanted kids. She would now have to make other arrangements.

Charlynne slept or pretended to sleep for an hour or so. She didn't say much until we were well north of Atlantic City. When we hit some heavy traffic near Strawfield, New Jersey, she sat up and opened up a little. The only thing I leaned that we could use was that Mel owed a lot of people money and that his wife had been tying up a lot of his liquid assets. This had put Mel in a bind. He had called the trip to Atlantic City a business trip. He spent hours at a time away from the room. He told her to go shopping and she did (the Caddy trunk was filled with the fruits of her foraging) but she got bored with shopping and had started playing blackjack. She did OK.

As we got close to the city, she sat up suddenly and looked for what appeared to be a compact case in her bag. Then she turned her back to me and bent down toward the seat. When she sat up straight again after a minute of fidgeting with something, she seemed wide awake. She began working her hands through her hair with quick strokes. I didn't see it, but I was pretty sure she had just treated herself to a wake up snort of the devil's own powder.

"How are you doing?" I asked her. "You want to stop for something?"

"No, thanks. I have to get back to house. I have to feed my cat,"

"Has somebody been looking after it?" I asked.

"Yes, but I told her I would be home tonight."

"Do you want to call anybody?" I said. "You can use my phone."

"I have mine. I don't want to talk to anybody right now. I think I have to let everything sink in a little."

"You must be still in shock," I said.

"I guess. It hasn't really hit me yet."

"Are the police involved in ... whatever happened?"

"Yes. They called me to let me know."

"Do they suspect foul play?" I asked her. I was trying to find a better term for murder, but all my brain came up with was the slightly formal "foul play.". It's a silly term, but handy at times.

"He was shot," she said.

"Oh." I said. Then there was a long quiet period. Then she said, "You don't think it will ever happen to someone you know."

"No, you don't," I said. She didn't offer any more information and I couldn't think of anything to ask.

When we got to her place, she said, "I'd invite you in, but ... you know."

I did. We shook hands.

21

"So what do you think?" I said to LT. I set his coffee in front of him. He looked at it with an appraising eye, noted that it was the desired color and the cup (not mug) was filled to the desired imaginary line and then he went back to his newspaper. A dead cigar, only half consumed, sat at a crazy angle in the Stork Club ashtray he inherited from his father. The story of how it was stolen from the club is one that LT likes to tell when he has had enough drinks to grease his tongue bearings.

"About what?" he said. He raised a single eyebrow.

"Mel Viktor's girlfriend is a coke-head. The way these things work, that means that Mel was probably a coke-head. So there is that whole drug world overlay stretched over this project. In the music business, drugs are not unknown. I understate for comic effect. Now, Dom Pancetta goes missing. He was once arrested for a couple of murders they couldn't make stick. We know what he is capable of. He's employed by Rodd Rock for security. Mel Viktor, who has taken twenty or so million dollars from Rodd winds up in a parking lot having eaten so much lead his teeth fall out. This happens on the same day that Dom goes missing. John Gnotto is Dom's silent partner. You would call that suggestive."

"It is. However, it is probably coincidence," he said blandly. I don't think he knew what he was saying. I looked at the coffee to see if any of Dickie's peyote buttons had floated to the top.

"You hate coincidence!" I countered.

"I hate taxes as well, but they still happen," he said. "I had a rather distressing phone call from Mr. Gnotto this morning. He was deeply upset to hear about Mel. I'm afraid he questioned my professional abilities. He expressed concern that I might have lost control of events."

"What did you tell him?" I asked.

"I said that Mel Viktor was the one who had lost control. In the end, his manipulations were futile and all the more desperate for that. His ego was such that he imagined he could continue dissembling indefinitely, that no one would ever catch on. Two of us were not fooled.

"Who is that?" I asked.

"Me and his killer."

"Who killed him?"

"We don't know yet, but I suspect the police will soon be able to tell us."

"Why do you suspect that?"

"Apparently there were a number of security cameras in the Casino parking lot. They have them everywhere these days."

"What about the kidnappers?"

"There were none," said LT blandly.

"Is that something you know, or something you suspect?"

"I am convinced of it. Mel made up the kidnappers to try to get me to release large amounts of cash for his own use."

"To pay off the person who killed him?"

"That is what I believe."

"So you are responsible for his death in a way."

"No. He is responsible for his death. He did not understand the world he thought he was manipulating."

"What about Gnotto?"

"I am not sure he was entirely mollified, but he is a realist. We shall see."

"Oh, great. Is there anyone who isn't angry with us?"

"You can add one to the list, two actually," he said to me, grimly.

"Wonderful, we need more enemies. Who are they?"

"I've sent the Mini-Cooper back to the showroom. The salesman called. I think he is annoyed that he won't be getting his commission."

"You said there were two?"

"Teddy isn't happy about it," he said. Then he hefted his coffee cup, poised it beneath his lower lip and sucked off some of the potentially scalding fumes to test the temperature.

"Well, if Teddy wants a Mini, she can afford her own Mini," I said.

"That's what I told her," he said with a miniature nod. Then he tilted the cup and allowed a small leak of coffee to enter his pursed lips. I had to look away.

"You don't like the Mini-Cooper?" I said, looking at the bookshelves.

"It's a fun car. I thought I would like it, but I can't have a fun car. Perception is four fifths of marketing."

"You need a car with gravitas," I said. He had put the cup down, as if it contained unstable nitroglycerine.

"Yes. Please don't use the word gravitas in my presence. It is a word used by the pompous to describe the self-important, but yes, I do."

"So…what are you looking at? A Hummer?" I asked.

"This is not the time for a Humvee. I'm not sure there ever was such a time. A lawyer in a Humvee is like an older man who publicly dates young girls."

"So?"

"I looked at a Crown Victoria," he said. His gaze shifted to a spot above my head. "But it seemed like an undercover car or a cab."

"Yeah." A Crown Vic is much too official for an eccentric back-room fixer surrounded by hired muscle.

"Same with the full sized Chevy," he said. "The Lincoln is well proportioned, but I would I look like I drove people to the airport as a sideline. So this afternoon I am picking up an Audi A8."

"All right! A *real* car!" I said. I was too enthusiastic. LT is the type who might change his mind if someone is too enthusiastic about a choice he has made. He views other people's enthusiasm with suspicion and distaste. He is prone to nearly violent enthusiasms of his own, of course.

"It seems to be well made, commodious, quiet and I am assured it will retain some of its value, as it should, since it is not inexpensive. I think it has a certain panache."

"I don't know what that means, but the car can move," I said. I was smiling. This was the one bright spot of news on a very dark horizon.

"You will treat it with respect," he said with a wagging finger of rebuke. "I don't want you abusing it. I fully expect you to drive it with consideration during the break-in period."

"Cars don't have break-in periods anymore -- real cars."

"I spoke with Gunter at Sunderland Restorations and he said to break the car in properly and that's what we are going to do."

"What color?"

"Dark blue, of course. What else could you imagine?" he said. Then he wrapped a thumb and fore finger around the cup handle and prepared to hoist.

"Not red, I guess."

"In the meantime we have some things to do with the Rodd Rock business," he said and then sipped.

"What's going on with Rodd? The project appears to be a complete loser."

"This project has been unusually messy. I have never, in my entire career at law, been involved with such a messy group of people. One might be happy to salvage some ragged remnant of professional dignity and what is left of one's reputation. I am thinking of abandoning Mr. Rock to his colorful milieu. Let them all sort themselves out."

"You want to fire the client? In the middle of a project?"

"It seems to be going nowhere."

"What about Arlene?"

"She'll turn up," he said calmly as he turned over his hand and pretended to inspect it.

"Why do you say that?" I asked. LT was talking crazy talk. I had never seen him like that.

"I have reached the limits of what I can do," he said. "I can not do that which can not be done. One of the most difficult things to understand about life is that there are things, and persons that cannot be fixed."

I stared at him. "What about Arlene's parents?" I said.

"Those poor people. My heart goes out to them. It really does."

"But they are your clients as well!" I said. His attitude was making me frustrated and impatient.

"Yes. I owe them, and will provide for them a full accounting of my activities on their behalf and what we have learned in the process."

"What *have* we learned?" I asked.

"That the media has become a power unto itself."

"Wait! People are dead and missing around here! Maybe Rodd did it! What does the media have to do with it?"

"Perception is everything," said LT. Then he sat back with a smug look on his face.

"I don't know what that means. Let's say Rodd had his wife … removed by … let's say, a carting service," I said. "Doesn't he deserve representation in both the courtroom and in the courtroom of public opinion? I'm just asking, because I would love it if you dumped him as a client. I would love to get Carrie out of there. He called her this morning to come in early because he's having some things moved to storage, mostly Arlene's things. I don't think Rodd gets the whole thing about public opinion."

"No. For a man in the public eye, Rodd has some very odd ideas about how to play to the public sensibilities. Now before I cast off the last remaining stern line tying us to the flaming wreckage of Rodd Rock's rapidly sinking career, I have to asses a small threat posed by Rodd Rock's bodyguard Marcus O'Brien. He has been overheard threatening some horrible revelation that he claims will be the end of Rodd Rock. The bodyguard was at the concert the night Arlene disappeared. He was not there when the concert ended and he did not accompany Rodd to the after-party as he always does and indeed, is paid to do. I want to know what he saw that night and what he is threatening to reveal. It may be critical. Before I cut us free from Mr. Rock, I have to know what his bodyguard is holding onto."

"He's a bodyguard," I said.

"That's right."

"He's five times my size."

"Yes?" said LT. He seemed genuinely puzzled.

"I'm not going to beat it out of him," I said.

"I should hope not. That's all this office needs is an assault and battery charge."

"How the hell am I going to get him to hand over his meal ticket?"

"Use your wits," said LT. Then he reached again for his coffee. I could tell that he thought there was nothing more to say.

"He's not going to tell me anything. Why would he?"

"I have every confidence in your ability. You will size up the situation and act accordingly. I have spoken to him. He is expecting you to meet him at the house at one thirty."

"He's expecting me? To come and pump him for his big secret?"

"I'm afraid I may have left in his mind the impression (however vague) that I am representing a publishing concern who is interested in one of those quickly produced best sellers that come out while scandal is still stinking and hasn't skinned over. He may have inferred the possibility of appearing on the David Letterman show to promote the book. You should take the tape recorder."

"I haven't seen the tape recorder in five years."

"I found it in the hall closet. Dickie is putting batteries in it. It's just for show."

"So the guy thinks you are selling out your client for a book deal?" I asked.

"Apparently he moves in circles where such disloyalty is not unthinkable."

"And you trust this character to come across with hard information, to me? Why?"

"You are on a reconnaissance mission. I just want an idea of what he has to retail. It's the last threat I can see. If we can neutralize him, we should be able to close this whole operation down."

"Are you going out on a limb there, a little?"

"I don't believe so. I will be much more at ease after you have spoken to the bodyguard."

"I don't have much hope, but I'll give it a shot," I said.

"Pun noted. Come straight back here when you are done. Things are in motion."

"What things?" I asked.

"Nothing that concerns you at present."

"You are not setting up one of your stunts, are you?"

"No stunts. I am merely maneuvering my forces," he said.

"That's what Custer said."

"He didn't know where the hostiles were. I am attempting to pinpoint them. You are going to be late."

I went.

I drove the Caddy. It wasn't like there was a choice. I was looking forward to the new Audi. I'm not a German car kind of guy, but I like to drive a well-made car and the Germans seem to know how to build them better than we do. Although not for nothing, you should check the reliability reports before you buy one. You might be surprised. You might even be shocked.

When I got to the house, the gate was closed. I called Carrie on my mobile phone. She didn't answer. I left a message. I called Rodd Rock's secret number. Rodd answered.

"Yes?"

"Hi. It's Max. I'm at the gate."

"I can't see you now, I'm in the middle of something."

"LT said I was supposed to talk to Marcus."

"Why?"

"I don't know. I'm supposed to talk to all of your staff, remember?"

"I'll send him out. Stay by the gate."

I wasn't going anywhere. While I sat, a news guy wandered slowly over to the car and asked me who I was. I told him I was the rat catcher. He asked if there were rats at Rodd's mansion. I looked at him hard for a second and said to myself, what the hell, and then I started describing rats that rode out from the city on the undersides of delivery trucks. The rats were almost as big as a man and had little beady eyes and had majored in communication and journalism. It took him a long time to catch on. He thought for a minute he was going to make some notes about the infestation of mega rats. A little file footage, a bubonic plague scare, a rock and roll millionaire and you got your lead story for the eleven o'clock news. When he got the joke, he said something uncomplimentary and wandered off.

Marcus came out of a small hinged grating cut out of big iron gate. When he opened it, the comedy mask swung out into the sunshine and glared gold flecks of light on the Caddy's old sandblasted windshield. Then he nodded to me and started over to the car.

I had actually seen Marcus play when he was with the Giants. He lasted two years. He wasn't that good and neither were the Giants in those days. A friend of mine who lost some money on them called them the Gi-runts. While Marcus was in the national eye, some bright promoter got the idea of having him make a rap video. It was called "I'm going to make your hip hop." It was a novelty thing. I guess Marcus took it seriously because he quit football to become an entertainer. He wasn't much better at rapping than he was as an offensive lineman. He made the usual TV appearances, had his hit and his 12 minutes of fame, and the next thing anyone knows, he is a hanger-on at the Rodd Rock mansion and people refer to him as a bodyguard.

"Hey, Max," he said. He flipped his head back in a quick up-nod.

"Hey, Marcus. Get in. We'll drive somewhere and talk."

He opened the door, looked for a moment at the seat to make sure there was enough of it to hold him, then he began to merge butt first with the automobile. The Caddy listed violently to his side. He must have weighed three hundred pounds. He was wearing the same outfit he had on at the concert. He also had some serious looking tattoos on his upper arms. He smelled like … I wasn't sure what.

"Are you wearing aftershave?" I asked.

"Yeah. Some stuff from France. Rodd gave it to me."

"Carrie said he also gave you a Boxster. You keep it here?"

"No. I like the car, but I have to lose some weight."

I started the engine and backed.

"Where to? You want to go to the beach?" I said.

"Naw. Let's go to Starbucks. I have to get me some lah-tay."

I reached behind me and grabbed the tape recorder and put it on my lap. I pressed some buttons and hoped that he didn't look close enough to see that the wheels were not turning behind the smoked plastic cover. He certainly noticed the act, but he didn't seem to care one way or the other.

"OK. So how did you meet Rodd Rock?" I asked.

"Mel Viktor introduced us. Poor Mr. Viktor. Sad about what happened to him. Do the cops know who did it yet?" he said and then he looked at me real hard. I got the tingle.

"Where were you when he was shot?" I asked. I hadn't planned to ask him anything like that.

"I was out," he said. I waited for more, but there wasn't going to be any more than that.

"You didn't like Mel Viktor?" I tried.

"He was part of my management team. He got me to record my hit single at Rodd's studio in New York. It was on the charts for three months. Did you see me on Leno?"

"Yeah," I lied. I don't know. Maybe I did. I saw him on TV doing his hit. He moved well for a big man. It might have been MTV.

"So what happened with your singing career?" I asked him.

"The money ran out and I couldn't afford to buy another hit song. I don't write music. You have to pay for that."

"Where did the money go?" I was pretty sure some of it went into Mel Viktor's pocket.

"The usual place. Mel told me they had to deduct for the studio time, the bus rental, and the sound system for the tour, and for this and that, and they deducted out everything so that at the end of that year they said I owed them two hundred and fifty thousand dollars for my hit single."

"Did you pay them?"

"With what? Pay them? Let me ask you," he said.

"What?"

"Do I look like a fool?"

"I don't think so. You scared the crap out of the Miami Dolphins."

"Yeah," he said and chuckled at the memory. "There was a guy on the Pats who hated to see me on the other side of the line of scrimmage. I could talk some trash in those days."

We both smiled at our memories of games gone past.

"You get respect from the brothers in that outfit?"

"No. This is for the suburban kids. I don't see many of the brothers out here in the Hamptons, or on the road. The people out here think I look menacing and that's what it's all about. That's what I get paid for."

"So what happened to all the money from the New York Giants? What about the per diems and the signing bonus and the rest of it? You must have had a couple a million dollars per season," I asked him.

"It's funny about the money. The government helped themselves to a lot of damned money. Mel Viktor helped himself to some of the money. That man just had sticky hands, may he rest in the eternal peace of the Lord. Money just seemed to stick to his hands. Everybody's money. I hate to speak ill of the dead, but that man had some sticky-ass hands. Then there was the entourage. You know what an entourage is?"

"Yeah."

"Well, I had one. I'd like to know where the damned entourage is today, that's what I'd like to know. Let me tell you this. If you hit the lottery, or if some old rich guy leaves you his fortune, the thing you have to watch out for is your entourage. You have a little bit too much to drink, and you find yourself asleep someplace, and then when you wake up, your entourage has grown in the night. An entourage likes to grow when you're not looking. And it likes to eat! An entourage can eat, and it don't like no fast food. You can't get by with a case of malt liquor and some wings, hell no. The entourage is fixing to throw down some filet mignon. Let me ask you."

"What?"

"Do you like the taste of champagne?"

"It's OK," I said. "I can take it or leave it."

"Me too. I can take it or leave it, but the entourage can't leave it, any of it. The entourage is all about cham-pagne. It costs a lot of money to keep an entourage happy. The entourage likes to go out to the club and sit in the VIP area and score some shit from some damned undocumented hustler. That's what the entourage likes to do." He fell silent.

I stopped for a red light. I put on my left-turn blinker. There was a chance I could sneak through on the next green, but it would be a while.

"So Mel Viktor got his sticky hands on some of the money?" I asked him.

"That man didn't like to let you see the books. Mel Viktor talked so fast that light couldn't catch up with his words. He always left you in the dark. The more he talked the darker it got and the less you knew. That man could talk. Mel Viktor got a lot of my damned money. When I needed some money to go back in the studio he wouldn't give me any. He wouldn't even lend it to me."

"So Rodd Rock gave you a job?"

"That's right. There was an incident with a stalker and Rodd called me up. He asked me if I would stay in his house and keep an eye on things, kind of look after him and Arlene. That's what I did, or at least that's what I used to do. Now the house is being sold and soon they will be moving everything out. He's not going to need a bodyguard one way or the other."

"What do you mean, one way or the other?"

"Either he's going to end up in jail or broke and turned out in the street. I have to think about my own situation."

"So, you must know what goes on at the house. You live in."

"For the past four years I lived in that house. I have seen things. Rodd Rock still has his entourage. He didn't have just one hit, he has a whole wall of gold records and platinum records and if they give out diamond records he's got some of them, too. So he can afford to keep the entourage happy, at least for a little while. But Mr. Rodd Rock has his troubles and there's only one thing that costs more money than an entourage."

"An ex-wife?" I asked.

"Well, then, two things. I was thinking about lawyers. Rodd has got three different dream teams. He has lawyers for the missing money and he has lawyers for his ex-wife cause she's got lawyers to get her share of his money and he's paying for them, too, so that's like four sets of lawyers and he's got this mess about Arlene and he's got your boss. He's got more teams than the NFL."

"Rodd lives a complicated life," I said.

"You can say that again. I have a lot of stories. I could write a book."

"It would probably be a best seller. You talked a little to my boss about some stories."

"That's right. It's pay or play time for Mr. Rodd Rock."

"What's the deal? If he pays, you are not going to publish? If you decide not to publish, where does that leave us?"

"Let me ask you," he said.

"What?"

"Do I look like executive material to you?"

"What do you mean?" I asked.

"Look at my face. Look at my arms. Look at all this tattoo shit. Do you see me walking into a business meeting with a briefcase? And what are all the other executives going to be saying, 'hey dog, word! Keeping it real. We bout to bust a move on General Electric?' You see any of that happening?"

"You didn't grow up in the projects. You're no home boy. The Giants drafted you out of the University of Colorado. You graduated. I know from reading about you that you grew up in Illinois and that your mother worked for the post office. She was a manager of some kind."

"That's right. She's retired now and lives in Boca."

"So what's all this gang banger paraphernalia?"

"It's my uniform. That's the thing. It's like football, it's about intimidation. You know people put on their game face 'cause you got to get respect. It's the same when you're a bodyguard."

"I don't know. The guys that guard the president, they wear suits," I said.

"They can afford to wear suits. They have fire power. I can't legally carry because of a prior."

"Conviction?" I asked.

"How do you spell fell oh knee?"

"When you were a kid?" I asked.

"Hell, no. One night after a personal appearance in Oakland I was driving the entourage in my white Escalade, man I loved that car, and some one was fooling around with my piece and it went off."

"Anybody hurt?"

"No, but some brothers in a Caprice decided to check us out," he said.

"Undercover?"

"I guess they were. And they brought in the dogs and the entourage was carrying all kinds of shit and they took my piece and they took the Escalade."

"They impounded it?"

"They just took it. They said it was used in the commission of a felony. My lawyers said to let them have it. They cooked a deal so I didn't have to do any time and they kept it out of the papers. But I have a record now. I can't vote. I can't do most anything. All I can do is look mean and crazy. And to tell the truth some times I feel mean and crazy."

That brought us to Starbucks. I powered down the big Caddy V-8 and we got out, slammed our doors and started walking to the door of the coffee vendor. As I walked along beside Marcus I could see the way people reacted to his look. He knew how to use his body and his game face. He could part the Red Sea just by scowling at it. New Yorkers don't give way easily, but they tripped over themselves making room for Marcus as he came through the door. And I have to say, I enjoyed it. If I ever needed a bodyguard I would call him. That's when I got the idea. I couldn't tell him about it until after we had grabbed our lattes and he had bagged up a couple of pounds of pastries. I paid for everything. He didn't say a word about it and didn't make a move to his pocket. Once we were back outside in the bright Hamptons sun I opened up the subject.

"Marcus, I have to level with you."

"Uh oh. That can't be good," he said. I sensed a lifetime of disappointment behind the tone of his voice. He had been built up and let down many times and it showed in his reaction.

"What would you say if I told you that there is no book deal?"

"No Letterman?"

"No Letterman," I said.

"Shit."

"But I think there should be a book deal."

"What are you saying?"

"You have a real story to tell. I think you should tell your story, the story of going to CU playing football, getting drafted by the Giants, the incident in Oakland and the music business. I know some people in publishing."

"I'm not a writer."

Two Masks

"You don't have to be a writer. We can take care of that. I have to warn you though, there's no money in writing a book."

"Come on. What do you mean?"

"What I mean is that you are going to need a day job. I know somebody that's looking for someone to hire. What was your major in school?"

"Communications," he said.

"Why?"

"I don't know. I thought maybe I could do color commentary someday," he said.

"Ever pursued it?"

"I couldn't get past the lady at the desk; any lady, any desk. Nobody ever returned my phone calls."

"It doesn't matter," I said. "I have to talk to some people, but I can guarantee you an interview and I think you would be perfect."

"What kind of work?"

"Similar to what you do now."

"All right," he said. He nodded once. "Make the calls."

"There's just one thing .," I said.

"What's that?"

"The terrible thing you know about Rodd Rock that could destroy his career."

"What about it?" he asked. He sounded suspicious.

"Could you give me a hint?"

"Oh ... it's not all that bad, but it would be the end of his career."

"You don't have to tell me, but I would sure like to know because we are about to drop Rodd Rock as a client. Now, you didn't hear this from me, but this thing has gotten way out of hand. My boss just wants to make sure there is nothing that could hurt our business. Is it anything like that?'

"I don't think so. I probably wouldn't use it anyway. If there's no expose' there's no reason to pay, I will tell my story another day."

"I'd sure like a hint," I said. "How's your latte?"

"Creamy, sweet and rich. That's how I like my women. I'm glad I don't know what they put in it." We sat in the Caddy and left the doors open. A black BMW pulled up in the parking spot next to the passenger door. The driver caught the look on Marcus's face and backed out to find another spot.

"Did you know that I went out with Carrie?" I asked him.

"Yeah. She talked about you. She was the one that persuaded Rodd to go with Mr. Close. She said he was a genius."

"What did she say about me?"

"You ain't no genius," he said and then lit up a sunrise smile. Then he wagged his great head and smiled some more.

"Can I ask you something … ah … a little personal?" I said.

"Like what?"

"Did Rodd ever … ah … come on to Carrie?"

"Don't ask me," he said. He put up a big defensive hand.

"Why not?"

"They was together a lot. It bothered Arlene. She told Rodd to fire Carrie during one of their fights. They had fights all the time. Arlene was the only woman I ever did see that could make Rodd Rock cry."

"Have you ever seen the stalker around Rodd's mansion?"

"Oh, yeah. I threw his ass off the property three or four times."

"Has he been around recently?"

"Not in the last week or so. I haven't seen him," said Marcus.

"He threatened Carrie the other night," I said.

"Just let me see him try something to hurt Carrie and watch what happens."

"You like Carrie?" I asked him.

"Everybody likes Carrie. Sometimes when Rodd is in one of his moods, she can talk him down. He listens to her. If Carrie wasn't there, there are two or three people that would just up and quit. She is always smiling, but she still gets her work done."

"What do you think happened to Arlene?" I said.

"I don't know what happened to that woman."

"Did you see her leave the concert?" I asked.

"I didn't see anyone leave. I was busting heads with the rent-a-cops in front of the stage."

"Why didn't you go to the after concert party with Rodd?"

"I was making a statement to the police. Two of the guys causing the trouble had records. It took about an hour to go through everything with the police. One of the kids called his parents and told them we had beaten him up for nothing."

"Did you?" I asked him.

"I beat on him, but not for nothing."

"You ready to go?" I asked, looking at his empty pastry bag.

"Let's sit for just another minute. You know this thing about Rodd?"

"Look. Don't tell me if you don't want. LT, my boss, set you up."

"LT! Lookit. There's only one LT and that's Lawrence Taylor. Don't you be talking about any LT unless you mean Lawrence Taylor."

"OK, Lawton Close, the famous consultant and my boss, set you up by making you think there was some book deal. Then he sent me over to find out what you know to see if it could blow back in our faces. He wanted me to scam you and steal your information. I can't do that. I saw you play against the Broncos. You guys murdered their defensive line. It didn't matter to me that you lost that game in overtime. You guys played with heart. Now if you had a quarterback who could throw to his own receivers instead of the Bronco secondary ..."

"There were some bad match ups in that game. We didn't have a winning season that year."

"You know what?" I said. "Most people don't. That's why we go to games. We want to see the winners and identify with them. And if our team can't win, we want to see them play with guts and determination and then we can go back to our own losing season and feel good about ourselves."

"Well, that's the thing." he said.

"What is?"

"What you just said."

"What did I say?" I asked.

"We want to feel good about ourselves. That's why I joined the church."

"What church?"

"The Holy Zion Fellowship Church," he said.

"Does it help?"

"Help? It saved my life. I am taking classes," he said.

"In what?"

"In the ministry."

"You are going to be a preacher?"

"Someday."

"You go to church every Sunday?"

"Got to," he said.

"And you are studying to be a minister?"

"There's a lot to know,"

"That's another uniform," I said.

"Yeah. They're not hung up on how you look. They accept me as I really am. I don't have to wear this shit when I go to the service. Anyway this isn't me. This is who I act like."

"A preacher! From the gridiron to the pulpit. That's going to be some book."

"There's one other thing."

"What's that?" I asked.

"Rodd Rock."

"What about him?"

"That's the story. If I open my mouth it's all over for Rodd Rock."

"What's the story?" I asked.

"He goes to church."

"What?"

"Arlene brought him to our church one night to hear the music and he's been coming every week since then."

'Where?" I asked.

"To the Holy Zion Fellowship Church."

"Rodd Rock?"

"If word gets out about this he's in the tank. Who's going to believe all that overlord of sex and drugs rap if he goes to church every week?"

"And you would tell this to the world?"

"Hell, no. I just wanted him to think I might. I got to eat."

"That's the big deal breaker? He goes to church?"

"Think about it. It's like Mr. Carlsen told us in communications class at CU. It's all about perception and the brand story. It's like he's a brand. Who's going to buy some Rodd Rock video where he's half naked singing to a bunch of bump-and-grind-gin-bang models if they know he goes to church every Sunday? If they know he's a Christian? People identify with a brand. It's a lifestyle thing. You can't go changing the story on people. They start feeling funny."

"What do they tell you in ministry class about blackmail?" I asked.

"They say don't bear false witness."

"And?" I prompted.

"It's all true! There's no false witness. It's the whole truth and nothing but the truth so help me God!"

"But if you threaten a guy and demand money …"

"Let me ask you," he said. He turned his head some more to get the full view of my face. Half his body turned with the head.

"What?"

"What does your boss do for his money?"

"He consults."

"Yes. And does he tell the bad things he finds out about his clients?"

"Of course not."

"And do they pay him?"

"Yes."

"So that's what I am doing. I am a brand consultant to Mr. Rodd Rock."

"You should have gone to law school," I said.

"I just follow the good book."

"Uh huh."

"And it goes 'render unto Caesar the things that are Caesar's but render unto God the things that are God's. I just want my share of the rendering around here. The bigger the spender the greater the render."

"We got to get going. Can I buy you lunch?"

"Yeah. I'm getting hungry."

"You can't be hungry. You're still eating."

"What? This? This is just an appetizer. I need some real food."

I put the key in the ignition and turned it. He had eaten the last of his pastries. He had scattered pastry crumbs all over his side of the car. I don't know why, but I liked seeing the crumbs all over LT's classic Cadillac creased blue leather seats.

22

WHEN I GOT BACK TO the house late that afternoon, I wrote up some notes of my meeting with Marcus O'Brien. I left out anything that LT would prefer to have verbally communicated. He doesn't trust computers not to rat him out after some shadowy governmental agency confiscates them to look for incriminating evidence of whatever they are looking for. I left out the big news, the deal breaker, the bit of information that could see Rodd Rock swept from the charts for all eternity.

I was a little amused by it, but LT was not. We were sitting in the summer office when I told him.

"He goes to church?" he exploded at me. I was expecting a chuckle.

"That's the big scandal."

"Every week?" asked LT. His face reddened a little. I thought it was odd.

"According to Marcus."

"And he's seen there?"

"Unless he goes in disguise."

"This is ... something I have not prepared for. This is ... the potential for mischief is ... I have to think. leave me alone for a moment."

I rose from the chair and went slowly to the doorway. I fully expected him to call me back. He didn't. I walked slowly into the kitchen and kept going to the refrigerator. Dickie was doing his puzzle. Something was steaming on the stove top.

"What are you making?"

"Fish stock," he said sadly. Normally I would have responded to his tone, but I had other things on my mind.

"Do we have any rice pudding?" I said. I was moving things around on the shelves looking for my little plastic tub with the deli sticker on the cover.

"Gone," he said. Then he sighed. Something was simmering on Dickie's front burner.

"Gone?" I said.

"Mindy and Mandy stopped in on their way to the beach."

"You gave them my rice pudding?"

"They asked," he said.

"How did they know there was any?"

"They looked."

"They looked in LT's refrigerator? You let them just open the door and poke around in LT's refrigerator?"

"One of them just yanked open the door and started looking. I couldn't do anything."

"Does LT know they looked in his fridge?" I asked. I couldn't believe what I was hearing.

"He has eighty-sixed them. They are no longer allowed on the premises."

"When did this happen?"

"While you were out with Marcus O'Brien. He said he couldn't stand their giggles."

"So, he eighty-sixed them?"

"He says forever. They are banned from the premises."

"And they went?" I asked.

"Not at first. There was a kind of a fight."

"LT had a fight with the Minder twins? Why do I miss all the good stuff?"

"It wasn't funny. At one point, LT told me to call the cops."

"What did you do?" I asked.

"I froze," he said.

"What do you mean?"

"I didn't know what to do. I just froze," he said with a shrug.

"How did it end up?"

"Teddy came in," he said. His eyes had a weird glimmer.

"And?"

"Teddy can get nasty," he said and then nodded to himself.

"Teddy took on the twins?" I asked. I was trying to keep up with the speculative mental images my daydream monitor was running like the coming attractions to a weird horror comedy.

"Teddy has a mouth on her," he said.
"And they left?"
"They didn't want any part of Teddy. It was scary."
"You didn't try any karate chops?" I asked.
"On who? Who was I going to attack? Who was I going to defend? It was horrible."
"They're gone now?"
"They called from the car. Oh. Mr. Kelly, I don't know what to do!"
"Are you still celibate?"
"I suppose, technically, but not entirely."
"How does it feel?"
"Not good. I remembered why I started celibacy in the first place. I just want my old life back. My father wants me to quit and move in to his guest house by the pool. He wants me to work on his boat. He says that all the publicity is going to be the end of Lawton Close. I don't know what to think. Everything has gone crazy. You know, Mr. Kelly, I enjoyed the simple life, I really did. Then this Rodd Rock thing started, and it becomes a big news item and people see it all over the world. Everyone wants to have a part in the big story. Girls I knew in high school show up out of nowhere trying to have a part in the big story. They want to go to bed with the big story. They think I am their portal to the big story, their way in and they want to sleep with me to be intimate with the big story, so they can claim it, but they don't know anything about me! They think I am the me that I used to be, that they can take advantage of, but I am not. I am the new me and they don't want to hear about it. I couldn't get them to listen to me. They just wanted to talk about the big story. I tried to tell them about my life since I got sober and all the things I discovered about … things, and they just laughed. They don't want to know the real me. They just want some souvenir to show their friends so they can say they have a part in the big story too.

"Then my father wants to take up where we left off. And we left off for reasons, good reasons. He says that the publicity is going to hurt his business. Like I'm supposed to feel guilty about what other people do to each other. He just wants me where he can control me again. I would rather fish for crabs in Alaska than live in his pool house. And crab fishing is one of the most dangerous and uncomfortable things you can do.

"What is it about publicity? Do people have to always be the center of attention? Man! What does that say about their self-esteem?"

"Good point," I said. Dickie was starting to make sense. I looked around the kitchen to see what they did with the real Dickie's body.

"What am I going to do about the twins?. I'm not used to this emotional stuff anymore."

"How was the sex?" I inquired.

"Mr. Kelly, in West Palm when I was growing up I was always told that there are things you don't speak of."

"That bad?" I asked.

"No. We never got beyond the kissing and fumbling stage. It took all my willpower."

"How was the fumbling?" I asked.

"Mr. Kelly…"

"Was it OK?"

"The fumbling was pretty great. while it was going on, but afterwards … you start thinking."

"Can I ask which sister?"

"That's the other thing."

"Both?" I asked. My eyebrows were at the top of their travel.

"Mr. Kelly!"

"Well, what then?"

"It was dark. I'm not sure which one it was. It has made my life a living hell. I was afraid to say anything at all, to either of them."

"This is a story I have to hear."

But I didn't get to hear it, at least not then. LT bellowed from the summer office, "Max!" The soundproofing only works when the door is closed. I should have closed it when I left the room.

I moved reluctantly to the sound of his voice.

When I entered the room I found him with his old office handset caught between his chin and his shoulder. He nodded me down into the chair with his head and eyes while he listened to whoever was on the phone. Then he spoke. He didn't bother to put a smile on his face like he always tells me to do. "They can hear the smile even if they can't see it," he says.

"I can not continue any further with you as a client. There is nothing else I can do," LT said into the phone. I knew from the tone that he meant it. Maybe the person on the other end could hear his frown. It was loud enough. "I am sending you a final statement of account. I have every confidence that you, as a professional, will pay it."

Then he listened for a moment. Then he continued, "No, quite impossible. There is nothing else to do."

Then he listened some more. The he compressed his lips and started nodding his head. I couldn't tell why he was nodding. Maybe he was pre-agreeing with what he was about to say and was impatient to get out. "If I may …"

There was another pause.

"If I may just …"

Another small pause.

"Mr. Rock. I am not open to blandishments. My mind is made up. I am handing the phone to Max. He will tell you what happens when I make up my mind. I have other things to do right now. I have already moved on. I suggest you do the same. Here's Max."

"Hello?" I said into the hand set after taking it from LT's sweaty hand. He never sweats.

"Max!"

"Hello, Rodd."

"Can you talk to him?"

"I don't think so. Talk is his trump suit. I could beat on him and it wouldn't take much in the way of blandishment to motivate me because I'm about ready as it is to pop him one, but talk is useless. He's a lawyer. You know?"

LT was frowning and squinting at me. I heard the rapid tapping of tasseled loafer heels on hardwood below the desk and I was pretty sure they weren't mine.

"I need him, Max. Everything has gone ... crazy. It's upsetting, all of it, but it's my wife who needs our concern right now. Talk to him. I need to be able to rely on him."

"Tell you what. I'll work on him. I am promising nothing because he is the most stubborn person I have ever met, and I've met some big time stubborn people. That's the best I can do. Would you please tell Carrie to call me?"

"Max!"

"I'm sorry, Rodd. That's the best I can do. I'm going to hang up now."

"I'm coming over," he said.

"No, you're not. The only way you could get in here right now is with your merry band of thugs and you are not on speaking terms with your thugs at the moment. I'm putting the phone down now."

I was following the phone down to its cradle with my mouth. From the earpiece I could hear increasingly loud protestations.

"Goodbye, Rodd. Be sure to have Carrie call me," I said as the handset came home and mashed down the button to end the call.

There was silence in the summer office for a full minute and some seconds. I looked at my watch face for something to do.

"Where's Carrie?" said LT, to break the growing silence.

"She's working at the mansion. I've got to get her out of there."

"The house has been sold," said LT. "I believe the closing is next week. Rodd will be moving into his apartment in Manhattan and I don't believe there is room for Carrie at the apartment."

"Well, I wish she would just quit," I said.

"Hm," from LT.

"You kicked the Minder sisters out of here today?" I asked.

"I don't want to talk about that sordid little episode. I won't."

"Dickie is heartbroken."

"The sooner the better. Those women are ..."

"What?" I asked.

"I'd rather not finish that. Dickie didn't come home again, last night."

"Did he have the night off?"

"Yes, but he always returns before midnight. I caught him sneaking in at dawn," said LT. He was slowly shaking his head.

"I think Dickie has had a setback," I said.

"I told those women they are not allowed on this property. They are not allowed to call here. I did it for Dickie," said LT. He was forcing optimism into his system using a tensed-up smile. LT always tells me the mood follows the set of the mouth. Judging by his smile, I thought that the mood would soon be tense. "He will thank me someday."

"Where's Teddy?" I asked him.

"She's out. She took her wallet. I don't expect her back before dinner time. When the going gets tough, she shops."

"What would you like me to do this afternoon?" I asked.

"Put yourself on standby. I am expecting a development."

"What kind of development?"

"I am not sure. There has been so much stimulation, the response or responses are beyond my ability to predict."

"So it's not over?"

"We'll see."

"I've never seen a case ... er ... project like this. Where is Tyrell? What's Bobby Dunton been up to?"

"Tyrell is in Atlantic City. He tells me that he has seen some of the video from the security cameras. Mel Viktor left the hotel in the company of a woman and two men. The police expect to have positive identification within a matter of hours. Tyrell pulled some strings to get in close with the investigation. There is an entire web of debts and favors in law enforcement that remains hidden from the layman. I find it incredible, but useful on occasion. Mr. Dunton is out of the area on field work."

"What kind of field work?" I asked.

"I am developing a line of action," said LT.

"Action? That's my department. What are you planning?"

"It is not ripe yet. You will be fully informed when you need to be."

"If the cops ID the people in the video, maybe we can wrap the whole thing up."

"What do you mean?" said LT, warily.

"If one of the men in the video is Dom, and we can prove a link to Mel's killing, then that pretty much proves that Rodd had Mel Viktor killed because of the money and had Arlene taken out of the picture to save half of what is left. You always tell me to follow the money trail. There it is!"

He just looked at me for a long time. He started to say something, then stopped himself. He shifted his weight in his chair and compressed his lips. Then he said, "We'll see."

"What is Bobby Dunton doing? He's still trying to find Arlene? Is he checking hardware stores for anyone buying contractor bags, duct tape, bags of lime and rubber gloves?"

"Something like that, but a little more subtle," said LT.

"Is he checking charge cards, cell phone records, ticket agents, in case she decided to flee the scene of her own wil?"

"That sort of thing," said LT, waving my comments out of the air like old smoke.

"What else?" I said. I was getting a powerful impression there was something else, something big.

"In the fullness of time," said LT. He was like an auctioneer closing out an item. The gavel had come down. That was all I was going to know for now. I have tried to talk him into revelations and it can't be done, at least not without cattle prods, a tub of water, two thumbscrews and the all-cast CD of *Cats*.

"What do you think happened to her?" I asked him. "You haven't really said what you think. We can scratch Mel Viktor off the list of suspects, can't we? Unless he was killed in revenge for having taken Arlene for some unknown purpose, maybe to force Rodd to back off on the twenty million dollar inquiry – naw. It doesn't make sense."

"Things rarely make sense if the true motivations remain hidden," said LT.

"But you stand to make some money from wrapping this up. What if it is another Hoffa deal where it can't be wrapped?"

"I have confidence that we will know what has become of the latest Mrs. Rock. I have some irons in the fire I have not pulled out yet."

"Like what?"

"They are still heating up. When they are ready ... I will pull them out and hammer them."

'You are in a poetical mood today."

"I am. Positively Wagnerian."

"The opera guy?" I asked. You never know with him.

"The opera guy."

It was later, just before dinner time, when Dickie came back from the village with some groceries. I didn't see it at first. Something registered, but my brain didn't stop what it was doing long enough to work on the significance of what had registered as mere sight data. Then he swung around at the refrigerator and my brain figured it out, and sounded the alarm.

"Dickie! What have you done to your hair?"

"I cut it."

"It's gone!" I said, staring.

"I went to the barber in town."

"You must have gone to the butcher or the candlestick maker because he was no barber."

"You don't like it?"

"Like? Dickie, your trademark is gone! Your ratty old pony tail is gone!"

"You know what, Mr. Kelly?"

"What, Mr. Douglas?"

"I got to thinking on the ride home, after the concert."

"Yes?"

"The past is the past."

"I can't argue with the logic. You want to expand on that?"

"Sometimes it's best to leave the past in the past and live in the moment, this moment right here."

"Yeah. These are pretty deep thoughts for a houseboy."

"I wasn't always a houseboy."

"Yes, Dickula, my eyes have been opened."

"But, see … I realized …"

"Yes?"

"This is the happiest I have ever been, here. My soul is at rest here. When we had the band in Florida?"

"Yes?"

"No one was happy because we were always trying to make it big and blaming each other and fighting about who played the wrong chord or who was pitchy on the chorus. We ended up hating each other."

"Yeah?"

"But the truth is we didn't have it."

"Have what?"

"It. We weren't good enough."

"So?" I asked. I didn't see where he was heading. I rarely do with Dickie.

"Then I had the bar. I made a good living. I always had my pockets stuffed with cash and cash is the most powerful of all the pheromones ..."

"Dickie! I have never heard you use such language. Your crossword puzzles are really working out for you."

"At two thirty in the morning, a couple of hundred dollar bills will pull chicks like a porch light pulls moths."

"What are you going to do with a couple of Franklins at two thirty in the ay em?"

"Nose candy, of course!" he said.

"Oh yeah. There's that."

"They weren't interested in me," he said. He was frowning a little, sad almost childlike frown.

"The chicks you were pulling?"

"I was just ... I was like one of those old vending machines with the candy bars, you know?"

"Mr. Candy Man! He can make a sunrise, sprinkle it with dew ..."

"Yeah. Do you know how much money I threw away?" he said. He was now looking right at me.

"I can only guess, Mr. Douglas, a lot."

"An inheritance, a large boat and a successful bar."

"Oh, Mr. Douglas. You would never have had to work again."

"No! That's the thing. I have to work, or I get bored. If I get bored, I get fidgety. I start thinking I need approval, someone who will tell me I'm special, really special."

"Yeah. We all look for that, sometimes," I said. Dickie was talking like I had never heard before. It was as if when they cut off his ponytail, his brain started to get oxygen or something.

"But if you have a band or run a bar you have to look for your approval at night, among the night people."

"Yeah?" I said.

"It's no good. They're night people; people of the night."

"Moths."

"That's right! So ... when I undertook the path of humility, I found contentment. I am not striving. My soul is at rest."

"In this loony bin? With LT and Teddy and Tyrell and ... and *me?*"

"I am but a humble servant. I am not invested in the craziness around me."

"I've never heard you talk this way. I didn't know you could talk this way. I don't think you should. You almost sound like you know what you're saying."

"I could never be a father."

"You have a medical problem?" I asked. His thoughts were all over the place like porgies around a chum pot in a heavy current.

"No. I don't have the emotional makeup and the patience."

"So?" I shrugged.

"So, I placed my foot on the path of celibacy."

"Well, you can have sex without ... the other thing."

"No, Mr. Kelly, you can't. You only think you can. The connection is cosmicalogical."

"Is that a word?"

"I don't know. But I realized once again that I don't wish to be stirred up. You know the reggae song, 'Stir it up?'"

"Yes?"

"I don't want to be stirred anymore. I don't like jamming, Mr. Kelly. I want ..."

"Yes?"

"Calm," he said with a sigh.

"But LT and Teddy are like a vortex of insanity. This is the least calm household I have ever seen," I said to him. Sometimes the obvious is hidden from those who look too deeply. The world is reflected on the surface of the pond. If you look below, you only see a muddy bottom.

"Not for me, because my job is simple. When I am chopping herbs, rubbing a chicken with olive oil, peeling a potato or making orange juice, I know what I am doing. I rise above the madness. I am on internal guidance. The way of humility and service is the way of contentment."

"Don't you ever get ... you know ... horny?"

"At first, but if you don't think about all of that, after a while ..."

"Yes?" I asked.

"It atrophies," he said.

"Not me. The longer I go without, the more I think about it."

"That's because you haven't found the path to humility and service. You can't have one without the other. You are still striving. You still think you can win ... that there is something to win."

"You're going over my head with this stuff and I didn't think that was possible. You stick to your cooking and I'll stick to what I do best."

"What is that, Mr. Kelly?"

"Whatever LT pays me to do."

"You are a young soul, Mr. Kelly."

"I hope that's a good thing, Mr. Douglas."

23

It was one of those times when the phone keeps ringing. We were all in the office watching the big flat screen TV that is usually hidden behind a fake panel. You would never know it was there. The fake panel was Teddy's idea. It looks just like the rest of the paneling, but if you press the lower right hand corner it goes in a little bit and then releases and pops out a half an inch. Then you swing the panel out to reveal the TV. The panel was swung wide and the TV was on. We were waiting to see a live report from the courthouse where Rodd Rock's new lawyer had participated in a preliminary hearing on the disappearance of Arlene Rock.

When the phone rang, I went to the kitchen to get it. Line one was blinking.

"Lawton Close and Associates," I said.

"Max," said Tyrell's voice.

"Hey! Where are you?"

"Just leaving AC. Tell LT that an arrest is imminent in the Mel Viktor murder."

"It is?" I asked him.

"Oh, yeah. Do you know that there are video cameras all over the place these days?"

"Yes."

"For security," he said. "All of the casinos have them in their parking areas. Trump's Casino security got a pretty good look at Mel Viktor getting in a car with a woman and two guys, one of whom appeared to be holding a gun. The time is right."

"So who are they?" I asked.

"The guy is a known drug dealer. The woman was once married to Bobby Roberts."

"The singer? The guy they call 'the art of the strip' because he spent so many years in Vegas?"

"Yep," said Tyrell. "I guess she has been trying to break into movies. What they have found out down here is that Mel Viktor was involved in a plan to finance her production company, but some of the money went missing. It's just like Rodd Rock, except these guys play rough. Some of the money came from a large drug deal. Guess whose name showed up in the investigation?"

"Carlito Penumbra," I said.

"Yep. Mel picked the wrong crowd to skim, this time."

"So there's no connection with Rodd?" I asked.

"They can't find any," said Tyrell.

"There's something I'm not getting," I said.

"Oh, yeah," said Tyrell. It was a weird thing to say.

"What does that mean?" I asked him.

"Look, I have to scoot. Tell LT that they have things under control in Atlantic City. He can relax."

"You coming here?" I asked him.

"In a little bit. I have to see about something first."

"You are being pretty darned mysterious," I said.

"Oh yeah," said Tyrell. "Let me give you a word of advice."

"What's that?"

"Don't count your chickens 'till they come home to roost."

"What the hell does that mean?" I asked him.

"Remember what I said," was his answer and then he killed the connection.

They all looked up when I came back in to the office. They looked grim, the three of them. Dickie was standing. He was playing with his apron. LT was behind his desk. Teddy was in the wicker chair that clients usually sit in. When I entered, LT held up his finger and shushed me. I hadn't said a word or made a sound. It annoyed me a little so I stayed by the doorway to the hall and leaned against the molding the way Tyrell always does. Tyrell should have been there. It was the bitter end and Tyrell should have been with the team when the season ended in defeat.

"… at the courthouse this morning, Rodd Rock appeared with his defense team, led by the flamboyant Alan Guttermucker. Rock refused to speak with members of the press. After the preliminary hearing, Guttermucker addressed the reporters."

There was a handheld shot of Guttermucker in front of a bank of microphones. Hands kept pushing little digital recorders into the picture. Guttermucker was smiling like he was running for office. Hell, maybe he was. "My client is completely innocent and he will be vindicated in court. The prosecution has no case and we have argued before Judge Trumble that there is insufficient evidence to proceed with an indictment. There is no weapon, no body, no witnesses, no forensic evidence and Mr. Rock staunchly maintains that he is completely innocent of any wrong doing, and has no knowledge of any foul play in the disappearance of his wife. Not only is my client innocent until proven guilty, there is no crime unless there is evidence to support the proposition that in fact a crime has been committed."

People started yelling to the lawyer, screaming out questions about Dominic Pancetta and other "facts" about the disappearance. The camera view was switched back to the studio where an anchorman looked sternly at his viewers.

"We have in the studio a legal expert, Doctor Roger Condonary. Doctor Condonary, what do you make of the press conference we have just seen?"

"Well, I have to say, my old colleague Alan Guttermucker has done a masterful job of pinpointing the key weakness in the prosecution's case. The local police are not used to this kind of high profile case. They have proven themselves not up to the job. Key evidence was missed. They did not search the parking lot where the woman's personal effects were found until 48 hours had elapsed. By that time the maintenance people had cleaned up, perhaps removing vital evidence. The woman's effects did not remain in their hands during that time. I think it's a disgrace."

"Do you think bad police work has crippled the case?"

"That would be my opinion. Yes. The first 48 hours in a disappearance are crucial. During that time the police did nothing except file a report. Those 48 hours allowed a person or persons unknown to remove evidence, to conceal or even destroy the body of the missing woman, assuming, as most do, that she was killed. All the evidence we do have, and it is almost entirely circumstantial, suggests strongly that this was done by professionals. This was a slick operation."

"As it stands right now, what, in your opinion, are the odds that Rodd Rock will just walk away from this a free man?"

"I would say the odds are very high that there will no trial. The prosecutor needs a breakthrough or for someone to come forward. Unless that happens, the disappearance of Arlene Rock is destined for the cold case files."

I didn't hear the rest because the phone started making noises. I looked around. No one moved, so I headed for the kitchen and picked up. It was line one again. I used my professional demeanor, the one that LT insists on.

"Lawton Close and …" was as far as I got.

"Max?"

"Rodd? Aren't you in New York?"

"I'm on the Expressway. Listen! Carrie has been kidnapped!"

"What?"

"Is Lawton there? I'm extremely upset."

"What do you mean *kidnapped*?"

"She was taken from the house at knife point. Put Lawton on the phone. I have to talk to him."

"Who took Carrie?"

"They don't know."

"Do you know?"

"Max! Nobody knows, but …"

"But, what?"

"They told me that the person who broke in, sprayed the cameras with WD40. They couldn't see anything in the video except blurry colors and the shine of what appears to be a knife, but …"

"*But, what?*"

"The person with the knife …"

"*Yes?*"

"Had red shoes."

"I'm going over there," I said.

"I have to talk to Lawton. The police are still at the house."

"He'll pick up. I'm going over there right now."

"Fine, the gate's open. Please put Lawton on the phone."

I punched the hold button and yelled, "LT!"

I ran to the office doorway, "LT!"

He turned to me. Half his face was blued from the TV screen. "What is it?"

"Carrie has been kidnapped. It looks like the stalker. Rodd is on line two. I'm going over there."

"Kidnapped? Why would he do that?" said LT. His voice was raised and tight.

"How the hell would I know? He's crazy. I'm going over there," I said. I was still shouting.

"What was he thinking?" said LT. It was a weird thing to say.

"I'll ask him. I'm going over to Rodd's. The police are still there."

"Do you think that's advisable?"

"He took Carrie! What does this have to do with advice?"

"The police ..."

"It's *Carrie!*" I shouted back to him. I was moving toward the stairs.

I ran up them and into my room where I grabbed my little Colt automatic, checked the magazine and put it in my pocket. Then I unplugged the cell phone from the charger and put that in my other pocket. When I cleared the bedroom door and started for the stairs. LT was standing at the bottom of the staircase. He was wearing one of his silly old smoking jackets that Teddy found for him at the charity thrift store. He looked batty and he was in my way.

"I don't think you should go over there," he said with his paws up. "You are just going to be in the way.".

My breath exploded. I took in some more and said, "I'm going to Rodd's."

"I need you here," he said.

"Tough. Carrie needs me there. If he touches her, I swear ..."

"Max!"

I pushed him to one side. He is surprisingly powerful. I forget. I had a clear shot to the door, but I hesitated. "What?" I said.

"I detest improvisation. Be careful. I don't know what we are dealing with."

"Did you ever?" I said. I shouldn't have, but I was upset.

"I thought ... now ... I don't know. Be careful. Keep your eyes open. Take your cell phone. Call me when you know anything."

I reached in my pocket and showed him the cell phone. I was only later that I realized that the housecleaner had plugged the charger into the switched outlet when she used the vacuum. All the outlets in the bedrooms have a switched upper outlet connected to the wall switch by the door. The lower outlet in each pair is always on. The outlet she plugged the charger into was switched off. It didn't charge. When I really needed the cell phone, it was dead. And then it was too late anyway.

The gate was open, but there was a cop there and he didn't want to let me in. I told him to talk to Rodd. I even tried to give him Rodd's secret phone number. He didn't want to hear it. He said there was no way I was going to go through those gates. I asked him to talk to the chief. He talked into his little shoulder mic, and managed to get through to the chief.. The chief said I could come in. Of course he did. He wanted to yell at me for destroying his career and then, pump me for information. Talking to the chief was like fencing with a three-armed guy. I wanted to see the video and he wanted to yell at me for making his life a living hell, scream questions at me about my relationship with Carrie, and demand that I tell him every detail of my meeting with Valderben in Montauk. I commiserated on the media coverage, answered all of his questions about Carrie and the stalker, the best I could. I didn't hold anything back. I wanted everyone to know everything because time was running out, and if there was any hope for Carrie, everyone involved had to be quick and surefooted.

He also asked me about her parents. I didn't know how to get in touch with Carrie's father, but I gave him the address I had for her mother in the Midwest. He told one of the officers to get her on the phone.

I did manage to see the video. WD40 does a nice job. It makes a blurry mess, but you could see the red shoes – not as shoes, but as red movement where shoes would be. So, was it the stalker? Or someone who put on red shoes to look like the stalker?

You couldn't see Carrie's features, but you could almost tell it was her. She was wearing a yellow top and you could see the yellow. You could also get a sense of her hair, and the hair color was her color.

You could see the glinting of the knife, but no details. You could get a sense of the struggle. He seemed quite powerful. Carrie can take care of herself, but she was just plain overpowered.

"Is he going to hurt her?" I asked the chief as we watched. It was anxiety talking. The answer to that question was locked in the cranium of a paranoid schizophrenic.

"I don't know. He left a video statement that we are supposed to release to the media."

"What does it say?" I asked.

"We haven't played the whole thing yet. I got a guy making copies back at the office. The part I saw, he just seems to be talking crazy about politics and world hunger and something he calls the machine. I turned it off and gave it to one of my guys to make copies. They'll go out within the hour to people who analyze this kind of thing."

"Are you going to release it to the media?"

"I don't know. That's already been taken out of my hands. My guess is they probably will because the media will want to play it. Crazy and violent is always good copy. I wouldn't release it. I don't see any good coming from it, and it might inspire other disturbed individuals to act out copy-cat fashion, *but I'm just a rude hick, small town dumb-ass and what the hell do I know?"* He started screaming again about the media and LT. His language got kind of colorful and I had to just stand there and take it.

After he vented, and the pressure had dropped out of the red and back into the yellow (it wasn't even close to green) he went back to questioning me. I don't think he had a plan. He was just throwing questions around the room in rage and frustration. That's the way it went until one of the radios in the room, and there were dozens, said something about the stalker's car. They found it abandoned on a little back road that runs past a couple of the surviving farms in the area. The chief started ordering people around. Then he had to talk on his phone. He was calling in reinforcements. He wanted forensics. He wanted the flatbed truck. He wanted additional coverage from other departments. He wanted the area sealed off. He wanted an ambulance with an EMT team on stand-by. There was a lot of purposeful confusion in the room. I used the sudden activity and distraction to slip out of the house. I had parked out on the street. I nodded to the cop guarding the gate. He nodded back. He was standing just beneath the mask of tragedy. I got the tingle.

24

I WATCHED THEM GO OVER the faded blue Saturn. I watched from a safe distance, where they couldn't see me. Whatever they were finding (I saw them take out a roll of cloth tape and some clothing) did not seem to point them toward the stalker in some other location. They seemed to be content with the car and the things in it. Nobody was walking away from it to look around. I stayed with them, out of their sight, until the truck came and they winched the car up on its flatbed and then they all left the scene. It was just me, the fading sun and some bugs.

I did nothing for a while. I just took in the scene. There was a patch of woods beyond an old barn. There were stacks of firewood in neat rows. The tracks for the Long Island Rail Road ran along the south edge of the farm fields. To the East, the tracks went to Montauk. In the other direction they ran to New York City. It gave me an idea. I got up and pushed my way through the waist high weeds toward the tracks.

I walked east for a while. The right-of-way just beyond the gravel roadbed was completely overgrown with weeds and small shrubs, but walking between the rails was easy. I scanned to my right and left. There wasn't anything to see except pieces of old white plastic bags, rusted cans, and items that had been in the weather so long they were no longer identifiable. The tracks smelled funny, of rust, of rotting wood and old creosote. The roadbed crunched underfoot. I had reached a place where the track ahead curved out of sight, when the rumbling started. There was a train coming from Montauk. I stepped off the tracks, and backed up into some prickly shrubs just as the engine came into view. The train raced past with a lot of wind and noise.

I hadn't turned on my cell phone because I know LT and LT would want me at his side, not to do anything, just to be there to soak up his anxiety. I didn't want that, or any of his tricks, so I kept the cell phone powered down. Now, I wanted to know if there was any news. I took out the phone and flipped it open. It turned on, but while I was dialing, it shut itself down. I turned it back on and saw the little battery icon showing me that it was out of power. It shut itself off again.

I started walking back to where I had parked LT's car. When I got to it, there were only a few minutes of light left in the sky. I decided to walk west along the track bed. It was just a feeling, not even strong enough to qualify as a hunch. It was just one of those little things we do in the moment. I walked.

I hadn't gone more than five hundred yards, when I saw movement. I could have been a deer, or it could have been a big dog, or it could have been a breeze in the weeds, but I didn't think so because I got a glimpse of red. I froze.

I slowly lowered myself where I stood and just listened. There was nothing. Neither of us moved for a full three minutes. It seemed a lot longer.

It was up to me. He could wait all night. I couldn't.

I started forward, as quietly and as slowly as I could. I was listening hard and scanning the area for anything. I kept moving.

I'm a city guy. I have finely tuned street reflexes. I can size up trouble in a subway car without even appearing to be awake. I can size up a public room for exits, threat paths and possible weapons that can be improvised from items close to hand, within seconds. In the city I read body language in a moving crowd, as if each individual had a name tag with intentions.

In the country, I'm not in my comfort zone. What's that bustling in the hedgerow? Raccoon? Wild dog? Stalker? I didn't know. That's why I fell for the second oldest trick in the movies. He threw something over my head. I even heard the fabric rub when he threw it, but when the thing hit behind me, I turned around. I couldn't help myself; noise – turn to the noise.

He was on me just I began to turn back to the sound of his feet racing at me. We both went down. Luckily for me, he didn't have his knife in his hand or this story would have ended here.

He was surprising powerful and he wrapped me up before I could do much. After the initial impact, I went limp, because my idea was to slowly reach for my gun. It was a good call in the huddle, but the stalker threw away my playbook.

"It's you!" he hissed in my ear. "Too bad."

"Where is she?" I said.

"You'll never find her," he said. That was it for conversation. I was about to say something else when his hands went around my throat. They were quick and powerful and they had an immediate effect. Both my hands came up to his. The gun could wait. I tried to pull his hands away, but he pressed harder and it hurt. Then he shook my head and I saw little flashes of brightness as everything else got suddenly darker. I had to do something and do it quickly. I scratched. He howled and pressed harder. I kicked my feet and arched my back, but he was too heavy to dislodge. I forced one of my hands to stop trying to get air, and to start getting the gun, but he didn't like the that and rolled me around and shook my neck some more. I was starting to gray out, when something horrible loomed up above him. It was ragged and muddy and wild in the early-night sky. It had a strange stick of some kind. It shouted something and the stick came down hard just as my sight failed.

I was only out for a moment, maybe five seconds or so. The hands around my neck released and the weight was gone. There was a rushing sound in my ears and voices that sounded far away, but were actually very close. Something went thwack, and there was a scream. Then the voices were shouting. I could hear the words, but I couldn't make sense of them right away. There was a little delay in comprehension. There was more shouting and the sound of something hitting flesh. I moved instinctively away from the commotion on my hands and knees. I shook my head to clear my vision. When my eyes began to focus, I could see the stalker kneeling and holding his head. Blood was pouring from between his fingers. Standing above him was Carrie. Her yellow shirt was covered with dirt and blood. She held a green snow-fence post in both hands like a samurai sword. One of her wrists was handcuffed to the post. The end of the post had dirt still clinging to it, as if it had been violently uprooted.

"Are you OK?" she said to me.

"I don't know," I said. "How did you get here?"

"I escaped," she said. I was too dazed to ask, "From what? Where?"

"Did he hurt you?" I said. I tried standing. It seemed to work.

"A little," she said. Then she showed me her wrists and the handcuffs and the snow-fence post. Her wrists were raw and her exposed skin was bruised. She couldn't drop the fence post. She was stuck with it until someone found a key to the cuffs.

I felt for the gun. It was there. I brought it out and turned to Thomas Valderben.

"OK!" I said to him. "We are going to need the key to the cuffs."

"Fuck you," he said.

"Thomas," I said. I was trying to keep my voice calm. "I really want the key to the cuffs."

"Find it," he said.

That's when the rumble started. I looked up the tracks to the West. There was one big, glaring headlight. We were about five feet from the tracks. There was no danger of being hit by the train, but it was a complication and I didn't need a complication just then. Valderben saw it as well. You could actually see him start to think about some new options. He looked around at his surroundings.

"Carrie!" I said.

"What?"

"Bring that fence-post within swinging range of Thomas." I didn't want to shoot him, and Carrie had already proven she could swing for the right-field bleachers. "Keep it cocked and away from his hands,"

She stepped up to the plate.

The train was blowing for a crossing. The rails were lit up by the headlight. They looked like spider silk; like the train was a spider made of light. It was getting close. Thomas was becoming agitated. He was going to try something. He looked up at Carrie – he was still low, but he had brought one knee up and shifted his weight. I needed to get his attention.

"Thomas!" I yelped at him. "Don't try it."

Now the train was blowing again, but it wasn't the road crossing sequence, it was trying to get our attention. Thomas looked at the train.

"Carrie!" I yelled. "Step back out of range."

Things happened quickly then. Thomas looked at her, and then he looked at me and stood up. Carrie stepped back a pace, but brought the fence post back in the fully cocked position. I gestured with the gun and started to yell to Thomas. He crouched slightly. He was going to go, but where?

Then the train was twenty feet away, moving fast. He made his move. He jumped toward the tracks.

"No!" was all I had time to shout.

At first I thought he made it. The train went by at about fifty, squealing with the brakes clamped down hard. Pinwheel showers of sparks circled around the hot wheels. The ground shook. The rails shook. There was a shock of hot iron wind. Sheet steel and lighted windows flashed past with back-lit faces pressed against the glass. The train's momentum carried it past us. It stopped another 100 yards up the track. For a moment, there was a strange quiet. I couldn't see sign of Thomas across the tracks. He seemed to have disappeared.

Carrie saw something first. "What's that?" she said, pointing with the fence post.

It was a red shoe, barely visible, like some weird cactus flower that only blooms in moonlight.

So, he hadn't made it.

It was close.

It was damned close.

But …

25

It seems that everyone on the train had a cell phone and they were using them. We didn't have to wait long for the first of the cops to show. I had a problem, should I go through Thomas's pants pockets for the key to the handcuffs?

I decided not to search him. It wasn't because of his condition, which was not good and entirely dead, but because I wanted the cops to see Carrie's condition. I wanted it on record.

They drove their strobe-flashing cruisers along the railroad right-of-way. They conveniently left the headlights on and the motors running. It wasn't long before I felt like I was back in the city. A lot of cop cars showed up. There was also a couple of fire trucks and an ambulance from Bridgehampton.

Some genius tried to get Carrie to sit in the back of one of the cars, but he soon figured out that the fence post had to be separated from the girl before she would fit in the car. I was being walked around the area by the first cop to arrive. I think his name was Dave. He had his Maglite out and he was shining its beam around the ground.

"Your friend said she was held in some kind of underground room," he said to me.

"There was a plywood roof, held up by snow-fence posts," I said.

"She said it was this way," he said and started walking behind the light of his flashlight.

"That's what she told me. It's just up by those shrubs," I said.

It wasn't far.

"This?" said officer Dave as his light found a dark patch.

"This is it," I said when we were standing over it. "He apparently liked 7-Eleven cuisine," There were bags and wrappers and empty coffee cups around. "Not the type for housework, I guess."

"Garbage in, garbage out," said Dave.

We sat on that comment for a few moments while he used his flashlight like a tour guide, to point out the architectural highlights

Thomas had made himself a little underground bunker by digging a trench in the earth. He laid green metal fence posts across the trench like beams and then roofed it over with old plywood (already gray with age and slightly de-laminated at the edges). The beams were additionally supported in the middle by a row of upright snow-fence posts. On top of the plywood, actual clumps of living weeds and grasses was used as a covering. It provided almost perfect concealment except where part of the plywood roof had caved in. Someone had wrenched out the center support. You could see a little crater where the post had been ripped out of the ground. That was how Carrie wrenched herself free from the underground dungeon. Before she ruined it, passengers in a passing train would have seen nothing, if they bothered to look out the window at all.

One of the remaining center posts had a sign tied to it with the picture of a bird and a warning to stay out of a piping plover nesting area.

Rolled up in a corner of the trench was a filthy sleeping bag. There were candles in various lengths stuck in the walls of the trench. There was an iPod and a small battery-operated radio visible.

"Home sweet home," said Dave.

"It was also a prison," I said.

"Yeah," he said quietly.

We started back to the big congregation of cars, trucks, cops and train.

Carrie was sitting in the back of the ambulance. She was being looked over by the EMTs. Her fence post had been removed. I broke away from Dave and trotted over.

"Hey!" I shouted to get her attention.

"Max! I keep telling them I'm OK, but they want me to go to emergency for observation."

"That's probably a good idea," I said. "I'll go with you."

"Hey!" said a commanding voice behind me. "Get down from there."

I looked around and it was the chief himself. He was motioning me down from the back of the ambulance.

"Where the hell do you think you're going?" he said.

"I'm going to go with Carrie to the hospital," I said.

"Bullshit!" he exploded. "You are going to stay here with me and you are going to tell me exactly what the hell has gone on here tonight." By then he had reached me, and he was pulling me out of the ambulance. He wasn't being gentle, either.

"I've explained to officer Dave ..." I started to say.

"And you will explain it to me and to whoever else is interested and you will explain it again and again until we are all satisfied," he said.

The ambulance driver gave him a look. The chief looked at Carrie and nodded. The EMT started to close the door. Carrie held up her thumb and pinky to her ear, the universal sign of "call me" and made a face at me. I nodded and then the door was closed.

The chief put his arm on my shoulder and started moving me back toward the grisly scene at the side of the tracks. "Maybe you should start from the beginning," he said.

26

"THEY MUST THINK WE HAVE no memory!" said LT. His checks were puffed up with indignation and in the blue light of the television, he looked like a weird Sesame Street character.

"Shhhhh!" Teddy was waving him silent so she could hear the talking face on the television.

"I don't think there is any hope," said the talking face, "of ever finding her now, dead or alive. There is some talk of bringing obstruction of justice charges against Lawton Close for the way he has interfered with the entire investigation. It was an employee of his who chased Thomas Valderben into the path of the oncoming train. Valderben has carried the secret of the whereabouts of Rodd Rock's wife with him to the grave. Is she alive or dead? There is still hope in some quarters that she may still be found alive, but it is a dim hope and getting dimmer with each day that passes.

"I think we see here, what happens when individuals attempt to get involved in the pursuit of justice. If the police had been allowed to do their job, I believe that Arlene Rock would now be found – maybe alive, maybe not, but at least there would be closure for her family and loved ones.

"The police had already found his car. It was in the process of being examined by professional, highly trained forensic experts. It was only a matter of time before Thomas Valderben's hiding place was discovered. Using the full complement of police resources, I have no doubt whatsoever that Mr. Valderben would have been taken into custody without incident, that he would have divulged the location of the missing wife of Rodd Rock and that he would finally have been able to get the treatment he so obviously required.

"If proper procedures had been followed, it is entirely probable, and it is my firm belief, that no one would have been hurt. Mr. Close and his associates have a lot to answer for. This is a tragedy that never should have happened. I am proposing ..."

There was a click and the screen went dark. Everyone looked around. It was LT. He had the clicker held out in front his face like a death-ray. He had just zapped the talking face.

"Lawton!" said Teddy, "we were watching that!"

"I have heard more than enough," said LT. "That man is a *ninny*!"

"What did you expect?" said Teddy.

"He is blaming *me*, *us* for the depredations of a psychopath!"

"Oh, excuse me, but yawn, where have you been?" said Teddy. "By definition, a psychopath can't be responsible for his or her actions, the person is *psychotic*. Ergo, someone has to be responsible. You were close at hand."

"I hate it," said LT, testily, "when you say 'ergo'."

"Why is that, dear?" said Teddy, with one eyebrow hoisted like a storm warning.

"I don't know," said LT. "It makes you sound like a lawyer, or a freshman in philosophy class."

"I see," she said. That was all she said. I was waiting for more.

"Yesterday, Rodd Rock was the villain of the piece," said LT, sounding a little like a teacher of freshman philosophy. "Today, the bar sinister has been painted over my shield and I'm the bastard! How do they know that Valderben had anything to do with Arlene's disappearance? Where is their evidence? If they had enough to convict Rodd Rock yesterday for his wife's murder, on what are they basing their ridiculous speculations?"

"You are asking this rhetorically," said Teddy. She phrased it like a statement, not a question.

"I am," he said.

"You are not looking for an answer."

"I am not," he said with finality.

"Well, then ..."

The room fell silent. I looked at Carrie. She looked at me. Dickie looked from his boss to his boss's girlfriend.

"I think I'll take Carrie's things to the spare room," I said. Dr. Hindus at the hospital had told us that she was in pretty good shape considering what she had been through. He suggested in a low voice to LT, Teddy and me that there might be some light scarring at the wrist and that she should see a counselor. He stressed that she needed rest for a week or more. Teddy insisted that she stay with us. I wasn't going to argue. LT tried. I think he actually almost finished his opening remarks.

"I'll help you," said Carrie.

We were ignored.

As I was getting to my feet, I held out my hand to Carrie. I drew her up and we turned to leave the room.

We were still holding hands when we cleared the threshold. I heard LT mutter out loud, "They must think we are idiots."

This was followed by a sigh from Teddy, and a quiet, "yes, dear." The last thing I heard was the sound of pages being turned.

27

Rodd Rock and Esmeralda were coming to dinner. LT and Teddy were trying to mend fences I guess. Carrie didn't want to be there when Rodd showed up, and I felt the same way. She hadn't seen him since the incident, nor had she been back to the mansion. She said it had too many bad associations. Now the mansion had a new owner. He hadn't moved in yet, but his work crews were busy on the grounds. The first thing they did was remove the two masks from the gate. No one seems to know what happened to the masks. Maybe they were sold, maybe they were thrown out at the dump. The new owner was a hedge fund guy and a recluse.

Time had passed and the media attention had moved on to other celebrities and other scandals. Arlene wasn't forgotten as much as ignored. The narrative had gotten skinny on a diet of nothing to report.

It was only briefly noted that Rodd had a new woman in his life. *Rumeur Monde* said her name was Esmeralda. She appeared (the only photos of her were taken from extreme distances with big lenses) to be Latino. There were some comments on the internet and a line or two in the back pages of the big dailies, but since Arlene's disappearance had been dumped in the cold files, Rodd was treated as a kind of media embarrassment. Nobody knew, or seemed to care much about Esmeralda. No one knew if she had a last name.

Dickie told me that Rodd was bringing his latest "conquest" (Dickie's term) in the hushed, conspiratorial tones that Dickie uses when he pretends to have deep and secret knowledge. "She's supposed to be very mysterious," said Dickie with a smug little nod.

"I don't want to see her," I said. "I liked Arlene."

I wanted to be with Carrie in a large crowd with a lot of noise. I didn't mind if everyone else was a stranger; in fact I preferred it. When it comes to faces in the crowd, the imagined story is often happier than the story learned. Carrie was waiting for me in the Cadillac. She had gotten anxious as the invitational hour struck on LT's grandfather's clock (it actually had belonged to his grandfather). I was just as anxious, but too slow. I was running down the stairs when Dickie came out of the kitchen in his apron to answer the doorbell. He opened it and there they were. I was caught in the middle of the foyer.

I made the best of it.

"Good evening, Max," said Rodd sticking out his hand like a salesman. The woman just smiled and nodded.

"Hi, Rodd," I said. I shook his hand out of a lifetime of conditioning. I can still hear Aunt Zila's voice saying (sternly) "Get on your feet this instant and shake the nice man's hand. And answer when you are addressed, young man!"

"You know Esmeralda?" said Rodd. He nodded at her, but she stayed behind his left shoulder. I'm glad she didn't try anything like a hug, because she would have been disappointed. Aunt Zila never said anything about hugging a brazen hussy.

"Hello," I said to her. Then I said to Rodd, "I saw a picture of the two of you in *Rumeur Monde*. You were just coming out of Pottery Barn. It looked real homey." I tried to get my voice to sound enthusiastic, but it ratted me out. Esmeralda looked pleased with herself. Maybe in her neighborhood a washed-up rock star is the big time.

By then LT was bustling in from the office. His smile was too big, he was too quick on his feet. I was disgusted.

"Rodd! Esmeralda! Come in, come in! Dickie has put on something truly special for you tonight."

"Will you be staying for dinner, Max?" said Rodd. The son of a bitch had a smile on his face. Everyone was beaming. It was creepy.

"No ... I'm ... I have to be elsewhere," I said.

"Is Carrie here?" said Rodd, looking around expectantly.

"No," I said.

"She was just here?" said LT, sounding puzzled.

"We're late," I said. I pointed toward the door. I was wishing that I was on the other side of it.

"Max has taken the night off," said LT. I made a face at him. I wanted him to drop the whole subject. Then I grimaced to warn him off, but of course it was already too late.

"Pity you won't be here. We could talk about old times," said Rodd.

Was he crazy? At that moment, I decided that his arrogance was truly world class.

"I don't feel much like stirring the ashes tonight," I said. I couldn't look him in the eye. Then I blushed, when I realized ashes was a poor choice of image. Unlike LT, I blush from time to time. It's part of not having a poker face.

"Carrie and Max have been through a rough couple of months," said Teddy, entering the room. "Poor dears. Hello, Rodd! And you must be Esmeralda! Rodd said you were pretty, and I thought he was exaggerating. On the contrary, he failed to do you justice."

"Oh, come on," said Rodd, to me. "Have a quick drink with us and I'll let you in on some interesting gossip."

"I'm sorry, Carrie and I don't feel too much like hearing gossip tonight. There has been far too much of the stuff around lately, especially if it concerns Rodd Rock."

"OK, old boy," said Rodd, throwing up his hands. "Done! Give a squeeze to old Carrie for me, won't you?"

"You know she was close to Arlene," I said. It was LT's turn to give me the warning face.

"Yes, she was," said Rodd. He had the grace to at least look sad for a moment. He even gave it two beats of silence before starting up again. "But Arlene is gone and ... life moves on. We move on. We must."

"Maybe you can move on," I said.

"It's wrong to live in the past," said Esmeralda.

I looked at her, but I didn't know what to say. I took a hard look at her for the first time. She was nearly the same height as Arlene, was a little bit thinner, but in every other way she couldn't have been more different. She had jet black hair and plenty of it. She had a sensual chest and it was clothed to excellent visual advantage. Her brown eyes were almost black. Her face was much more sculpted. Her cheekbones were prominent and her lips full. She was something to look at. I couldn't blame Rodd for getting caught up with her. I would have if she had batted her brownies my way. It was everything else I blamed Rodd for. He had, one way or the other, been responsible for Arlene's disappearance. And LT was putting aside his morality and considerable dignity (with which he liked to threaten me on occasion) for a ... what? An aging has-been with a shadow of murder over his twilight years. I had to get out of there.

"I'm sorry, but I'm running late," I said.

I bolted for the door. I didn't offer my hand to shake. As I was almost to the door I heard Teddy start in with her excited pleasantries. The laughter made my skin crawl.

I was halfway to the car when I realized I had taken the wrong set of keys. I had taken Teddy's set in my haste. My set has a miniature LED flashlight on the key ring. When I saw that there was no little light, I groaned out loud. It meant I had to go back and exchange them. I stopped, let myself cool off for a moment and turned back to the house. There was already candle light coming from the dining room. They were probably seated. Dickie was probably bustling in and out of the kitchen with his little starter course items and the little maroon plates with the gold rims that used to belong to LT's mother.

I tried to open the front door without making a sound. I didn't want to have to face any of them again. I can be dead quiet when I want to be. I had the closet door open and was about to grab for the keys when the sound of laughter came from the dining room.

The laughter alone was bad enough. These people were acting like vampires. A young woman was missing and presumed dead and they were acting like they were at a fraternity party, and had nothing more to worry about than a possible poly-sci pop quiz.

Then I heard my name and there was a little tittle of additional laughter, or at least a broad chuckle. I froze. The key ring dangled from my thumb and finger. It glinted in front of me like a hypnotist's prop. I was concentrating on the sounds from the dining room. I was beginning to make out individual words. One of those words came from Esmeralda and the word made me jump like I had touched the hot lead of a dangling wire. The keys tinkled in my hand. Suddenly things made a totally new kind of sense. Damn!

I walked very quickly, but without making any sound, to the doorway of the dining room. I hesitated for just a moment. I had no idea what I was going to say. Then I moved in to the room. I didn't pay any attention to the rest of them. I walked up to Esmeralda and stopped in front of her. She spun around. She still had some leftover smile on her face from the previous chuckle.

"Max!" said LT.

"Uh oh," said Teddy.

"Max, old thing," said Rodd.

"Arlene!" I said to Esmeralda.

"I'm sorry?" she said.

"You are Arlene. I don't know why I didn't see it immediately. You have the hair and the dark contact lenses and you've had some work done, but you are Arlene."

"Max!" bellowed LT. "Arlene no longer exists. Sit down."

"It's a good job. You fooled me and I am supposed to be a trained observer, but you gave it away when you used the word 'spiffy' just now. Then all the little subconscious nudges came together in one big kick in the ass. The whole damned program is a scam. And you all have been scamming since day one. And I'm right in the middle of the whole thing and I don't have any idea what's really going on! You people should be ashamed of yourselves."

"Max! Sit down at once," said LT.

Teddy patted the empty seat next to her. Her eyes were twinkling with little glints of Teddy merriment. She loves games of any kind. The swinging door swung. Dickie appeared carrying two plates of something. He saw me and his eyes nearly exploded in their sockets. The son of a bitch was in on it. He backed out through the swinging door with his plates.

"I feel like such a ..."

"Max," said Teddy, as she reached for my hand. I started to withdraw it, but ... well, you would have to know Teddy. "We all had our parts to play and you played yours brilliantly."

"But I wasn't acting."

"Exactly," said LT. "That is why we had to keep you in the dark about this. You are entirely without guile."

"You've got to see the fun side of this thing," said Rodd. "I mean those chaps in the press were falling all about, foaming at the mouth ... mind you, there could be some nastiness if word of our little melodrama gets out."

"Not from me. I get it. It's one of LT's anti-advertising deals. He thinks he invented the technique. It's how he keeps the walk-in trade from barging into his office on Madison Avenue. It's the same idea on a much bigger scale. You have made yourself somebody the press no longer cares about. They have moved on and left you alone. I get the whole picture. Arlene ..."

"Esmeralda, please get used to the name," said LT.

"OK. I'll say Esmeralda. Who came up with that name?"

"You don't like it?" said Arlene/Esmeralda. She looked hurt.

"It's a great name. You picked it out, didn't you?"

"I always wanted to be an Esmeralda," she said dreamily.

"You should have consulted LT first," I said.

"You really don't like it?" she asked. She frowned.

"It's great. It's a nice name. I'm just saying ..."

"I'm sorry you had to find out this way," said Teddy.

"Well ... what the hell? It's not the first time LT had had a deal going behind the deal. Do her parents know about this?"

"Yes. They were in on it from the first meeting. I got you out of the room so I could discuss it with them. They handled it very well. They were rather relieved to know that Esmeralda was fine."

"You son of a bitch. And you! Rodd Rock! Throwing your career away and your reputation away ... and ... all those kids that have your poster on the wall! They all think you are a killer! People hate you! The media made you out to be worse than Sweeney Todd! And that's all people will remember."

"Max. Let me say a few things. As far as the career goes, I'm not a young man and I'm feeling my age, every minute of it. I never thought I would see thirty. And here I am ... my God ... I still can't believe it. I never took care of myself. I never saw the need. I was a rocker, a hard rocker at that. But the fun has gone out of it for the most part. I love plinking away on some old blues bits, but doing Underground Rider at my age ... I mean, I have to bite my lip to keep from laughing. You know the lyrics, 'Underground rider, I'm a shadow in the night, Got my underground rider and she treats me so right, she knows all the tricks that her mother wouldn't tell, she's only fifteen and she's halfway to hell ...' I mean what am I doing? Mind you, it's the number one request when we play for one of the big venues. People shout it out. The scream for it. Crikey ... I was eighteen when we recorded that!

"No. I've had it with the treadmill. I didn't know how to get off. So many people depended on me for their living. Rodd Rock is like an institution. Everybody wanted to be part of it, but who is Rodd Rock? Who is the Underground Rider? The Blue Roller? Not me. There is no Rodd Rock. Rodd Rock was creature of a marketing man's three martini lunch, and I can tell you who that marketing man was. He's gone these last ten years, but it was Arthur C. Greenberg.

"'Porkhouse?' he said to me, "we've got to give you some balls. Perception is everything. I want you to lose the pompadour and the leather look. That's not where it's at today. And you need a name. I can do miracles but I can't sell anything called Sidney Porkhouse. It's just not on. I have come up with some names and they've tested well with the youth.' Can you imagine? They have tested well with the youth?

"I had my choice of three names; Jackie Stark, Rodd Rock and Morgan Dread. Can you imagine? Of course I picked Morgan Dread. I rather liked the idea of being Mr. Dread. But they said Rodd Rock tested better. Morgan had public school associations, they said. It did? Well, why the bloody hell ask me what name I wanted? Water under the bridge.

"But I was never Rodd Rock ... oh, for a time I got into it. I mean, kids will. I was boozing and drugging and what not, and with the ladies, and I started feeling like there was this actual person who was above and beyond convention, and who had transcended all the dos and don'ts, you know? You've just been done by Rodd Rock, now, off with you. It was fun. Rodd Rock had the time of my life. He rode the big ride. I tell you, it was giddy for a year or two and then there are the plunges. But I was never really Rodd Rock. I was still Charlie Porkhouse's boy from down the lane.

"When my dad died ... well, it brings you up short, doesn't it? Charlie Porkhouse, dead of emphysema. I wasn't there when he died. I didn't think I liked him, when he died. We never got along very well, but when he was gone and it started to work on me. Who was I?

"I was a middle aged, divorced musician with arthritic hands, a voice that had lost half its range and a good deal of its power (thank God for digital so they can shift the notes up to where they belong on recordings) and who had to keep up the front at all times. Being famous is a round-the-clock job. You can't relax when you are in the public eye because the public wants to see Rodd Rock the stud, the wit, the hard drinking man.

"I started to realize that three in the morning was getting later and later and later.

"Then I met old Arlene here - Esmeralda. She was different. She saw through Rodd Rock. She peeked in and saw little Sidney Porkhouse hiding behind the blown out spandex and here's the part that still gives me chills, she didn't run screaming into the night. She kind of liked him.

"It was time for Rodd Rock to leave the stage. Sidney Porkhouse wanted his life back. But the world will have its way. The world has its own agenda. Rodd Rock was condemned like the Flying Dutchman to sail on and on and never rest, doing the world's business, being the world's plaything.

"Arlene couldn't take it anymore. She wanted a normal life and I could give her anything her heart desired except the only thing she wanted; a normal life. We were splitting up. We had nearly signed the papers. Somebody said I better see a lawyer, a good one, before we started signing anything.

"Then Carrie suggested I see Mr. Close. People said he could get the devil out of hell if the money was right. I thought, why not?

"You remember the night we came to dinner? You took Carrie home for me? While you were gone, Mr. Close said, what if we killed off Rodd Rock's reputation, and I said go on, and we started talking about it. One thing led to another. We conspired to murder Rodd Rock!"

"What about Paul Williams?" I asked.

"After we decided to strip Rodd of his powers, we didn't need security anymore. Paul became redundant. The whole security apparatus became redundant. That's why I didn't get excited by his being in the house. I can't tell you how freeing it all was.

"Part of me didn't believe that Mr. Close could pull it off. Then somebody started leaking items to the press and put the entire project in jeopardy. That gave me some sleepless nights, I'll tell you."

"Paul Williams?" I asked.

"Mel Viktor," said Teddy.

"Was the leaker?" I asked.

"He desperately needed money," said LT.

"Wasn't he rich?" I asked.

"That's the thing," said Rodd. "Old Vic had a cash flow problem. When the cocaine shipment was hijacked, he had to make good on the loss to the supplier. His partners thought he had cut them out of the deal. They demanded their share of what should have been the proceeds, but there weren't any. That's why they killed him.

"The leaking was a problem and we had no idea where it originated. Then LT decided that if we couldn't control the leaks, we should exploit them. It's like in jujitsu when an opponent comes at you. You don't try to stop him, you step to one side and use his momentum to trip him up. That's what LT did. He came up with the idea of a counter leak. He said it was used a lot in the '90s by some of the big boys in Washington. It's like setting a back fire to burn the fuel before the forest fire can get to it and use it to continue growing. "

"Disinformation," I said. Dickie was closer than he knew to the truth of the matter.

"Not really," said LT. "Arlene did actually go away. I merely planted on item, more of a doubt really, in the *Herald*. I told Marty that there was more to the Arlene story than was being reported. The rest was supposition, conjecture and assumptions."

"I have spent my entire adult life in the public eye and I had never seen anything like it," said Rodd. "It was a little unnerving, really, and more than once I wondered if he had let the thing slip out of control, but LT was solid. He's the real rock. Here's to you, Mr. Close and to you, Teddy, because you put up with him. Chin Chin!"

We clinked glasses. I took one of Teddy's wine glasses that was still half full of some white California wine.

"He's a bloody master mind!" said Rodd.

"I only have one other problem," I said. "You have all lied to the American People and to history and the music business."

Rodd shrugged. Esmeralda put her head down. Teddy smiled brightly and LT leaned into the table and met my eyes with his.

"No!" said LT. "Never. Not one word."

"You faked Arlene's disappearance. What do you call that?"

"Nothing fake about it. She disappeared. She didn't want to be seen until the bruising and swelling had gone away. Esmeralda has a normal woman's vanity. It is no business of the world's if a woman wishes to have a little cosmetic surgery."

"She changed her name! And her identity!"

"So did Sidney Porkhouse," said Rodd, somewhat sadly I thought. "It's all about entertainment."

"But, people have completely the wrong idea about what has happened. You are allowing lies to stand for truth. If you do nothing, then you are complicit in the lies. Right, LT?"

"You have been hanging around lawyers too long for your own good. You have a valid point. Go in the kitchen and ask Dickie if you can borrow his lap top and go on the Internet and type in "thetruthaboutroddrock.com"; all one word," said LT.

"Maybe I will. What will I see there?"

"The entire story with comparison pictures of both Arlene and Esmeralda," said LT.

"Whose website is it?"

"Mine," said LT.

"Why isn't everyone talking about it?"

"That's the great joke," said Rodd. "Everyone assumes it's just another Internet crackpot conspiracy. It's too wild to be true."

"But it is true," I said.

"But it doesn't fit the established narrative," said LT. "So it is ignored."

"Just as you planned?"

"I have discharged my duties to my conscience. I can't be held responsible for what people choose to believe."

"People," said Rodd, "will believe anything."

"People have moved on," said Teddy. "The people are being force fed stories about Thomas Valderben and his sad childhood."

"Was it sad?" I asked.

"No more than mine," said Rodd Rock.

"But that's the narrative again," said LT. "They have to make Thomas a sympathetic character because they have already demonized Rodd and myself."

"And me!" said Teddy. She was not smiling.

"Yes," said LT, as if he was thinking about something far away.

"What was Tyrell doing?" I said.

"After Thomas Valderben surfaced, I sent Tyrell to stay with Esmeralda. Bobby Dunton handled the daylight hours and Tyrell was there at night. I couldn't take any chances."

"So they were both in on it? And I wasn't?"

"I'm afraid so," said LT. "I didn't want to presume on your straightforward nature."

"I'm never going to hear the end of this," I said. "You have given Tyrell and Little Bobby Dunton bragging rights over me for the rest of my life."

"I wouldn't worry about it," said Teddy. "You saved Carrie's life."

"And more importantly," said LT, "you ended the last threat to the entire operation. With Valderben out of the picture, we were free to shut it all down and go about our lives."

"I didn't push him into the tracks, he ran. He was trying to get the train between us to make his get-away."

"I know that," said LT.

"The news guys said that I chased him into the path of the train."

"Yes," said LT. He looked pained.

"The narrative," said Teddy.

"They could screw up someone's life," I said.

"It happens every day," said Rodd.

"Carrie!" I said. I suddenly pictured her in the car, getting anxious.

"What is it?" she said, coming through the doorway. "I got tired of waiting. Did you forget about me?"

"Hello, Carrie," said Rodd.

"Carrie!" I said, "Esmeralda is Arlene!"

"I know," said Carrie. I couldn't tell from her face what she was thinking. "Dickie met me at the door and filled me in so there wouldn't be a scene."

"Dickie," said LT.

"Hello, Arlene," said Carrie. Arlene/Esmeralda stood and the two women embraced.

"It's Esmeralda now," said ex-Arlene. "I wanted so to tell you, but you were too close to Max."

"Yes," said Carrie, and then she looked at me funny. What the hell, it was a funny night.

I pulled a chair from the wall for Carrie and she sat. Dickie asked her if she wanted something to drink and she asked for white wine.

Then there was more rustling in the hall and we all looked toward the door where Tyrell soon appeared. He had a giant sized smile on his face. He went right to Esmeralda, bent down low and got a long hug with patting. Then he straightened up, looked at me and shook his head. The smile hadn't dimmed any. Rodd rose to a crouch holding his napkin with his left hand and they shook hands across the table. Then Tyrell gave Teddy a hug. LT merely nodded gravely from the head of the table. That's the LT equivalent of hugs and pats.

"Sorry I was late," said Tyrell. "The wife made pork chops, and I had to eat one before she would let me out of the house. Hey Max!"

"Hey, Tyrell,"

"Hello, Carrie," he said. Then he turned to the wall, picked, picked up one of the chairs and set it down next to Teddy.

Dickie came back in the room with plates of prosciuto and melon for LT and Teddy and something that looked like tofu in a sauce for Rodd and Esmeralda. Tyrell waved Dickie away, saying he had eaten and just wanted a beer. Dickie raised his eyebrows at us and I told him that we weren't staying.

"You are quite a sight," said Tyrell to Esmeralda. "This is the first time I have seen the whole package together. You are looking goo-ood."

"Thank you, Tyrell. I am sticking to the diet."

"Now wait a minute," I said to LT. "What about Arlene's permanent record, her social security, her driver's license and tax forms?"

"That's a bit of bother," said Rodd. "Esmeralda will have to forfeit all of her social security money, but we don't really need the money. The government can have it for expenses incurred; fine with me. We don't need that much to live on these days. There's no gardener, no staff at all, no bodyguard."

"What happens to all of them? What about Jorge?"

"He always wanted to start his own company. I invested in it. I am now a partner in a landscaping business. We've got business booked through next summer."

"What about Marcus?"

Rodd laughed. "He gave me two weeks notice. He called some woman that you told him about, Carol somebody."

"Carol Prankham," I said.

"That's the one. It would seem that our Marcus is going into the detective business, thanks to you."

"Pica?"

"She and Jorge are getting engaged. They are planning two weddings, one in East Hampton for their new friends, and one in the village they came from, for the relatives. I gave them both a nice engagement gift."

"What about Esmeralda? How is she ... how are you going to get a new Social Security number, a driver's license and all the rest?"

"That's the beauty part. She's currently undocumented so your boss has arranged for her to take advantage of the latest amnesty."

"You're not serious!" I said.

"Quite serious, actually. It is something the government is willing to offer."

"You'll need a lawyer. It will take years to go through the whole system."

"We have a lawyer." He nodded at LT, who smiled and nodded back. "I don't give a rat's hide how long it takes. We're not going anywhere, are we, Muffin?"

"No, dear," said Muffin.

"They'll find out. It will all come out. You can't keep something like this secret," I said.

"Oh, it will come out in the end," said Rodd. "I don't care. Rodd Rock is finished - the victim of murder most foul. Rodd and Arlene Rock had to die so that others could live!" He reached out for Muffin's hand and she took his hand in hers. Their eyes glittered at each other. Carrie put a hand on my shoulder.

"People like to poke around, though, "said Rodd, "and sooner or later there will be a book, I expect. Someone will connect the dots. Who knows? The True Story of Rodd Rock! When all will be said and done, it shall be revealed that he was neither the overlord of sex and drugs nor poor shivering little Sidney Porkhouse. He was a man like any other who enjoyed making tunes and managed to get caught up in everyone else's expectations until he was divorced from his own."

Epilogue

Rodd Rock had the first of many curtain calls a couple of months later. Carrie had moved into her own place by then and had accepted a job with working for Carlton Boyce Barlton. He made billions in hedge funds and just built a forty-three room mansion in East Hampton. You might have read about him. Carrie went where Barlton went and he was planning to spend part of the winter on his yacht in the Bahamas.

We all piled in the Cadillac to see the first of many last appearances by Rodd Rock. Dickie got the hump. Teddy drove and she put her foot in it. Our destination was a little bar called Outlaws. It was a dark den of human frailty on Rt. 25 near Riverhead. There were biker bikes out front, and a neon beer display with a clock face in a grimy little window next to the entrance. A hand written sign taped to the door read, "Rodd Rock Live 2 Nite No Cover!"

We sat with Esmeralda. No one in the place paid her any attention. She was just another customer. LT had a whisky, neat. Teddy had a Baily's something that made the bartender groan out load. I don't know how she stays so thin. I had a Sam Adams. Carrie and Esmeralda each had a white wine, a Zinfandel blend. Let me give you a small piece of advice you may never have to use, do not order the house white in a biker bar. Stick with the margarita mix.

Rodd started with a little blues number. He chose a National steel guitar from his little rack and he put a harmonica around his neck. He began slow and quiet and built it up bit by bit like an old brick house. The song began in Africa, settled in the Mississippi Delta, moved on to Chicago and got electrified, then leaped over the ocean to Birmingham England and was now alighting for just a moment on the disreputable fringe of the Fabulous Hamptons. It was a song about the things that slip through cupped fingers, the things that can't really be held, just grabbed. Here was a man, not a young man, and he was singing about those things he had seen in a long life. He had seen a lot. He sang about those moments when you want someone so bad it makes you sick and crazy. And he sang about those moments when you've stayed past the longing and there's a road just outside a closed window, and it goes somewhere else. He sang about those moments when you find out you cannot have the thing you counted on having. Carrie reached for my hand under the crusted plywood of the Formica table. Teddy (of course!) noticed. I looked at Carrie. She was looking at Rodd and concentrating. She was in some funny mood. I squeezed her hand. She squeezed back. There was something starting at the corner of her eye, something gleaming in the neon bar-glow.

Teddy touched my foot softly with hers, so lightly I almost missed it. I looked at her. She nodded at LT. I looked at him. He had his eyes closed. He was leaned back so that his closed eyes pointed toward a distant low sky. His head, LT's head, slowly rocked with the beat. Where was he?

Rodd was playing simple music. It was made like rough cloth from only three chords. The way he handled the music was subtle. Simple music seems easy to play, but it takes a master to play it well and get some new juice from a well-squeezed lemon.

I looked around at the others.

Half the people in the room were talking. The music went around them. Some of the rest were listening and moving their heads or feet in time. Everyone had a drink close by. Some had a lover close by. I looked into every face I could see. I saw three faces that reflected back the song. Those three people were each at a personal crossroads. The song was expressing something immediate and personal to each of the three. I could tell because of the tears. Tonight it was for them, and for us, but the song … the song is forever.

Breinigsville, PA USA
11 November 2009
227422BV00003B/50/P